PENGUIN BOOKS

COUNTING THE STARS

'Striking, memorable' *Sunday Times*

'Assured, addictive and captivating' *Daily Telegraph*

'A moving, passionate tale of two people in love' *Independent*

'Richly evocative' *Daily Mail*

'Dunmore at her most innovative and daring' *Time Out*

'Marvellous' *Scotsman*

'A superbly crafted foray into ancient times' *Mail on Sunday*

'Thanks to generous helpings of corruption, promiscuity, hedonism and celebrity, the Roman Empire feels startlingly modern' *Psychologies*

'Elegant, transfixing character-driven historical fiction' *Financial Times*

'Her narrative moves in sensuous leisure . . . the landscape is exquisitely realized' *Literary Review*

'Fascinating . . . Dunmore's skilful scene-setting and characterization ensure that the action always grips' *The Times*

'Dunmore vividly recreates ancient Roman society . . . with intricate detail and tormented love, it's a must-read' *Elle*

Counting the Stars

HELEN DUNMORE

PENGUIN BOOKS

PENGUIN BOOKS

Published by the Penguin Group
Penguin Books Ltd, 80 Strand, London WC2R ORL, England
Penguin Group (USA), Inc., 375 Hudson Street, New York, New York 10014, USA
Penguin Group (Canada), 90 Eglinton Avenue East, Suite 700, Toronto, Ontario, Canada M4P 2Y3
(a division of Pearson Penguin Canada Inc.)
Penguin Ireland, 25 St Stephen's Green, Dublin 2, Ireland
(a division of Penguin Books Ltd)
Penguin Group (Australia), 250 Camberwell Road, Camberwell, Victoria 3124, Australia
(a division of Pearson Australia Group Pty Ltd)
Penguin Books India Pvt Ltd, 11 Community Centre, Panchsheel Park, New Delhi – 110 017, India
Penguin Group (NZ), 67 Apollo Drive, Rosedale, North Shore 0632, New Zealand
(a division of Pearson New Zealand Ltd)
Penguin Books (South Africa) (Pty) Ltd, 24 Sturdee Avenue, Rosebank, Johannesburg 2196, South Africa

Penguin Books Ltd, Registered Offices: 80 Strand, London WC2R ORL, England

www.penguin.com

First published by Fig Tree 2008
Published in Penguin Books 2009
1

Typeset by Rowland Phototypesetting Ltd, Bury St Edmunds, Suffolk
Printed in Great Britain by Clays Ltd, St Ives plc

ISBN: 978-0-141-01503-3

www.greenpenguin.co.uk

Penguin Books is committed to a sustainable future
for our business, our readers and our planet.
The book in your hands is made from paper
certified by the Forest Stewardship Council.

For Jane, Mary and Eric

whoever wants to number
your thousands of love games
let him first count
each sand grain of Africa
and every glittering star

One

This is how it begins.

In the bolt-hole Manlius lent us: you remember it, of course you do. Your blank, blind stare doesn't fool me for a second.

You didn't think much of it.

'What a dump,' you said that first time, looking around the room while my heart thudded with the terror of having you there. Cold fire ran over my skin. My hands trembled. Metal clanged in my head as if someone were beating out a sword there. It was so loud that I could scarcely hear the words you said, let alone speak to you.

Manlius' little villa looked out of place next to the apartment blocks that towered on either side of it. It was a piece of the country in the city, a remnant of family history from long ago. It's gone now. There was a fire – a very convenient fire – when the slave janitor happened to be absent on his master's business. So no more villa, just a tasty, smouldering piece of land that was immediately snapped up by a property developer. Manlius probably took a rock-bottom price from him, not realizing the value of the plot, and never suspecting that his steadfast old slave might be pocketing a backhander.

That's Manlius' world. Slaves are treated well, and in return they offer loyal service. Wives are discreet, faithful and fertile. He's only broken the rules once in his life, when he married a girl who 'wasn't really one of us'.

You are such an innocent, Manlius. They've already thrown up a five-storey building on the site of your villa, to match the apartment blocks on either side. I don't need an abacus to reckon up the profit that the developer made. As usual the new place has a handsome façade, and not much behind it. It's built on air, held up by a few beams here and there and a random scattering of brick. It'll fall down in a decade or two but until then it'll hold dozens and dozens of juicy tenants. They'll be squeezed until the profit gushes like blood. They'll be crushed flat like bedbugs when the floors collapse, or burned alive when fire traps them on the top storey. That's how we build in Rome these days.

Manlius' little villa was planted in the earth, like an olive tree knotted into its soil, taking flavour and colour from it. No one had lived there for years, apart from the old slave. The fountains were dry, and there wasn't a single flower growing in the courtyard.

'We've got nowhere to go,' I'd said to Manlius one day. 'She can't come to my place. I can't go to hers. It's driving me mad. Sometimes I think I'd rather not see her at all than carry on like this.'

Manlius had the villa opened and cleaned for us. The slave brought in bundles of bed linen, wine, a basket of cakes, a basket of figs, and then he was told to clear off for the day. Even ancient hobbling slaves can run fast enough to the market-place with a ripe piece of gossip. Manlius knew I wouldn't want the janitor around when you arrived.

You weren't quite as thrilled as I'd hoped when I told you about Manlius' offer. You weren't used to poky little villas in the wrong part of town. You stipulated that a separate room must be prepared for you to bathe, dress your hair and restore your make-up afterwards.

Afterwards! That's my girl. Always so practical. You would never go back to your husband smelling of another man, with the carmine smudged on your cheeks and your hair in a rope down your back. No, you played your part in the game which had nothing to do with concealment and everything to do with appearing to have made the proper effort to conceal.

You didn't come alone. With characteristic discretion, you brought Aemilia, not in the litter with you but scurrying along

2

behind in full view. She was quite recognizable, Aemilia, with her strange eyes and loud laugh that went off like a fart at all the wrong moments. I think she laughed like that because she was afraid. She had plenty to be afraid of, didn't she? Your husband finding out, for example, and whipping her flesh to ribbons for her complicity, or having her tortured to squeeze out the details of what you'd been up to.

– Or indeed your fury if she used the wrong colour eyeshadow on your lids.

But I think Aemilia was afraid of the whole set-up, where she had nothing to do but cower in the next room with her hands over her ears, waiting for us to be finished. She knew right from the start that none of it was a game. We were in earnest: deadly earnest, you might say. Up to our necks. You'd have to admit that much, wouldn't you?

Manlius put a roof over our love. Aemilia connived, tittered, dropped things and made the place smell of fear. In fact, when I look back, the only one who wasn't afraid and who behaved with perfect naturalness at all times was you.

That first time, I was pacing up and down the bedroom before you arrived. Yes, really pacing, like an actor in a bad play. It may be a cliché but it's what your body makes you do when you're wound up so tight with love and fear that you have to keep moving, up and down, up and down, because something in that rhythm stops the choking of your heart in your throat. I heard my own footsteps, but all the time I was listening for the heavy slap of your slaves' feet.

At last they came. I heard the shuffle of their sandals as they steadied the poles of the litter to let you down. I imagined you stepping out quickly, wrapped in your cloak. You wouldn't want anyone to see you as you flitted to the door.

I stood still in the bedroom and heard your footsteps. The tap and echo of your toes and heels on the stone. It's bad luck for the bride's feet to touch the threshold.

You'd already been a bride. I didn't want to think of your

wedding, of your husband waiting to lift you into his arms while the torches flared and the crowds shouted and sang, and children scattered to grab the nuts that were thrown to them. In a rush of air your husband had lifted you out of your old life and into the new. Your feet in their saffron-gold bride's sandals never touched the threshold on your wedding night. Your husband is a man of tradition. He'd have made sure that everything went as it should.

Tap and echo, tap and echo. Your steps were quick and firm as you entered Manlius' villa.

'The bearers had a hell of a time finding it,' you said, staring round with your eyebrows raised. 'Aemilia couldn't keep up; I hope she hasn't got lost. What a hole.'

'Aemilia?'

'Yes, Aemilia,' you said impatiently. 'She's a genius with hair, but she's got no sense of direction.'

Your hair looked as if you'd reached up your hands and knotted it casually at the nape of your neck. Natural; perfect. Bunches of curls dropped from the knot. I hadn't yet seen Aemilia's fingers at work, making nature what it should be. Your hair shone. The shallow curve of your cheek was as perfect as a shell.

You burned so brightly in Manlius' villa. I could barely look at you.

'You don't seem very pleased to see me,' you said, unfastening the pin to take off your cloak. Before I could answer, Aemilia arrived, panting and apologizing. She'd had to run to keep up with the litter, but even so she'd lost sight of it and taken a wrong turning.

She dumped a big basket on the floor, and you frowned and said, 'Carefully, Aemilia,' in the way I would come to know well. Harsh, but intimate. Aemilia knew every crevice of your body. She knew everything you did.

Aemilia was sweaty and out of breath. She looked like a clod of earth, next to you. You let your cloak slip off your shoulders

4

without even glancing behind you to see if she were there to catch it. She caught it, folded it and laid it over one arm while she picked up the basket in her free hand. She vanished into the little room that led off the bedroom.

I thought that the gods had infused your clothes with your own grace. Your cloak could not help falling into exquisite folds, even in Aemilia's hands. You could not help being beautiful. The hours you spent with saffron, carmine, chalk and antimony had nothing to do with it.

You taught me all your arts in time. *This is the brush for eyeshadow, but foundation has to be blended in with the fingertips.* I would lounge and watch you, not wanting to miss a grain of powder as it fell from the brush – and yet at the same time I was bored, bored, exquisitely bored, bored to death – yes, really aching all over with it –

True boredom is next door to desire. It stretches you out and makes you ache until you'll do anything to stop the pain. That's before you learn that the pain doesn't ever stop, it only changes. I was alone with you and I was afraid to look at you.

The rooms had been sprinkled with fresh water and swept, but they still smelled of distant lives that weren't being lived here any more. Before you arrived I thought of crazy things. Why hadn't I sent for ice from the Alps to cool the Falernian? Why not cover the bed with rose petals? It was such an ordinary oak bed, and it creaked when I sat down. Get used to it, little bed, I thought, you'll creak a lot more before we're through with you. I'd arrived so much too early that I was almost sick with boredom and desire by the time you came.

I heard your footstep on the stone, bringing our own bad luck with you. Our bad luck that's exactly like anyone else's bad luck, but feels different because it belongs to you and me. I should have offered you fire and water, as a bridegroom does to a bride when she first comes to his house. The thought never crossed my mind. It wasn't my house. You were not my bride, but the wife of another man. I was very literal-minded, for a poet. I had no idea that these facts could be changed, or that you and I might be equal to such a transformation.

When you came into the room the dry, dusty, used-up air of Manlius' little locked-up villa changed utterly. You brought the smell of roses with you. I thought it was part of you, and I'd be able to lick it out of you when I licked the sweat from your skin.

Of course I soon knew better. You had to have attar of roses from Turkey, so expensive that even your husband's eyes must have watered when he saw the bill.

'I suppose it will have to do,' you said, testing the bed with the flat of your hand.

You wanted me, and I wanted you. It was very simple then. Aemilia faded out and disappeared. You untied your girdle, whipped that sea-green silk tunic off your body and threw it on the floor like a rag. There was nothing 'sexy' about you and nothing timid. You weren't wearing underwear. You couldn't bear it that day, you said later. The silk of your tunic touching you here and there on your naked body was enough for you.

You wore your cloak to come to me, and no one else saw through that transparent tunic, made of silk from Kos. I liked to think of you sitting in the litter, wrapped up tightly, as anonymous as a parcel, with just your head poking up from the folds of the cloak like a bud from the brown earth. Or like the little girl you'd have been before I was even born, when you were eight years old and sitting by a brazier in the courtyard in winter.

Who knows what you were really like, even at eight? Who knows if you were innocent, even then. That is, if innocence can be lost by what is done to us, as well as by what we do ourselves. You were a child, and they say your brother came to your bed, for comfort at first. He was two years younger than you, but always big and strong for his age. *'They say Pretty Boy Clodius was a grown man at eleven.'* There you sat, wrapped in one cloak with your brother, feeling your cheeks grow hotter and hotter. Pretty Boy and Pretty Girl.

6

Don't let's think of all that. Back to the day, the first day. My beautiful girl. That's how I remember you, sitting up on the bed, naked, careless, showing me everything with a look that wasn't even flaunting. It was more: 'Here I am. This is what I'm like.' You drank from your cup of wine and then you laughed. There were wine stains on your teeth.

I've called you a lot of things. Bright-shining goddess, tart and whore, ball-breaker, heavenly visitor. But on the happiest days you were just my girl.

After you'd left, wrapped up in your cloak again, I wandered around the villa in a daze. I kept stretching myself, pulling back my elbows like bird wings, flexing myself because I had to make sure I still had a body, after all that.

Amazement, disbelief, bliss – yes, of course I felt all those things. It was like waking up on one of those May mornings long before the heat sets in, when the shallow hills of our city are bathed in rosy, misty gold. Everything's ahead, everything's waiting, nothing is soured or used up yet. There haven't even been any quarrels. The last wagons have rumbled out of the city after making their night-time deliveries, and day's about to begin. The mother pulls her baby to her and smiles as its lips latch on to the nipple that's bursting with milk.

You came to me, and of course you left me longing for you. One more touch, one more glance. A whole abacus of kisses, with the beads flying from side to side as we tried to count them. The smell of you after sex: salty and gamey. The hiss of silk as you dressed. Even as you walked to the door with Aemilia lugging that everlasting basket behind you, I was already begging for you again.

But not aloud, Clodia. I had some dignity then. Or perhaps it was just a pinch of good sense that was soon to dissolve in the tide of my hunger for you. Maybe I guessed even then how quickly your scorn could corrode what you'd once caressed.

I wandered out into the dry courtyard. The slave had swept it clean, but now, in one corner, there was a little heap of rubbish.

I went over to it, saw it, and a ghost walked through my body, leaving a shudder in its passing. A torn loaf of bread lay on the shards of a broken pot. There were tattered poppies strewn over them. The quiet corner of the courtyard was set up like a tomb, with offerings left there for the dead.

Aemilia's done this, I thought. Someone's put her up to it. I bent over the offering. I wanted to kick it away, but I couldn't touch it. The bread had been sopped in wine, and the smell of it was already staling. Flies buzzed thickly. The trapped air of the courtyard was stifling.

What motive could Aemilia have? Besides, a slave wouldn't dare to challenge the gods with a mock funeral. Suddenly I was sure that this death offering had been left here for me. *'You think you're at the beginning, but you're at the end. Your love is like the flesh of a dead man. Soon it'll rot and stink.'*

Now I believe that it was the slave janitor who left those offerings. Who knows what lay buried there, deep under that courtyard? A child of his, perhaps. A slave baby who had taken a breath of human air, sneezed, thought better of the fate it had been born to, and died.

We thought we'd come to an empty villa, a blank wax tablet on which we would write our own story. We were wrong.

I was wrong. I was the one with delusions. Imagine, Clodia, I thought your past didn't matter. The heat of our passion had burned it off like mist. A good simile, but not, of course, the truth. You were thoroughly married, and you had your daughter, safely removed from Rome for a 'good old-fashioned country upbringing'. You'd had the same good old-fashioned country upbringing, but with some unusual elements. Brothers and sisters growing up together, all so close. Too close in some cases, if rumour was right. And now the adult siblings were showing their claws in the big arena of Rome. Your favourite brother – Pretty Boy Clodius – had become one of the most ruthless political operators in the city, with his own private army of thugs to back up his ambitions and start a riot whenever he wanted one.

I knew all these things. Becoming Roman isn't just a question of where you live, or whom you know, or what you do. It's a state of mind. I believed that I was Roman now. I'd left the provinces and plunged into a life that kept on seducing me even when it no longer dazzled me. Gossip, poetry, bathhouses, sex with girls, sex with boys, theatre, music, who's in, who's out, epigrams, satires, new books, new clothes, old wine, new friends and even newer enemies. I was a long way from Verona, and swimming as strongly as anyone; or so I thought.

– Coming to the law courts this morning? Calvus is defending.
– Coming to Ipsitilla's? She's having a party tonight.
– Coming to dinner?
– Coming with us?
– Coming, Catullus?

Yes, I was very Roman. I went everywhere and knew everyone. I knew all about Clodia's past, but I didn't believe it could affect 'us'. The calendar began afresh on the day we met.

I can't get Manlius' villa out of my head. Its clean proportions and sober history, a piece of old, plain, heroic Rome in our modern city of palatial villas and roaring, rickety tenements. It's gone, as it had to go. That hive crammed with dozens of tenants has replaced it.

I walk past there sometimes. In my head I see the villa, more real than any ghost. But the tall building looms above me. The apartment tenants eat, drink, make love, scrabble enough together for a fat bet on their favourite chariot team, argue and die without the slightest idea that you were once there, on that same piece of earth, gracefully sweeping your silk tunic over your head in one movement and then kicking it aside as you walked towards me, naked, for the very first time.

Two

Noon. The white hour, when ghosts walk. May, the month when Rome's heat is still just about bearable, although the stink from the slums of the Subura grows richer every day.

There's water in the villa's fountain now. Manlius has given orders and the sluices have been opened. The janitor has brought in pots of lavender and marigolds.

'Since you're coming here so often,' said Manlius, with a grin that transformed his dark, sober features, 'let's get the place into shape.'

But 'so often' is only a couple of hours one day, then a blank for a week. Catullus and Clodia have never spent a night together. She may be reckless, but she's busy, too. She has friends to meet, books to read, poetry to write, bets to lay, massages and hair treatments to be fitted in, visits to her dressmaker and her chiropodist, travels to plan, new dishes to consider. Their chef is a true artist for whom her husband paid a hundred thousand sesterces. All the running of her great household takes up time – let alone the managing of her great husband –

Clodia's life is like her jewel box, opening to reveal a dozen separate ivory-lined compartments. When he said this, she flashed with anger.

'And what about you? What about all those poetry evenings with your friends? You're up half the night with Cornelius or Calvus, you drink until dawn, and then you spend whole days lounging around the Forum and the bathhouses. Wherever there's a crowd, *you're* the centre of it. And don't think I don't know about all those girlies you visit in the afternoons. If that's pining for me, then you're an excellent actor, my dear poet.'

Her anger dissolved, and she laughed as if his deceptions pleased her, but he was stunned. Was that how he seemed to her? No, she was the one who was acting. She preferred not to admit his passion, and how it coloured every hour of his life.

'You have your life, and I have mine,' Clodia continued, snapping shut her hinged silver mirror. 'Everyone's like that. We're together now, so why think about what goes on when we're apart? It only spoils things.'

'Not spoiling things' is one of Clodia's unspoken laws. She likes to live in the present; she's at home there.

'We are not everyone,' he said, with equal anger.

The fountain in the courtyard chinks water into its basin, over and over, until even the sound of coolness becomes part of heat's monotony. She has been with him for an hour. They lie together, wiped out, sealed to each other by sweat. He looks at her profile, a few inches from his eyes, but far away. Her eyes are half shut. He can see the shine of them, but not what she's looking at. Nothing, maybe. Maybe she is thinking of nothing.

It's too hot to speak or write or move. The bedroom is airless. Even her sparrow is still, in the corner of its cage. Clodia has got into the habit of bringing her sparrow to the villa. She carries its cage on her lap in the litter, and covers it with a cloth so that the bird doesn't cheep.

It's too hot to speak or write or move, but with sudden decision she gets up, swings her legs over the side of the bed and walks away naked through the thick warm air as if she's wading through the sea.

Aemilia will have heated water to bathe her mistress. She's set up the little room next door like a boudoir. She'll be ready to stand behind Clodia, dressing her hair as she sits in the basketwork chair Manlius has produced from somewhere or other. And now for the make-up. It's Aemilia's job to return Clodia's bruised, swollen lips to an even carmine, to smooth on foundation paste and massage it into her face, to wipe away the smudged cosmetics and replace them with subtle grey eyeshadow and kohl to create Clodia's famous 'Hera' eyes.

He prefers her without make-up. When he says this, she laughs. *That's rubbish.* The woman he fell in love with is the woman whom Aemilia helps to create. *I'd be a poor draft of myself without my make-up. You'd want to rewrite me.*

But he loves her naked face. It's true though, that when women haven't got their make-up on they'll look sideways, or down, as if to hide themselves. They're like soldiers, he thinks, building fortifications of mascara and kohl to defend the cities of themselves. He smiles. The sparrow is still watching him. Sometimes, disconcertingly, Catullus will glance up over Clodia's body when they are making love, and catch the sparrow's eye. Its keen darkness might mean nothing. A sparrow cannot think. It can only hop and chirp and take crumbs of cake off its mistress's palm.

The sparrow is watching him with suspicion now, as if it knows what he's capable of. After all, he's only just finished groaning, thrashing and shuddering over the body of its mistress.

Sometimes she's on top of him, fluid as a fish, her teeth bared. Sometimes she dives and clutches the bed linen as he straddles her and then her muffled, raucous cries make the sparrow hop nervously from one end of its perch to the other.

There's not far to hop. The perch is narrow and the cage ungenerous. It doesn't matter, because Clodia is always taking her sparrow out to play. She's so familiar with the catch of the cage that she undoes it without looking, opens the little door and puts her hand inside. The sparrow hops on to her wrist and fastens his claws delicately on to the bone at the base of her thumb. He chirrups as she draws him out of the cage, transfers him from her wrist to the palm of her hand and brings him up to her face.

She brushes his body against her cheek. His wings are folded tight. He never attempts to open them, not at this moment. His body is slim and she passes him over the smooth warm flesh of her cheek in the direction of his flight feathers, so nothing ruffles. His beak touches the contour of her lips. His taut, sharp little beak, still closed, like his wings. It outlines her lips, pressing a little. She laughs. When she laughs it's the signal. He nips the cushiony fullness of her lips, quite gently.

After a while she takes him away and holds him at arm's length, her hand curved now, holding him inside her palm so that his body throbs there, hidden. Only the dark bubbles of his eyes show, and his closed beak. She laughs in her throat, and squeezes very gently, so that the sparrow feels the pressure of her hand. He doesn't struggle.

Catullus loves to watch Clodia with her sparrow. She's gentle, warm. She can hide those qualities, as she hides the sparrow in her hand, but they're there. He believes in the real Clodia, revealed in tenderness. Or at least, he tells himself that he does . . .

But sometimes there's something disconcerting about Clodia and the sparrow. His naked, eager girl, and the little bird. The way she moves the sparrow's beak over her lips.

'He's my true friend,' she says. 'I believe every word he says. How many friends can you say that of?' And she laughs.

The sparrow is probably laughing too. The man flings himself on to his back and lies with his head pillowed on his folded arms.

Sometimes, if you take up a position of relaxation, you trick yourself into believing that you are relaxed. He plays the part of a man at his ease, enjoying a siesta after sex, on a day when the heat is so intense that it's almost frightening. The streets will be empty. Dogs will lie in slices of shade as thin as crescent moons. No man of sense would do anything but lie on his bed, on his back, pillowing his arms, to dream and listen to the fountain.

What a lie it all is. He's listening out for her, of course, trying to catch the tiniest laugh or chink of a glass bottle-stopper. She's disappeared into her inner sanctum, and he can't follow her there because he knows exactly the cold, hard, slightly scornful stare that will greet him if he does. Aemilia will be wiping Clodia's temples with alcohol, or reducing the flush on her cheeks. Both women will be rapt, intent on their rites.

He knows exactly what goes on between them, because of course he's watched through the doorway when Clodia's left the door ajar. Only a few weeks ago she was still happy to let him watch, or even mess about with the precious little jars and bottles and their stoppers. But then she said that Aemilia couldn't concentrate if he was there.

'You're putting her off, my dear poet. You have no idea how alarming you are when you stare like that. It's worse than a cat watching a bird.'

Clodia still left the door open the next few times. He watched as if he were watching a play not from the auditorium but from a space of invisibility right on the stage, close enough to touch the actors. He watched as if he were to be cross-questioned in court on the techniques of make-up. He watched the way Aemilia dipped a tiny brush into grey powder, brushed a line above the lid and smudged it carefully with a minute sponge-tipped applicator, while Clodia lowered her eyes and kept perfectly still. He watched while Aemilia massaged her mistress's gums with a special paste made of orris, mint and salt, and while Clodia rinsed her mouth and spat into the bronze basin.

But why not watch a woman, when you've only just finished anointing every crevice of her body with sweat, saliva and semen? What is left to be secret? Nevertheless, Aemilia closes the door on him now, with a prudish, triumphant look. It has to be on Clodia's orders.

Aemilia pours perfume slowly, with a care that would seem exaggerated if you didn't know the price of attar of roses, or the quick flare of Clodia's temper. Clodia raises her hands and rubs the perfume into the loose, glossy thickness of her hair. But she only rubs it a little this time, perfunctorily, and then she gets bored and gestures to Aemilia to finish the job. Aemilia flushes with pleasure. She loves perfuming her mistress's hair, and Clodia, from spite or contrariness, rarely allows it.

With her strong fingers Aemilia massages Clodia's scalp, parting the hair and dividing it into sections so that every lock can be dealt with in order, in time. She massages first with her fingers, and then more strongly, with the heel of her palms. Finally, with butterfly fingertips, she strokes Clodia's temples. Who would have thought Aemilia's touch could be so delicate?

The room fills with the smell of Clodia's hair, warm and damp after sex. Clodia's eyes are shut. After she has massaged her mistress's head for about a quarter of an hour, Aemilia takes an ivory comb and begins to comb, spreading the strands out across the air and then letting them fall against Clodia's bare shoulders. When she finds a knot she teases it out gently, watching Clodia's shoulders for the signs of tension that mean she is about to lash out with a sharp, stinging slap.

But today, there is no slap. He'd hear it if there were, even through the door. Clodia is no weakling, and has no inhibition to make her pull her punches. She's like one of those pets or children of whom their carers say fondly that 'she doesn't know her own strength'. Those on the receiving end of the bite or the slap are quick to know it. Aemilia's tactic is to burst into noisy tears and throw herself on the ground, sobbing, until Clodia says, 'Here, Aemilia,' and pops a square of quince paste into her slave's mouth. It's a game, and they both know it's a game. After such a storm, Clodia will allow her body slave to perfume and massage her pubic hair.

'One of these days you'll kill me, you will,' moans Aemilia. 'You don't know your own strength, my lady.' He wonders if she's right. Could his girl be capable of killing, and if she did kill, what expression would cross her face? He used to think that he knew all Clodia's expressions, but now he's not so sure.

Sparrow, sparrow. Beautiful little sparrow, dear little sparrow that my girl loves more than her two eyes. A shocking poem has been doing the rounds, which hints that his girl uses her sparrow to do more than caress her cheeks or her lips. After all, it's completely tame. Clodia believes he wrote the poem. She has faith in his malice.

He rolls on to his side, in the ruck of sweaty bed linen, and stares at the bird. So smug in its cage, so sure that it's wanted, treasured, possessed. Hop up and down, then, little bird, and believe whatever you want to believe. You can even believe your mistress is kind if you want.

Kind? She wouldn't recognize the word if it came out of her own mouth. She'd kick it out of the way, as one kicks a broken twig off a raked gravel path.

That bitch Aemilia is still with her. A pity the door is so thick, too thick for him to listen to them giggling, whispering, moaning to each other. That shut door is a piece of business he can't fail to understand. It says: *You think I need you, but I don't need you. I can climb straight off your prick back into my own world where what matters most is whether the perfume that my steward ordered from Turkey is of the same quality as last year's from Syria. And my world is where I love my sparrow as much as I love you. Or more. A thousand kisses, and then a hundred more. Kiss kiss kiss kissy-kiss kiss kiss until the mind gets tired of counting.*

But a man has to count every one of your kisses, Clodia, when they are given to someone else.

Yes, you may well look at me like that, little sparrow. Your mistress will be back soon. Even she won't be able to drag out the ritual much longer – the slaps and the tears and the crushing scent of cosmetics, and the reek of Aemilia's sweat because she never washes her armpits properly no matter how sharply you order her to do so. And perhaps she knows that you like it really, don't you, Clodia, that rankness of Aemilia's? You told me so once, when we were lying so close together I thought we were one body, one blood. You didn't even seem to me like a woman any more. I held you as I would have held my son, handed to me washed and wrapped after birth. Yes, it's comic, isn't it?

I held you like that. You were so fragile, warm, tender, coupled to me by the sweat of sex as if you'd been joined to me by the blood of birth. I have never loved anyone as purely as I loved you then. Even your thoughts seemed as breakable as eggs, to be cupped in my two hands and cherished. Suddenly you stirred a little, and opened your lips. I even drew you closer, my Clodia, so I could taste your words as they formed like miracles out of breath and spit and whatever else it is that words are made from.

'You know, that smell of Aemilia's armpits,' you murmured, 'it's sexy, isn't it, in spite of the goatiness? Really, it's quite a turn-on . . .'

And then you lapsed back into those thoughts I'd been cherishing, no doubt with a foolish smile on my face. A smile like that is a sign of weakness, and it has to be punished.

The sun went in, Clodia. It's always like that with you, isn't it? A beautiful morning, a stretch of mist over the rosy countryside – and then the gods wake up belching and farting and there's a rain of hailstones like dirty eggs. Harvest's ruined. Everybody runs for shelter, cursing.

He rolls on to his back again, and stares up at the ceiling. The best thing to do would be to get up, manage a calm, affectionate parting and go off to the Baths to sweat it all out of him. Meet friends, catch up on the gossip, get asked to dinner somewhere, drink too much, finish off the night in a blur where anything might happen and it doesn't really matter if nothing does. Go and see another woman, Cynthia maybe, or Ipsitilla. The task is to be happy without Clodia. And if that's not possible, he can at least seem happy without her, just for one evening. He managed it for years and years before he knew she existed. It would be nice to see Ipsitilla . . . she has such a beautiful laugh, warm and dirty . . .

The door opens. Sometimes he's sure Clodia can hear his thoughts. Just as the rope that holds him begins to slacken, she pulls it tight again.

'Let's go to Baiae,' she says, smiling at him from the doorway.

'Baiae?' he repeats stupidly.

'It's time to get out of Rome. The heat is worse than ever this year. Everybody will be gone by the middle of next week. I want to have at least six weeks in Baiae before we go to the hills.'

'Everybody? Even your husband?' he asks unforgivingly. 'Is he going to Baiae, too?'

'Of course he isn't going,' she replies coolly. 'He always makes a tour of the estates in late May and June. Besides, can you imagine him in Baiae? There's so much to disapprove of, he wouldn't know where to look first.'

'But you would.'

'I would look at you,' she says. She crosses the room to him, kneels at the side of the bed and kisses him gently on the forehead. It's impossible to believe that her soft, wide gaze could ever harden. 'Let's. Do let's. Come to Baiae. We'll have such fun. Of course we'll have to be sensible – but you know how much more relaxed things are down there. I'm going to take a course of thermal treatments.'

'Thermal treatments?'

'Rheumatism in my shoulder,' she explains. 'It's been troubling me more and more since about – when was it? – last September?'

'Yes, last September,' he murmurs.

'I haven't been sleeping properly. And I've lost weight – look. Every night I dream and I toss back and forth, back and forth – and sometimes I cry out –'

'And so your husband sends you to Baiae.'

'I send myself,' she says. 'I've given myself a thorough examination and considered all my symptoms.'

'Which are?'

'Feel my pulse. No, not there, there. Can't you feel how fast it's beating? That's a sign of fever. And my lips have never been so dry. I'm thirsty all the time. I want something and I don't know what it is.'

'Don't you?'

Her eyes narrow. Her softness vanishes. 'You think it's you. You think you've caught me, don't you?'

'We've caught each other. Why can't you admit it?'

She laughs, not very pleasantly. 'You think you can put me into a cage, like my sparrow, and I'll hop about until you come along with a bit of cake and let me sing for it? But even my sparrow is wiser than you think. He tells me things that no one else knows. Sometimes I think I love him more than anything else on earth.'

He sits up with a jerk and turns his back on her. 'I've got to go.'

'Why does every little thing make you angry? It doesn't hurt you if I love my sparrow.'

'You go too far, Clodia. You know what you said. I'm not one of your pretty boys who'll swallow anything.'

'I assure you, my friend, any swallowing that takes place isn't done by them.'

'You bitch.'

'That's not what you said two days ago. "A thousand kisses, and then a hundred more, and then another thousand . . ." Wasn't that it?' With a swift, sudden movement she climbs on to the bed, curls around him and puts her arms around his neck. 'Why are we arguing?' she murmurs. 'Why not just come to Baiae? I'm a good doctor – I can prescribe for you as well as for myself. Let me see . . .' She unclasps him and takes his face between her hands. 'You're pale, and you've got shadows under your eyes. Do you remember the first time you saw me, at our dinner? You were so handsome. Your skin looked golden. Every time I moved I felt your eyes on me. And you were so funny – you made me laugh so much –'

It floods back to him. The table was loaded with lobster, mullet, a whole sucking pig. He ate almost nothing. He thought he'd been struck dumb by her, but no, he'd made her laugh. He'd felt raised up and full of power. Words would do whatever he wanted. He could weave them into spells which would bind her.

Her husband had eaten some plain dish of roast meat. The elaborate feast was for his guests. A man of the old school, with hard, trained appetites, that was Metellus Celer.

'Everybody wanted to talk to you,' Clodia continues. 'You were twice as alive as anyone else at the table, as if you had a secret no one else knew. Even my husband thought it was quite a coup, getting you to recite after dinner. "The most brilliant of our young poets" – he said that afterwards. "People who claim there's nothing in this 'new poetry' are not using their ears."'

'Did he really say that?'

'He'd have been repeating what someone else had told him. You brought lustre to our table, my dear poet, and my husband is a man who can respect something for which he has no personal feeling or even liking. But now look at you. You're pale. You aren't well. I prescribe . . . now let me see . . . yes, the perfect medicine for you is a course of treatment at the Baiae thermal baths. And you must drink the waters. The air's so good down there, you'll soon turn golden again.

'Listen. You can't imagine how beautiful it is in the evenings. when it's not quite dark, but the first stars are coming out. The frogs croak and the crickets chirp under the myrtles. You point at one star, and then another, and suddenly there are so many you can't count them, and before you know what's happened the moon has risen too. And then – this is the best part – you wander along the shore until all the villas are behind you, and you've got rid of all the heavy-breathing old senators who think that because they're lumbering around like elephants in short tunics every woman in Baiae is longing to see what they've got underneath.

'You find a little beach, and slip off your clothes, and walk into the water. Water feels quite different at night, did you know that? But of course you must have a friend with you, because it's dangerous to bathe alone. And your friend walks into the water too, and you reach out your arms and find him.'

'Yes,' he murmurs, and reaches up, and pulls her down to him.

'Hold me like that,' she says. 'Just like that.'

Three

The calm surface of the sea quivers in the late-morning light. He disturbs a viper, coiled in the dust of his path. It uncoils like a whip and glides into the scrub. He must remember to tread more heavily, so that the snakes feel his footsteps and make their escape.

He's been in Baiae for ten days already. A small routine has established itself. He gets up early, eats bread and cheese or a few dried figs, and then settles on the vine-shaded terrace with his stylus and tablets. It's very quiet. He has few visitors and he pays as few visits as possible. He's come down here with the minimum of slaves. Lucius, his steward, has stayed behind in Rome.

'There'll be nothing for you to do in Baiae, Lucius. I shan't be entertaining. I'm going down there to take the waters, and write.'

Lucius looked doubtful. 'All the more reason for me to be there and run everything, if it's peace and quiet you want.'

'I need you in Rome. I can't trust anyone else as I trust you.'

Lucius nodded, acknowledging the case.

So there won't be many parties, but Catullus doesn't mind that. All the friends he really wants to see are in Rome or the countryside. Baiae is too flash for them – or simply too expensive.

His true friends, the ones who'll read the twentieth draft of a poem as keenly as the first. And he will do the same for them. He thinks of them with a flush of affection. His dear Calvus, with his grasshopper body and lofty, brilliant mind. Fabullus, to whom you can tell everything, because, as he says, 'I'm the grave of every secret'; Veranius, with his Gaul-green eyes glistening with laughter. Friends who know when to praise a poem, and when to rip into it:

– It's got two good lines, and it's as light as a drum technically, but you've written the subject to death. What we don't know about Juventius' honey-sweet arse and what you'd like to do with it could fit on the point of this pin. Even you are bored by it.

– Boredom's a good subject for a poem. And to be bored by an arse is original, at least.

– Yes, but *bored writing* is unforgivable.

Calvus, Fabullus, Veranius. His people, the ones he writes for. The ones who know where poems come from, how they work, and where they fail. They know the mystery well enough to see the wheels turn in its heart.

He writes, erases, writes again. The words tease like mosquitoes, out of reach. Today he'd rather do anything but this. Even a morning trapped with one of Rome's really celebrated egotists – Sestius, perhaps – would be better than this itch of words that just won't let him scratch.

A light breeze shakes the oleanders. Their deep red flowers shiver, then are still. Everyone raves about Baiae. He sees that it's beautiful, but doesn't feel it. He'd so much rather be at Sirmio, on the shore of his own northern lake. Rather anywhere than here, where everyone's so ostentatiously having a good time and he can't get away from the sight of Clodia, in her thinnest silks, her head flung back and her throat bare as she laughs. She seems to be always laughing.

He'd like to know what there is to laugh about. Her husband, the upstanding Metellus Celer, with his soldierly stride, his practical grasp of every situation, his power and glory and his way of seeing a joke a few seconds after everybody else and laughing loudly, dutifully to make up – Yes, her husband, against all the odds, has come to Baiae this season, just as Clodia promised he wouldn't.

Perhaps he just wants to see the splendid villa that he's been pouring money into for years, without ever bothering to stay there. Or perhaps he's more clued-up than he looks. It might be dangerous to take at face value his air of nobly noticing nothing that his wife is up to. He may not be all that quick-witted, but he's used to power. His hands are on all the ropes of Rome, and no doubt he intends to keep it that way.

Something's made Metellus Celer break with his iron personal traditions and come to Baiae, instead of making the usual dignified progress around his many estates to receive diligently prepared accounts from his many stewards. Clodia says her husband is quick to spot any fudge in the figures. Maybe he's spotted a fudge in the facts of her life, too.

You really shouldn't keep bringing up my name in front of your husband, Clodia. It's not very clever. You think that as long as you attack me, you're safe. But don't you think he notices how often my name is in your mouth, and how your eyes sparkle as you heap insults on me and my work?

'How sublimely self-centred he is, just like all the other "new poets". Their conceit is the most original thing about them. They take themselves so *very* seriously, beneath the jokes. He was fun at first, but I know how bored *you* were the last time he came to dinner. Positively glazed over, weren't you, my dear?'

But how does your husband answer?

'I wasn't bored, my dear.'

You didn't take warning. You reported the conversation to me as if it were a game you'd won. You went on playing, and you scoffed at the idea that your husband might be playing, too.

'And now I've discovered that he's here in Baiae for the whole season, when we simply want to relax. And when I've finally got *you* to Baiae for once – Why don't these young men ever go home and visit their fathers? But I suppose we'll have to ask him to dinner.'

'Why not?'

You rolled my name around in your mouth, Clodia, and then you spat it out. I'm sure your husband hears more than you think. But he greets me with his usual impeccable politeness.

The point is, though, that he doesn't leave you alone. He remains in Baiae, sitting it out.

He's even organized a boating party today. I can just imagine it. The entire villa party will sail along the shore until they reach a private beach with artfully rustic couches set up for them under canopies of vine leaves and myrtle branches. The unpretentious table will be covered with a snow-white cloth. Lobster with asparagus, roasted capons, pickled quails' eggs in a salad of mint and lettuce, gamey slices of roast boar with spiced apple relish, strips of tender kid seethed in the milk of its own mother, pomegranates, preserved quince paste, dates and apples of Hesperus –

Good, plain food, everything of the first quality. Metellus Celer will permit no tasteless *nouveaux* exaggerations at his table. There'll be no gimmicks and no surprises.

'I'm a man of simple tastes,' he'll say, with an offended stare, if any innovation is suggested. 'I leave that sort of thing to other people.'

Clodia ought to smuggle a couple of dancing-girls into her husband's 'simple picnic, with just a few close friends'. That would make them all sit up, those senators dressed in daringly short tunics and creaky holiday smiles. They'll all be goggling at Clodia as the breeze blows her silk dress over her body and moulds it to her breasts and thighs. There's no doubt that she's a damned fine woman, they'll say to themselves. At the same time they'll thank their stars that their own wives know how to behave and are safely at home, upholding the strictest standards of Republican matronhood, and speaking only to approve their husbands' utterances.

Or maybe – just maybe – those wives are rolling around in the matrimonial bed with a handsome steward. While the senator is away, the senatresses do play. Let's hope so. Those senators deserve to pay for licking Clodia all over with their lascivious glances, and for the way they'll toss themselves off in their sleepy villas at siesta time, dreaming of her thighs . . .

What a boating party! He laughs out loud, harshly. A lizard takes fright, and runs away up the wall. Clodia has sent him an invitation, naturally, but he's not going to go. He has no desire to spend hours watching her preen in sexual attention, dressed in one of her fetchingly simple 'seaside' outfits, laughing, teasing, dropping back into silence as she trails one hand in the water and mesmerizes some other poor fool with the darkness of her dreaming eyes.

Yes, her eyes are dark, although they seem bright. Her enemies call them cow eyes, or pretend to praise her by saying that her eyes are as lustrous as Hera's. And who did Hera take into her bed but her brother, Zeus? Clodia is almost as fortunate as Hera; she may not have Zeus for a brother but she's got Pretty Boy Clodius, the handsomest sibling any girl could ask for. What a fine pair they make.

Always the pretend praise, followed by insinuations. Clodia says she takes no notice, it just makes her laugh. She has all the annihilating pride of the Clodii and now of the Metelli too, and with it a quality which is hard to define because it seems to change day by day as the light of his imagination plays on it. She follows a path no one else sees. She seems to walk freely.

Once, before she was married, Clodia made a pilgrimage to Paphos. She'd had a dream, she told him, in which Aphrodite had appeared to her in a chariot drawn by sparrows. The goddess had said nothing, but had held up her right arm and beckoned to Clodia as she was swept to earth.

'She wanted me to come and worship at her shrine.'

He looked at her hard, suspecting her. Clodia had wanted a voyage, maybe. She'd grabbed the chance to enjoy freedom in the guise of a pilgrimage, before her family married her off.

'Did they want you to go to Paphos? Your family?'

She shrugged. 'Of course not. It was very inconvenient for them. It meant delaying the wedding.'

'But you went anyway.'

'Better to start marriage with a blessing than a curse. If a goddess calls you, you must go.'

He applauded her inwardly. Those must have been her exact words. They would have stopped family opposition in its tracks.

Her face was as smooth as rock. He wanted so much to believe that she had really believed in her pilgrimage: that she hadn't used – or invented – her vision to get her own way. She'd braved the voyage for the sake of something, whatever it was. Dark seas, late-season storms, the taste of salt day after day, whenever you lick your lips. The sea makes everything else unimportant. Even Rome recedes . . .

(He should travel. He should get right away, Baiae is no good. It's Rome-on-Sea, with all the same old faces, the same old gossiping and politicking. Even when you're face down and naked on the slab at the thermal baths, being pummelled by the best masseur in Baiae, you can't let up. You've got to keep your wits Rome-sharp.)

It was a long voyage for Clodia, though, all the way to Cyprus. There's enough weather in April to make a ship bucket, even though the waves are bright. Something must have driven her there. The thought of her marriage, perhaps. Clodia was to be handed from the Clodii to the Metelli: it was an alliance between cousins, of the kind that keeps Rome strong. Patrician families must marry with care, to advance the power and honour of the clan. They got more than they bargained for with Clodia, he thinks with a grim smile.

She must have been about fifteen. Maybe sixteen. Virginal, innocent.

(Or perhaps neither, if the rumours are true. The things a girl should hope for had already happened to her in secret.)

What was she really like then? It gnaws him, because he'll never know that fifteen-year-old Clodia. All he can know is the Clodia of now: lovely, urban, ironic, guarded when she appears most free.

Maybe she lay awake at night, when she knew her marriage was fixed and she would have to take the next step, and then the next, towards a future that belonged to a man she scarcely knew. Maybe she had spots and puppy fat and she thumped her pillow and tossed from one side of the bed to another, praying for a way out. And that was when she heard the wings of Aphrodite's sparrows, beating the air as they brought the goddess's chariot to earth.

Something slid in his heart at the thought, like a key opening a place which he hadn't known to exist.

Once Clodia's ship docked at Paphos, she would have rested before she was taken by litter to the precincts of the shrine. There, she would have dismissed her slaves. Girls don't prostitute themselves for the goddess these days, but the tradition is still that they go to the shrine unaccompanied. No one would dare to molest a girl on her way to the goddess, carrying her offering of flowers. Even a hardened rapist would let her pass.

Clodia, alone, on a narrow dusty path between olive groves, within sound of the sea. His girl carried a basket of blood-red anemones, to offer to Aphrodite in the name of Adonis. It would have been late spring, the voyage safely made after the worst of the winter storms. He pictures Clodia in a white tunic embroidered with red, the shade of anemones and of blood. She would have been alone, but there would have been many other girls, on other winding paths, making for the shrine.

Aphrodite herself bathed there, long ago, where a spring of pure water bulges out of the earth and fills a stone basin. Clodia, too, would have bathed at the shrine, and left her flowers there as an offering.

This is how he wants to think of her. Not at the shrine itself, bustling with the commerce of priestesses, oracles, votaries and offerings, but alone in the sunlight. Not yet married, her face round, serious and at peace. He wants to think of her laying down her flowers, making an invocation and truly believing that she sees the shadow of Aphrodite's hand above her bare head. Before anyone had touched Clodia; before she'd touched anyone.

If there ever was such a time. They say her brother stayed in the habit of visiting her bed, even when they were too old for it to be decent. He took her virginity, or else she took his.

The gossipmongers love Clodia. They're like dogs snuffling under her skirts. His own foot itches to kick them away. The Clodia they talk about has nothing to do with his girl.

'I don't listen to all that stuff,' Clodia says, with the small patrician shrug. 'Whatever I do, people will talk. They always have. It means nothing.'

Sometimes he wishes she'd had smallpox in childhood, not badly but just enough to mark her so that she wasn't perfect any more. So that people would glance her way and then pass on, uninterested. Or maybe a minor accident . . . A broken nose or a scar above her right eye . . .

Not that perfection is Clodia's charm. He's deluding himself if he thinks a scar would make any difference. Some girls need to be perfect, or their beauty vanishes: those pure, classic 'white' beauties mustn't have a mark on them. But even with a broken nose and smallpox pits on her cheeks, Clodia would find another way of being the woman everybody can't help wanting.

Her critics tear her apart. Her eyes are too large – cow eyes. She walks too fast. Her figure isn't symmetrical enough for beauty. She laughs too loudly. But they can't take their eyes off her. She's public property – not anyone's Clodia, but 'our' Clodia. *Clodia nostra . . . Lesbia nostra.* In his poems he hides her name without hiding it. The stress and quantity don't change. Our Lesbia – *Lesbia nostra* – that Lesbia, *that* one.

She's in everyone's mouth and everyone's eyes, but they don't see what he sees. They see themselves instead: their own doggish greed and the smart little jokes that fall flat when she meets them with a cold stare. People whom she wouldn't let into her house tell stories about 'what Clodia's really like'.

She has the power of changing to suit anyone's eyes. If they want to see a great lady, she'll be blue-blooded and arrogant. If they want a whore she'll rustle, giggle and snatch at purses. She'll play in the gutter better than anyone.

He shifts on his seat. Leaf shadows are falling on him now, through the vines that spread over the pergola. The shadow is cool and sweet, scented with verbena and with those small, tight, dark red roses that open for a day and then die. As he watches, a rose dissolves in a shower of petals.

He looks down at his stylus and blank writing tablet, and grimaces.

'You've got to come to Baiae, my darling. I'm down there for weeks and weeks and I'll go crazy if you don't come. He never comes to Baiae. It'll all be so much easier than it is in Rome. People do turn a bit of a blind eye in Baiae. When we can't be together, you'll get on with your writing. You'll have complete peace.'

And boating parties, she said, and picnics, and midnight bathing, and expeditions to a little farm where you can milk goats, drink new milk and take away cheeses wrapped in vine leaves.

'I can't picture you milking a goat, Clodia.'

'You're so wrong! I was an expert when I was little. We used to be sent off to the country every summer, to my father's old tutor. He'd been freed and given some land near Formiae. My brother and I milked the goats, teased the bull and climbed every tree for miles around. He was two years younger than me, but he could always keep up with me, he was so tall and strong. We even trod the grapes at harvest. You should have seen my feet – I wore away a whole pumice stone on them before the stains came off.'

He thinks of her bare feet, treading down the mass of grapes. Her child's face, sunburned and laughing, before she learned to whiten her skin.

'My brother and I did everything together. If one of us cried, the other cried in sympathy, even if there was nothing wrong.'

Her words eat at him now. He's jealous of the years that have gone before he knew her. He's jealous of everything about her that belongs in other people's memories, where he can never reach it. Even Pretty Boy Clodius – vain, violent, power-mad Pretty Boy, who won't be satisfied until he's running Rome as his personal fiefdom – he can't be dismissed along with all the other politicians, because he possesses something of Clodia that Catullus will never have.

'Come to Baiae – you'll have complete peace!' What a joke. He hasn't known peace since he met her.

He'd like everything to dissolve, except for the present tense. Clodia here, now. Clodia belonging to the moment, and to him. Yes, if she were here now, sitting on the cool marble bench, then he could be happy.

When the next rose fell apart, he would brush its petals out of her hair. He'd like to lose all those years, all those men. Lose them all in a drumbeat of kisses, hypnotic, repetitive, cancelling out everything but their own rhythm.

> *da mi basia mille, deinde centum,*
> *dein mille altera, dein secunda centum,*
> *deinde usque altera mille, deinde centum.*

Da mi basia – give me kisses – give me a *mille*, give me a thousand – then give me a hundred – and then another thousand, a second hundred, and then another thousand with them, and then a hundred –

> *da mi da mi da mi*

Like a child following its mother, whining and dragging at her heels. Like a greedy shopkeeper reckoning on his abacus. *Give me give me give me.* It's the only thing in the world. It's what we all desire. *Basia.* Listen to the sound of it. It makes your lips join and then softly blow apart. Exactly like a kiss.

Kisses flying like beads flying across the abacus. Centuries of kisses wouldn't be enough for him.

da mi basia da mi basia da mi basia Lesbia Lesbia Lesbia Lesbia mea puella

My girl, he calls her when he's closest to her, when Clodia

Metelli and Gaius Valerius Catullus cease to exist. Their freight of name and reputation sinks to the bottom of the ocean. They are melted into each other, dissolved into *basia*. Thunder beats in their ears and their eyes are full of darkness. He's still counting, counting, until all the figures fly apart.

> *You ask how many kisses*
> *Lesbia, how many kisses will be enough?*
> *Lesbia, count each grain*
> *of Libyan sand that sifts*
> *through silphium-rich Cyrene,*
> *count from Battus' tomb*
> *to Jove's hot-blooded oracle;*
> *or reckon up the stars*
> *watching over the hidden*
> *loves of humans while night is silent:*
> *that's how many of your kisses*
> *would be enough for your possessed Catullus,*
> *so many that the spies fall silent*
> *so many that no evil tongue*
> *can worm its way into them.*

The frame of the pergola thuds. Rose petals rain down on him.

'I could of broke my neck on that blessed step,' announces Aemilia. 'You think they'd get a stonemason to fix it, the rent you'll be paying. A person could break an ankle too, and then where'd you be when you wanted a message? Waiting and waiting, like the girl whose best boy said he'd marry her once he'd given her a good try-out. Oops, mind, you've got rose petals all over that – here, let me give it a wipe clean for you.'

He snatches the writing tablet away before she can rub out his poem. Aemilia has lost her fear of him all too thoroughly, at least when she's alone with him. In Clodia's presence she remains subdued. Now she lunges at him again.

'My mistress said I was to tell you on the quiet, when no one else was by.'

'Tell me what?'

'This party they're giving, it's going to take up most of the day, and half the night, too. They're having recitations and musicians and dancers –'

'Dancers!'

'Not what I'd call proper dancers. It's those ones that strike poses according to the lyre, and look as if they've got no blood in their bodies.'

'Oh.'

'And I don't know what else they're having, once the boats bring the party back. So my lady won't be able to get away today. She says, why didn't you accept her invitation?'

'I'm working, Aemilia. I came to Baiae to work.'

Aemilia flicks a quick glance over his writing tablet.

'I dare say. But she says tomorrow's all right. There's a doctor down from Rome who's good on digestions, and my master's booked with him the whole morning. He suffers terribly with his digestion. So she'll meet you up by the old Marcian villa. Which I don't agree with,' adds Acmilia, as if to herself.

'What?'

'As soon as she's had breakfast. You know the place, it's that old ruin up above the Lepidan rocks. It's always supposed to be being renovated, but no one's ever going to want to live in it. It's miles from the Baths. Miles from anywhere if it comes to it. Nasty old place, full of rats and snakes and cockroaches, and they say it's haunted, that's why nobody goes there. There's a little bit of a beach just below it. You go down through the olive grove. That's where my lady'll be.'

'What don't you agree with?' he asks abruptly.

She looks straight at him. 'It's not safe. Anyone could come. Everyone knows my lady, and she says they know you as well.'

'You think that the olive trees are going to tell tales?'

'It's not trees I'm worrying about. And it's me that's got to come scrambling after her. Never mind that it's bad luck to disturb such places.'

She makes a quick sign against the evil eye. He's not sure if it's really ghosts she's afraid of, or Metellus Celer.

Clodia will protect you, he wants to say. *You're a genius with her hair, she won't let you be flogged and sold off.*

He has a sudden vision of Metellus Celer's face. Not genial now, but judging, condemning. And Clodia at his side, her face as hard as his.

'No one's going to see anything,' he says.

Aemilia gives him the strangest look, and her lips open, as if she's about to speak. But she says nothing. Suddenly she is formidable. She outfaces him, squat and sure. He could believe she's been standing there since earth began, guarding the gateway to love and beauty, trampling down trespassers. But it's only a moment, and then Aemilia's gaze falls. She's herself again, the daughter of a home-bred slave who was mated to a Syrian bought at Antioch.

'Tell your mistress I'll be there,' he says.

Aemilia still doesn't respond. She stands and waits as if the message hasn't reached her ears. Of course, he thinks in relief, she wants money. That's what it is.

'Wait,' he says, and picking up the writing tablet he goes into the villa. Money, money, why has he never got any when he needs it? He feels in the dry, scratchy innards of a pot where he sometimes drops coins. Yes. He shakes a few into his palm, then goes out to the terrace and the waiting Aemilia.

She disappears the coins into a fold of her cloak. 'I'll tell her,' she says, and she's gone, barging into the pergola as she goes, shaking the vine leaves and knots of roses.

Four

The little beach is made of grey-white sand. It's littered with driftwood which is also grey-white and as dry as the bones of a sheep which have been picked clean by winter. A couple of basking lizards whisk out of sight as they feel his footsteps.

He's early. The water laps very softly, as if it's already tired out. He explored the empty villa before coming down here, but Aemilia was right: no one was ever going to want to live in there, not even for a brief summer season. It's badly built and there are already cracks in the ambitious portico. Its mixture of meanness and ostentation sets his teeth on edge. The situation looks good at first sight, because the villa is set high on the rocks and commands a view of blue water, olives tumbling down rocky promontories, and in the far distance the outlying villas of Baiae. But you would always take the brunt of the wind there; cold in winter, parching in summer. The olive branches would knock and moan all night through. Even today there's a dry, itchy, irritating breeze.

The villa wasn't locked when he tried the door, and there wasn't a single slave to look after the place. It was abandoned, after all the waste of building it. He thought of the houses that children build in a morning, before the sun gets too hot. The children are called inside, and they forget about the carefully piled earth and pebbles, and their wilting miniature gardens made of daisies, marigolds and olive twigs. The sun blazes, the petals blanch and shrivel. By the time the children come out to play again, in the cool of evening, they've lost interest and they kick the walls apart without a qualm.

He thought that there were so many different kinds of

emptiness. Manlius' villa gave the impression that it had been startled in the middle of a long but living sleep. But this place was dead. Bricks, concrete and marble hadn't fulfilled their boast. There'd never been any life here. No one had been born, or made love, or died. If you ate food here, it would turn to powder, clogging your mouth.

He wouldn't bring Clodia inside the villa. When Aemilia had mentioned the place, he'd hoped that maybe it could be a retreat for them. All they needed was a corner that belonged to no one, where they could pitch their camp of love.

Camp of love! Flattering yourself again, he thought. Building your own little villa of metaphor, and standing back to admire it. You are fucking another man's wife, let's not get too fancy about it.

As soon as he smelled the air in the villa's dreary vestibule, he knew it was no good. He looked up, and saw that the ceiling was cracked right across, as if the whole place knew that the best thing for it was to fall down as quickly as possible. Scrabblings came from the inner rooms. Those rats of Aemilia's, perhaps. Not snakes. Snakes are silent, unless you're very, very close. Crows would roost here, and lizards would cover the walls. Owls would nest, bringing bad luck.

He shivered. The atmosphere was getting to him, making him tired, depressed. Maybe Aemilia was right, and the place was haunted. Sometimes land doesn't want to have a house built on it, because too much has already happened there. Suffering; death.

But he was being absurd. The olive trees around the villa were well tended. He noticed the black-tarred nets, carefully stored in little stone shelters against the day when they must be spread for the olive harvest to be shaken down into them. Nothing ghostly about them. Most likely the neighbourhood boys and girls found their way up here at dusk, and giggled as they proved themselves in these empty rooms. Big, strong peasant girls like Aemilia would be happy enough to flaunt their fertility before marriage.

Wedding songs kept running through his head like an obsession. Girls and boys raising high their wedding torches. Flames the colour of crocus flowers, licking the dusky sky. The whole day rushing towards this moment when the bride meets the groom, like a river rushing towards the rocks where it will become a waterfall.

The torch-bearers, musicians and attendants have to back away and close the doors on the couple, because there's no place for them in the bedroom. No one has the right to intervene in this sacred mystery that seeds the human race until the couple's children's children's children's children are as many as the stars –

But he and Clodia would never have a child.

He looked around quickly and felt heat rise to his face, as if someone had overheard his thoughts. Just imagine what his friends would make of them. Calvus, especially, with his sharp tongue: '*Sacred mystery of marriage! This is even worse than the sacred mystery of the golden fuzz around Juventius' balls. You should have stayed in Rome with us. You're going to seed down there in Baiae. Hay-seed, in fact. Big-bellied country wenches and clodhopping bridegrooms. Our lovely Lesbia as a blushing virgin – sharpen your wits, my friend.*'

The rats rustled again, like the leaves of long-dead trees. There are places that make a horse swerve, and you don't know why. Blood-soaked fields where wheat grows tall and strong, but there's a taint in it that makes the grain worthless.

He came down the steep path where brilliant patches of light quivered as the olives stirred in the breeze. There were dozens of yellow butterflies. He still had a sense of darkness at his back, but he was walking towards water and into the light.

She'll be here soon, and then everything will be all right. But she's late. Maybe her husband decided that the doctor was a quack, and cut his treatment short. Maybe something distracted her –

Clodia is easily distracted. How quickly she lights up at something new. When you are that new thing, it's overwhelming. You can hardly breathe.

He hears them. A giggle, and then a sharp, imperious voice. His Clodia. But she's not coming by land, she's coming by water. Their boat is rounding the little point that shields the beach, skimming so close to the rocks that the side almost scrapes. The inexpert handler of the oars is Aemilia, the passenger with a white scarf thrown gracefully around her head is Clodia, who shades herself further from the sun with a green parasol.

There's a broad patch of sweat on the back of Aemilia's tunic. She must have rowed all the way from Baiae.

It's crazy. They could hardly have found a more conspicuous way of getting here than in that dumpy little boat that looks as if Aemilia's stolen it from a not-very-well-off fisherman.

But Clodia, graceful and glowing, half stands and waves to him.

'Sit down, my lady!' shrieks Aemilia. 'You'll have us all in the water!'

With much ladling of her left oar, she turns the boat and heads inshore. Catullus has already unstrapped his sandals: now he kicks them off and wades into the water.

'Stop rowing! I'll pull you in.' He braces himself. The boat is heavy and the water holds on to it. 'Get out on the other side, Aemilia, and help me bring it in.'

Aemilia sploshes into the water, soaking him but fortunately not Clodia. Together, they haul up the boat, and Clodia steps out on to the grey sand. Her radiant smile passes him so close that it seems to scorch his cheek, but it's a routine smile, one of those that Clodia flashes just to show that she can.

She's not in the best of moods. The plan of bringing her sparrow has not been a success.

'He was terrified, poor darling. I've never heard such pitiful cheeping. Look at him cowering in the bottom of his cage. It's the first time he's ever been out on the water.'

'We should of put a cloth over him, my lady, then he wouldn't know any different than he was still in your room,' suggests Aemilia, who is already unpacking rugs, bags and baskets from the bottom of the boat, and lugging them to the part of the beach where overhanging olives give some shade. 'This blessed rug is damp,' she grumbles.

'No wonder, the way you kept catching crabs,' snaps Clodia. 'Spread it out on that rock and it'll dry in no time. We'd have been here in half the time if I'd been rowing.'

'Can you row?' he asks curiously.

'Of course. My brother and I had a boat when we were little. There was a lake near that place in the country I was telling you about. We used to time ourselves, rowing across. We'd each have a turn, and the other one would count. But you had to count fairly. One-and-two-and-three-and . . . You couldn't just count one two three, that was cheating.' She laughs.

'You should have rowed,' he says. 'I'd have liked to see it.' He feels another stir of jealousy, of her past.

'What, me row Aemilia past all those villas? You're mad. They were out on their terraces staring as it was. This isn't the most graceful of boats, but it was all I could get at short notice.'

'Doesn't your husband have a boat?'

'It's not suitable,' she says shortly. 'Oh, look, he's beginning to perk up! He's looking at me.'

She opens the cage, puts in her hand and lets the sparrow hop on to her index finger. Carefully, she begins to withdraw her hand.

'Won't he fly away, out in the open?'

She nestles the sparrow against her cheek, her eyes shining. 'Why should you think he wants to leave me? Is it because *you* want to fly away?'

'You know that's impossible.'

'Kiss me. Kiss my lips.'

'You'll have to move that bird.'

'He won't hurt you.'

He hesitates for a moment, then leans forward and meets her lips. They open, and his body shudders. He can smell sparrow, the dry mousey mustiness of the bird, mixed with the scent of Clodia's skin and hair. The bird's wings stir uneasily against his face. He moves back.

'Put him in his cage,' he says.

'Why?'

'You know why.'

She looks at him, measuring him. The sparrow cocks its head to one side and regards him with one bright black bead. Clodia's lips part again and her teeth show.

'I do like you,' she says. 'All right then, have it your own way. I'll put him back, and we'll eat. I'm hungry after watching Aemilia row so badly.'

Aemilia lifts her sweating face. She's already unpacked the baskets and laid out dishes which contain olives, lettuce, a cold roast chicken that smells intoxicatingly of truffles, a jar of pickled capers and another of preserved pears. There is oil, wine, and a white linen napkin folded around a loaf of barley bread.

'I love simple country food,' says Clodia. 'Wait, Aemilia, did you forget the thrushes?'

'Thrushes?'

'Yes, you fool, the thrushes that were delivered yesterday.'

'I didn't see any, my lady. Kitchen would've told me if we'd had thrushes. The master must of ate them.'

'What, in the middle of the night? No wonder his digestion is so bad. Never mind, Aemilia, pour the water.'

Aemilia unseals the jar of water she's brought to wash their hands before eating. The scent of lavender fills the warm air as she pours a stream into his cupped hands, and then into Clodia's. They rub their hands, and Aemilia dries them carefully with a napkin.

'You should wash your own hands, Aemilia,' says Clodia, 'since you're going to eat with us. Here, give me the jar. Hold out your hands.'

Aemilia looks uneasy, almost fearful. 'It's not right for you to wash my hands, my lady.'

'Nonsense.' Clodia smiles into Aemilia's face. It's one of those sudden, bewitching smiles that transform everything he's ever thought about her into a stab of love that makes him catch his breath. Even Aemilia's heavy features catch light from that smile.

'You and me, Aemilia,' murmurs Clodia, pouring water over her slave's hands, 'we've been together a long time, haven't we?'

Aemilia nods, moving her fingers clumsily in the stream.

'I was a girl when my father bought her for me. Aemilia dressed my hair on my wedding night, did you know that?'

He turns away, and digs his teeth into a chicken thigh.

'There now, Aemilia, eat. Go on, you must be hungry, and remember that we've got to row all the way back. You'll need your strength.'

He watches as Aemilia takes bread and olives, modestly. She's smiling now. Does Clodia know what she's doing, he wonders, when she binds people to her so easily with a few words or a smile? He's seen her do it so many times now, randomly it appears, at a party or in her husband's house. She can lapse into an almost childlike conspiracy with some dazzled youth, or with a disapproving old man who will never credit any gossip against Clodia again once he's felt the force of her spell.

Perhaps it isn't random. There's a plan, or at least a pattern. She disarms people, and turns them into allies. She seems to sense the exact moment when her charm is wearing off. She knew that Aemilia was hot, tired and resentful. And now Aemilia's happy again, well fed with intimacy as well as olives.

And even with chicken – there's Clodia now, offering a piece of breast from her own plate to her slave, and laughing softly as if the two of them share a secret.

In a minute she'll realize that *he's* slipping away, and call him back into her enchantment. He wants to be called. He wants it so much. He smells lavender, and the smell of Clodia's hair. She's let the white scarf slip off now that she's in the shade.

A few curls break loose from the knot on top of her head, and cling to her neck. Her body is curled gracefully sideways and her feet are tucked under her. Her toes are perfect: slim, straight, tipped with rosy nails.

'You're not drinking,' she says to him, raising her cup. 'Why aren't you drinking?' Yes, she's noticed that he's on the outer reaches of her spell, and she's drawing him back. 'You should drink,' she says, 'because tomorrow you may not be able to.'

'What do you mean?'

She glances at the glittering brightness of daylight on the water.

'It might not be day. It might be night. Day for other people, but night for us.'

'You aren't going to die, Clodia,' he says.

'Of course I'm going to die. My best friend when I was a girl, she went to bed one night and when she woke she was spotted with the plague and she couldn't recognize anyone. Her mother said she was terrified. She thought she'd gone blind in the night. But it was death coming for her, closing up her eyes so that she wouldn't see him.'

'What was her name?'

'Livia. She was very small and soft, like a bird. But she had a loud laugh. You'd never think a laugh that size could come out of Livia's body.'

'I promise you, Clodia, you're not going to die tomorrow.'

'Are you sure?' she asks, laughing at him, but he notices with something like joy that her eyes are wet with tears.

'Come here. I'll hold you, and then you'll be sure, too.'

'The day looks bright, but there's night all round it. Such a mass of night that all our days are just a speck of brightness in it. Night's always there, waiting for us, saying: *Go on, live, live as much as you want, do everything you choose, ignore me if you like. I know how to wait.*'

'You mean death.'

'Yes, death.'

He strokes her hair, looking out over her head. Her hair is warm. It smells of perfume, and faintly, sharply, of her animal self. He feels such tenderness for her. Such a desire to cherish her, as if she were his own child. He's never felt like this about any woman before. Such love. And then such hatred when she turns on him, as blank and blind as a painted goddess, with lies glittering on her face.

She wants to keep people in boxes, separate. Only Clodia can hold the keys. Her husband in one box, him in another. Who knows how many more there are? He tells himself it's the price he's got to pay, because how would Clodia be Clodia otherwise? Even Aemilia has her own box, which Clodia alone can open. And the people in the boxes are so grateful when the lid lifts and Clodia's face shines down on them.

He will not be grateful. He will not be pitiful. Enough. His hand tightens on her hair, and he forces his fingers to relax. Don't spoil the day, he reminds himself. She is here now, with you. She's in your arms, entirely given up to you, not thinking of anyone else.

They are on a journey together. It began when she looked across at him for the first time, in her husband's house. He looks back at himself and can't believe how careless he was, how much at ease. He was free then. He went to that dinner as 'one of our most brilliant young poets', a literary lion who could roar or not as he chose. He didn't care about any of it: all he cared about were the poems. That was what made him strong. Perhaps it was what made Clodia want him. She had so much – beauty, poise, a Roman-salon elegance that was still just a little daunting to him as a young man from Verona – and yet she wanted him. She laughed at his jokes and he shot epigrams across the table to her so that she could turn them back on him. And then she looked across at him, straight at him, and his tongue failed.

He still doesn't know where they are going together. It's only the journey that matters, rocked by her, caught by her, lifted up with her, raising himself on one elbow sometimes to watch the world fly past as if they were racing in a chariot to the thunder of a crowd that has bet everything it's got.

He closes his eyes, and the darkness sparks with life. If only Aemilia would disappear. Stop scouring that little pan with sand, and vanish into the trees like the most solid and lumpish of wood spirits. But then why should all dryads be graceful? A knotted olive tree, that's Aemilia. Blown so hard by the sea winds that she's twisted out of whatever shape might have been dreamed for her at birth – beaten for her fruit and condemned to live long years, gripping the earth . . .

He opens his eyes and looks at Aemilia. Really looks, for the first time. Her eyes are on him. Her busy hands cover her watching, listening self. She doesn't like him. He sees it fully. She doesn't trust him and she wishes he'd go away. She stops her scouring, picks up a lump of bread and bites into it.

She's seen too much, that Aemilia. She's been in places with Clodia where he'll never go. To how many other men has she given that long, measuring stare? It says: Yes, I know, for the time being my mistress can't do without you. But we'll see: we'll see.

Aemilia and night are hand in hand, just biding their time . . .

You've got to stop this. Another sleepless night is on the way if you're not careful. Tossing and sweating, listening to the cicadas give way to the owls. Wanting her so much you end up tossing yourself off like a goat scratching itself against a post. And then lying there with sweat drying in the dawn chill and still thinking of her, still thinking of her quick, small hands and the laugh stifled in her throat.

He strokes her hair. It is so alive. When Aemilia draws the comb through it before it's oiled, Clodia's hair rises in a cloud and spits out blue sparks, while Aemilia purses her lips like a votary tending a flame.

Her eyes are closed. She looks shadowy, as if she's more than halfway to the other world. He could ask her what she's thinking of, but she'd say, 'Nothing.'

'Listen, Clodia,' he murmurs, 'let's be together tonight, even if it's only for an hour. Surely you can manage an hour?'

But she twists away from him. Her eyes snap open and she changes into another Clodia, commanding and vital.

'Let's go out in the boat. There's a breeze over the water – see how it's picking up the surface. It'll be cooler there. Aemilia!'

Obediently, Aemilia champs her mouthful of bread, swallows convulsively and scrambles to her feet.

Five

Clodia doesn't want to leave Aemilia behind on the beach, although it's plain that with three in the boat they won't be able to breathe, let alone talk or touch, without Aemilia being part of it. But this doesn't seem to bother Clodia.

'Aemilia's used to it,' she says, and he doesn't want to probe what she means.

'But you can't leave your sparrow here alone,' he says guilefully. 'Someone might steal him. A fox might get him.'

'In broad daylight?' she scoffs, but he watches the thought darken in her eyes.

'Or a lynx,' he adds, guessing that she wouldn't know any more about the creatures of these woods than he does. 'If we left Aemilia here, she could fight off a lynx with no trouble.'

Aemilia makes the sign of the evil eye. 'The gods forbid any such creature come near us,' she says, 'but I'll find a stick to beat them off.'

'All right,' says Clodia, 'Aemilia can stay.'

'You'll need more than that little sunshade, out on the water this time of day,' says Aemilia, 'if you don't want to burn black as an Egyptian.'

Familiarly, she touches Clodia's cheek, showing off to him the complexion which she has helped to make. Clodia smiles and shrugs.

'Fix something up then, Aemilia.'

He watches while Aemilia rigs up a canopy over the boat, using pine branches and the linen cloth she spread for their meal. She dips the cloth in water before she stretches and knots it to the branches – *to cool that blessed breeze down for you* – and then she hoicks the canopy into place, wedges the upright supports, and lashes them into place with the cloths she used to wrap the food. He has to admit it is clever, but Clodia seems to take Aemilia's ingenuity for granted.

'There, that'll keep the sun off you,' says Aemilia with satisfaction, looking at her handiwork.

He thinks it might be hard to row without knocking the contraption into the water, but Clodia is as skilled with the oars as she claimed. Easily, falling into rhythm together, they manoeuvre their odd little boat out into deep water.

Clodia has wrapped her white scarf around her head so that her face is half concealed. There are no other boats anywhere near them. Everyone will be sleeping out the hottest hours of the day. They're hidden, not by night but by the extremity of day.

Sun glares off the water, although a small breeze makes its burning heat bearable. Waves cluck and slap under the hull. The oars are shipped, and the boat drifts, rocking. He feels under the bench for the anchor, drops it over the side and listens to the bump and rattle of the chain until the anchor finds its depth and settles there.

Already the shore looks like another world, shimmering in the heat haze. His head throbs, and he stares down into the depths, into the silky, clear, dark water. To the right of the anchor there's a bulge of rock. A quivering shoal of tiny fish hangs above it, and then suddenly darts sideways. They must have felt the boat's shadow. If this were his own lake, instead of salt sea, and that promontory his precious Sirmio, he'd know exactly what fish they were.

'I had a dream about Livia last night,' says Clodia.

'Did you?'

Before today he never even knew of Livia's existence, and yet she's important enough to live in Clodia's dreams as well as in her memory.

'Yes. I was with a crowd of people. My family; friends. I think that you were there. We were by the water.'

'Here?'

'Not here,' she says impatiently. 'Livia never came here. It was by that little lake I told you about, where I raced with my brother. But in the dream the lake was larger. Everybody was talking and laughing when Livia appeared. She asked me question after question, and I answered all of them carefully. It was a while before I realized that no one else could see her, or hear her. Livia knew it too and she was smiling, as if we had a private joke together.'

'And then what?'

'I don't remember. She had her hair dressed like a woman. But Livia was only ten when she died.'

The boat rocks at anchor, and the ripples push their way under the bow. He takes her hand but she doesn't respond.

'How did the dream end?'

She shrugs. 'The usual way. In a muddle. You don't expect dreams to make sense.'

He's quiet for a while, then he asks, 'What questions did Livia ask?'

'How can I remember that? How can anyone know what the dead want to know?' she bursts out.

He tries to put his arms around her, but as he reaches out Aemilia's canopy sags, threatening to collapse on them. Clodia recoils, staring at him angrily. 'You're always after the same thing, aren't you?' she says. 'All right then.'

Her hands tear at scarf, linen cloak, tunic, belt. She rips off her underwear, making the boat wobble violently as she wrestles with the folds of breast-cloth and loin-cloth.

'Clodia!'

She won't speak to him. In a panic he realizes that she's done what he's always wanted her to do: in speaking of Livia, she's opened up her past to him. And all he's done is make a grab for her.

Clodia kicks her clothes into the bottom of the boat, and huddles on the wooden bench naked but for her bracelets and the circle of gold around her neck, glaring at him.

'You don't want me now, is that it?'

He reaches for her wrists, and she springs sideways. The boat tips, the canopy falls on them, tangling them both in linen and pine branches.

'Get this bastard thing off me!' shouts Clodia, but Aemilia's too far away to leap to her rescue. And he can't help it: he laughs and keeps on laughing as he drags the canopy off them.

It all happens in a second. One minute she's on the bench, the next she's fought her way out of the tangle, braced herself with both hands on the side, and vaulted into the water. He lunges after her and there she is, going down, her hair streaming up to him, her body sinking. A flash of panic races over him. What if she can't swim?

Fully clothed, he throws himself overboard. The water churns with bubbles and he can't see anything. He thrusts his face down, kicks as hard as he can and forces himself underwater. He opens his eyes and sees her below him, twisting, half hidden by her hair. He dives after her.

He hasn't taken enough breath. He touches her ankle, then she slips away. His chest burns as he swims after her. She's turning. She's upright, and now she's rising to the surface. A strong kick from her foot catches his shoulder. She's swimming, not drowning. He hauls himself free of the water and bursts into daylight with his ears ringing.

And there she is, treading water, sleeking her hair out of her eyes.

'You bitch, I thought you were drowning.'

She laughs. 'I could easily swim from here back to shore if I wanted to.'

He glances behind him. There's the boat. Lucky that he dropped anchor.

'Clodia – let's get back in the boat.'

'Why?'

'So we can row in. Look, there's Aemilia pacing up and down at the water's edge. She'll be scared to death.'

He hasn't even glanced behind him. He has no idea where Aemilia is, and cares less.

'You're such a liar. There's no one on the beach.'

'Maybe that lynx ate her.'

'Much you care,' she says. She looks quite different like this, with only her face showing above the water, her make-up washed off and her hair plastered to her head. He swims closer.

'If I hold you, will we sink?'

'Leave me alone, I want to swim.'

She dips her head under the surface again and it comes up streaming. Through the transparency he can see her breasts, pale and distorted by the surface glitter. Her body dwindles away to her feet. She lifts her hands and pushes her hair back again.

His tunic clings. His heavy belt and sandals drag at him.

'Let me hold you,' he says.

He puts his arms around her. She feels dense, solid, slippery. Her hair swirls and fills his mouth, and water rises, touching his lips, his nose, his eyes. They hang for a few seconds, and then they start to sink. She lets go of him and kicks, shaking her hair back so a shower of drops beats through the air.

'Let me hold you,' he says again.

She holds him tight and he feels that she's laughing. He goes with her, down, down and then at the last minute she peels herself away again and they shoot back to daylight.

'Why aren't we able to keep afloat?'

'Because you're pulling me down.'

'Let's try again.'

This time she wraps her legs around his waist and they sink even more quickly. She clings like a monkey, even when he has used up all his breath. He starts to fight. He pushes her and pulls her head back by her hair. She still grips him. And then he lets go. He doesn't care any more. Let her do what she wants. Let her drown them both and let them be dead and together.

– *Clodia*, he whispers inside the hollow of his head. Her name echoes, growing smaller. *Clodia, Clodia* –

But his body won't let him drown. It seizes her, drops his head, opens his mouth at her white shoulder, and bites.

When they come up to the surface, she is crying.

'You hurt me.'

There is a deep ring of tooth marks in her flesh.

He coughs up water, unable to speak. His body convulses, expelling the last dangerous drops.

'Don't touch me,' she says. 'I want to swim on my own.'

He swims slowly after her, to the boat. He's exhausted. The side of their little boat looks as formidable as a cliff. She treads water, still weeping, too upset to clamber in. At least the boat has swung round and they are hidden from the shore. Wherever Aemilia is, she can't see him.

He raises himself, grabs hold of the boat and then drags himself over the side, scraping his flesh. Shivering, he drapes the canopy over the side of the boat so she'll be protected when he pulls her up. He kneels, reaching over the side, and grasps her under the arms. She lets herself be grasped.

He can't lift her weight unless she helps him. She must push against the side of the boat with her feet and he'll be able to lift her.

Slowly, draggingly, they get her into the boat. She isn't really helping herself. Even when the blaze of the sun touches her, she shivers.

'You're cold. You must get dressed.'

She nods.

He sits in his wet clothes while slowly, tremblingly, she puts on her long tunic and ties her girdle. She doesn't bother with her underwear.

'I've lost my bracelets,' she says, when she is dressed. 'They must have gone to the bottom.'

We could have gone with them, he thinks. He tries to remember what her bracelets looked like.

'Were they gold?'

She nods indifferently. 'Throw the canopy into the water,' she says. 'It'll only get in our way.'

'Aemilia could untangle it.'

'Let the fish make a home out of it.' She seizes the tangle of cloth and wood, and heaves it over the side, but it refuses to sink. It lies across the water like the sail of a capsized boat.

'Someone will find it, and try to guess what's happened,' he says.

'They might think there's a body wrapped in it.'

'Baiae's certainly got a reputation,' he agrees. 'All those late-night parties and nude bathing. I had great expectations when I came here, but so far it hasn't lived up to them. I'm surprised how tame it all is.'

'Baiae is famous for adultery,' she says, with an air of defending the town's reputation against unjust attack. 'There are far more adulterers here than in Rome, proportionately.'

'Proportionately?'

'Yes, they're cram-jammed into Baiae like slum-dwellers in a tenement. Don't ever let your wife come here for the summer season, if she's an upright Roman matron. Which naturally she will be. Even the purest of them will change when the Baiae wind blows through their hair. They soon discover that you can find anything you want at the bathhouses.'

'My wife!' he says quickly, stifling a desire to ask her for more: which bathhouse, when, and how does she know? 'What makes you think that I'm going to marry?'

'Of course you'll marry. It's your duty,' she says, as if she's twenty years older than him instead of only ten. 'You have to secure the family name. Your brother has no children, has he?'

She sounds like one of the matrons she's just mocked.

'Was it *your* duty to marry, Clodia?'

'Of course. What else is there for a girl but to marry? Even her virginity doesn't belong to her. A third of it belongs to her mother, a third to her father, and only a third to herself.'

'Did you believe all that?'

'You'll believe anything when you're fifteen. I was young for my age in some ways. But let's row in. This sun is beginning to burn me. Look, your clothes are almost dry already.'

She rubs the cloth of his tunic between her finger and thumb. The bite on her shoulder is hidden. Her husband will see it, he thinks. That ring of tooth marks is unmistakable. But she seems unperturbed. She'll manage it, he supposes, the way she manages everything else. Aemilia will paint it with paste, and bandage it, and say it's an infected insect bite. What man would ask to spy under his wife's bandages?

'So who introduced you to Baiae?' he asks. 'Your husband?'

She makes a quick, dismissive gesture. 'He's broken the habit of a lifetime to come. Haven't you heard that he only came for his health? He'd be far happier talking to the farmers about the prospects for harvest.'

'Surely he has stewards to do that for him?'

'But he likes to do it himself. He counts things over in his mind. That's how he is. Position, property, people. Not gold: that's too base for him. He has accountants to know about that. I am part of his counting, and again, that's why he's here this summer. Maybe his doctors did warn him to ease up and take the waters, or maybe they didn't. But something tells him things aren't quite right. He's got wonderful instincts; I never make the mistake of underestimating them. I must be reckoned, like a sheep who has got out of the fold. I must be counted back into it.'

'Shall I take both oars, or would you like to row with me?'

'You row.'

She trails her hand in the water. There is no hurry. Her skin won't burn, even without the canopy or the parasol. She has wrapped her scarf so that her face is completely protected, and her light embroidered silk shawl covers her arms and shoulders.

He can't see her expression. He rows slowly, rhythmically, heading not directly for shore but in a wide circle that will bring them gradually to the little cove. He doesn't want to let go of her.

'Yes,' she says out of nothing, 'I was married and since then my life has been the same.'

'You gave birth to your daughter. You've written poems.'

She sits up. 'Poems? You and I know the worth of my poems. Next to yours they are like grains of dust in a field of stars.'

He considers the simile, mildly approves it, then takes her meaning.

'They are not as bad as that,' he says, truthfully.

'No. You're right, they're not as bad as all that. If they were, I'd stop writing them. But isn't it interesting how we keep on dancing, or playing the lyre, or writing poems, even when we're perfectly aware that the performance is really not that good compared with what others can achieve? And one daughter, that's not so bad either. But not quite so good as to satisfy my husband. Look where you're going. You're heading for the horizon, not for the shore.'

He digs his right oar in, and the boat begins to turn. The light has changed. It's no longer the white heat of midday, which strikes the back of the neck like an axe. It's thickening now and becoming more golden. They must have been out on the water longer than he realized.

He wants to ask her: *Are those rumours true, about you and your brother? Pretty Boy Clodius and beautiful Clodia . . .*

No, of course he doesn't want to ask her. He's learned by now, surely, not to ask questions when he may find the answers unbearable. This is one lesson that Clodia has taught him thoroughly.

Clodia at fifteen. He'd have been – what? – five, perhaps six. Even if he'd been brought up in Rome and not Verona, even if he'd known Clodia and talked to her, he wouldn't have noticed her. She'd have been a grown-up; a pretty lady. If he'd been one of the crowd of children in the street outside the bridegroom's house, he would have tried to join in the chorus of the wedding songs, and scrambled to pick up the nuts when they were scattered. Would anyone have taken any notice if a little boy had cried out, *'No! Don't marry him! Wait for me, Clodia, wait for me!'*

She would have worn a wreath of marjoram flowers, a saffron-coloured veil and saffron sandals. She'd have been nervous. Or perhaps she'd have been in control, as she is now, casting down her eyes only because this intensifies their sudden, wide, lustrous lifting.

No. Not completely in control, not then. But he'll never be able to reach or touch that Clodia who really might have been shy, frightened and at a loss.

> *your golden feet –*
> *lift them over the threshold*
> *with bright omens*

At a loss, because everything in the ceremony celebrated her virginity, and they say she was not a virgin. She'd been used by her brother, who was *'fully a man at eleven'*. Penetrated, and left fearing exposure on her wedding night.

Or so they say. It could easily be a lie. Pretty Boy makes enemies as fast as he makes friends. Scheming, ruthless, ambitious and magnetic, what Pretty Boy wants Pretty Boy usually gets. His private army grows more dangerous month by month. His power-base among the plebs is formidable. Even Catullus, who's in the habit of dismissing politicians – 'They're all the same – corrupt and power-mad' – has to admit that Pretty Boy Clodius is in a class of his own.

But Clodia loves her brother. Everyone knows that. Whatever he does, she shrugs and accepts it. Why shouldn't her brother run Rome, if he chooses? He has passion, at least. He loves the people and wants to defend their interests. Of course all the conservatives hate him for that.

Catullus thinks that 'passion' is the wrong word. Pretty Boy is wilful on a scale that takes your breath away. Those eyes stare through everyone. He doesn't love the people, but he knows how to manipulate them as skilfully as any actor. With the backing of his rabble of thugs, runaway slaves and gladiators, he intends to give Rome what it thinks it wants. He gets away with everything. Even dressing up as a woman and penetrating the secret rites of the Good Goddess hasn't destroyed him. He sailed through his trial for blasphemy and left people shaking their heads not in horror but in perverse appreciation. They'd have given something to see Pretty Boy in his women's clothes, his beautiful eyes glittering as he picked up his skirts and outran his pursuers.

Clodia loves her brother, whatever has happened between them. And what did Metellus Celer make of his bride? He could have thrown her out, if she was not a virgin. He'd have had law and custom on his side.

But perhaps the bridegroom loved the bride. That's something Catullus hasn't considered. Perhaps his love was so great that it lifted itself like those golden sandals and crossed the threshold of that night when the virgin proved not to be a virgin.

> in him no less the fire
> than in you the fire
> but it burns inward, hidden

Of course it's not true. The marriage wasn't a love match, but an arrangement between cousins. No fire burns between Metellus Celer and his wife, as it burns between Catullus and Clodia. The same fire consumes them both.

He lifts his oars and a stream of water glitters off them, reducing itself to drops just before the oar plunges back. He has his back to Aemilia but he's sure that she's there, waiting on the shore like a future neither of them can escape. He's had his hour or two with Clodia. It's childish and unreasonable to expect more. An affair must not become strident and force itself in the faces of those who are trying to uphold standards.

Hypocrisy is a beautiful thing, he thinks, looking at Clodia's dreamy, downturned head.

There's sweat on his back. He's like a slave at the oars, going to a destination he doesn't want and hasn't chosen. Back to the familiar, the *familia* where Clodia belongs. And she won't break out. She wants her husband and the court she holds in her house on the Clivus Victoriae. She wants her poet, too, and the borrowed bolt-holes, the midday sweat and the insistent cheep of a sparrow that can't believe it's being, for once, ignored. She's like her brother, who wants to be swept to power on the shoulders of the mob while he retains the privilege of Rome's ancient ruling families. They want the gutter and the crown. They want everything.

Sweat trickles down his forehead and into his eyes. So she knows that her poetry is not much good. He hadn't thought she would admit it, or even be aware of it. She is surrounded by flatterers, who praise her dancing, her singing, her poetry. She has grace in all she does, but no more than that. *A field of stars*. That's what she is to him, and she doesn't know it.

'You should marry me,' he says.

Six

By early evening the wind has begun to blow. The sun is clouded and brassy. The heat is stifling. There's a storm coming.

The slaves are closing shutters, barring windows. A devil of dust and dead leaves leaps across the terrace. All the way along the coast, from every villa, a dog howls. From the olive groves there is an uneasy clamour of birdsong.

The sky is darkening. Catullus will not allow them to close the dining-room shutters: he wants to see the storm. They serve dinner but he is almost too restless to eat. Besides, who wants to eat alone? Suddenly his deliberate solitude seems crazy. It has nothing to do with poetry.

The first growl of thunder is far away. Antonius stands still, counting, with a platter of roast mullet in his hands.

'Still five or six miles away.'

Lightning flickers, cutting through the gloom.

'Shall I light the lamps?'

'No, Antonius, let's see the storm.'

He takes a few mouthfuls of the fish. It's fresh and good, but he has no hunger for it. Antonius looks pleased as he carries the plates away. They will appreciate mullet in the kitchen.

A jagged zizz of light, a couple of seconds' pause, and then a clap of thunder. The storm has reached them. He gets up and goes to the window. A few big drops fall on the courtyard, kicking up a sharp smell of dust, but the real rain still hasn't come. The sky is dark as metal, with pale rims around the heaped thunderclouds. He drops his napkin, leaves the dining room and goes out of the villa on to the terrace.

The wind is blowing hard now, hot and suffocating. His tunic flaps against his body. A crease of light runs down the livid sky.

Another crack of sound, but still no rain. He goes to the edge of the terrace and looks down through the olive trees which thrash in the gusts of wind. Their leaves flail, silver against black. Another streak of lightning splits the sky, and he thinks he sees a figure, deep in the olives, cowering for shelter. A woman, wrapped in a long cloak. The branches whip backwards and forwards, hiding her.

Clodia.

The thunder breaks, almost on top of him. With a roar, the rain comes, whiting out the trees. Within a few seconds, his clothes are plastered against his skin.

He runs downhill in a white confusion of lightning and rain. A spate of loose stones and washed-away soil rushes after him, as the dried-up stream grows into a torrent, frothing white at his feet. He heads for the trees where the woman was. Lightning comes down the sky like a ladder at his right hand, almost touching him. He smells something hot, metallic, acrid. It's sulphur: the smell of lightning itself. Something has been struck. Thunder bursts above him, shaking his whole body.

He cannot find her. She is somewhere inside the storm, close to him. He pushes through the branches, reaching out for her.

'Clodia!'

He sees her in another explosion of lightning. She is under a tree, crouched against it, rain running off her.

'Clodia!'

He's found her. He has hold of her. He lifts her up, into his arms. She smells of rain and she is cold. He pulls her into his own body, sheltering her, protecting her.

'Don't you know how dangerous it is?' he demands, angry with her for the risk she's taken with herself.

Lightning flashes again and on top of it comes a blast of thunder, silencing them. Rain hisses through the leaves, so thick and white that everything is invisible to the two of them except themselves. He holds her tight, as if to fold her into his own body and deceive the storm into thinking she isn't there.

'I wanted to see you,' she says.

He is covering her face with kisses, consuming its wet coldness, the clotting of her eyelashes with rain, the shivers that run up and down her body and into his own.

The paths are dry again, and pale with dust. The inner flesh of the umbrella pine that the lightning split open has turned from creamy white to yellow. Time is already undoing everything that the storm accomplished a week ago.

It's two days now since he last saw Clodia. He sticks to his routine, even though he has lost faith in it. Up when the morning is empty, to write out the whiteness of a sleepless night. His limbs ache as if he's going down with marsh fever. His eyes burn and his throat is dry. He reaches for a cup of wine and water mixed, and takes a long draught, but it won't slake his thirst.

He knows what she's up to. She's playing games with him, confident that her hook is embedded deep in his flesh.

He's a fool, wasting love on someone who thinks she wants it but doesn't even know what it is. She wants the feeling of being loved, and that's why one lover is never enough. Clodia doesn't kill for food, she kills because it's her nature.

He hates her and he loves her. He doesn't know what is happening to him or why it's happening. He came to Baiae because she asked him to, for fuck's sake, when he'd rather have stayed in Rome, or gone to the country. Rome's where he belongs, not Baiae, not even Sirmio any more. Rome is his, because it's where he's made his life.

Two nights ago she was at a party where he didn't expect to see her. She'd sent him a message that she was going somewhere else. *'Some incredibly tedious do that I can't get out of. Thank your stars that you're not forced to sit through it.'* He hadn't been disappointed. He had his Clodia. He preferred to hold her safe in the memory of the storm.

He'd only gone to the party out of boredom, and because Ipsitilla kept going on about it. Ipsitilla adores Baiae, and she's thrilled that Catullus is here this season. *'The atmosphere's wonderful: you'll see. So different from stuffy old Rome with all the respectables pulling long faces whenever they see anyone having fun.'* Ipsitilla has a new 'protector', as she calls the favoured client of the moment, and they're throwing a party.

'Do come tonight, sweetheart, we need you. I'd so love you to recite. It lifts the evening on to altogether another plane.'

'Which plane are your parties on as a rule, Ipsitilla?'

'Nasty insinuations, darling, don't cut any ice with me. I bring like-minded people together, that's all. If they make friends and go off and enjoy themselves, then so much the better. What's life for, if you can't help your friends to make friends? Promise you'll recite, just for me. One of those gorgeous Sappho translations?'

'Maybe. If I'm in the mood. Or I could write a poem about *you*, just for the occasion.'

'Hmm. I'm not sure about that, bearing in mind some of the poems I've heard you write about us girls. I'll have to hear it first.'

> lingua sed torpet, tenuis sub artus
> flamma demanat, sonitu suopte
> tintinant aures . . .

'Sweetie, I'm not fooled for one second, you most certainly didn't write that one for me. I'm not quite as badly educated as you seem to think. But it's gorgeous, isn't it? So exactly how you feel at that moment, you know, when you're falling in love and you don't know anything at all about the person . . . And after that it all starts to go off.'

> I can't speak,
> thin fire runs over me,
> my ears pound
> with the thunder of my blood . . .

'I wonder where it all goes?' asked Ipsitilla.

'Where what all goes?'

'That feeling about someone, as if nothing else matters or ever will. Because it always does go . . . Sad, isn't it?'

'Yes. But then someone else comes along. Especially at one of your parties, Ipsitilla.'

'Go away, you spoil everything. You're getting so cynical. I know who's to blame for that. Look at you, you're supposed to be on holiday and you look as if you haven't slept for a week. And not *nice* not-sleeping either. She's such a mega-bitch, darling – No, don't look like a thundercloud. Everyone can see it except you.'

'For fuck's sake, Ipsi –'

'Don't get cross. What I mean is, all those thoughts you've got about her, they've got nothing to do with what she's really like. That's the trouble with you poets. It's all very well being brilliant, but you end up miserable. You ought to listen to me. I knew you ages before she did and I always made you happy, didn't I? You always used to leave me with a smile on your face. But you will come tonight, won't you? Promise?'

So he came, not intending to stay. And there Clodia was, on a couch in a shadowy corner, reclining half in the lap of a boy he didn't recognize at first. Anger scorched him. Ipsitilla must have known. She must have planned this, wanted it.

But no. Ipsitilla wasn't like that. Clodia would have come on impulse, and Ipsi would have welcomed her just as she welcomed everyone who 'knew how to have a good time'. She didn't turn anyone away, as long as they behaved themselves. Plenty of 'respectables' came to her parties, when they wanted to 'let their hair down' – as they so grimly expressed it.

If Clodia saw Catullus she gave no sign. Her throat gleamed in the lamplight as he stared at her: her head was flung back as if in ecstasy. But it was false. She was the best of mimics; he already knew that. She even knew how to mimic herself.

He scanned the shifting roomful of bodies, but her husband was nowhere to be seen. It wasn't his kind of party. Either he was at the do Clodia had mentioned, or she'd made the whole thing up and he was at home, dining with himself. There was nothing here for Metellus Celer tonight. No hairy-legged senators, no Baian regulars who loved a spice of impropriety. Only the serious party animals who were the hardcore of Ipsitilla's little gatherings.

At the Baths earlier in the day he'd heard that Ipsitilla had discovered a Nubian dancer who just simply took your breath away. She'd been booked for that night. But he still hadn't really made up his mind whether to go or not. He'd been drinking at dinner, but not much, brooding on Clodia. And then she was there, with her unexpectedness and his unpreparedness changing the sight of her into a knife that sliced him to the heart.

He would have left straight away, but she released herself, stood up and came to him. She moved just a bit too carefully and defensively, as if the table might have a mind to get in her way. He knew immediately that she was drunk, although he'd never seen her drunk before. Clodia sipped her wine, she didn't swill it.

When she smiled at him her teeth were stained with wine. The failure of her smile – and her not knowing about the stains – made her seem fatally close to him. He could have coped with her usual beauty, but not with the way she staggered and caught at his hand to steady herself before quickly dropping it again.

'I told you about Baiae,' she said. 'Don't say you weren't warned. People don't come here to be – to be *boring*.'

He smelled the alcohol on her breath. Her eyes were glittery and she had that look of a person spoiling for a quarrel and not caring with whom it came. He'd do.

'You did tell me,' he said.

'So now you can – you can write a poem about it,' she said derisively.

'You flatter yourself,' he said. 'Give him a blow-job right now, in front of me, and then you'll deserve to be transfixed in my iambics.'

For a moment she gaped at him, then she spat back: 'Be careful what you ask for. You might get it.'

He made himself shrug.

'It's a pretty picture, isn't it,' she said. 'Two people who love each other, meeting unexpectedly like this.'

'But not quite pretty enough to be worth immortalizing, Clodia. You'd better get back to him. He might get jealous.'

'Then why did you come? You only came because you knew I'd be here, and now you've found me.'

She was telling the truth. He hadn't really come because of the Nubian, or because of Ipsitilla. He'd heard another flick of gossip at the Baths. *'Our Clodia was at one of Ipsitilla's late-nighters a couple of days ago. She'll probably be there again tonight. She's got her eye on a little milk-fed lamb she found there, maa-ing for his mother.'*

'It's true that incest has never been a stumbling-block to the Clodii.'

'More of a stepping-stone, wouldn't you say?'

And then laughter. Greedy, uneasy laughter. She was too much for them. Too much for Baiae, even. Flaunting it with her Princess of the Palatine hauteur, and then drunk on a couch with a near-stranger's hand on her breast. And what her husband thinks, fuck only knows. No one dares bring up the subject anywhere near him.

'So where's your husband tonight?' he asked her.

'Resting, after a course of enemas,' she pronounced carefully, unable to resist a small smile of triumph when she gets the word 'enema' out without stumbling.

'Clodia –'

'Don't touch me.'

'I must see you tomorrow.'

'It's impossible.'

There was the dancer after all: he hadn't noticed. She had long, polished limbs, and she wore an elaborate twisted red-and-gold headdress that emphasized the carriage of her neck. When she flexed her fingers they seemed to make the music swell and then fade. She cared nothing for him, for Clodia, for Ipsitilla, for Rome even. She seemed to mistrust even the air around her and to breathe it only because she had no choice.

He'd like to go over, take her hand and walk away with her. 'It's impossible,' repeated Clodia, but this time, maybe because she sensed the Nubian in his thoughts, her voice was less final. A little space began to exist, where the impossible might change to the possible – perhaps – if he played the game right.

He couldn't resist. He hates her but he loves her. There's no room for anything else.

'You should go home,' he said.

'We only came because of the dancer,' she replied.

We, you bitch, he thought. Well, go on – have him, and then see how he looks in the morning light.

The dancer stirred. Flute, cymbal and drum rose, clashing out a noise that stirred his blood. A shiver of music ran through the Nubian's body. She seemed languid at first but then she quickened. Her long red tunic almost covered her feet, and was cut severely high at the throat. The fabric swayed in the lamplight. Her face was stern, with its strong, tilted planes. The whites of her eyes were faintly yellow, and the irises and pupils fused in darkness. She could have been Clodia's sister, if one looked only at those wide, dark, distant eyes.

Clodia was looking, too. At him and then at the dancer. The dancer noticed and stared back for a few seconds, impervious. For her, Clodia was no witch, no princess, no equal, even. She was just another punter who might, in the way of these Romans, have so much money that she didn't know what to do with it.

The Nubian moved her hips faster, answering the shrillness of the flute. Both he and Clodia vanished from her attention as the music took it.

'She's like you,' said Clodia.

He laughed incredulously.

'She *is* like you,' Clodia insisted, 'and that's why you can't take your eyes off her.'

'How?'

'Look at her.'

Clodia gestured towards the dancer. People were watching Clodia now. She made a disturbance, just by standing there. She was as strung-up as a charioteer at the start of a race, with his reins lashed around his body and his knife ready to cut them free in case of a smash.

But there was nothing to win here. Only the smoky lamplight, and Clodia tense with a passion that was going nowhere. She was everything to him and she had everything that belonged to him, but it meant nothing to her.

He wanted to hate her, but his heart could not do it. He thought of the rage that burned in her. *Lesbia . . . mea Lesbia . . .* Her rage, that became a depression smouldering in her for days, not to be lifted. Days when she would sit blank, her face unmoving except when her sparrow chirruped from between her breasts. But even then her sadness didn't really shift. Sometimes she stared at the sparrow without seeing it.

Clodia had no race to run. '*I'm going nowhere,*' she said at those bad times. And then, because he loved her, he wanted some bright object to appear before her – some apple of the imagination for her to run after – *et tristis animi levare curas – and lift the weight from her unhappy spirit –*

Unhappy wasn't right. It was something less curable than unhappiness. Clodia seemed lifeless as she sank down into a world that had no welcome for anything or anyone –

'Come back, you bastard.'

'What?'

'You're thinking of a fucking poem again. *This place makes me sick!*' said Clodia loudly, as if the wine had suddenly doubled itself in her veins. '*She's* safe in dance-world, *you're* safe in poem-world, the rest of us can *go – to – hell*. Don't lie to me, I know you. Is it too much to ask for you to be present, *really here*, just for a single hour?'

'It wasn't for my presence that you came here. What about *him* – what's-his-face? – no, don't tell me, it'll come to me. Decimus, isn't it? Did he come trotting down from Rome because you crooked your finger? How many more have you got lined up, waiting?'

'At least he's *here*. At least he's not thinking about resolution of the fifth foot into spondees.'

'I don't think of such things. I discover afterwards that I've accomplished them.'

That boy was watching her with hot, aggrieved longing. There was something babyish about him, too, as if he wasn't quite sure what the grown-ups were up to. But he stayed on his couch. He wasn't going to come over and make a scene. Catullus turned back to the dancer.

'Look at her eyes,' Clodia repeated, more quietly now. 'She doesn't even see us.'

She was right. The dancer was lost inside the music. Her right hand, holding a pair of wooden clappers, came up slowly. The sleeves of her tunic fell back to show her oiled bare arms. The fall of her sleeve, the slight, perfect movement of her fingers, and the ripple of clapper beats joined into something so beautiful that he had to catch his breath. The sound of the flute rose again from the trio of musicians behind her, harsh and compelling.

Clodia was a dancer, famed for it in her circle. But she was nothing compared to this, and she knew it.

She would sit for days now, her spirit clouded. She'd go out at night and take one of her boys with her, the type who can only stammer with pleasure because he's sitting next to her. And each morning he, Catullus, will be gnawed to rags by the thought of what she's been doing. Picture her looping her long legs around another man's back, or spreading honey on her nipple and letting him suck. All her little tricks.

He'll try to stick to routine. He'll go and sit on the shaded terrace of his rented villa, and struggle with a first draft. The words that might have made poems will shuffle about in his head like criminals. He'll be sick with jealousy. Shaking with it, close to retching into the bushes, and then furious with himself.

Why does she do it? Why does she make them both live in the grey, shivering, when the sun could be glowing down on them? They have given each other everything. They've gone beyond pleasure into an ecstasy so still that moments pass like hours, ripe and perfect. He's sure, dead sure, that she, like him, has never known happiness like this with anyone.

But she'll go back to the boy. As if driven by devils that always get the better of her, she'll do it. Her chariot will clip the post, she'll overturn in a splintering of wood and a thrash of hooves. Her eyes will stare at him out of the wreckage, still furious.

But the real Clodia, his Clodia, is somewhere inside those eyes. Words stir in him.

Vivamus mea Lesbia, atque amemus

vivere = to live

vivamus = let us live!

mea Lesbia = Lesbia mine, my Lesbia (my girl, my darling, my only one)

mea: let it roll, slow and voluptuous but at the same time sweet and simple. Mine.

Lesbia = my name for you, my name that shields your identity (even though everyone knows it's my name for you that gives a name to the fiction I have of you)

and *Lesbia* because sometimes I borrow the voice of Sappho who loved so much that she saw nothing, heard only the drumming of her blood in her ears, and felt fine fire under her skin –

atque = and with that – yes, and also

amemus = but first let's listen: *am em us* – No, you can't say that word without putting your lips together and kissing it. Let's do it. Let's fall in love. Let's love. Let's kiss and kiss until the word is almost rubbed away between our lips.

Vivamus mea Lesbia, atque amemus
Got it. Listen to this, Clodia!

And at that precise moment she turned. She stalked away from him, with the dignity of someone who was holding her drink well. Her body melted on to the couch and she was beside that baby again: Decimus. Her eyes were as wide as Hera's, her voice cooing while the scent of all Venus' spices breathed from her skin. *He* was meant to see it, hear it, smell and taste it all. To feel as if the hand that she was dragging slowly down the side of the boy's cheek was dragging his own guts out of him.

Her eyes turned on him, as hard as stones. 'You've got your poems. This is what I must have: this boy who doesn't remind me of anything except how potent I am, and who stares at me like an ox about to be slaughtered, because he can't believe how lucky he is. Now leave me alone with him.'

> *nec meum respectet, ut ante, amorem,*
> *qui illius culpa cecidit velut prati*
> *ultimi flos, praetereunte postquam*
> *tactus aratro est*

> *tell her not to believe my love*
> *is as it was*
> *but blame herself*
> *that it has fallen like a flower*
> *at the far field's edge*
> *under the plough*

He's up in the dead of night again, with one lamp burning. His eyes sting, his body is stiff with lack of sleep. Even the owls have gone to bed. She'll be sleeping, he's sure of it. Arms flung back behind her head, face to one side, breath coming heavily because of the wine the night before. She'll sleep on steadily until long after the sun is up and then she'll call for Aemilia. Her skin will be bright and clear. They'll gossip in the warm sunlight, while Aemilia washes and dresses Clodia's hair, and neatly dodges a slap when she pulls a lock too tight.

'Did you have a good evening, my lady?'

'You were asleep in your chair when I came in. I told you not to wait up for me.'

'It's the master's orders.'

'Just don't let me catch you yawning today, that's all. It's like having your hair combed by a corpse.'

'Shall I sing you a song, my lady?'

'As long as it's a nice one.'

They both laugh. After a moment's thought, Aemilia bursts out plangently:

> Mother, make a bed with straw
> Mother, fill a cup with gall,
> For your son has come home
> Like a colt from distant pastures
> Stumbling to shelter,
>
> Look from your doorway, he's coming
> Over the fields, faltering
> Where love has poisoned him,
> Lay him on straw and cover him,
> Bring gall to his lips
>
> For love has laid death on your child,
> False love has murdered your son –

The comb clatters to the floor as Clodia pulls her head away.

'For pity's sake, Aemilia, can't you sing something else?'

And she does, of course: some ditty about Cupid flitting bare-naked around the heads of the gods and getting his little willy tweaked by his mother. But later, Aemilia will hum her own song again as she cleans the combs and brushes:

Love has laid death on your child,
False love has murdered your son –

He's not guessing, he's remembering. He listened to that exact scene through the open door, long ago, while Clodia dressed. In happier times, when he lay curled in a drowse of contentment, breathing the smell of sex from the bed linen. Then, the only question in his head was whether he should drift away again into sleep, or reach out for that cup of wine on the little oak bedside table that Manlius' janitor had dragged in from somewhere.

Happiness calls everything to it, he thinks. Misery drives everything away. Leave it, Catullus! Time to break it off. You make as much of a fool of yourself with your hatred as you did with your love.

Leave Baiae: that's the first step. There's nothing for you here. Seaside resorts are intolerable when you can't share the shrieks of pleasure. The water is calm, the sun is hot, the beautiful people are strolling the promenades after a morning of massages and facials. The Baths are full of steam, gossip, the sharp smell of herbs and the busy self-importance of doctors who have decamped from Rome for the season in pursuit of fatty livers, rheumatism, migraines, bladder inflammations and those more intimate difficulties which respond so well to the stimulating air of Baiae. According to Clodia there's a new Greek fertility specialist with some very unorthodox theories and a bronze speculum the size of a shoe-horn, who is attracting patients by the dozen. She half-thought of visiting him herself; veiled, of course.

His smile dies. Every thought of her comes back to the same place. He is raw with scratching it.

Leave Baiae. He could go to the hills like everyone else, but perhaps he'll punish himself, go back to Rome and sweat out the heat there until the city comes to life in autumn. The summer seems endless but even that will pass, and there'll be a fresh start. Dawn chills, bright days. Savoury patties piled high on food stalls, braziers burning on cold nights, and the ebb and flow of a thousand thousand unknown faces. He'll be safe in the womb of the city. There's always something new to talk about. A new scandal as ripe and steaming-hot as a fresh turd on a frosty morning, a catastrophically bad actor in the lead part of a new play, a pretty boy who has hit sixteen and has everybody running after him. There'll be friends to meet at the Forum, dinner invitations, an abjectly tedious recitation to avoid, or a bright, breathtaking new poem from dear Calvus. Cinna's never-ending epic will have grown by a verse or two and they'll tear it to pieces and then put it back together.

Yes, a fresh start. Politicians, orators, arse-lickers, idiots, plotters, poisoners, back-stabbers and buggers from Caesar downwards. All the bastards who make Rome the incomparable fountain of entertainment that it is. As long as you're not looking for those beggarly old virtues that have to scuttle around the streets without a rag on their backs, there's everything the human heart could desire. Surely Rome is enough to fill a life, if he can just get free of this obsession that has robbed everything of meaning except itself –

But she'll always be there. He won't be able to escape her. Even if he can stop meeting her he'll never be able to avoid hearing about her. Their circle is too small an island in the sea of Rome. Her name will follow him everywhere.

She's in his blood. He's not even sure if this is still love. He needs new words for her. He'd like to drown all the Tullias and Quintias with their flowing hair, white ankles and radiant blushes, so they'd never be able to simper their way into a love poem again. He's got to seize the subject and shake it until all the lies fall out like insects from winter bedding.

Clodia, I'm talking to you. *Listen.* Love and hate, that's what I feel for you, love and hate so fused together that I can't drag one from the arms of the other. You want to know how that's possible? You say it doesn't make sense? You're right. There is no sense left in me: only sensation. Feeling tears me apart.

Do you remember Crassus' crucifixions, after the Spartacan revolt? Of course you remember: you're older than I am. Maybe you went to see them. I was only thirteen, living back home in Verona, but even there we heard about Crassus' punishment. It made me shiver although I knew it was never going to happen to me. I wasn't a slave.

A man crucified every fifty paces, the length of the Appian Way. Six thousand slaves hanging there, stinking and rotting in the midday sun.

Blood and crap and piss and sweat and screams until at last, one by one, they had the luck to die. Crassus left them up on those crosses until the worms and vultures had seen to every last ribbon of flesh. A stew of flies and maggots simmered for miles.

That's what I'm like. Pissing and bleeding and sweating and screaming because I'm being torn apart. You hoisted me up here, Clodia, and no one can get me down. Crucifixion stinks. People couldn't walk the Appian Way for months.

You won't walk my way now, will you, *mea Lesbia*? It stinks and you're repulsed by it. You have to wrap layers of cloth over your mouth and nose so as not to gag. I've been torn apart and I'm hanging here in rags. Love is one arm of the cross, Clodia, and hate is the other.

But let's cut the long-winded crap. No one wants to listen to a moaner. Let's set the words on fire, Clodia, until even you can't shut out what you don't want to hear. Let's make your ears burn.

> *Odi et amo. quare id faciam, fortasse requiris?*
> *nescio, sed fieri sentio et excrucior.*

> *I hate and I love. Maybe you want to know*
> *how that trick's done? I know nothing.*
> *I feel crucifixion.*

Seven

Back in Rome. Back among familiar comforts, and, just as he hoped, things seem better. He's getting his balance back. Two quiet months in empty Rome – empty, that is, apart from a few hundred thousand plebs and slaves – and he's not happy, but at least he's calm. All his friends have gone to the hills, where the air is cooler and they can relax in the deep shade of carefully planted groves, or ramble in orchards, or fish in rivers that never dry up like the muddy trickles on the plains around Baiae.

The muggy, tormenting heat of the city rules Catullus' days. He sleeps best just before dawn, when a faint, cooling breeze cuts through the heavy air. The rumble of carts and wagons in the streets seems to make the nights even hotter. Babies cry for hours, and guard-dogs bark at the end of their chains. The cicadas chirr so loudly that it's like the filing of metal in his ears.

Sometimes, when he can't sleep, he pulls on a tunic and wanders out into the courtyard. The fountain splashes. He dips his hands in the water then pours it over his head and body until the tunic is soaked. Soon the dawn breeze will blow and the evaporation will cool him. Then, perhaps, he'll be able to sleep. The household will wake soon. Lucius gets up before anyone, to oversee the slaves' rising and to take charge of the day as he takes charge of the house. If he finds Catullus sitting out here, he'll worry.

'Couldn't you sleep? Do you feel ill?'

'I'm all right, Lucius, it's only the heat.'

'Tomorrow night you should have a massage before sleeping. It will relax you. You looked very tired yesterday.'

'You know I never sleep well in summer.'

'You sleep much better at Sirmio than you do here in Rome.'

He should have gone to Sirmio, that's what Lucius thinks. It was his duty to go to Sirmio for the summer, back to the family home. But he's not going, not even for a day.

His father has freed him from paternal authority. *You have the right to do as you please, and I must trust to your own judgement.*

Whenever Catullus receives a letter from his father, he puts it aside for a while before opening it, to brace himself. To read a letter from his father is like pressing on a bruise.

But at least his father is in Sirmio, and he is in Rome. His father's cold disappointment, like a cloud, grows smaller when Catullus is at a distance. When he's in Rome, he can blot it out. He is not the son his father wanted. That ideal son, his infuriating twin, has followed him all his life. His father's son is high-spirited but pious, writes clean Latin in a decent old-fashioned style, sows his wild oats (none of your cold-hearted, prissy, calculating youths!), but once these are satisfactorily scattered he's ready to settle down with a girl of our type. 'A girl like your mother,' that's his father's ideal. His mother, dead, embodies all the virtues, but she no longer laughs.

Catullus remembers a different woman from the figure of his father's recollections. Less pious, fond of jokes, a woman whose eyes often gleamed with private amusement, and who would creep into her children's room with a handful of honey-cakes when they had been sent to bed without supper.

His father can make an ideal of her, now that she's no longer there to tease him out of it. Catullus, however, is all too alive, a flesh-and-blood contradiction of his father's desires.

The ideal son understands business without having any of the grasping, commercial spirit which is so alien to his father's standards. Wealth is something to be husbanded. You must not squander, but equally you must not grasp. In their position – not quite patrician, but at the very top of the equestrian tree – they have serious responsibilities. They must lead Veronese society, and negotiate effectively with the powerhouse of Rome (without, of course, becoming seduced by Roman values).

They must exploit and if possible extend their landholdings at Sirmio.

The ideal son knows all this. He is modestly eager to learn everything his father has to teach him about the management of the family's estates and of their trading interests in Bithynia. He understands that his chief purpose in life is to advance the family, protect its interests and defend its name.

(Extraordinary, when you come to think of it, that his father and Julius Caesar are such good friends. Caesar, Rome's leading adulterer and bumboy, ruthless exploiter of every opportunity that comes his way; Caesar, who could put the whole world on his plate and still be hungry —

— His father doesn't see it. His Caesar is an ambitious but virtuous man of ancient family, a loyal friend. The image of what a man ought to be physically: Caesar's tough, tireless body never spares itself. His splendid seat on a horse is often singled out for especial praise. But perhaps what his father most enjoys are their conversations. 'A man of vision,' his father comments approvingly, 'A man of vision who is also a man of action. That's a rare combination, as you boys will discover.')

The ideal son, of course, would have sat at Caesar's feet.

Even his brother, Marcus, who does almost everything else that their father wants, does not like Caesar. Marcus is the favourite son, or at least he's the son whom their father understands. He has stayed in Sirmio, he's married to exactly the right kind of girl, he is loyal and thoughtful towards his father, intelligent and hardworking as he takes on more and more of the running of the estates. Sometimes, though, Marcus seems not as happy as he should be. Perhaps even he feels the shadow of the ideal son darkening his own life.

'Why do you try so hard to please the old bastard? He's never satisfied,' Catullus had asked once.

Marcus had been shocked. 'You shouldn't speak of Father like that.'

'Why not?'

'It's wrong.'

'You mean, the gods are going to strike me down with fire from heaven?'

'Of course I don't mean that, it's just – not right. It sounds ugly.'

He had felt ugly for a moment, after Marcus said that.

No, Catullus will put off going to Sirmio for as long as possible, even though he loves it more than anywhere else on earth. His life is in Rome now.

And suddenly, between one day and the next, the nights are cooler. The day's heat is golden, rather than white-hot and choking with dust. Clodia is back in Rome. She stayed on in Baiae for a few weeks after Catullus left (he has his spies) and then she went up to the hills with her husband.

She's back in command on the Clivus Victoriae now, no doubt packing in a punishing schedule of dinners, poetry readings, dance classes and musical soirées. He can't help hearing of her almost every day.

But even the most ardent gossips get bored. Doesn't Clodia realize that? They still want to know the latest, but *'It's all getting a bit same old same old with our Clodia, isn't it?'* They've licked her hands and now they're getting ready to bite. *'Great show but we've seen it all a hundred times, darling.'*

His heart is mean enough to take pleasure in seeing the dogs snap at her ankles and begin to believe that she can be brought down. She's been arrogant for so long, with her head set at the Clodian angle that she shares with her brother, her power to promise and to punish, and the quick blank stare that shuts offenders out of her magic circle.

So this is what love has brought him to: he sides with her enemies now. At the same time he wants to destroy them as they grin and roll her name on their tongues. Knock them to the ground, make them eat dirt until they choke on it.

He hasn't seen her. He'd rather walk through the warren of the Subura at night without protection, through filthy streets that swarm with drunks, pimps and muggers, than risk passing her threshold.

The less dramatic truth is that he hasn't been anywhere because he's been ill. At first it was the usual autumn cold, but annoyingly, his cough and sore throat refused to go away. He was plagued by a fever that sank down sometimes like the flame in a dying candle, only to leap up again. He was wrung out by nightmares and night sweats until each morning he woke exhausted. In the hopeful hours of daylight he thought he'd be better tomorrow, but the nights went on getting worse until Lucius insisted on sending for a doctor.

Lucius has been with the family since long before Catullus' birth. He was given his freedom on the death of Catullus' grandfather, but he's so much part of the family that it's hard to imagine how they would live without him. At one time, Catullus remembers, there was talk of Lucius starting his own timber business with money loaned by the family, but it came to nothing. Lucius didn't want it, perhaps. He was content to be their steward, rather than to scrabble for riches in the way so many freed slaves did. Lucius never seemed to care about money.

They couldn't manage without Lucius. He knows everything and everyone. He oils the machinery of the year so deftly that they don't even notice him doing it. Lucius belonged to the family once, and now they belong to him. They owe him more than they could ever repay.

When Catullus' mother died, it was Lucius who made life bearable for the boys. They saw him grieve rather than become silent and angry like their father. They remembered how often their mother had laughed with Lucius, and how rarely with her husband.

Their mother had become a shade. She had gone to join their ancestors, those terrifying ancestors whose wax death masks were stored in the atrium. You couldn't love an ancestor. Your task was to live up to him.

Their mother could not come back, ever. They tried to remember her as she was, but their father talked about a different mother from the one they knew. Only Lucius remembered the small things that brought her to life again.

'You are like your mother, both of you, you have a taste for salt,' he would say, removing the jar of pickled capers before they could gobble them all.

Lucius recalled little rhymes that their mother had remembered from her own childhood. He had her knack of telling stories, so that if the story were about a spider you would seem to see the thread spinning from its body.

Their mother had stood between her boys and all the dark shadows that scared them, but then she turned into a shadow herself. Catullus remembered pressing into her skirts, against the swell of her thigh, snuffing her smell through the cloth. He was shy with strangers, and his father hated it.

'Don't cower away like a slave! Stand straight, stop snivelling and look at me.'

'It's nothing. He'll grow out of it.'

His mother sounded gentle. She was gentle, but her hand was firm across his shoulders, supporting him. She had power in her and his father subsided.

Only Lucius still carries the cargo of the brothers' childhood inside him. To Catullus' father, childhood was over and done the day his boys put on their men's togas. He saw the outer shell, not the inner life.

Lucius knew everything about them. He even knew that their skin smelled different when they had a fever, and he would heat up the brazier, grind herbs in the pestle and prepare medicines just as their mother used to do. Lucius never criticized their father, but sometimes he'd be silent in a particular way, if their father had lashed out at them.

Lucius' brazier is burning again, but his medicines are not working.

'That cough has really taken hold,' he says, 'and neglecting it

79

isn't going to make it go away, nor is going out drinking till all hours the way you did two nights ago. Death knows your name just as he knows everyone's. I'll send a message to Dr Philoctetes tomorrow morning.'

'It's only a cold.'

'That's for the doctor to say. I blame myself: I've been too soft. If you'd had me in Baiae with you, instead of making me stay on here to look after an empty house, you wouldn't have come back looking as if you'd been doing time in a salt-mine, not a spa.'

'All right, all right, I'll see him. It's not the medicine I object to: it's the sublime superfluity, my dear fellow, of matchless, made-to-measure mellifluousness.'

'He's a good doctor. You let him talk. It does you no harm, and it makes him happy. There are patients queuing up to see Dr Philoctetes since he treated Julius Caesar's wife for inflammation of the bowel.'

'*That's* a new name for it.'

Lucius frowned, and ignored the remark with his usual air of stern, experienced chastity.

'Well, we all know what a bumboy Caesar is, Lucius. He must have forgotten himself and inserted his eminent tool into the wrong backside . . . Why are you looking at me like that? The Republic isn't going to dissolve because our great general doesn't know who or what he's shafting.'

'Our own lives, that's what we've got to think of, never mind the shortcomings of others. As long as we know our duty, we shan't go far wrong.'

Catullus lay and watched Lucius move around the room, putting it in order. It wasn't his job. One of the slaves should do it, but Lucius always had to check that the drinking water was cold, the bed linen changed after another night of fever and sweats, and that the bunch of rosemary that hung over the door was freshly cut and not shedding its narrow silvery needles. And it was soothing to watch Lucius. He had a way of putting things in their place that made them seem sure not to slip out of it again.

Long ago, Lucius had lifted a two-month-old calf high above his shoulders, not even for a bet – Lucius never took bets – but just to amuse the children. How well Catullus remembered the calf's offended bleating, and the bellow from its mother, who would have trampled them all to death if she'd been able to get out of her pen. He and Marcus had squealed with laughter and hopped around, close to wetting themselves with delight.

Lucius stretches up to trim the wick of a lamp. How puny his upper arms are getting, where the muscles used to bulge. He wouldn't be able to lift a calf now. He's in late middle age . . . No, it's no use deceiving yourself. Lucius is growing old.

He's feverish again for sure. The barriers between *then* and *now* are coming down. The day seems endless, but suddenly it's night and all the hours have finished unwinding, as if a spool of thread has rolled this way and that until it's empty. He almost thinks he hears his mother's footsteps outside the door, hesitating, and then going on, quickly and lightly, to see why the lamps aren't yet lit.

'Lucius?'

'Yes?'

'Did you hear someone, just now?' he asks, feeling his tongue thick in his mouth.

Lucius gives him a narrow look but replies calmly. 'There's always someone coming and going. We've had trouble with the heating today: a blockage in one of the pipes, so they've been faffing about with spare parts. We've got to get that fixed before the winter comes.'

'It sounded like a woman.'

'Could be. Now let's get you sitting right up. It's time for that negus you don't care for.'

'Negus is a complete waste of perfectly good wine.'

'But it settles the stomach, as well as strengthening you up,' says Lucius firmly, buffing the pillows and then laying them in his special way, two pillows crosswise with the third supported by them. Catullus lets himself sink slowly back on to them.

'That's so good. That's the way you used to do it when we were little, you remember?'

Lucius laughs. It's a spare, dry sound, as if to say: How can you think I'd ever forget a single detail?

'It's crucially, not to say vitally, important to keep an even temperature in the bedchamber,' says Dr Philoctetes, gazing at the ceiling, 'and apart from the daily visit to the Baths, for purely hygienic purposes, no other excursion can be considered appropriate or advisable at this juncture.' He rocks a little from heel to toe, like a happy child. 'The Baths, with their cleansing and purifying properties, will effect some ameliorative improvement to the patient's immediate symptoms. Naturally the patient must be transported there in the utmost tranquillity, in a closed chair. However, should the condition of the patient deteriorate to any degree, then these visits, advantageous as they may be, must be suspended.'

Dr Philoctetes speaks the florid, expansive Latin of a Greek who prides himself as much on his linguistic sophistication as on his medical knowledge. And who never uses one word when three can be vanquished at a blow.

'This cough, my dear young friend, has taken root, as it were, in a specific area of the lung: just here. Allow me the liberty of sounding your chest again for your elucidation and indeed enlightenment. You hear it? Ah, perhaps not, it takes a certain trained understanding: penetration, one might say. A pulmonary system that is completely free from obstruction, you understand, gives back an echo of a different timbre to one which is congested by disease.

'Not that I speak of disease in the organic or morbid sense: no, this condition is eminently treatable – eminently localized, responsive and put-right-able. Patience, my dear young man, patience and perseverance with the correct procedures and prescriptions are all that is required if this minor medical mis-adventure in which we find ourselves enmired is to be resolved as swiftly and optimistically as we require it to be.'

With Dr Philoctetes no patient ever suffers alone. The enjoyment of the first person plural is one of the perks of his treatment. More worryingly, Catullus has noticed a growing fondness for alliteration in Dr Philoctetes' speeches; but perhaps this is no more than the effect of trying to treat 'one of the Muses' most cherished sons'. For Philoctetes loves poetry. Very probably he writes it. The thing is not to find out for sure.

'Breathe in – hold it – and now breathe out. Go-oo-od. And again.'

The only sound in the room is suddenly his own breathing. It sounds loud and harsh, as if some suffering animal is inside him rather than his own self.

'Do either of your parents ever suffer from a cough such as this?' asks the doctor, with sudden directness.

'Yes. My mother.'

'And – you'll forgive me – how did her case respond to treatment?'

'She died when I was eight.'

'I see,' says Philoctetes abstractedly, and continues to thump, to tap, to sound the entire canvas of the chest. 'And now turn over if you will . . . thank you. And breathe in. Deep breaths. Good.'

Catullus is not sure whether to be glad of this outbreak of plain speech, or to be afraid of it. Philoctetes, who is after all a very good doctor, perhaps senses the tensing of his diaphragm.

'Of course we are not sufficiently inexperienced,' he adds smoothly, 'as to make any immediate connection, my dear sir, between the maternal malady and that which troubles you for the present. A little knowledge is a dangerous thing.' He laughs lightly, while his fingers continue their expert probing.

At last the examination is over.

'Stay indoors for the present, my dear young sir. Regard it as an unmatched opportunity for uninterrupted, unchecked – nay, untrammelled! – composition. I shall give highly specific orders to your household, above all to your excellent Lucius, regarding diet, room temperature and ventilation. The most minute attention to all particulars is an essential element of the holistic healing process.'

Lucius nodded agreement, with the air of one who recognizes his own excellence but sees no reason to bask in it.

'You must not risk the seasonal miasmas that rise from our great Tiber at present,' continues Dr Philoctetes. 'You young men are apt to congregate at the Forum, enjoying your discussions, favouring the cut-and-thrust – or should I say the play? – of ideas, in the youthful exuberance of intellect. News of the moment, the ins-and-outs of politics – the very spice of life, in short. Even, perhaps' (he lowers his voice reverentially) 'even, perhaps, a meeting with some kindred spirit who also wanders the green slopes of Mount Parnassus. But you will stand too long in the wind, and then you will be tempted, no doubt, to frequent the bookshops and linger in the arcades. I consider all this highly injudicious, imprudent and injurious for your health at present.

'Shun the vicinity of the Rostra, my dear young friend. Rest, relaxation, restoration are my recommendations, together with a most exacting adherence to the prescriptions which I shall have made up and sent round to you by this evening. All this being in hand, so to speak, I make bold to predict that within a few days you will begin to feel the benefit of my regimen – and perhaps – dare I say it – a few lines will emerge to delight and astonish all who love poetry?' He brings his clasped hands together in front of his stomach and shakes them hard, like a priest delivering good news from the entrails.

Sometimes Catullus is sure that Dr Philoctetes is mixing him up with someone else. His poems – surely – can't be much to this genial and prolix taste? But the idea of sickness acting as a poetic laxative has its appeal. Those few lines, easing themselves out – He smiles.

'There, you see, it's not such an unpleasant prospect.'

Dr Philoctetes lingers by the bedside, apparently not in the least of hurries in spite of the crew of supplicating patients that Lucius claims are always at his heels. He takes Catullus' wrist again, finds the pulse and begins to count, silently.

'Everything will go swimmingly, my dear young sir, if you will just put yourself in my hands.'

His words fall lightly, as if from far away. *Put yourself in my hands.* Yes, it's safe to do that. He's a good doctor and Lucius was right to send for him.

Let go, sink down, think of nothing. Dr Philoctetes has taken charge of his little ship and is ready to steer it masterfully between rocks and whirlpools. Yes, Lucius and Dr Philoctetes are in this together. '*Yield,*' they murmur. '*Yield, and be cured.*'

And so, later, when Aemilia comes to the outer door, he doesn't hear the kerfuffle except vaguely, as a matter of raised but distant voices with which he doesn't need to trouble himself. Lucius will sort it out. He closes his eyes and rocks on the waves which will carry him back to health, but the noise won't go away. Lucius is arguing. Other voices join in and he recognizes them vaguely. His household is massing for a fight. But what about? It's crazy to be shouting so loudly in the middle of the day, when no one's even drunk yet.

A woman's voice, harsh and piercing, rises above the others. The next moment Lucius hurries in, his face tight with annoyance.

'There's a woman at the door. She says she won't go without seeing you.'

His heart turns over. It's her. He can't breathe.

'She says she's come from the house of Clodia Metelli with a message for you. She says it's urgent.'

Not Clodia herself. Of course it couldn't be. It was only fever that made it seem possible.

'Shall I tell her to go away?'

'No, tell her . . .' He fights to gather himself up. 'Can't she give you her message, Lucius?'

'She insists on seeing you personally.'

'Then bring her in.'

Lucius stands there, radiating disapproval, then nods stiffly and goes out.

It's Aemilia, of course. He should have recognized her voice. She's wrapped in her cloak, and a fold is pulled right over her face. Lucius stands at her side like a gaoler.

'It's all right, Lucius, you can leave us now.'

'Well, if she gives you any trouble, I'm only outside. And no more of that shouting and carrying on, young woman,' he adds sternly to Aemilia, 'or you'll have me to answer to.'

Lucius leaves, but sure enough, his footsteps stop as soon as he's out into the hall. He'll be listening, because it's for the family's good that he knows everything about them. How else can he best protect their interests? And he knows that Catullus knows he's listening. Lucius is no snooper.

'Pull back your cloak,' says Catullus. 'I can't see your face.'

'There's no call for you to see me, is there?' asks Aemilia.

He feels a surge of anger. 'No, and there's no need for me to listen to a word you have to say either. I'll call Lucius back.'

'Don't do that!'

'You've got a message for me: right, let me see you deliver it.'

Slowly, sulkily it seems, she pulls back her cloak and he sees her face.

'Who did that to you, Aemilia?'

'No one. It was an accident.'

There is a raised weal down her right cheek. Her nose is swollen, and her eyes puffy. Her injuries are so fresh that the bruises haven't come out yet.

'Who did that to you?' he repeats.

She shrugs her shoulders. 'You've got to come and see my mistress now this minute. She's in a bad way. That little bird of hers has took and died.'

He stares. 'Her sparrow?'

'Yes. She found it at the bottom of the cage this morning, on its back with its claws sticking up.' She shudders. 'I can't abide the look of a dead bird, nasty things they are.'

'And she did that to you,' he says, not making it a question.

She shrugs again. 'She can't help herself.'

'I'll come,' he says.

Immediately, Lucius is back in the room. 'Don't you understand that this is a sickroom? Gaius Valerius Catullus cannot possibly leave the house.'

Catullus does not want to contradict Lucius in front of Aemilia. 'Wait outside,' he tells her, and when she has gone, 'Get them to order a litter for me, Lucius. I'm going to the Palatine.'

'You heard what Dr Philoctetes said. It's serious. You can't play about with your health.'

'I'm twenty-six years old, Lucius.'

'And how old was your mother when she died?' asks Lucius, his voice strange and hard.

'Why, Lucius!'

'She was twenty-eight years old, that's all. She should have lived to see you with children of your own.'

He has never thought of it like that. He is almost as old as the age his mother reached, and Marcus has passed it. Lucius' hands straighten the bedclothes, folding and patting them smooth, then folding and patting again.

'If she'd taken care of herself – but no, she didn't choose to. She was pulled down like a deer.'

He has never heard this note in Lucius' voice. There's an edge to it, acute, personal and suffering. But he can't think of that now. He needs all his strength to get to Clodia.

Eight

He's here, where he didn't want to be. At her house on the
Clivus Victoriae, where the long forbidding frontage says: 'Here
is power.' He is admitted, and asked to wait. There's still some
fever on him, which makes the brilliant tiles of the entrance-hall
mosaic pulse with colour. Diana stands there, arm upraised. She
has loosed her punishment on Actaeon, and his human flesh has
been swept away into the substance of a stag. Now his own
hounds will hunt him down. Actaeon's human spirit is still alive,
trapped behind stag eyes that watch what is happening with
horror. He leaps into the air, arching his neck to get away from
the jaws of his hounds.

Catullus stops, and looks into the eyes of the man-stag. There's
no escape for Actaeon. His hounds raven around him, snarling
as they prepare to leap for his throat. Behind him, trees crowd
together, blocking the paths. Diana watches intently. Her concen-
tration is pitiless, pure and beautiful. She stands close enough to
hear the crunch of bone and gristle when the hounds destroy
Actaeon.

This mosaic artist has broken all the rules. Diana isn't wrapped
in a cloak hastily thrown over her by her maidens when they
spot Actaeon's human eyes on her. She remains naked, as if to
show the man that she's invulnerable, no matter what impious
crime he's committed in daring to see her body. Let him see it
as the dogs tear out his throat.

The mosaic bristles with horror. The naked, ruthless goddess,
the man clothed in a stag's flesh. Actaeon's fate is terrible, but
his knowledge of it is worse. The goddess is about to feed the
man to his own dogs.

Catullus bends to examine the work more closely. What an artist. It seems almost impossible that such drama could be made from thousands of pieces of coloured stone. How come he has never really noticed the mosaic before? He must have walked over it a dozen times, on his way into a dinner or an evening party, and yet he never saw how beautiful it was.

'Clodia commissioned it when we rebuilt the front of the house.'

He starts. Clodia's husband is there, on the other side of the vestibule, watching him. How long has he been standing there?

'It's a superb piece of work.'

'Crassus introduced us to the mosaicist. He's done a remarkable Leda at Crassus' summer retreat – you know his little place near Formiae?'

'You'll have to narrow it down. Little places in Formiae are his speciality – the last time I heard, he had a dozen.'

'He has a good eye for property,' says Metellus Celer with a tinge of reproof in his voice.

Oh, for fuck's sake, thinks Catullus. So we can't say that good old Crassus is a greedy bastard who won't be satisfied until he's bought up half of Italy. No, let's keep up the pretence that wealth drops into his lap – and ours – and that we're all too high-minded to notice what's going on. We can just about be bothered to pick up the booty.

'You've been unwell, I hear,' says Metellus Celer.

'It was just a cough.'

'You must take more care of yourself. Where would we be without your poems?'

Where indeed? In your case, to be without my poems would be a positive advantage, since so many of them are addressed to your wife –

But it's unlikely that Metellus Celer has seen those. Why should he have done? Unless someone's been malicious enough to pluck a lyric out of private circulation . . . In Rome, of course, malice has to be factored into every equation of human be-haviour. The pseudonym he gives to Clodia in his poems wouldn't hide her from anyone who knew her.

He's sweating. It's this damned fever again. Standing up for so long makes him feel dizzy. He's weak as a cat, and there's Metellus Celer looking exactly like what he is: a strong, upright, hairy-thighed pillar of the Republic – or indeed of any other system that would put him where he deserves to be, at the top.

'You look as if you should be at home in bed,' says Metellus Celer. 'It's very good of you to pay this visit of condolence to my wife, in the circumstances.'

Pillars don't know about irony, surely? The man's face is impassive. *My wife.* Well, why shouldn't he say so? It's true. Clodia is his wife and the mother of his child, and they both belong here, in this palace on the Palatine. She is part of him, just as the rare, naked Diana is part of the floor. Men like Metellus Celer don't moon over what they want, they act decisively and they get it.

An immense weariness and discouragement washes over him. He is dissolving, like Actaeon, into something he is afraid to be.

– Oh, yes, his verses are marvellous, apparently, although I can't say I see it myself. Verging on the scatological, and so *short*. As soon as you start to grasp what it's about, it's over. Give me something I can get my teeth into – Have you read Volusius' *Annals*? Immensely worthwhile, in my humble opinion. But Catullus . . . chaotic lifestyle of course, that goes with the terri-tory. Clodia Metelli had quite a thing going with him for a while, you know. Yes, of course you knew. Not one to bother with discretion, our Clodia. What her husband makes of it, as usual, no one has the first idea. Yes, he's very dignified, isn't he? Hidden depths. Such a marvellous family tradition of service – I must say I do so *admire* him. He makes all those artists and whatnot look very flimsy.

Flimsy is what he feels now, all right. And tawdry, too. He's in Clodia's house, and her husband is judging him. His *visit of condolence*. Yes, that's about my mark, isn't it? Traipsing in here, bringing my nasty cough along with me, to pay my respects on the occasion of the death of a sparrow.

'My wife's maid will be along shortly. I can't stay, I'm afraid. Pressing business at the Senate. Duty calls.'

Excellent. Keep on talking like that, and you'll soon wipe my conscience clean. I'll be free to dislike you, my dear Senator. The only pressing business we all want to know about is which pair of downy buttocks is currently the recipient of our noble Caesar's prick –

But all the same, Metellus Celer owns this mosaic.

'It's the detail that makes it so remarkable,' says Catullus abruptly. 'See that dog there? He's lost interest in the hunt, just for a moment. He's scratching for fleas.'

Metellus Celer bends, and looks closely. 'I had never noticed that before,' he says, and his face folds into a slow, unwilling smile.

Metellus Celer has gone. The hounds encircle Actaeon, but they will never leap. No, it's worse than that. They will all remain frozen in that slice of time which can't release them. Actaeon's terror will never end in death.

Art is a monster, he thinks suddenly. Poetry is the same. It stops the work of time. All the love and suffering in the world is trapped in it.

Aemilia nudges him. 'My lady's waiting for you.'

'What?'

'Didn't you hear me say? It's this way, through to the blue reception room.'

She bundles along at his side. Slaves glance as they go past, then duck their heads or sidle off through doorways. One unlucky girl drops a pile of linen and scrabbles to pick it up. She glances at Catullus fearfully, as if he might be qualified to punish her.

'Report yourself,' says Aemilia. 'That lot will need to go straight back to the laundry.'

'Swear you, mistress, z'not a mark on it, s'as good as new,' gabbles the slave in an accent so thick that at first he doesn't recognize that she's speaking Latin.

Aemilia's face darkens. She kicks the linen out of the girl's hand and wipes it across the floor with her foot. 'You want me to put the dirt of the earth next to my lady's skin, do you? Wait till I tell her.'

'Oh no, mistress, mistress, I beg you, mistress – '

'Report yourself, girl!'

The girl backs away with her soiled bundle, sobbing. Aemilia's face is calm, and curiously content. She's passed on the blows Clodia gave her, he thinks. The girl will be flogged and Aemilia will be satisfied. Aemilia seems older and more powerful in the Metelli house.

'So a slave calls you "mistress" in this house,' he says to Aemilia.

She glances sharply at him. 'She knows nothing, that one.'

The blue reception room is empty. After a moment a child comes in, a little Moor who wears a scarlet loincloth and a fine gold necklace. Catullus has seen the boy before. He's a favourite of Clodia's, and he runs messages around the house. He also feeds Clodia's pet monkey, and picks up its shit. Clodia has no interest in the monkey, which was a gift from her husband, along with the little Moor. No one has bothered to house-train the animal.

'Where's my lady?' demands Aemilia.

'My lady's still crying,' answers the child.

'You'll have to come to her chamber,' says Aemilia to Catullus. The boy gives a high bubble of laughter, looking from one to the other of the adults, and then he leans back, back, back until his hands touch the floor behind his head and his silky belly is stretched to a tight hoop.

Aemilia's face glistens. Swiftly she bends and tickles him just above the navel. The child collapses, giggling, then springs to his feet again and says, 'I'll never learn my routine if you keep doing that.' His Latin is strongly accented, but perfect. Children are sponges, Catullus thinks, they soak up everything.

'You'll never learn your routine anyway. You're lazy,' says Aemilia. 'If you ever learn to tumble fit for the guests to watch at dinner, I'll give you a denarius.'

'*You* haven't *got* a denarius,' he answers, and dances away from her.

Aemilia's face falls, heavy again.

'It's this way,' she says to Catullus, leading him.

He doesn't want to go with her. It will all start up again, and he's not strong enough for it at the moment. His breath catches, and he has to lean against the doorpost. If he could just cough freely he'd be able to breathe better, but it hurts to cough.

He can't stand here, propping up the house. He must see Clodia, and then get out.

'She'll be in her room. Go on, go on.'

The bedrooms open off a colonnaded garden, full of splashing water and shade that will be rich in summer time but feels dank now in the Roman autumn.

'Here, this is the door.'

She almost pushes him through the doorway. He has walked too fast. Dr Philoctetes was right: his heart is hammering and there's sweat all over his body. He shouldn't be out in the world.

The room is dark. The shutters are all closed and only pallid lines of light squeeze through. There's a faint smell of vomit.

In the centre of the marble floor, she's sitting cross-legged and bowed forward. She lifts her face as he enters. It looks shocked, slapped.

'So you're here,' she says.

'Yes, I'm here.'

'Did Aemilia tell you my sparrow is dead?'

'Yes.'

He sees that she has the bird in her hands. It is lying on its back, showing its claws and its pale fluffy belly. He kneels beside her. She pushes the bird a little way towards him, showing him. He touches the claws with a finger, gently. They are stiff, and they catch on the skin of his forefinger.

'I thought he was sleeping. He had his cloth over his cage. I didn't want to disturb him.'

'I know.'

'I went to wake him up and I found him like this.'

Aemilia stands over them. 'It's too dark to see, my lady. Will I open the shutters a bit?'

Clodia stares up at her. Her face is wide and blank. 'Do you think we ought to, Aemilia?'

'We can't see to him without we have some light, my lady.'

Aemilia unfastens the catch, and swings a shutter open. Clodia doesn't stir. She strokes the sparrow's belly with one finger, while light bathes her exposed face. Her eyes and nose are swollen. Her hair hangs down roughly, as if she's been tearing at it. Her cheeks are scratched.

'She's cried herself half blind,' observes Aemilia, as if talking of a child.

But Clodia stares up at her slave, frowning. 'What have you done to your face, Aemilia?'

'You know what it was.'

'Did I do that?' asks Clodia in a tone of pure wonderment.

'You know what you did, my lady.'

Clodia's stare switches to him. 'I hurt her. I didn't mean to.'

'You were out of yourself,' says Aemilia, as if commenting on a flaw in Clodia's skin.

'I'll make it up to you, Aemilia. I promise.'

Aemilia looks down, with a dark, indescribable expression. He almost thinks she's going to smile, but she doesn't. 'Let me take the little thing,' she says, 'you can't sit there holding him all day. And I need to clean you up, my lady. Look at that stain on your dress, where you were sick. It's not very nice, is it?'

'I saw him in the bottom of his cage,' says Clodia, 'just like this. Just as he's lying now. But how could he have died like that? Birds never lie on their backs. Do you think he was trying to roll himself over?' Her face contorts with anguish. She brings the sparrow close to her lips, as if to kiss it, then lets her hands drop to her lap again. The sparrow's body bounces a little. 'What if he was trying to roll himself over all night, and he couldn't?'

'No,' he says, 'birds lie on their backs when they're dead. I've often seen it.'

'There was nothing wrong with him last night. He was perfect. He hopped all the way up my arm and then he came and talked in my ear. He was chirping just as usual, wasn't he, Aemilia? You heard him, didn't you?'

'Yes, my lady.'

'How could he die so quickly?' Her eyes fill with tears again. 'How could he be all right in the evening, and dead in the morning?'

'Let me take him now,' he says. 'We need to bury him, Clodia.'

'Do you think we should?'

'Yes. It's the right thing to do.'

'I don't want my husband to know he's dead until we've buried him,' says Clodia quickly.

But he knows, thinks Catullus. One of the slaves must have told him.

'She don't want the master seeing her little bird like this,' explains Aemilia.

'*Doesn't*, Aemilia. You're not a farm girl any more.'

'Doesn't,' repeats Aemilia, but Clodia has already slumped back into grief.

His head is spinning. The floor feels icy through the fabric of his tunic. He wants to be back in his own bed, under the spell of Dr Philoctetes, not here. Clodia looks desperate, awful. His heart clenches with pity, but he still wants to be anywhere but here. What a coward he is.

'Have you got a piece of silk we could wrap him in?' he asks.

Clodia doesn't reply.

'Silk,' he says. 'Something beautiful for him to take into the other world.'

It catches her attention.

'Do you really believe he is in the other world?'

'Of course. That's why we have to make him beautiful, so that he can show all the peacocks and popinjays that a sparrow is finer than them all.'

She smiles faintly. 'More beautiful than all the peacocks,' she mutters. 'Aemilia, cut a square from my blue silk evening cloak. Cut it big enough to wrap him. And then empty my amber jewel box, and line it with the same silk.'

'You mean your embroidered cloak?'

'Yes.'

'The one with the pearls sewn into it?'

'You heard me.'

'Well, if you say so,' says Aemilia, and goes out of the room.

'Poor little sparrow,' Clodia says, 'poor little pippety. But do you think we should bury him? Maybe it's wrong to shut him up in a box.'

He was in a box when he was alive, he wants to say. *His cage was a box, and besides, you never let him hop more than three feet away from you.* But Clodia's poor swollen face suffuses him with tenderness. 'You can visit his grave,' he says.

'Where? I can't bury him here. My husband will find out and he'll dig him up again.'

'He wouldn't do that.'

'You don't know him. You don't know how much he hated my sparrow.' Her eyes dilate. She goes on in a low voice, 'Maybe he did it.'

'What?'

'Maybe he killed my sparrow.'

'Why would he do such a thing?'

'Because I loved him. That would be enough reason. You don't know my husband. No one does.'

He moves back from her a little. The stink of vomit and the

musty smell of the sparrow are making his stomach churn. He wipes his forehead.

'You're sweating,' she says, really looking at him for the first time. 'Are you all right? Are you ill?'

'Yes, a little.'

'Because of me?'

You flatter yourself, he wants to say, but instead he tells the truth. 'Maybe.'

She smiles fleetingly. 'You should have stayed with me at Baiae.'

'I couldn't do that.'

Her spell is so strong. It's working on him, in spite of everything. She's calmer now. Her face is more beautiful to him like this, without make-up, without a thought for beauty. The rims of her eyes are red. She stares at him for a long time.

'You do love me,' she says at last, like a good doctor making a diagnosis.

'You know I do.'

Carefully, so as not to touch the sparrow, he moves to her side and puts his arm around her. Her shoulders feel thin.

'It's all right,' he says. 'Listen. If you're really worried about your husband, I'll bury the sparrow. I'll find somewhere beautiful, a place where he won't be disturbed.'

'Will you come back and tell me about it?'

'Of course.'

'Don't mark the grave. Just tell me, and then no one else will be able to disturb it.'

It's the sparrow's burial that really does for his chest. He should have stayed in the chair and supervised the burial from its shelter, but he would have been ashamed not to dig the hole himself. Aemilia had given him a little trowel.

He ordered the men to carry him to the Caelian Hill. He knew the perfect spot, near to an ancient oak that was dying from the inside, dissolving back into the earth it had known since long before Rome was founded. Wild violets flowered there in spring. He'd be able to tell her about the thick, twisted oak roots, and the smell of the orange fungi that clung to them.

The ground was harder than he thought. He broke out in sweat as soon as he started digging. One of the men offered to help but he shook his head. He was afraid that they might be tempted by the jewel box, and so he told them that he was burying one of Venus' sparrows as an offering to her, in propitiation after a curse she had put on him in a dream. They stood back, and made the sign of the horns. At least they hadn't seen the silk burial cloth, thickly seeded with pearls. Curse or no curse, he's not sure they'd have held back from those pearls.

The soil was full of sharp pieces of rock. He dug deeper, smelling sharp, sour earth, hollowing out space until the hole was big enough. The effort made him cough and he had to sit back on his heels until the spasm passed. The men watched him expressionlessly. That harsh tearing sound was back in his chest again. Dr Philoctetes was right: he ought to have stayed out of the wind. It was starting to rain, too: the thick, slanting rain of early winter. But never mind. She had let him bury her sparrow. She trusted him that much.

He scattered the dried rose petals she'd given him. Their faint smell of dead summers blew into the air, and vanished. He laid the box carefully in the grave, settled it, and scattered more petals over it. Suddenly he saw the bird in his mind, as clearly as if it really had been one of Venus' sparrows. It was hopping and chirping over the sunlit floor, making its way to Clodia, who watched it smiling. Now he wasn't pretending for the sake of the men: he was making an invocation. As he rattled soil on to the lid of the box he seemed to hear wings.

Nine

The journey home from the Caelian Hill is a blank. He must have climbed into the litter, and given orders to the men, but he can't find any memory of it. Maybe they had to lift him in. They could have robbed him, bludgeoned him, left him out in the rain to die, but they brought him home. Fever has left holes all over his memory. He feels as if he's been drunk for weeks.

Dr Philoctetes comes only once a day now. Catullus is officially 'making progress'. For a long time the doctor's clever, ugly face seemed to be at the bedside every time he opened his eyes, day or night. Dr Philoctetes' cool fingers were touching, probing. It hurt to be touched, and he tried to roll away, but he was too weak.

The strange thing was that during those days the loquacious Dr Philoctetes barely spoke at all, except to murmur 'Goo-ood' or 'Excellent' whenever he took a pulse, measured a fever, or spooned out a new decoction. He dominated the sickroom with the stripped-down urgency of a wrestler who has just perfected a new throw. Dr Philoctetes was going to outwit death, get him off balance and bring him to the ground.

Catullus needed a champion. Death was very close. He knew it with mathematical certainty, and tried to say so aloud – *math-e-mat-i-cal* – because he needed to tell Dr Philoctetes that there was an equation which would reveal how Death and Life belonged to each other. It could all be demonstrated in a few lines, as sweet as a nut. But he couldn't speak; he couldn't even lift a hand. He was completely helpless and all he could hear was the gods muttering in his ears. Just then he had another revelation. Poetry and mathematics were the same thing. It was only human beings who made different words for them. When you understood it properly, everything was connected and belonged together in a pattern like the patterns of the stars. If Dr Philoctetes knew that, then he'd be able to heal anything. But no revelation could get past Catullus' swollen tongue, and all Dr Philoctetes said was, 'Don't try to talk.'

Death was in the knife that turned in his chest each time he breathed. Death was there in the pounding of his heart while he coughed. Death was in the sweat that soaked his sheets, the dizziness that swam over him when he moved his head, and the nausea he felt for everything but plain water.

'Has the family been sent for?' he heard Dr Philoctetes ask Lucius one night.

'His father is being kept informed. A letter was sent to him two days ago.'

He won't come, thought Catullus. He won't come because I don't want him here. He'll know that. His voice is too loud. He hurts my head when he says, 'Well, my boy,' and waits for an answer. I've never known the right answer to 'Well, my boy.' He's afraid of illness. He was afraid of Mother when she was dying. Maybe he said, 'Well, my girl,' and she didn't answer.

His head hurt, even though his father was not there. Lucius must have written the letter to his father without telling him. He must have thought it was his duty.

If I die, my father will be sad. He had to piece his thoughts together from a hot, confused place at the back of his head. *But I don't want him here. Why don't I want him here? He'll be sad if I die, so why is he never happy that I'm alive?*

For a while death waited to take him away, as if Catullus had been sold to death like a slave at market, naked as the day he was born. He lay in the familiar bedroom, on the clean sheets that Lucius kept changing day and night. But he was also slipping away into the shadows. He was in the shadow of the doorway. He was high up above his own bed, watching his own struggle as the gods watch the struggles of men. How puny he looked.

His body was a husk. Why go back to it, when it was so easy to look down, free from pain?

Without a doubt it was Dr Philoctetes who pulled him back. It hurt to re-enter his own weak, suffering flesh. He hated the doctor and tried to escape into the darkness again, away from the hands pummelling his chest, lifting him up, forcing him to take medicine. There were poultices strapped to him that burned and kept him in his body. He was trapped. And there was Lucius on the other side of the bed, propping more pillows under him, rolling him sideways to wash him with long strokes of a warm sponge that smelled of eucalyptus. Lucius carried away his shit and piss and vomit, and the doctor carried away the vessel of blood he'd taken from Catullus' arm at the height of the fever. His body didn't belong to him any more. He let it go, and other people looked after it.

He thought that the opposite wall had become a tablet on which a long stylus was writing all by itself. What it wrote was better than the best lines he'd ever composed, but when he tried to read them out to Lucius, no words came. The stylus froze, teasingly, and then the writing began again. As fast as the letters formed, they melted into the wax of the wall.

The day came when he was better. No one else spotted it, but he knew. He was lying on his back, and Lucius must have taken away some of his pillows, because he was looking at the ceiling. There was no sound, but there was light. Very slowly, with great effort, he turned his head towards the source of the light. His head still hurt, but not as much, and he didn't become dizzy. He rested for a while, then moved again. This time he saw the candle flame, burning steadily upright. Behind the flame there was Lucius, slumped sideways on his stool, his head propped against the wall. He blinked, and Lucius' face dazzled.

He remembered everything. Clodia's eyes.

I've been ill, he thought carefully. I've been ill for a long time.

He was better, he knew it. His fever was gone. He felt happiness rise in him, so intense that the only word for it was 'bliss'. He must have muttered something because the next moment Lucius snapped awake.

'What? What's that?'

But Catullus couldn't answer. He was too weak. He just gazed at Lucius as the anxious eyes in the lined face came closer, hanging over him, reading him. He wanted to smile but it was beyond him.

'You're awake?' asked Lucius, and his voice sounded frightened. A hand came down and touched Catullus' forehead. Then the face did something strange. It twisted, and the eyes almost disappeared in a fold of lines. A harsh coughing sound came from him.

He thinks I'm dead, thought Catullus. He wanted to make a sign, lift a finger, smile, do something to show Lucius that he was still there; but he couldn't stir. Lucius swung the candle up, and Catullus' eyes must have shown that he was alive. The light hurt, and he blinked. He felt Lucius seize his hand. He wanted to speak but the distance between them was still too wide to be crossed. But he could move a finger now. If he summoned up all his energy he could move his hand a little inside Lucius'. And then Lucius was kissing his hand all over.

He must have fallen asleep again. When he woke something had shifted decisively. Dr Philoctetes was there. He held out a drinking vessel with a long silver spout. Catullus swallowed a little: it was wine and water mixed. Dr Philoctetes gave him a little more and then Lucius bent over with a sponge soaked in water and moistened his lips.

I can do that for myself, Catullus thought. Slowly he moved his tongue, and licked his lips. They felt dry and cracked. Lucius applied the sponge again.

He'd be able to speak to them now. They weren't far away on the opposite shore of a wide river. They were with him, in the same room, and time wasn't slipping about any more. No, it would move only in one direction now, creeping slowly forwards. Out of the corner of his eye he saw his ragtag of visions fade.

'I'm better,' he said.

He has had a letter from his father, welcoming news of his recovery. There are only two sentences in it that seem at all personal.

'Remember, my son, not to usurp my place as your father. I am counting on you to demonstrate filial respect by outliving me.'

He read that sentence many times, and it still seemed possible that his father had made a joke, a stiff, creaking joke perhaps, but a joke nevertheless. He rolled up the letter carefully, and put it away.

This is the first day he's sat at his desk. He still can't recall a single line that the stylus wrote on the wall while he was ill, but he does remember something. The poem wants to hide from him. As soon as he tries to look at it directly, it vanishes. It's to do with Clodia and her sparrow.

He buried Clodia's sparrow, but he left Clodia sitting on the floor. His girl. She needed him, and he didn't help her. It was a moment that wouldn't come again. Clodia grieving, Clodia alone and looking for consolation. She'd even sent for him. What a chance that could have been if he'd stayed there with her, instead of wanting to get away. Yes, he'd buried the sparrow, but his offer to do so had been a pretext. Really, he'd wanted to escape from her red, swollen eyes and the black cloud of grief that had swallowed her.

All the things that he hated about her had crowded the Clodia he loved out of his mind. Now he remembered her, sitting in the little courtyard of Manlius' villa while her sparrow hopped in and out of her lap, pecking up crumbs of the honey-cake that Clodia scattered for him.

'Aren't you afraid he'll fly away?' he asked.

'He won't fly away. He knows I love him.'

It sounded so simple; so gentle. How his friends would laugh if he said that Clodia Metelli was gentle, in her secret self. They thought she was as hard as she was gorgeous. He was deluding himself while she manipulated him. She was never going to give up her status or her husband. She was playing with Catullus, couldn't he see that?

'He won't fly away. He knows I love him.'

He's got to write about Clodia and her sparrow. He can't write about her without finding that she's in his heart again, folded away and nestling there. He hears her words so clearly, and sees her red eyes on the day the sparrow died; the day when he didn't know how to comfort her. He's got to write about her, but not as Princess of the Palatine, calculating sex goddess, or imperious mistress. Not as a lady lapped in Koan silk, not as a whore dancing for cash and attention.

She sits on the floor with her hair tangled and her face bare. She has torn her tunic in grief. Her dead sparrow lies in her lap. That's what he wants. He can begin in the high style, but then bring it down, as the grey, intimate light of dawn replaces the flare of torches. Only the simplest words fit her now: *mea puella. My girl.*

> *Mourn, all goddesses of love, and love's children*
> *on earth and in the heavens, put on mourning,*
> *for my girl's sparrow lies dead*
> *my girl's sweet sparrow, her darling*
> *for whom she'd have torn out her own eyes*
> *and left herself blinded;*
> *He was her honey-familiar, he knew her*
> *as a child knows its mother,*
> *and as a child lives at his mother's skirts*
> *he hopped and peeped this way and that*
> *chirruping only for her.*

But now he hops and peeps by way of shadows
into that darkness which returns nothing,
dark devouring death
has torn our small sparrow from us
beautiful as he was.
Poor little pipsqueak! – and now my girl's eyes
are red with weeping, almost blind
with what death has done.

. . . *flendo turgiduli rubent ocelli* . . . It's finished. He sits back. There he is, Clodia's little sparrow, hopping away into the dusk of death's shadow, pecking this way and that, hoppity-hopping with a sparrow's small concentrated cheerfulness. He cheeps as if Clodia can still hear him. He doesn't know that death's path has already closed up behind him.

Enough. He rubs his eyes to wipe away the sight of the bird. He's still so weak that writing drags the guts out of him. He leans forward, and rests his head on his folded arms.

'Are you all right?'

It's Lucius, coming up swiftly behind him.

'I'm fine. Just resting.'

'You shouldn't be trying to write. You need complete peace. A change of scene. Remember what Dr Philoctetes said. You must accept that a full recovery takes time. You have to recuperate properly, if you want to root out the disease rather than leave the seeds of it dormant in the system.'

'Yes, I know, Lucius. I've heard quite enough of Dr Philoctetes and his mixed metaphors. Don't fuss.'

Even as he speaks, he remembers something else Dr Philoctetes said: 'After an illness of this type, irritability is a regrettable but alas an all-too-common – indeed an unwelcome but yet unavoidable – symptom of a particular stage in the relationship between our patient and his malady. Or, as I should say, his recovery.'

The double-barrelled adjectives were back in force. He really must be getting better. And so Dr Philoctetes had been proved right: he'd just snapped at Lucius, who would give the blood out of his body for either of his boys.

'I'm sorry, Lucius. I'm tired and it makes me cross.'

'Just think how delighted your brother would be if you went out to Bithynia to visit him,' says Lucius, striking while the iron is hot. 'The voyage would do you good, too. Dr Philoctetes was talking about the beneficial effects of sea air.'

'I tried sea air at Baiae, and look where it got me.'

'It wasn't the air that did you harm,' says Lucius.

'Have there been any messages for me?'

'There've been inquiries all morning. Gaius Licinius Calvus called, but when I told him you were writing he told me not to announce him. Two more baskets of fruit from the Camerii. Oh, and a slave came from the Metelli house.'

'From the Metelli? Who?'

'No one we know. He wouldn't leave a message. Wanted to speak to you but I told him you weren't to be disturbed.'

'Lucius, you know that's not what we agreed –'

'When a child puts his hand in the fire, and gets burnt, he doesn't do it twice.'

'I may have been ill, Lucius, but I haven't regressed to child-hood. You'd like us both tucked up in our cosy beds before sunset, wouldn't you? Me first, and then Marcus because he's older. It was perfect then, wasn't it? – go on, admit it, you don't have to pretend with me.'

'At least you were safe. But "perfect"? I don't know.' Lucius stares down the years, his face clouded.

What had he wanted, thinks Catullus suddenly, wanted and never had? Lucius had never married, although of course he'd had women, discreetly, none of them lasting very long. No wife, and no children either: only his boys. He didn't approve of Clodia.

'I did my best,' says Lucius at last, slowly and a little heavily. 'I promised your mother I'd stay with you.'

'Did you?' Everything that Catullus has believed about his own past shifts slightly, as if there's been an almost imperceptible earth tremor. He's always thought that Lucius grew into the family like a graft to a living tree. But perhaps it hadn't been inevitable. His mother had asked Lucius to stay with her children. Had she not trusted his father to love them? 'Did she ask you that when she was dying?'

'Yes, when she knew it. No one else was by. We were alone.'

He says those three words, and Catullus knows. *We were alone.* Alone, but not alone, because with Catullus' mother Lucius was 'we' not 'I'.

And he'd never known it. Never even begun to guess it. He almost doesn't know how to begin to feel. Affronted – curious – No. Stop all that. Leave Lucius with his three words. Say nothing.

'Listen, Lucius, if anyone else comes from the Metelli house – *anyone* – they're to be admitted. I want to see them.'

Ten

Even before he hears the news, he realizes that something big has happened. Knots of people are gathering around the shops outside the Basilica Sempronia. They're not even looking at the displays. Passers-by lock on to the clusters like bees joining a swarm. Someone brushes against him, and apologizes.

'Oh – I didn't expect to see you out and about. I'd heard you were ill. Good to see that you've recovered.' But the look doesn't match the words. A furtive, appraising head-to-toe sweep, and a nervous flash of dazzling teeth.

'What's up, Egnatius?'

'Haven't you heard?'

'Evidently not, since I'm asking you.'

'The word is, Metellus Celer has been taken ill, suddenly. *Very* ill.' Egnatius pauses theatrically for the reaction. A punch of feeling hits Catullus' stomach. Metellus Celer is a pillar, as tough as they come. Men like him don't fall sick.

'Who says so?'

'I heard it from Arrius.'

'Since when has he been worth listening to? H'Arrius doesn't h'even know where 'is h'aitches h'are.'

'He was at the Clivus Victoriae this morning, just by chance, to pay his respects. He had the news from the Metelli steward himself. The whole household's devastated.'

Catullus glances around. Faces are tense, excited and fearful. The bad news is flying from mouth to mouth, like dust in the bitter January wind.

'*And* he was seen in perfect health at the Senate yesterday,' adds Egnatius. In case Catullus hasn't got the point, he adds with heavy emphasis, 'From the Forum to death's door in less than twelve hours, that's what they're saying.'

Catullus pulls his cloak more closely around him. How he dislikes this man, with his teeth as white as a pipe-clayed toga, and his habit of flashing them into a grin on every occasion, just so no one misses the sight. White flash: saliva spray: white flash again. Someone's mother has just died: grin. Best friend loses a fortune when his ships go down: grin.

'I see you're still following the old Spanish custom of swilling your mouth out with urine, Egnatius. It certainly whitens the teeth – but perhaps it doesn't do as much for the breath.'

Egnatius' face mottles with temper. 'Don't blame the messenger, my dear boy, just because you don't like the message. Our Clodia's tearing her hair out, naturally.'

'Don't call her that,' he snaps.

'No offence meant, old chap, as you know it's just an affectionate little soubriquet we all use.'

Catullus fights down his temper. Don't let this buffoon get under your skin, for fuck's sake. 'What kind of illness is it?'

'Who knows?' says Egnatius dramatically. 'Illnesses like this, which come on so *very* unexpectedly, are always alarming – don't you think? Especially when the victim – the patient, I mean – is well known to be as strong as an ox. Perhaps it's something he ate.'

'Food poisoning wouldn't cause this kind of panic, Egnatius. It must be something more serious.'

'I don't believe I mentioned *food* poisoning.' Egnatius raises his eyebrows and flashes another smile. No doubt he imagines that he looks the perfect man-about-town, with his carefully draped toga and nicely curled fringe. Such lovely thick hair. No doubt he washes that in piss as well. 'But don't take *my* word for it. Ask around.'

More and more people are gathering. He leaves Egnatius, and skirts the crowd, searching for friendly faces. He's still looking when someone taps his arm.

'I thought it was you. Have you heard?'

It's Calvus. He seems his usual self, neither excited nor fearful. He looks at Catullus searchingly.

'You're not fit to be out.'

'That cretin Egnatius made me lose my temper, that's all. He was hinting that Metellus Celer has been poisoned.'

'He's not the only one.'

'I've got to see her.'

'Wait.' Calvus' hand is on his arm. 'Don't rush in before you know what's going on. Listen, Cicero went to the Clivus Victoriae this morning. According to him, he was admitted to Metellus Celer's bedside. He came straight back here and gave one of those lethal little impromptu speeches of his, from the steps of the Curia. You only just missed him. He really pulled in the crowds. They were shouting and stamping by the end of it.'

'What did he say?'

'You know what he's like. All very formal and full of restrained feeling at first, and then a swell of emotion which he fights to master – but it's no good, natural feeling *will* fight its way through – but on he goes, bravely, until the final drop into sorrowful silence. I suppose he might have some genuine feeling, but it all sounded pretty calculated to me.'

Already, Catullus' fears are lifting. This so-called poisoning will turn out to be yet another *canard*. Cicero's making a meal of it – that's a sure sign that the whole story is bogus. A political hare, started by one of those factions Catullus can never quite keep up with – Cicero has always been thick with Metellus Celer. A duck and a hare at once, in fact. He can't help smiling.

'You're just jealous,' he teases his friend. 'You'll never match old Chickpea in the law courts. He's the king of advocates.'

'And the king of character assassins. It works like a charm every time, that's the problem. Why shouldn't he go on sweeping the strings of his lyre until we're all in tears? On and on about how his dear friend Metellus Celer was in the Senate only two days ago, radiant with health, in the flower of manhood, fulfilling his duty to the city he loved so well, and so on and so forth. And now he's been struck down in his prime and he's lying on what may be his deathbed, but still he thinks of nothing but Rome.'

'You're such a cynic, Calvus.'

'Not at all. Just showing my appreciation of Cicero's flourishes, as one orator to another. Where was I? Oh, yes, there was the poor old bosom friend of Cicero, barely able to speak above a whisper, but still thinking only of Rome and how he couldn't bear to leave his beloved fatherland without his protection. You can imagine the break in Cicero's voice on "fatherland". Nothing vulgar or showy, of course, just a restrained stumble to indicate his unbearable emotion. What an actor that man is. And the worst of it is that he doesn't even know he's acting. He believes every word of it, while he's speaking.'

'Show some respect, please.'

'If I could kick him into the Tiber and throw stones at his head while he bobbed about, uttering *pitiful imprecations* and with any luck not knowing how to swim very well, it would be the happiest day of my life. I hate the bastard. He's got the gift of the gods and he flogs it to the cause that pays best. He's power-mad as well. God knows which delusion he's chasing now: Cicero, defender of the ancient virtues of the Republic; Cicero, the great wit; Cicero, guide and mentor to Crassus, if not Caesar himself; or Cicero, ally and confidant of Pompey – what a joke. He's like a rabbit playing with wolves. All three of them are completely ruthless and at least twenty moves ahead of Cicero. Pompey's raring to be Emperor of anywhere. Crassus would buy up hell if he thought he could make some money out of it. Caesar will fuck or fight anything that moves, up to and including that mare he rides so outstandingly, with his handsome head held high enough for the entire army to see it.'

'He can't help being tall,' says Catullus.

'He could crouch down a little, surely?'

Catullus laughs, almost completely reassured. Calvus is bitching away as normal. Nothing serious can have happened. Tomorrow – or perhaps the day after – Clodia's husband will be laying down the law in the courts again, Cicero will be preparing a speech on a completely different subject, and there'll be another Forum drama on the boil. A touch of food poisoning, that's all this will turn out to be.

'*Stop laughing*,' says Calvus, in an undertone. 'People are looking at you.'

'What?'

'For fuck's sake, don't be so naive. Your name's linked with his wife and you're laughing your head off in public, on the day he's said to be dying.'

'Dying? What, really dying?'

The wind was in his eyes, full of grit.

'Haven't you been listening?'

It was really happening. Clodia was in the middle of it. Clodia might be hurt, in danger –

'I thought you said Cicero was talking it up?'

'Yes, he was, he was making capital out of it, but that doesn't mean it's not true. There've been plenty of other reports confirming it. Be careful, my dear friend. Or if you can't manage that, be just a little cautious. You've made enemies. People don't like being mocked; they'd rather be hated.'

'I can do both.'

'Be serious, for fuck's sake,' says Calvus, grasping his elbow. 'Can't you see that this is their chance? Think how easy it's going to be to make it look as if you're in this up to your neck. And then think of all those pompous fuckwits you've skewered in your epigrams. They'll be having orgasms at the chance of shitting on you.'

'You'd rip me apart if I mixed a metaphor like that.'

'It's a physiological fact.'

'I've got to see her.'

'You'd be crazy to go there now. All the Metelli are gathering.'

Someone jostles Catullus' back. The crowd is thickening. Bad news brings everyone to the Forum. If Metellus Celer dies – if this is true and real –

Calvus would never talk like this, unless it were true. Clodia will suffer. Whatever happens, she's going to suffer. She'll be weeping. It's her husband she's losing this time, not her sparrow.

Will she grieve for him? His heart is thudding. He can't picture it. Clodia, a widow.

A man is dying. At this moment his hands may be losing their sense of touch. But yesterday he was walking and talking. He was a winner, he had everything. Dull and pompous, that was what I thought. Standing there like a pillar with his broad shoulders and thick legs. The kind of man my father approved.

Clodia will be a widow, free, as I have always wanted her to be. But I never meant it to happen like this. Even in my most secret thoughts, I never asked for Metellus Celer's life.

'What else is Cicero saying?' he asks Calvus.

'He's very clever, you have to grant him that. Plenty of orators can think on their feet, but only our Cicero can be inspired by breathing in the groans of a dying man. There was a lot about his dear friend banging on the wall.'

'*Banging on the wall?*'

'It's all part of the image Cicero's trying to create. You remember how Quintus Catulus used to live next door to Metellus? So, logically enough, poor dying Metellus Celer tries to summon up his old ally in the optimate faction. You know how it is with Cicero's speeches. Everything is in them for a reason. He wants to link the way Metellus called for Catulus, saviour of conservative values, with the way he sent for Cicero. Putting them on the same footing, you see?

'It's always the same with Cicero, he can't resist self-aggrandizement, even when a man he calls "one of his dearest friends" is dying. Can't you just picture it? Cicero, Catulus and Metellus, brothers-in-arms against all the dross and riffraff who are just itching to take over and destroy the traditions of Rome. What a joke. Cicero wouldn't last five minutes against Pretty Boy Clodius. He goes around boasting that his evidence destroyed Pretty Boy's reputation at the blasphemy trial – but what he seems to forget is that *Pretty Boy got off*. His transvestite gate-crashing enterprise earned him no penalty at all. But our Pretty Boy most certainly hasn't forgotten one word of Chickpea's speech for the prosecution. Cicero has no idea how much a truly vicious man can enjoy the wait for his revenge.'

'Was he saying that Clodius might have something to do with Metellus' illness?'

'It was more subtle than that. You know how Cicero plumes himself on his implications. Very stupidly, in this case, but the man is a mass of vanity. He's completely missed the fact that our Pretty Boy is going to get him one of these days, implications and all.

'The Metelli are another matter. They don't waste time pluming. They're men of action, and they look after their own. So that's why *you've* got to be careful. Remember *your* role in all this, my friend.'

'I'm about as political as a – as a sparrow.'

'No one's above politics at a time like this, O composer of exceptionally indiscreet and adulterous hendecasyllables addressed to the wife of the dying hero. The word in the marketplace is that Pretty Boy is in this up to his neck, and his sister, too.'

'That's impossible. She would never –'

Calvus' face gleams. 'How someone who writes such outrageous poems can remain as innocent as you is one of the eternal mysteries.'

Even Calvus is caught up in the drama of it. How terrible that the dying of a man brings such a glow to the faces of those who knew him. They've dined at his house, enjoying his ample and rather impersonal hospitality. They've curried favour with him, pretending to remember every word of his Senate speeches. His front-runner toadies will be up at the Clivus Victoriae already, and soon the whole pack will follow.

Catullus has a sudden, sickening memory of the mosaic. The lead hounds make ready to leap, while the more timid circle the man they called master and will soon call meat. Clients, dependants, the dozens and dozens of professional friends that any rich, influential man gathers around him. They'll be crowding the entrance hall, 'making inquiries' while they ensure that the slave sends in their names correctly. Terrified, some of them, or distraught, or swiftly planning ahead, deciding what to do if he lives, and what to do if he dies. Getting themselves into position, like charioteers calculating how they'll shave a few seconds off at the turn.

Metellus Celer has given a fine feast to his friends this morning. Even his enemies can count on their share. This is a table where the host has no power, and can exclude no one.

Calvus is probably right. It's best to keep away from the house on the Palatine. But all the same, he's got to go.

The wind seems to be growing stronger. It whisks more dust into his eyes, and they blur with tears. He grasps Calvus.

'Have you ever thought what it must be like, the moment after you realize that you've swallowed poison?'

'I ate some mushrooms once, without bothering to check them properly. A foul taste gushed into my mouth, like the pus from a rotten tooth. I broke out in a sweat. I remember looking for a knife. I thought I'd rather slit my wrists than die on the floor, frothing like a dog. But it was all right. I wasn't important enough for anyone to poison me.'

'But *he* is.'

'Yes. Take my advice for once. Stay unimportant. Keep out of it. We can't afford to lose you. But if you're still pig-headed enough to go looking for trouble, then let me come with you.'

Calvus is a head shorter than him, but strong and compact. A man no one could easily overturn. A friend who won't run, who'll fight back to back with you if he has to. But I'm going on my own, thinks Catullus, because I've got to see her alone.

Scavengers, well-wishers, messengers from fellow senators, clients and every shade of what the word 'friend' might mean: the whole ragbag of Rome seems to be heading for Metellus Celer's house. The big entrance hall is so crowded that some spill out into the street while others are still trying to force their way in.

How to get through the crowds? He's standing irresolute, flanked by his slaves, not wanting to push into all that flesh, when someone hails him. He turns, and it's Dr Philoctetes, moving forward with the quiet authority of a grain-laden ship coming into harbour.

'Let me pass now – quickly, please – let me pass. How are you, my dear young friend? But I need not ask on an occasion so oppressive – nay, overwhelming to the spirits – Stand aside there, my good fellows! Let us pass now – quickly –'

'You're his doctor? I didn't know that,' says Catullus.

Dr Philoctetes allows a small smile to escape him as he glances back over his shoulder. 'In a case of urgency such as this, you understand, nothing can be thought of but obtaining the best advice. Established practice goes for nothing, and rightly so, given the need for swift, decisive, authoritative intervention by the most astute and robust of medical skills – But I must leave you, my dear young friend, since duty calls, delightful as it would be to me to prolong our present encounter. Stand here, against this pillar, and you will not be discommoded by the antics of the vulgar mob.'

Catullus leans against cold marble, catching his breath. Philoctetes has already disappeared. At the far end of the hall a line of heavily built men blocks the way into the main house. He doesn't recognize them as slaves of the household. And there's Aemilia, not three yards away, shouting at a ragged fellow who's dared to arrive with a petition at this inauspicious moment, and at the slave who for some reason has allowed him in.

'Don't you know what's going on here? I'll have you flogged for your impudence, and you as well, Stephanicus, how much did he give you to let him in?'

The ragged man doesn't take a blind bit of notice. He's here to deliver his petition and deliver it he will. He begins to chant it out in a high-pitched wail: 'And so if my lord wants to know what's being done in his name, that is to say, the agent's crooked, time and again we've begged him to see to the drains and now the sewer's backed up and overflowing all over the floor, and there's six of us in the room, what with the new baby as well, only the women say it's not likely to be long for this world, poor little mite, and the smell of it is something awful, especially with my wife not being equal to scrubbing the floor given her situation –'

'Drains!' shrieks Aemilia. 'I'll give you drains. Wait until you're put out on to the streets for not paying your rent. You can whistle for all the drains you'll find there. Drains! Trying to get out of paying the rent more like. Well, it won't wash with me.' Her face flares. Metellus Celer and the grief of the house is forgotten. She couldn't feel it more keenly if she owned the wretched tenement herself. 'You don't know how fucking lucky you are!' she screams into the petitioner's face. The slave, Stephanicus, knuckles his forehead and watches sullenly.

Catullus would never have thought that the quiet, inflexible orderliness of Metellus Celer's house could break down inside a few hours. This uproar must be loud enough to reach the dying man's ears.

'Aemilia,' he calls, and she turns to him, plunges forward and grabs his arm as if he's about to run away. Her face is pallid, swollen.

'Have you come to see my lady?'

'I'm here to inquire after the health of Metellus Celer, like all these people.'

She sniffs with contempt. 'You think that's what they're here for? Vultures, more like. They come flapping over from the Esquiline Hill at the first whiff of sickness.'

But vultures don't attend sickness: they feast on death. A slip of the tongue, maybe. When tongues slip, the thoughts behind them show.

'He's very ill, then?' he asks in an undertone which will carry less than a whisper.

She glances around quickly. 'Come with me,' she says. 'Leave your slaves here, the fewer in this house the better, the way things stand with us.'

He tells his slaves to wait for him, and follows Aemilia as her big solid body barges forward. He doesn't greet any of the half-familiar faces that sharpen as they see him. They watch his back as Aemilia leads him away, and he feels the heat of their curious gazes.

– I didn't expect him to show up.

– Wonder what he's here for?

– Can't you guess?

Aemilia speaks to the men guarding the inner entrance. They are heavily muscled, with the hard, set faces of centurions or gladiators. No one's even attempting to get past them. They let Aemilia and Catullus through, and as he glances back they close ranks into a solid wall of flesh. He's trapped. But there's another way out, he calms himself. There's always another way out.

'Who were they?' he asks Aemilia as they cross the atrium and pass the doorways of the formal rooms.

'Trainee gladiators,' she says with satisfaction. 'You can hire them by the day. They're glad of the money. It was my lady thought of it.'

Not quite so prostrated with grief that she can't think straight, then. She knew there might be trouble.

He tries to think straight, too. Her husband is sick, maybe dying. All their stratagems and secrets are suddenly meaningless.

What if Clodia is beside herself with grief, as she was for her sparrow? He will have nothing to say to her.

They go through the courtyard gardens, past the fountain, to the little reception room where the Moorish boy tumbled, on the day of the sparrow's death.

Eleven

There is no one in the room. It's bare and blank, but it feels as if something's happened there only a second before. The air seems to quiver with shock. There's a slap of feet, running away.

'Come back here this moment!' yells Aemilia, and the feet stop. A frightened slave puts his head around the door. 'Where's my lady?' Aemilia demands.

'She been with the maister,' mutters the slave, head down. He's dressed in a rough brown tunic, and his face is weather-beaten. A garden slave, who shouldn't be in the house at all. Suddenly he raises his eyes boldly to Aemilia's face. 'They do say maister's slipping fast,' he says.

To Catullus' surprise, Aemilia doesn't flare with rage. The two slaves look at each other, a long look full of calculation. They are in this together, locked into the fortunes of the house.

'So my lady's left him now?'

The slave nods. 'And such a scouring and cleaning of pots in the kitchens as you've never seen, all by my lady's orders.'

Vaguely Catullus thinks this must be some women's rite he's never heard of, to cleanse the house as death approaches. Maybe Clodia hopes to appease the gods, and persuade them not to take her husband.

'The smallest scrapings offen the floor, they'm to be burned. So they tellt me. Herbs is to be burned in every room, so I been a-chopping and a-gathering, along with all of us garden lads. But seeing as how I'm foreman, I'm the one a-bringing it all into the house.'

Aemilia considers this in silence. A door bangs in the distance, they hear more running feet, and a babble of scared voices.

'I must see her,' says Catullus.

'Best you see *him*,' says Aemilia slowly, 'best you see my master.'

Both slaves nod judiciously. She's right, of course. Catullus is here to express his grief at this sudden, terrible illness of a great man. Metellus Celer is his friend. He's been a guest in this house many times – an intimate, almost. What other reason could he have to come here, if not to sympathize?

And now Catullus truly wants to see him. Wants to take the man's hand. He didn't will this sickness, let alone want it to end in death. The most he ever dreamed was that one day Clodia might be divorced.

'Yes, I'll go in to him, if it's allowed.'

He has never been inside Metellus Celer's bedchamber. As they go down the corridor towards it, he sees a knot of people at the door. Family: he recognizes a brother, and an uncle. They don't even notice him. All their attention is focused on Dr Philoctetes, who has lost his smooth calm air for once, and seems to be arguing with them. His hands gesture vehemently, palms upward. He looks very Greek. Aemilia has slipped away, leaving him to fend for himself. She's scared of drawing the family's attention to herself, and no wonder. The house must be seething with rumours of conspiracy and counter-conspiracy. The Metelli would be within their rights to seize Aemilia and have her tortured for information.

He'll go in alone, he decides, but at that moment Dr Philoctetes glances down the corridor and sees him. He makes a sign to Catullus to wait, while he carries on talking to the family. Catullus is close enough to hear the words.

'The excessive salivation is a symptom which gives rise to considerable concern, but my energies must be chiefly directed to relieving the breathing problems that cause most perturbation to our patient.'

'But can't you do something? He's suffocating.'

'I am doing everything that can be done. May I suggest that

this is a most propitious and proper point in time for the afflicted family to gather and make an offering? Perhaps some prayers for the intercession of the illustrious ancestors?'

He wants them out of the way. So Metellus Celer isn't going to die just yet. A group of older women comes out to join the men: more family. They are marked as clearly by their Metelli features as by their grey, haggard faces. They must have been up all night, in and out of the sickroom. One of them catches hold of the doctor's sleeve.

'He's in terrible pain, doctor, isn't there anything you can do?'

'I beg of you, dear ladies, to join your noble relatives in the tablinum. I assure you, it is the most fitting aid that you can offer to your dear one at this time. I must return to my patient immediately.'

'But if things are taking a turn for the worse, then we've got to be present. You understand, doctor, the rites –'

'I give you my word of honour, most esteemed lady, that you will be informed immediately if there is any question of that. But in my judgement the crisis is not absolutely immediate.'

The flock of relations turns uncertainly this way and that, and then steadies itself. They don't know what to do, but the sight and sound of one another gives them strength. Whatever happens, they won't panic. They are Metelli, and the determination to survive is cut into their faces as strongly as their sufferings. They'll retreat, regroup, and ready themselves to advance again.

He can almost feel the slow thick pulse of the Metelli ancestors beating through the house. The clan is greater than any one of its members, and will outlive them all. Hope dies for a son or a brother, but the Metelli will never die.

'We will invoke the gods,' says one of the uncles, and a murmur of agreement sweeps over them. The flock turns and hurries away to the tablinum.

They haven't noticed him; haven't recognized him even. All they can see or think about is Metelli business. That's their salvation, and it might be his, too. They're in no state to question his presence, or call him to account. But Dr Philoctetes, of course, knows him, and has taken in the situation flawlessly.

'My dear young friend, I must warn you that this is no ordinary sickroom. I must have your absolute assurance that you will remain calm, whatever your emotion, for the sake of my patient. Such a death is easy neither to suffer nor to watch.'

They are alone. Once again, in a crisis, Dr Philoctetes' florid phrases and circumlocutions drop away. He is full of force.

'He's dying, then?'

'Of course he is dying,' answers Philoctetes, almost angrily. 'He has no alternative. His vital signs are weak. His pulse, his breathing, his temperature, his reflexes' – Dr Philoctetes numbers each sign angrily on his fingers – 'all of these are failing. He cannot live, but he has some way to go before he can die. Now come if you are coming.'

Catullus follows the doctor through the anteroom and over the threshold. It is a large room, full of gloomy magnificence. The shutters are closed, and only one lamp burns at the bedside.

The smell is terrible. Vomit, blood, and a seeping smell of faeces. Metellus is lying propped up, with his face turned to the right, away from the door. An old woman is crouched over him, wiping his face.

'It's all right, my dearie, nanny's here to look after you, you'll feel as right as rain by tomorrow, nanny won't let it go on like this.' Her voice is feeble, gasping. Tears run down her beaten old face. She wipes away the saliva that pours from the sick man's mouth. Such a stream of saliva! – Catullus has never seen anything like it.

Metellus looks unconscious, but suddenly a terrible groan of pain escapes him. He tries to draw up his knees.

'I'll put a hot stone on your tummy, my angel, that'll help the pain,' blathers the old nanny.

'I'll try the sedative again,' says Philoctetes. He steps to the bedside, grasps a long-handled drinking cup and eases it into the half-open mouth. 'Try to swallow, my friend. It will ease you.'

A gargling sound comes from Metellus Celer's throat.

'No swallowing reflex . . . paralysis of the windpipe, I suspect,' Philoctetes murmurs to Catullus, as he comes away from the bedside.

'Where's that slave who was cleaning him?' he asks aloud, sharply. 'He ought to be here constantly. A man can't lie in his own dirt.'

'I'll do it and glad to,' says the nanny, 'many's the time I've cleaned his little backside for him,' and she struggles to rise.

Philoctetes puts his hand out, stopping her. 'Go and get that slave. He should be flogged for leaving his post. It needs a man's strength to lift the patient without hurting him.'

The old nanny stumbles out, and Catullus steps round to her side of the bed. Why he wants to see Metellus Celer's face, he doesn't know. Perhaps because he thinks it will be as it has always been: powerful, if a little unimaginative, the face of a soldier and a statesman of Rome.

But that face has gone. Metellus Celer is unrecognizable. Even to use the name 'Celer' seems like a bad joke. Swift! – he can't move. His face seems to have caved in. His skin is grey and filmed with sweat. The only sound that comes out of him is a gargling moan, deep in his chest. The smell of shit grows stronger.

I shouldn't be here, thinks Catullus. He wouldn't want anyone to see him like this.

He steps back into the shadows. Philoctetes leans over his patient, taking his pulse and then lifting his eyelids. There is nothing to be done, that's obvious now.

Cicero was lying. How could a man in this state speak of the affairs of Rome? It wasn't the real Metellus Celer whom Cicero preached about on the steps of the Curia, but some ideal Roman of his own actorish imagination, dying nobly without vomit, piss or shit. Most likely Cicero never even came into this bedroom. He'd be careful to hold on to his illusions, because they were the foundation of his career.

This man is real. Catullus has never felt so close to him, as if he were a brother going out into a winter storm on the mountains, barefoot and without a cloak. But better to freeze to death than to die like this. If what they say is true, then this is the face of poison. It's not quick or neat. It doesn't resemble any of the stories he's ever heard about it. How could a man do this to another man?

'I'm sorry,' he whispers, so quietly that even Philoctetes won't hear. No one answers. The sick man gives out shuddering gasps, from his stomach. The nanny has come back, and is keening quietly to herself. He glances round and sees a tall, burly slave waiting. His hands hang at his sides, ready to wash the shit off Metellus Celer.

Perhaps Metellus would have wanted to be seen as Cicero saw him. He'd have wanted to die in the Roman style, stoic and unyielding, thinking only of the public good. Perhaps inside that suffering, destroyed body, he really *was* thinking only of the public good, and was glad that his throat was paralysed so that he could not speak the wrong words, or betray himself by crying out.

Metellus Celer is so entirely alone. All those clients and dependants might as well be in Egypt for all their noisy presence means to him. Even his family and the gathered shades of his ancestors can't help him. Here, everything has stopped. Soon, the breathing will stop too.

'I'm sorry,' Catullus says again. Sorry for being alive when you're dying, for putting thoughts into your head and words into your mouth. For triumphing over you, not by sleeping with your wife but by having the power to walk out of this room into the sunlight, and live another day.

'The family will finish their prayers soon,' says Philoctetes. Catullus should go now. The family won't want to see him here.

Philoctetes walks with him through to the anteroom, and to the door. No one is about. They can hear the muffled clamour of Metellus' clients and dependants, but the gladiators are doing their work well, and the corridors are quiet. From the tablinum there comes the sound of chanting.

'Mushrooms, I think,' Dr Philoctetes says quietly. 'It is of course the characteristic excess of salivation that points to the culprit – here we are speaking of culprits in the vegetable kingdom, you understand. Of the type I am not precisely sure – it is not my field of expertise. But perhaps one of the amonitas. However, my dear young friend, believe that I say this only into your sympathetic ear, knowing that I can trust absolutely to your discretion. I have no wish to find myself suffering symptoms similar to those that our friend endures, one of these fine nights or days. And you, I trust, will be equally circumspect on your own account.'

He turns and looks into Philoctetes' eyes. They are moist and gleaming – but with what emotion? A man is dying behind him and he speaks so coolly of culprits and symptoms. Does he not feel it?

'Shouldn't you be attending your patient?' asks Catullus, rather coldly.

Philoctetes shrugs that Greek shrug of his, that says: Things are as they are, not as we wish them to be.

'My attendance now is of no value, except to the family. They need to know that every conceivable course of beneficial action is being carried out. It is for this reason that they sent for me, knowing of my reputation. But the old woman – the nurse – she is of more use to my patient now than I. He is beyond amelioration, so he might as well hear words of love. Do you know, my dear young friend, that the sense of hearing is the last to fade? You must be very careful what you say at the bedside of a man who is dying.

'So, quickly, my dear poet, leave these noxious, nay threatening miasmas of the sickroom and return to the health which you have tried so severely and so recently that you cannot risk it again.' Philoctetes lowers his voice. His eyes glisten with a relish which even the darkness of the chamber can't dim. 'In Rome we need our poets, you understand, more than we need soldiers or politicians. We have plenty of the latter.'

Philoctetes vanishes back into the sickroom, while the chanting continues. Stability, that's what the chant represents. The Metelli going on and on, whatever happens. Stability is what Cicero was after too, with his fictions about the torch of the Republic being lifted out of Metellus Celer's dying hand.

Perhaps it doesn't matter if something is true or not, Catullus thinks, if it's seen as true. And it's true that the Metelli are what they've made themselves. They uphold the standard, and the sufferings of one melt into the well-being of all. A great family, which has a right to believe in itself.

But I don't believe in it. I believe in shit and blood and vomit. I believe in the darkness waiting for Metellus Celer. The rest is a lie.

Philoctetes will fetch the family soon. Metellus Celer can't last long. As life slumps in him the family will surround his bed. If they follow the old ways, they will lower him to the floor, the closest he can get to the earth that bore him. He has no son to perform the rituals for him, and his daughter is only a child, safe on their estates with her nanny, far from the complications of her parents' lives.

Metellus Celer's brother will kneel to kiss him as he breathes out for the last time. And then the family will call out his name, so loudly that everyone waiting in the anteroom will know that Metellus Celer, the swift and strong, is dead.

He's forgetting Clodia. She'll have to be there, surely, weeping, tearing her clothes and pulling down her hair. But he can't quite imagine it. He can't see Clodia washing her husband's body for burial. She is used to organizing great occasions. She'll organize this one, all the way from the lying-in-state to the magnificent funeral that a man of his stature deserves. Perhaps she has already ordered the embalmer. Washed, anointed, embalmed, dressed again in splendour, his body will be ready for its journey, with a coin under his tongue to pay his passage to Charon for ferrying him across the Styx. Clodia will play her part. She won't give way to grief in public.

No, he can't imagine Clodia washing her husband's body. He knows his girl. She'll be frightened of the dead man, and she won't want to touch him.

The family would think it shameful for Metellus Celer to be laid out by paid hands. Perhaps his aunts and sisters will ignore Clodia's arrangements, and let no one but themselves lay him out. That old nanny would be the best one to take care of him. She loves him, and still sees her child in him. She wouldn't leave him.

Death takes everybody to where they don't want to be. Even Clodia will have to pay service to it, and sink herself into the tribe of the Metelli. She'll be in mourning, with her path laid out for her.

He won't be able to see her. But he's got to see her. He's got to grasp her, hold her, press her against him until all he can smell is her skin and her hair. And swallow her greedily, the touch and the taste of her, until there's nothing else in him.

It felt right that she wasn't keeping vigil at her husband's side. At least she's not a hypocrite. She doesn't love him. He would know that. Besides, thinks Catullus with a cold, flat accuracy he rarely achieves in his thoughts of Clodia, she's not what her husband would want now. You have to be strong to cope with Clodia's bewitching, disturbing, betraying presence. At the point of death, an old nurse might be better.

But I would want you, Clodia. I would never want anyone else. If you were dying I'd sit by you. I would wipe your face and if you pissed yourself I'd wash you very gently and I'd lift you up so that it didn't hurt you. Nothing about your body could ever disgust me, don't you know that? You could shit and vomit and I'd look after you. Whatever happens, I will always want you.

But he's not going to see her. Not now, under this roof where Metellus Celer is dying horribly. Wherever she is, she's keeping away for a reason. Aemilia's bound to have told Clodia that he's here.

The chanting rises, cold, stately and imploring. The gods won't listen. Metellus Celer is already on his way down the shadowy path. Not very swiftly, poor man; not nearly as fast as he'd like. He crawls and stumbles and he longs for the journey to end and for the blessed dark to wash his eyes.

Nobis cum semel occidit brevis lux,
nox est perpetua una dormienda.

Sounds good, doesn't it? It sounded good while he was writing it.

Our sole short day is set
into enduring night.

And the little sparrow which pecked and tapped its way down the death path – that sounded good, too.

qui nunc it per iter tenebricosum

ten-e-bri-cosum – as shadowy as a spider's web in a dark corner, and as clinging. And what a brilliant contrast between his mimicry of the sparrow's sound and movement –

> *sed circumsiliens modo huc modo illuc*
> *ad solam dominam usque pipiabat.*
> *qui nunc it per iter –*

– pip pip pip it it it – and the marvellous word that wipes it out for ever: *tenebricosum.*

The gladiators let him pass. It's their duty to stop people getting in, not to prevent them from getting out. But one of them says to Catullus out of the side of his mouth, 'Had enough, eh? Bet that poor bastard in there would like to walk out, too.'

Perhaps the gladiator didn't really speak. It was probably his own overheated imagination. He shoves through the crowd, finds his slaves and steps out into the clean, cold air.

Clodia loved that poem. She cried when he recited it to her for the first time. She was poet enough herself to understand everything he was doing.

'It's my sparrow exactly, as if he were alive again. It's just how he used to hop here and there, always staying close to me. *it per iter* – it's so sad, my darling. But it's perfect. Thank you, I shall never forget it.'

He won't be writing any poems on the death of Metellus Celer. Some fool will, cloaking reality in fine words about fortitude, sacrifice and steadfast service to the ideals of the Republic. He ought to have his papyrus stuffed down his throat, until he chokes for breath as Metellus Celer is choking now.

Twelve

The funeral is huge. Fitting for a son of one of Rome's great noble families, a man who was both praetor and consul, a military leader who turned back Catiline in the Apennines, a man who was already crowned with honours and would have earned greater honours if he'd lived. One of the old school, who really believed that *pro bono publico* meant something.

The Metelli clan has gathered in force, along with all those under its protection. The roots of the clan flex invisibly in the soil that nourishes it, drawing on a rich humus of favours asked for and given, of protection offered, services rendered, loyalty tendered. The blustery grey day with flurries of rain deters no one. Every Metelli client, dependant and hanger-on is here, with his children at his side and even a grandchild sitting on his shoulders to mark the passing of their patron. To see and to be seen is the thing. No one should be able to say, 'And where were you, at his funeral?'

The spirits of the Metelli ancestors, wearing their death masks, are making ready to lead the litter that carries the dead man. Musicians are tuning their instruments. Hired mourners, the pick of their profession, are drinking hot wine with honey, to lubricate their throats. Their voices will have to hold out through hours of wailing dirges. Heralds have been criss-crossing the streets since dawn, to announce the funeral and the route of the procession. Everybody knows it already, but when they hear the heralds they rush to get a good vantage point among the crowds that line the streets. It will be a long wait, but worth it because on a day like this you don't want to miss anything.

The death masks of the Metelli ancestors are famous. When they ride the streets in their chariots it seems as if the dead breathe again, and the old days have returned. Great feats of ancient heroes come to life. Captured elephants from the wars against Carthage bellow in fury, trampling the stones of the Forum. Temples are raised overnight, and the blood of Rome's enemies streams like wine. The ancestral spirits gorge on the sight of the Rome that they have helped to create, and then, satisfied, they go back to their places of honour in the Metelli house.

The ancestors will be proud to recognize their son, and to welcome him into the Underworld. He deserves to join them. His death mask has been made, and he will be numbered and remembered among them for ever. They are generals, lawyers, politicians, governors of faraway provinces, men who by wit and force spread Roman power like a tide over the world. The life of Quintus Caecilius Metellus – Metellus Celer, Metellus the Swift – joins the lives of his ancestors in an eternal present, which is also the eternal present of Rome. At the next Metelli funeral, his spirit will stand in its chariot, masked, watchful for the honour of the clan.

Metellus Celer's formal elegies will be spoken in the Forum, in the presence of his family and the great men of Rome with whom he belongs. The people crowding the streets have stories of him, too. They liked him, on the whole, although he had no charisma and never cared to woo them. Wooing was not a part of his political vocabulary. He was stern, straight, orthodox, and he did what he said.

He'd helped to fight down the Catiline conspiracy, which everyone knows would have brought ruin on Rome. Murder and arson and eating little children – or so they say. It's Catiline's enemies who do all the talking now, his friends being mostly dead. Old Catiline made his worst mistake when he made an enemy of old Chickpea. Didn't he know that was the way to get his name blackened for generations? He'd have minded that even more than getting his head chopped off after the last battle against Marcus Antonius. They brought that head all the way back to Rome. A man can only die once, but a reputation dies a thousand times.

They brought back that stinking head because they wanted to make sure we all knew just how dead Catiline was. *He* had charisma all right. Bucketloads of the stuff.

Still, he's dead, and maybe we're all the better for it. When you listen to old Chickpea your heart's so swayed that you believe Catiline was first cousin to a viper. And then you remember other things, like the way he never cared for gold, and the way he loved his friends, and you wonder. But it's not worth going over the ins and outs of it; not if you know what's good for you in today's Rome, the Rome that really exists rather than the one that might have happened. Best just to pass the time of day, and stick to the subject of the dead man we've come out to honour.

– Metellus Celer, he was a fighter all right. One of the old school. Not given to a lot of smiling and soft-soaping his enemies.

– He had his enemies all the same.

(Let a silence fall. Don't follow that one up. There are rumours everywhere that it wasn't a natural death. Poison, they're saying. But you never really know who you're talking to, out in the streets, or which faction they belong to. This bloke looks all right, but discretion is the better part of valour, as they say.)

– He'd've been all right. They were going to make him Governor of Our Province.

– A nice little plum to drop in your lap. Lovely juicy trade routes, just waiting to be squeezed.

– But you've got to bear in mind all those nutters up north. Whoever gets Our Province has to deal with them as well: your long-haired Gauls with the trousers. There's your Avernians, your Helvetians, your Aedui – they're supposed to be our allies now, but don't count on it, they're slippery as fuck, the Aedui. The further north you go, the worse it gets. All those lunatics in Germania – terrifying they are, racing along with these ponies they train to fight, according to what I've been told. I never saw them myself. Once the Germanii get the Bellovaci going it'll be time to pack up shop.

– You were posted up there, then?

– That's right. Stationed at Massilia for five years. We were sent up to the border for six months, because the Avernians were making trouble. That was far enough north for me. Leave them alone to murder each other in peace is what I say, the plunder's not worth the aggro. All we need now is some Governor getting the idea it's up to him to pacify Gaul. Thank the gods I'm out of it. There's nothing that your Gaul likes better than plotting against the tribe next door, making treaties and breaking them, getting blind drunk and swearing vows which even Hercules couldn't keep, only *they've* got to because a vow's sacred with them, you see.

– Well, fair enough, so it is here.

– But what I'm saying is, *we* don't go making vows we can't keep. But your Gaul, get a few cups inside him and he's rampant, quarrelling with anybody and swearing oaths on his mother's life. And their chiefs are the worst. 'I vow to avenge the honour of my third cousin once removed by marriage by riding my horse through six Legions.' That's the kind of lunacy they come up with, and next thing all the rest are standing up and yelling that they'll do the same. So, just when you think everything's calm, the alarm sounds and the Gauls are hammering at you, screaming out gibberish, red hair all over their shoulders, great big shields in front of them with what look like hundreds of snakes wiggling about all over them, and a spear that's got your name on it. It stands to reason, in the long run they haven't got a hope in hell and they all get slaughtered, but in the short term they'll have your head on a pole. So it's lucky for us that they're half the time at each other's throats. Your Gaul's a fighter. If that lot ever got together and "developed the concept of a common purpose", as old Chickpea keeps saying we're the only ones in the world who know how to do, then those Gauls'd be over the Alps like they were jumping molehills. Never underestimate your Gaul, that's what I learned in Massilia. *(I'm going on a bit. Get me started on the Gauls and I can't stop. He seems to be following it, though.)*

– So who do you reckon they're going to give Our Province to then, now Metellus has gone? *(He was following all right. He's not stupid, this one. Knows that's the big question. Whoever gets Gaul, gets to raise an army as big as he can prove himself fit to lead. Once you've got an army like that, it'll go with you to Hell's gates if you tell it to. And who's going to stand in your path, then? But keep it casual.)* Could be Julius Caesar, from what I heard.

– Caesar? You reckon?

– Think about it. Listen, you hear that noise? They must be getting close.

They are getting close. The sound of pipes shrills above the keening of the mourners. There's a rumble of chariot wheels. People count the chariots as they appear, bearing the chief mourners and the masked ancestral figures. After the mourners, the body of Metellus Celer himself, propped on its bier, dressed in a purple-edged flowing toga.

The embalmer has done a superb job. Even after lying in state for days, there is no mottling of decay on the face. Perhaps he was not poisoned after all. People say that a poisoned corpse corrupts fast, and often the family are forced to hold the funeral immediately. But Metellus Celer has lain in state in the Metelli house for five days. His body has the air of something neither dead nor living. The grey-yellow face has already become a mask. It represents the man who has gone, rather than revealing him to the public gaze one last time.

The eye sockets are shrunken. The skin is stretched tight, and the jutting nose has the look of a scaffold that holds the structure together. The magnificence of his clothing, the glitter of his bier and the freshness of the flowers heaped up on him contrast strangely with this mummified relic. (And where did they find such flowers, in grey January? How many riders have galloped from the south, at the Metelli command, with a sheaf of lilies in one hand, and a sword in the other?)

A sigh ripples along the procession route, chasing the bier. This is what it all comes down to, all the glory and wealth, and being one of the great ones who rule Rome. This is what happens at the end of being able to go where you like and do what you like and think of what you'd like to eat for dinner and be sure that you'll find it on your table.

Metellus Celer was known for knowing where his money came from, and where it went. Not tight-fisted exactly; just prudent. But even for him, the time has come when the only coin he can use is the one set under his tongue, to pay Charon so that he'll row him across the Styx. There's no skimming across that river in a glamorous private pinnace. No, it's Charon's creaky old boat for everybody, and he grumbles as he picks up the oars.

Somehow you see it more clearly, the mystery of death, when it's a great man who dies. It makes going home all the sweeter, with the prospect of a beaker of something hot to warm you up, and then a fat roast capon with fish sauce. Even if all you've got to look forward to is pottage, you're still better off than Metellus Celer is now.

Catullus follows the crowd as far as the Forum, and then he turns away. She is inside, with all the Metelli, hearing the funeral orations. There will be long elegies on her dead husband, followed by speeches in praise of the ancestors whom her husband has joined.

It's one of those weighty occasions that define Rome to itself. The dead man isn't just a man any longer, great or insignificant; he's part of Rome's public story. Every virtue that Metellus Celer possesses will reflect back on to Rome.

Catullus has no place there, and yet he couldn't keep away from the funeral entirely. He stood and watched them all go past, and saw the blank, blind face of Metellus Celer go past, too, seeing and recognizing nothing.

Although Catullus is wrapped in his warmest cloak, there's a chill that nothing can keep out. He's alone. He didn't want to share this spectacle with friends. He can't shake off the feeling that he's helped to ambush an unarmed man. Clodia is inaccessible and will remain so for nine days after the funeral feast. Even after the purification, there is a year of mourning to come. And how are they to meet, with people watching every move she makes? Rumour will harden into accusation if she isn't careful.

But he is sure that she had nothing to do with it. She could never plan a death like that. He sees her run across the room to him and throw her arms around his neck. Her arms are strong and slender and her breasts press against him. She is quick and warm, laughing, and then she pushes him away from her and says, 'Let me look at you.'

Clodia's there now, this minute, gazing ahead and thinking her own thoughts. The speeches will go on for ever but she'll keep a mask on her face, like her husband. She will be attentive, sombre but controlled. She will know that people are watching her reactions.

Before they put Metellus Celer inside the family vault on the Appian Way, custom demands that the dead man's eyes be opened one last time. He's not sure why. Maybe, long ago, people thought it was necessary to be sure that the dead were really dead, before they were separated for ever from the land of the living. Who will open those eyes? One of the male Metelli: it will have to be. He hopes and prays that it will be. But the image that haunts him is of Clodia herself, leaning over her husband, lifting his eyelids with her thumbs and then staring into his eyes, and of his eyes staring back, sightless and accusing.

It is also the custom for one of the family to kiss the dead man for the last time. Over and over in his imagination, Clodia's warm lips meet that grey-yellow flesh, and taste its decay along with a faint tang of the embalmer's gypsum.

Thirteen

There is poison everywhere. It jumps to his ears and his eyes. It's like the time eight months ago when Clodia thought for a week that she might be pregnant. Everywhere he went, women's bodies swelled ripely under their tunics, when he could have sworn that only the day before they'd been flat-bellied girls. Babies howled all night long. Friend after friend sent messages, proud and bashful, to announce a wife's pregnancy.

It can't really have been like that. He's a poet, he makes things up. He even makes people up. Clodia accused him of that once. 'You don't know who I am! You only know the woman in your poems.'

But she loved the poems. He knew that. No one, not even Clodia, could fake that slow, warm, delighted smile.

Poison. He heard Lucius berating the cook for buying mixed wild mushrooms from a market stall instead of from their usual supplier, who came in from the country with a basket over his arm and knew every mushroom like his own child.

'Are you trying to poison us? In this household, false economy is not a virtue!'

Then there was that imbecile Egnatius in the bathhouse yesterday, telling some rigmarole about a girl who sent poisoned sweets to her rival, but the younger sister whom she sent to deliver the basket peeped under the cloth, saw honey and almonds, and swiped just one.

'Just *one*, and she was rolling on the ground in agony. It's true, I had it from someone who knows the girls' aunt.'

A flash of teeth and a roll of the eyes to see just how much he's the centre of attention. Yes, you're like a child, my dear

Egnatius. A grown man with a sodden mass of napkins hanging around his knees.

Later on, in the Forum, a group of pompous baldheads debated the niceties of an inheritance case that had been dragging and droning its way through the courts for longer than even they can have been alive. One of them hee-hawed confidentially, nodding his head like a donkey which has been tethered outside a school of rhetoric for so long that it thinks it's a polished debater: 'And then – hee-haw – it has to be said that there was some question – hee-haw – of potentially improper interference in the *sequence of events*, if you understand me, the *sequence of events* leading to the decease of – hee-haw – the deceased.'

And they were off, muttering about decoctions, potions, preparations and symptoms –

The decease of the deceased. You barbarian. Ye gods, if language were ever granted a triumph, you should be led in rags and chains in the procession. The populace of Rome should hurl the contents of their chamberpots over your heads, until the outside matches the inside.

All the grave donkey heads bobbed up and down, as solemn as the judges they longed to be. Wag away, you impotent, prating word-slaughterers. If you want to see the decease of the deceased, you've only to look in a mirror.

Wherever Catullus went, poison haunted him. He passed two little boys sharing a pie on a doorstep. In a flash, sharing changed to fighting.

– Give it back here, you bastard!

One snatched, the other snatched back and half the pie fell in the dust. One boy was left holding a good-sized piece, the other none. Quick as a flash, the pie-less boy gobbed on the pie.

– Go on, eat yer pie then, he jeered.

But the other boy, pale with fury, kept his head. 'Think I want to poison myself?' he said, and dropped the remainder of the pie in the gutter.

It's as if Catullus has been asleep, and suddenly he's woken up to what everybody else knew all along. A nod and a wink. Poisoners can become celebrities, masters of their profession. Rome is full of them. Even Dr Philoctetes said so, when he was measuring out a dose of digitalis for Catullus, at the height of his fever. 'If a physician is not precise, he will soon see the other side of the drugs he employs. Medicines' – and he stared at the ceiling with a lofty expression – 'medicines are Janus-faced, my dear young friend. They turn one way to heal, and the other to kill. There is no country for poisoners like Rome; even Egypt must acknowledge that we are masters of those profane arts.'

But did Philoctetes really say that, or is Catullus imagining it? His obsession with poison corrupts everything.

He must find out more. He wants facts that will bleach away these filthy suspicions like the hard midday sun. Clodia is ignorant, innocent. Philoctetes must be wrong. *Mushrooms, I think*. That's what he said, and then something about that gush of saliva from the dying man's mouth. But what kind of mushrooms, and how could they have been put into the dish of one man alone? The same sauces were placed in front of everyone. People chose what they liked: their choices couldn't be predicted. But only Metellus Celer had fallen ill.

Relief sweeps over him. There could not have been a dish of poisoned mushrooms on the table: the risk was too great. If the poisoning didn't take place at dinner, then when? Metellus Celer was not the type of man to eat a dish of mushrooms simply because it was brought to him. He took pride in living an old-fashioned Roman life where dinner was dinner and if you were hungry, you waited for the proper time. Metellus Celer wouldn't titillate his appetite with savoury snacks.

But Dr Philoctetes has no motive for diagnosing poison if there was none. He's too good a doctor. Catullus wants to forget his words, but he can't. His fear grows like the evening shadow of an umbrella pine, sprawling until it swallows a field. Dr

Philoctetes wanted to warn him to keep out of it. *Leave these noxious, nay threatening miasmas . . . In Rome we need our poets.* Perhaps Philoctetes was afraid of what the family might do if they suspected that Catullus was implicated in Metellus Celer's death. Philoctetes might believe that a clan as rich and powerful as the Metelli could lash out at anyone close to what he would no doubt call 'the scene of the crime'. And it's true that Catullus has slept with Metellus Celer's wife . . . but that wouldn't be enough. No one, looking at him, knowing him, could ever imagine him to be a poisoner. Surely?

Or perhaps Philoctetes was afraid of someone else. Pretty Boy, possibly. He's as good a candidate as anyone, if you're looking for motives. Political motives, of course, Catullus says to himself quickly, stopping the thought that rises like some vile misshapen creature of the deep: *He has cause to hate the man who sleeps with his sister as his lawful wife.*

He must stop thinking. All he's got to do is find out what the poison was and how it came into Metellus Celer's body. If there was a poison at all, he adds rapidly. He needs to talk to an expert.

Asking around could be tricky. He'll say that he's writing a play, and needs to do some research. Bathhouse slaves know everything. He'll start at the bathhouses, and then move on to the brothels.

'Cynthia, you know everyone. I'm writing a play, and I need help with one of the scenes.'

'A play! I thought you only wrote poetry.'

'"Only"?'

'I didn't mean it like that, I'm sure you'd write wonderful drama.'

'You must think I'm as vain as that idiot Volusius. *"I've been turning my hand to, for want of a better word – ahem! – our great epic tradition."* That bastard is enough to make tradition cower like a slave before a beating.'

'So are you really going to write a play?'

'It's a career option I'm considering.'

She pulls a face. 'Don't talk like that. You sound like a politician. I get enough of them.'

'It's just to rile you . . . But maybe poets *should* be more like politicians. Practical . . . down to earth . . . self-confident, not to say self-satisfied –'

'Not to say in love with themselves, at least the ones I get. And as for down to earth, they spend so much time plotting what if this and what if that – They end up with less idea of what's real and what's not than a six-year-old child. You can tell them any lie you like, and as long as it's flattering enough they'll swallow it.'

'Mind you, that's not completely untrue of men in general, now, is it, Cynthia?'

'Don't put words in my mouth. Tell me about the play. I'm always at the theatre, if I get the chance of a free afternoon. I don't know if I ever told you, but when I was little I wanted to be a mime. I used to drive my mum and dad crazy, doing the death of Electra one day, and Iphigenia at Aulis the next. And dancing and acrobatics too – I don't know what the people in the downstairs flat used to think. I learned how to do back-flips and cartwheels and I don't know what else. But it's hard to get proper training. You've got to have contacts, and it's all kept in families. We didn't know anyone.'

'This play I'm writing has a poisoning in it.'

'Is it about Medea? Just imagine playing that role. You wouldn't dare go to sleep at night in case you killed yourself with your own wickedness.'

'Medea's been done to death. This is contemporary.'

'I love the way you write. It's so sharp and funny – just like real life. And the way it all fits together like a craftsman's box. I wish I could speak lines like that – No, don't start looking all embarrassed, my darling, I'm not after a part. In my dreams, that's all. Maybe I'd have been no good, even if I'd had the chance. But if you haven't, you can still hope – Maybe you're better off not knowing.'

'You'll have seats in the front row, Cynthia, if I ever finish it. But I'm stuck on the research. I need to talk to someone who knows all about poisons and how they work. It's the detail that makes the difference. If it's not believable, people start throwing things.'

'And you think I'm the right person to know about poison?'

'No, of course not. But you do know a lot of people, Cynthia.'

'Yes, I do, don't I?' She wrinkles her nose.

'That's not what I meant,' he says quickly.

'I know.'

Even a couple of years ago, Cynthia was still a golden girl. She'd been like that for ever, friends told him when he first came to Rome. One of those women whom time can't touch. But suddenly, within a bare few months it seems, she's changed. Her breasts and hips are spreading. Her hair, although beautifully dressed as always, is dry and lustreless. There are lines on her face that don't go away when she stops smiling.

She doesn't smile as much now. It all dates back to the accident her boy had last year, when he was playing with friends, jumping off a high wall. He fell badly and broke his leg, high up where the thigh joins the hip. In spite of Cynthia pouring out money on doctors, the bones didn't set right. The child limps badly now. Still, he's good about doing his exercises, Cynthia says, and he goes to that physiotherapist your doctor friend recommended. There's a big improvement. And he's ever so bright, loves his studies. His private tutor thinks he's very promising. Maybe he'll be a lawyer one day.

Cynthia fosters him out and rarely sees him; it's better so. He's getting old enough to notice what goes on. When he was a toddler he used to come here sometimes, and all the girls used to pet him and give him sweets.

She works as hard as ever, but her price is going down. That means taking on more clients, and not such good ones. She's done well in her time and she ought to have savings, but they're melting away, what with the boy's injury and his education.

'Don't worry about it, Cynthia. I'll ask around.'

'No – wait. Listen. I do know someone – that is, I know *of* someone. But you'll have to be careful. Really careful, I mean it. She has protection, and if they think you're snooping around to inform on her, they'll make sure you don't live to do it.'

'Bodyguards – seriously?'

'There's a lot of money in what she does. She's right at the top. She can do anything, and they say she's got a client list that would put us girls to shame.'

'What's her name?'

Cynthia glances around quickly, even though there are only the two of them in the room.

'Gorgo,' she says quietly.

'She's Greek, then?' The name sounds and echoes in his head. One of Sappho's rivals was called Gorgo –

'She's been here in Rome for ever. I think she came from Lesbos originally, or her mother did.'

'Lesbos!'

'Yes, I think so.'

'How old is this woman?' Hundreds of years, perhaps, he thinks, a woman from Sappho's island with its apple branches, dappled shade, roses, dill and violets . . . 'Have you ever met her?'

A flush rises through Cynthia's skin. 'What do you mean? What are you accusing me of?'

'Cynthia, please! It was an innocent question.'

'Putting somebody out of the way, I would never do that. The gods forbid it, since our lives are theirs, and not our own.' Sudden seriousness darkens her face. For a moment he seems to see into the core of her being, the incorruptible Cynthia. 'It was for a different reason,' she says, and, getting up, she begins to rearrange a vase of anemones, with her back to him.

He remembers an evening long ago. Cynthia and he were drinking wine in her room. She had a carved couch covered with embroidered silk then, not this workaday little bed. The two of them lay there, warm and tired, gossiping like the old friends they were slowly becoming. He'd always liked her company. Considering her trade she was surprisingly – almost touchingly – unimaginative in bed, as if she'd never had any training at all. But with her warm soft skin and her beautiful breasts, the touch of stolidity in her didn't matter at all. Cynthia had had a good room then, not this stuffy little cubicle. She never complained about the change, or even appeared to notice. Something fierce drove her on, and burned away any other feelings she might have had. He supposed it was the child.

But to downgrade her like this is harsh. She won't get good clients if her importance is so evidently diminished. She'll get the ones with bad breath, or vile habits.

And here he is, thinking he's the gift of the gods, while she might feel that she's drawn the short straw with him.

He laughs softly.

'It's no laughing matter,' says Cynthia angrily, 'but I suppose you wouldn't understand. It's easy enough for *you* to walk away.'

Anemone petals drop to the floor. She is pulling them apart: Cynthia, who loves flowers so much that he always brings her whatever is in season, ridiculous as it looks to enter a brothel like a suitor.

'Don't take it out on the anemones, Cynthia. I wasn't laughing at you, but at myself.'

'It's no joke, when a girl gets into trouble. Especially not here.'

That was for a different reason . . . Yes, of course. A mistress of poisons will know all about the drugs that women need.

'One of the girls, one of the new ones, she panicked. If she'd come to me I could have helped her. At least, I could have told her where to go. About Gorgo, that is. But she kept it secret from us and went off to some quack who tells her that black hellebore will do the trick. Before we know anything about it she's swallowed enough to kill an ox.' She shudders. 'That was a night, I can't tell you. I've never forgotten it.'

'What happened?'

'She died, of course. Then there are all these other things the girls try. Gorgo's expensive, and they don't want to pay up until they have to. But these herbs and so on, you've got to know what you're doing or they turn your guts inside out, you're ill for days but at the end of it you're still pregnant. Clyster's all right: that works for some girls. The Greek girls all swear by silphium. But someone like Gorgo, she knows. She really knows. It's not just having the right ingredients, you see, it's how you mix them, and the quantities. It takes years to learn, and it's all kept secret, they won't tell you.'

'Just like doctors,' he says.

'You're right, it's exactly the same, except for the end result. They say that Gorgo has medical training, although how she came by it, I wouldn't know. The story is that she dressed as a man.'

His curiosity quivers. 'She sounds like the one I need to talk to.'

'Yes, but be careful. Say what you want and why you want it. Don't try any of your stories on her.'

'But you love my stories, Cynthia.'

She turns around to face him. 'You won't get any more flattery from me today. I'm not in the mood.'

'I can see that. Listen, let's have another drink.'

She goes to the wine cooler, lifts the flagon, wipes it and then pours wine into their cups.

'Don't put so much water in mine. That stuff you drink – it's water bewitched.'

She tilts her cup, looks down into it. 'Once you start letting yourself drink in here, really drink, not just a cup between clients to relax you, there's no end to it. I'm not going down that road.'

'How's Titus doing?'

She sighs, and comes to sit on the bed beside him. Her heavy, perfumed body rests against him, as comforting as the wine. If only he could rest like this, with Clodia, now. But Clodia has taken him too deep, into places he never dreamed of before he knew her. Sometimes they seem not to be in their bodies any more, but to be lifted out and beyond themselves as if at the point of death. And yet at the same time he's so intensely conscious of her body that he can taste every drop of her sweat, feel each hair on her head, catch the double beat of her heart as if it's his own.

He must have sighed, too. Cynthia says, 'You're thinking about her again.'

'No, I'm not.'

'I can always tell.'

'Leave it, Cynthia. I was asking you about Titus.'

'His thigh muscles need a lot of work. They've wasted, you see. The doctor says it's muscle wastage that's causing the limp to be so bad, as much as the break itself.'

'Are you all right for money?'

'I'm all right for now. I can pay the doctor's bills because, look, I haven't really got any living expenses.'

'But what about your flat, Cynthia?'

'I've given it up. I'm living here now.'

There's nothing to be said. Her light, pretty, flower-filled flat: he's never seen it, she never takes a client there. She wants to keep her two lives quite separate. But she's described it so often that he could walk around it blindfold. It is on the third floor, not too noisy, quite private. There's a little balcony, and she keeps her pots there, with thyme, marjoram and parsley as well as flowers. She's made her place lovely, over the years.

'So you go to visit Titus, now? I mean, he doesn't come home at all?'

'He never did, much. It's best not to disrupt his routine. You see, he's got a life there – I don't want to disturb it.'

'No, of course not.'

She has given up the flat. She lives here all the time, with the coming and going of clients, the girls gossiping. Who's coming up, who's going down. And only this little room, stuffy and flowerless.

'It's nice to have time to chat,' observes Cynthia. Her face remains smooth, but he thinks she sounds anxious. He is a good client. When he comes, he always pays for a full afternoon. Maybe she's afraid that he too is going to give her up for someone younger.

But he won't. It's no virtue in him: he likes to be with Cynthia more than he can imagine liking to be with any of the other girls. They go back a long way now, to the innocent days before he met Clodia, when he was new to Rome. And all he saw in blood-soaked, plot-ridden, power-broking, death-dealing Rome was poetry. There was no poison then . . . He was like a naked child playing around the dugs of a wolf. A proper little Romulus.

But of course that isn't entirely true. He came to Rome for a reason. He was on the make, like everyone else, although in a different way; he wanted to make himself as a poet. He wanted to know everything, feel everything. Long before he met Clodia, he wanted her. He wanted to feel as Sappho felt in the presence of her lover. He wanted cold fire to run over his body, transforming him.

'Yes, it's nice,' he agrees, 'I look forward to our afternoons.'

'Have you got any new poems?'

'I've got one. Pour me some more wine and I'll recite it to you.'

She pours the wine, climbs back on to her couch and sits gracefully cross-legged in a pose she must have learned from one of the Egyptian girls.

'Go on.'

> Cup-boy, pouring out the best Falernian,
> mix mine as strong as you can
> by the law of the lady of the house
> who is drunker than drunkenness itself;
> but you water nymphs who dilute everything
> and turn strong wine to piss
> bugger off and join the virtuous –
> here Bacchus mixes it with no one!

'Did you compose that chez Lesbia?' asks Cynthia sweetly. 'It's very good, of course, but I hear so many drinking songs that I get a bit sick of them.'

'Cynthia, that's uncharacteristically bitchy of you.'

She gives him an innocent little smile. 'I don't like to watch a handsome young man turn into a purple-nosed old bore. I've seen it too often.'

'Trouble with you, Cynthia, you've seen too much of everything. You've got a caution for every occasion.'

'Yes, I suppose that's true,' she says thoughtfully, then leans over and gives him a quick, apologetic kiss. 'There's nothing worse than a tart preaching virtue, is there?'

'I didn't mean that.'

'I know you didn't, otherwise I wouldn't have kissed you. You have these little pockets of innocence in you – I love putting my hand in them.'

'*You* don't need to steal innocence.'

To his amazement, her eyes fill with tears.

'I think that's the nicest thing anyone ever said to me,' she says.

They lapse into silence. She's lost in private thoughts, and he doesn't want to spoil the moment. He'd like to stay here for ever. Or at least, for a long series of afternoons, with just enough wine to make the hours slip by easily, like this . . .

How has he got to this place? Not to Cynthia's room, but to *where he is now*. Metellus Celer has died in agony, struggling to draw breath, shitting and pissing himself in a dark room. Clodia is hidden behind a veil of family mourning. He doesn't see her or hear from her. Even if he did see her, it would be like staring into a mask that wears the face of the dead man.

This little room is like a boat. He would like to stay here, drawn up high on the sands in a secret cave –

But of course he can't. He likes Cynthia, but he doesn't love her. He can't love anyone. Nothing can touch him now, except

Clodia. She is his food and without her he will starve. Even if it poisons him, he's got to have her.

He'll leave in a moment. He isn't meant to have a refuge. He's got to go wherever Clodia's path will take them. First to see that poisoner, Gorgo, and then to the house on the Palatine. How surprised that green boy from Verona would be, if he could walk into this room now and see where poetry has led him.

'Cynthia,' he says, 'I'd like to give you some money.'

'You don't need to worry about that, it's just the usual arrangement.'

'No, I mean I'd like you to be able to get your flat back.'

'Well!' She sits back on her heels and stares at him. 'But what's the point of that, when I'd only have to let it go again?'

'I mean real money, Cynthia.'

'I never know, with cl – I mean I never know with anyone, what they mean by money. Whether you're really rich, for example. All those poems you write about your purse having cobwebs in it and not being able to put a dinner on the table . . . Don't get me wrong, I know you always pay what's due.'

'We've got what they call "extensive property and business interests at home and abroad". We've been in Verona for generations, and then there's the estate at Sirmio. My brother manages the Bithynia property – you know he's living out there at the moment. What I'm saying is that I could give you enough to buy the lease outright.'

'But why would you do that?'

'Why? I don't know why, Cynthia! I'm only saying that I'll do it.'

'I don't understand you.'

'You don't need to. Think of it like this: your flat – I feel as if I know it, you've talked about it so much. I'd like to think of you being there again, with your flowers.'

'But listen, you have to understand, I've never had gentlemen to the flat.'

'I'm not asking for that. It won't be my place, it will be yours.

I shall never go there, I promise you. The lease will be in your name.'

She is silent for a long time, then she says, 'Are you doing this because you're going to stop coming to see me? Because you feel sorry for me?'

'No! I swear to you, Cynthia, this isn't a Trojan horse. I don't want anything out of you. It's just a lease. And besides, no one who knew you could ever feel sorry for you. They could only feel envious of you.'

'Envious! You know what my life is like.'

(Or perhaps you don't. You think you do, because you're free to come and go, paying your way so carelessly, making me laugh. You can do what you want. What does that feel like? One day, will you say to your son: 'Go to old Cynthia, she's getting on but she's a decent sort, you'll be safe with her'?)

Cynthia drops her eyes. He is a good client. A friend, almost. 'Envious,' she repeats, with a touch of irony.

'Yes, but inside, in your mind, you're at peace. You've done everything right.'

She gets up and starts to tidy the cups and straighten the bedcovers. 'Just lift up a minute – there. That's better.' She bends down quickly to pick up her slippers, but not before he's seen that she's actually crying now, without sound.

'Cynthia, I'm so sorry. I didn't mean to upset you.'

'It wasn't you. It's the worry with Titus. It gets to me some-times. I know he's in good hands, but I just want to see him –' Her shoulders heave. Her face is suddenly blotched and swollen with tears. 'See him walking – like he used to – all straight – and *running*. He used to run so fast it put my heart in my mouth.'

He says nothing. Her grief is beyond him. For the second time in the past month, he's glad that he has no children. The first was when he saw Metellus Celer's nurse in the house on the Palatine.

That green boy from Verona wanted to know everything, feel everything. As if he had any choice, poor fool.

Fourteen

Lucius and Catullus are in the study, poring over papyrus. Lucius has found a new copyist, a real craftsman, and has brought back samples of his work.

'Remind me, Lucius, why are we leaving old Balbus' work-shop?'

'His eyes are not what they were. There's a film growing over the right eye, and the left will follow.'

'But he's got a team of copyists, surely; he hasn't done the work himself for years.'

'He watched over it like a hawk. He wouldn't let anything less than perfect go out of the workshop. The training he gave was the best in the city. But then, these past few months, everything's gone downhill. Two of his best copyists have been bought. The gods alone know why he allowed it, but I suppose the bid was so high he couldn't refuse. And now he's cut his own throat. Look at the fourth verse of the epithalamium: here.'

'I agree, it's still not good.'

'It's not fit to be circulated. Balbus' prices are the highest in the city, and he used to be justified in charging them, but not now. I returned the first copies to Balbus, if you remember, with your authority. And now this is what they've sent us. In my opinion it's not worth the waste of papyrus, to be copying and re-copying and getting results like this. You may want to give Balbus another chance.'

'No, of course not, Lucius. You're dealing with it. You know what I want better than I do myself.'

Lucius bows his head, closing his eyes for a moment as he receives his due. 'I've been making inquiries and visiting workshops. This one, I think, is the pick of the bunch.' He takes up a roll of papyrus, inscribed with sample text, and shows it to Catullus. 'His name is Alexandros – a Greek – and he has three slaves working under him, all personally trained. I spoke to each of them and questioned them carefully. They're well-educated, highly skilled men. I spent two or three hours there, watching work in progress. The consistency is first-rate, and they have an excellent client portfolio. Alexandros assured me that he would take charge of all your copying in person.'

Catullus studies the papyrus. Beneath the sample text there are four verses from the epithalamium he wrote for Manlius' wedding. How long ago that seems now. A day of unreturning innocence. He can almost hear the shrilling of the flutes, and see the flare of the torches. A happy marriage. But Lucius is talking.

'This is the house style, but if you're not happy with it, they will copy any style you select. In that case we can visit the workshop together and discuss your preferences.'

'It's very fine. Shall we pay him what we paid Balbus?'

'Why not, if he can produce a result like this. I gave the same verses to each workshop I visited, to make it a fair trial. And there you are: each stroke as clear-cut as a diamond, yet the words flow like water.'

'I think you're the poet here, Lucius.'

'Consider the width of these downstrokes – here – and then the upstroke. We haven't seen work like this from Balbus for a year or more.'

'No, you're right. It's true. Go ahead, let's give this Alexandros a commission and see how it goes.'

Lucius nods, satisfied. These are his happiest hours, in the study, intent on details which would mean nothing to an outsider. The brazier is burning apple wood today, and the lamps are lit although it is only late afternoon. But the day has been grey and cold, with a wind from the north. He would like to prolong the moment, but his sense of duty is too precise. The discussion is over. Lucius rolls up the papyrus samples and puts them away carefully, except for the one that his master is still studying.

'I'll have to become more productive,' says Catullus, 'if I'm to do justice to the art of this Alexandros you've found.'

Lucius smiles. 'The Muses do not permit anyone to take them for granted,' he says. 'We must be happy that they choose to visit our house as often as they do.'

A bizarre, almost comical picture forms in Catullus' mind. The Muses in all their grave glory knocking at his door, and Lucius ushering them in, taking off their sandals himself and ordering a slave to bring warm water scented with orris-root for foot washing, and a golden tray with goblets of grape juice mixed with crushed ice. Lucius would bring out all the household's jewels and plunder the ice-house for the Muses, but he would expect them to sit with decorum, and leave after the proper interval.

It's good to see Lucius looking more relaxed. Catullus' illness affected Lucius badly, and then there was the death of Metellus Celer. For years, Lucius was the man and Catullus the boy who looked up to strong arms, a broad, deep chest and pillar-like legs. But suddenly, when you are not paying attention, things change. At first you almost believe that they can change themselves back if they want. That grey hair, those thin old-man flanks can't be permanent: they're part of an elaborate pretence. Soon Lucius will clap his hands for the game to end, whip off the disguise and laugh the booming laugh that used to go through you like the rumbling of Jupiter when you were curled against his chest.

'You should be wearing a warmer tunic in this weather,' says Catullus abruptly.

'Me? You know I never feel the cold.'

I know that you never did, thinks Catullus, but you're thinner now and you don't move so fast. 'Stay a while, Lucius. Let's have more wood on the brazier, and we'll get them to bring us a jug of spiced wine. I like the smell of this apple wood; it reminds me of Sirmio. Do you remember when we cut down the old orchard there, and all the peasants brought offerings to appease the dryads?'

'It was time to cut down those trees. They had almost stopped bearing.'

'And we burned the wood all winter. Whenever I smell apple wood I am back in that winter. Mother was still alive, do you remember?'

'Of course.' Lucius rises. 'The day the orchard was cut down was the day after the doctor came from Rome to see her. You remember, your father wasn't satisfied with any of the Verona doctors.'

But Catullus doesn't remember. He can't quite see his mother's face. The apple trees are so clear, and the fires, and Lucius throwing on another log so that red sparks shoot up. His mother is there somewhere, off to one side and shadowy. Perhaps she was in her room.

Such a beautiful orchard, on the slopes that run down to Lake Garda. Some of the trees had their feet almost in the water. The tree trunks were knotted and grey and he used to play hide and seek there with his brother. After the trees were cleared, a little vineyard was planted. Beautiful, beautiful Sirmio, loveliest of all islands and near-islands, standing out into the lake and catching every summer breeze and every winter storm. How he had loved it as a child. He had stood on the terraces of the villa so many times, wrapped in a frieze cloak when the storms came, feeling that he was on the prow of a ship, voyaging, voyaging.

He could compose on it. It could happen now, here. The water parts, the outline of the poem shows for a moment, immense and slippery, and then it dives. He knows where it is. It will come again, he knows it will come again. His mind stretches, reaching for what it has failed to grasp. Lucius is at the door, talking to a slave. Catullus goes over to the brazier and warms his hands. Lucius comes back across the room, his face warm and pleased, ready for talk.

'The wine will be here in a minute.'

'Good. It's just the thing on a cold day.'

'And she's bringing some of those sweet almond biscuits you like. They were baked this morning.'

Yes, Lucius, you will have given orders. Sweet almond biscuits, a new copyist, and apple wood in the brazier. All the true, familiar notes of home must be struck, to keep away danger. There are rumours that the Metelli have vowed revenge against 'those responsible for our sorrow'. In public they say nothing. Everybody sticks to the story of sudden, tragic, unavoidable death, a great man cut down in his prime, an irreparable loss to our city, and so on and so forth. So many words that they seemed to bury the man for a second time.

'Ah, here she is!'

Virgilia carries the tray with its two steaming cups. Sure enough, there's a plate with a pile of almond biscuits, pale fawn and then golden brown at their crisp edges. A smell of honey and spices mingles with the apple-wood smoke.

They lift their cups and toast each other.

'Health and happiness!'

'Health and happiness! And to my dear friend, the most indefatigable of copyist-discoverers!'

They drink. Lucius sips; he has always been abstemious. A faint flush rises in his cheeks. 'We must think of ordering more household wine down from Sirmio,' he observes.

'Perhaps we'll go there ourselves. Would you like to see the old place again, Lucius? Are you growing tired of Rome?'

'Rome is demanding. I'm not convinced that it's the best place for your health. The air at Sirmio has always suited you. You put on weight there, and you've a better colour.'

'Poets have to live where there are people who want to hear poetry.'

'That may be, but to write poems at all, poets first have to live,' says Lucius. 'You don't know how ill you were. More than halfway to the dark kingdom, even Dr Philoctetes knew he had a fight on his hands. You won't escape so easily next time.'

He knows what Lucius is hoping: that the scandal of Metellus

Celer's death will bring an end to his relationship with Clodia. Catullus will come to his senses. There are enough beautiful young women in Rome who would jump at a young man of wealth and good family. And only two brothers to divide the property – what could be a more suitable match? And he's not bad-looking. This is the most Lucius has ever been willing to allow to either of the brothers. They were not bad-looking, he'd say, they looked as they ought and they were not a disgrace to the family's name. They even wore their togas acceptably, now that they had at long last learned that it wasn't in the least fashionable to drape them like tablecloths.

When Catullus looks back, it is Lucius who figures in all the important memories, not his father. The day he put on his man's toga, it was Lucius who adjusted the folds. Where was his father? Surely he must have been there, but Catullus can't remember him.

The brazier gives out its sweet smoke. Yes, Lucius is happier now than he has been for months. There have been no messages from the house on the Palatine. No Aemilia wrapped in her cloak, ineptly conspiratorial, ill at ease with Lucius and trying to talk as if the two of them were on equal terms. He'd snubbed her, but she didn't even notice. What can you expect from a woman like that, no matter how far she's wormed herself into her mistress's confidence?

Lucius has almost persuaded himself that Catullus' passion has burned itself out, as all fires must which are too fierce to give long-lasting warmth. Now, the life of the house can proceed. The brazier burns steadily, predictably. Lucius is no prude. He has been young, although in his youth he was still a slave, and that changes everything. But the same blood burns. All young men drink too much and want to get under the tunic of every half-good-looking girl they see – and won't say no to lifting the tunic of a pretty boy or two, either. Let them go to brothels in the afternoon, and then drink and feast all night in decent company, where they belong.

Lucius has always prided himself on the welcome Catullus' friends receive in the house, and on his own skill in ordering feasts for them in the style that he learned long ago, when Catullus' father was young.

'Shall I order another cup for you?'

'Why not?'

Lucius rings for Virgilia and orders more wine to be brought. All the girls are well trained; no household in Rome runs more smoothly, although ostentation has never been their style. Theirs is old money, which doesn't need to shout to draw attention to itself.

He'd been a little hurt by that poem about Catullus having a purse full of cobwebs, and nothing to put on the table. And to cap it all, the poem was addressed to Fabullus, who's had more hot dinners in this house than Lucius can count.

> You'll dine well at my place, my Fabullus,
> and soon too, the gods willing
> – but only if you bring
> the dinner with you, fine and plentiful;
> and why not bring a pretty girl as well
> plus wine and salt and all the jokes –
> yes, my old mate, you bring the whole bang-shoot
> and you'll dine well; for your Catullus
> has nothing left but a fat purse of cobwebs . . .

As if it were possible for such a thing to happen! The poem seemed to throw a cloud on Lucius' own management of the household, and over the fine evenings, mellow with the best Falernian, which the poem's readers had so often enjoyed. Maybe they'd forgotten, as they laughed, how smoothly the wafer-thin slices of cured, spiced beef had slipped down throats already coated with oyster sauce.

But the poem wasn't meant to be taken seriously. A rich man might make himself out to be a poor one. A poetic device, that was the name for it, and as such not to be wondered at, or injured by.

All Catullus' friends know Lucius and greet him with respect. He doesn't care what goes on, as long as there's an end to skulking about in dingy love nests with a married woman who's not only ten years older than his master but also possesses the worst of reputations in a city where there's stiff competition for that honour.

Love! Lucius glances sideways at Catullus. The boy thinks that he knows everything about love. But he and Lucius have a different idea of it. The love where you 'burn with uncontrollable fire' and forget the rest of the world, and don't eat or sleep or work – that's just one type. You can love and work as well. You can fulfil your duties, and behave like a man, not a child. Why, if Lucius had let himself go – if he'd shown a thousandth part of what he felt – he'd have lost his life, his work, the children, his home. You have to guard yourself. Guard your eyes and your tongue, watch where you walk. And feel it all the while, like the fire that they say burns deep in the earth. He never even let himself say her name aloud in the safety of his mind. She was always 'the mistress'.

The boy has let himself be possessed by that woman. He looks like his mother: he has her eyes. But she belonged to herself; she would never have let herself be captured.

The Metelli creature's talons seem to be losing their grip. The boy put his whole heart into the discussion of the parchments. He's coming back to himself. This is his true home: a warm room, yellow pools of lamplight, companionship, poetry –

'Lucius,' says Catullus, looking down into the lees of the wine, 'I need to go to the Street of the Màster Tanners tomorrow morning, at first light.'

Lucius' throat tightens.

'The Street of the Master Tanners,' he repeats, to gain time. 'What can you want there? It's no place for you. There's a mugger on every street corner in that part of the Subura.'

'That's why I'll need two slaves to go with me. How about Niko and Antonius? Can they be spared?'

'Of course they can be spared. You are the master in this house,' says Lucius bitingly. He knows immediately that this must be Clodia business. Nothing else puts that hot, distracted look into Catullus' eyes. The Street of the Master Tanners! It's come to something when one of the Metelli drags a great name in the dirt down there. But she's like that. Everybody says so. Greedy for the gutter. She doesn't love his boy. A woman like that is incapable of love, and wants only to degrade him as she has already degraded herself. The boy can't see it, because he is obsessed with her. And now she's set up a rendez-vous among stinking courtyards full of tanning vats.

'I'll ask Niko to cut bunches of mint for you,' he says.

Catullus looks at him without understanding.

'You've never been there,' says Lucius. 'The smell in that quarter is enough to make you vomit. The vapours rise to your brain, and do harm. Hold the mint in front of your face, and breathe that.'

'I see. So, big sticks for Niko and Antonius, and bunches of mint all round. Is that everything we need for protection?'

'It is better not to go at all,' says Lucius sombrely, 'but there's no stopping you, I suppose.'

'It's not what you think. I'm going to meet a lady –'

'I know that –'

'Excuse me, Lucius, you don't know anything at all. I've never set eyes on her before. She has some expertise in medicine, and I want to consult her.'

There *are* a few lady doctors in Rome. They call themselves specialists in women's problems – another name for upmarket abortionists, thinks Lucius. But what doctor would choose to practise there in the tannery quarter? And what patient would go there for a consultation?

Suddenly he doesn't want to know. There's no stopping Catullus now. Childhood is far away. Those two boys who

160

scrambled on to Lucius' shoulders for rides don't exist any more. His mother's eyes are clouded with obsession. Best to accept it, and do what he can to save the boy from himself.

If he *were* still a boy, how easy it would be. The brothers had looked to Lucius as wolf cubs look to their pack leader, long ago. The master was a good enough man in his way, but difficult. Not the kind who knew how to value what he had. A critical man who never shone a light inwards to judge himself. How surprised he'd been that his wife had hidden her illness from him.

'I don't want him to know, Lucius,' she'd said, when he came on her in a fit of coughing that went on and on until the veins bulged in her forehead. 'He'll only fuss me with more doctors.'

She'd already seen a doctor, secretly. She was taking medicines, but they didn't seem to be working. Lucius had helped her to her room. By some miracle none of the slaves was about. She leaned on him. He smelled her body, spent and sweating. It was the only time he ever touched her.

'Thank you, Lucius,' she said. 'I'm glad you were there.'

She was soft on others, but hard on herself. She even tried to draw back from her boys, so that they wouldn't miss her as much when she was gone. It didn't work, of course. There they were, those two little boys, huddling together after their mother's death. Their father let them grieve for as long as was proper, but then he began to get angry with them. In fact it was obvious that he couldn't stand the sight of their unhappiness. Soon he decided that he had to go out to Bithynia – which was true enough in its way, given the extent of the family's interests there – but there was another truth in it, too. He had to be away from the children.

Lucius could see it from his point of view, to some extent. As head of the family he had fought down his own grief. And he felt genuine grief, you couldn't deny it. He had put duty first, and he didn't want to be surrounded by whey-faced, miserable children.

That summer, Lucius showed the boys how to begin to be

men. Marcus was ready for it, and the little one tried to copy him. Every night he'd curl up in Lucius' lap and listen to stories, and take comfort. Soon they were both bold and noisy again all day long. He taught them about danger, and how to get out of it. They rowed with him on the calm waters of the lake, and he taught them what to do when a sudden fury of wind blew down over the mountains. He taught them to skin rabbits, to make fires in the open that would stay burning all night long, and how to defend themselves. Even the little one needed to learn that the world was a rough place that wouldn't let him sit in its lap. But a child doesn't learn through bullying, Lucius was sure of that. They got enough floggings at school.

All his teaching is of no use now. His boy wants that woman as a drunkard wants his wine, and the more he tastes her the worse his thirst becomes. Only the gods know what crimes that woman has committed. It will never be spoken of in this house, or even alluded to, because if you bring evil into the open, it grows stronger. But in the market and in the bathhouse, Lucius hears everything.

Why is it that the boy seems to want this madness? It's not a happy thing. It's nothing to which Lucius would give the name of love. He looks at the careful rolls of papyrus, and the taste of disappointment floods his mouth.

'You'll be better going with four slaves,' he says. 'There are too many street gangs roaming around the Subura these days.'

'And there will be, as long as there are thugs like Pretty Boy Clodius to keep them in business,' says Catullus harshly.

Lucius says nothing. Old, deeply ingrained slave habit sits on his tongue, the habit a freedman never quite manages to scour away. You don't talk politics, even when people try to talk politics to you. But the real reason he doesn't speak is that the words he'd say would come between them for ever.

You're right, that woman's brother is the worst of them. Corrupting decent men, working up his pack of criminal scum until they're ready to murder anyone to fulfil his ambitions. Starting riots in the streets.

He's her brother, you poor innocent, don't you realize that they are vipers from the same nest?

It's night now, and Catullus is alone. He can't sleep. He thinks of Sappho, sleepless too, hundreds of years ago, lying awake until the moon set and even the stars disappeared. She was alone. Her life was passing like the night. Youth had gone. But it was a speaking loneliness. He knows it; he has inherited it.

He gets up and lights the lamp. The room feels safe and familiar. He wishes he had been nicer to Lucius. Lucius sat drinking that spiced wine with the light of happiness in him, and then it was snuffed out.

She will be awake, too. Suddenly he is sure of it. Awake and alone, without her sparrow and without her husband. Her daughter may still be there, but she's almost a stranger to her mother. More likely, Clodia has already sent the girl back to the country.

He's glad that Clodia is alone. He would like her to suffer, as he has so often suffered. The thought rises, and then sinks back. He can't want to hurt her, no matter what she does. He wants her here, now.

What became of all Sappho's girls? No one knows. They're alive in the poems, and nowhere else. Lovely Cleis, the daughter who was like a golden flower; Timas, who died young and far from home. Her age-mates cut the soft curls of their hair in mourning. Only Timas' ashes made the long voyage home to her family, instead of their living daughter. There was Anactoria, making wreaths of violets in the woods; and Sappho's island itself, Lesbos, with its chirring crickets, its girls weaving at their looms, its bare-legged goat herds; its glossy, galloping horses.

The poem is beginning to rise. His poem. Tomorrow he will meet the poisoner who has the same name of one of Sappho's girls. Tonight, he'll write. His own island, the almost-island of Sirmio, begins to show its back above the waves.

Paene insularum, Sirmio, insularumque
ocelle –

But something stands in the way of the poem. The Street of the Master Tanners. He'll be there in a few hours now. Poison is a cruel way to kill a man. He wants to write his poem but the face of Metellus Celer rears up in his mind. Such puttyish contorted features. All that's left of a handsome man.

Paene insularum, Sirmio, insularumque
ocelle –

Of almost-islands, Sirmio, and of all islands
the apple of my eye –

It's no good. Leave it, Catullus. The Muses are already halfway up the street, making their getaway. It's stupid to feel so abandoned. All you've written are five words, for heaven's sake! Yes, you had the sound of the lines in your head, but you lost it. It'll come back one day, maybe, when you're not looking for it.

Sometimes a poem isn't ready to be written. Sirmio will always be waiting for him, half-island, nearly-island, almost-island . . .

But his father is there too. He looks bleakly at his son, the difficult one, the disappointing one. *Poems are all very well*, says his father's face, *but our ancestors expect more.*

Beautiful Sirmio is growing small. Soon it will have shrunk into a dot and he won't be able to see it. All he can see now is the face of his father, which keeps dissolving into the face of Metellus Celer. He must roll himself up in a blanket and think of nothing, and perhaps, if he's lucky, sleep will come.

Fifteen

The slaves don't like coming to this part of the Subura. The streets are narrow and twisting, and you can't see what's around the next corner. Or who. You feel as if you're being watched. Streets like these are where Pretty Boy Clodius recruits his thugs. They've got nothing to lose and they'll do anything the boss tells them to do. Ambush a man, set fire to buildings, murder a stranger or knock down someone's house.

Antonius, Niko and the lads keep close to their master, thinking that he looks much too soft and gentry-like, peering round this way and that way as if he's having a day out at a beauty spot. The gentry don't come down here. They've no call to, and besides it's dangerous even during the day. You can get your throat slit for a purse with a few pence in it. Walking around on your own in a good-quality woollen tunic and cloak is asking for it. As for a toga, that's tantamount to suicide. But then, no one could call their master streetwise.

Antonius has had a discreet confabulation with Lucius, to ensure that Catullus will be wearing a plain brown cloak and a pair of old boots. If he came down here dressed as usual he might as well be carrying a placard that says 'Cash over here, come and get it!'

Lucius put it well to the master. 'The streets will be running with filth. You don't want to ruin a decent cloak. As for boots, you'll only have to throw them away afterwards. Better wear these old ones.'

But there's no disguising the milk-fed look of a man who's been brought up knowing there's a solid wall of money at the back of him. It's there in the quick, bright, fearless way he faces the world, like a lucky child instead of a grown man who's had enough blows to teach him what's what. He looks as if the world belongs to him. Which I suppose it does, thinks Antonius, or as much of the world as anyone has need of. How that might feel, he can't begin to imagine.

'A proper rat's nest this is,' says Niko with disgust, stepping over a heap of stinking fish heads. There's rubble blocking the next corner, where part of a building has collapsed. No wonder, given the way they throw up these tenements.

Thousands and thousands of lives are stewing here. The buildings are warrens, four or five storeys high and blocking out the light. They pass a burned-out block with staring, blackened holes where its shutters were. Lucky the whole street didn't go up in flames. These places are death traps. Fire jumps from building to building and you can't get out in time, once the narrow stairways fill with smoke. Your best chance is to throw the children out into the street and pray they land in a pile of horse-shit.

The streets are filthy. The sun can't squeeze its way down to cleanse them with its ferocious summer blaze, and no one seems to cart away the rubbish on a regular basis. Every so often people must shovel out the cesspits, Antonius supposes.

They make their way over heaps of rotting food waste, the carcass of a chicken gnawed by rats, a pile of building wood guarded by a dog with yellow eyes that runs at them until it is yanked back by its chain. It's just after dawn. People are swarming out of the tenements. Dirty barefoot shrilling children clutch the heel of a loaf, men with work to go to make for a pie-shop to break their fast, men with none slouch down the streets, red-eyed from the night before.

They pass a tavern where a thin, tired girl is sweeping wine-sodden sawdust out of the entrance into the street. Vomit spatters the ground outside, and someone has smashed the pot of daisies set beside the doorway. The roots are dry and the flowers have wilted. The girl stoops to gather them up, holds them in her hands for a moment as if wondering whether it's worth trying to plant them again, then drops the daisies back into the dirt and sweeps them away with the shards of the pot. But not very far away. They join the sawdust in the middle of the street.

Catullus wonders if she planted those daisies.

'Hi! Get out the way!' A woman on an upper floor swings a pot over the balcony rail. Yellow liquid shoots past Catullus, spreading out in the air like a flag as it falls. He jumps back, and the woman cackles. It would have been so easy to tip the pot straight on to their heads, without warning, just for a laugh. But she's in a good mood this morning. She shoulders her pot, and goes back inside.

There's washing everywhere, flapping from balconies, pinned to lines that zigzag across the street. Wherever a line can hang high enough that mud won't splash it and thieves can't reach it, there's washing. Although who would want to steal such a lineful of rags, he can't imagine.

'According to my reckoning, we're about two streets away from where the tanning yards start. And then it was the master tanners you wanted. I'll have to ask, I don't know this patch,' says Antonius.

The other two boys jostle each other as they stare back at the tavern.

'I reckon we could just be sitting down to a nice game of dice,' one of them whispers to the other.

'You 'member old Varro, he could really roll 'em.'

'Get a move on!' Antonius orders them. They're big, raw-handed lads, fresh down from Sirmio, home-bred slaves. Strong enough, but pig-ignorant. To them, a sawdust tavern in the Subura is the bright lights.

They stop to buy bunches of mint from a market stall. The leaves have the dull look of winter, but Catullus crushes one between his fingers and the sharp, clean smell of mint rises strongly. The tanning yards are close now. Their acrid smell hanging over the surrounding streets gets into his throat and clings there, in spite of the mint. Antonius has got directions from the stallholder and he leads them confidently left, then right, and through a narrow street with openings off it that lead into tanning yards. Workers are moving around on the raised edges of the stone tanning vats. They have poles in their hands to press the hides deep into the tanning solution. They are young, no more than twelve. You'd have to be young, to be so quick and sure-footed on the narrow stone edges.

'It's not this entrance, it's the next one,' says Antonius, and barks, 'Keep up now, what do you think you're here for?' to the boys who have forgotten their duty to protect their master and are gaping at the tanning vats. They couldn't look more like bumpkins if they let their mouths hang open and stuck straw behind their ears, thinks Antonius with annoyance. They show up the whole party. Niko, as usual, is letting it all wash over him. He lives in the present, that one. Does what he's meant to do, and seems not to think beyond the day. If he gets a spare moment he whittles out little wooden figures that he calls by name. Says it's what all the boys did back home, round the fire. Niko comes from a Greek mountainy tribe. He's a captive, must have been ten or eleven when the master bought him. He whistles while he works away with that little knife in his hands.

Maybe it's the best way to be. Niko doesn't look as if he has this file rasping away inside his mind –

'Here we are.'

The entrance to the Street of the Master Tanners is just wide enough for a donkey cart to pass through. The stink is abominable. They raise their bunches of mint in front of their faces and breathe through the leaves. Even so, it is fetid. You would take this smell home with you. You'd never wash it out of your clothes. Maybe that's why the boys around the vats are naked but for loincloths. The tanning vats are open to the sky, breathing out their acids. Not good to fall in there.

The master leatherworkers' stalls must be behind these streets somewhere, Antonius decides. Now that would be worth seeing. He'd like to spend a day watching a first-class saddle-maker at work, or a man who knows how to turn a belt into a jewel without putting a single stone in it. Just to study a craftsman at work is a pleasure. It makes you feel different: lifted up. What if you were a skilled man, with a trade: now that would be a life. But no, all they'll see are the stinking old tanneries.

'Which house was it, master?' he asks quietly, not wanting to startle the master, since he seems to be lost in thought.

'Gorgo's,' says Catullus, 'ask for her by name, and if they don't know her, say that she practises medicine.'

Does she indeed, thinks Antonius, funny sort of doctor to set herself up down here. She won't get many patients knocking at *her* door. He goes into one of the workshops, where a slave is sprinkling water on the floor to settle the dust before he sweeps.

'All right, mate? I'm looking for a lady, name of Gorgo, lives in this street.'

The lad takes a step backward and makes the sign of the evil eye.

'You know her, then?' Antonius continues blandly. It's only what he expected. No decent woman would set herself up down here. The strength of the slave's reaction is a bit of a surprise, though. Probably reckons she's a witch.

'Six doors down, opposite the sign of the money-changer,' mumbles the sweeper, ducking his head so he won't have to look at Antonius any more, and kicking up a storm of dust with his broom.

Oho, thinks Antonius as he goes to rejoin the others, got a bit of a reputation all right, our Gorgo. That lad was scared shitless.

They reach the sixth door down, opposite the money-changer's. Its shutters are closed. The street is empty, which is natural enough, since everyone's in the tanning yards, workshops and offices, but Antonius is sure that they are being watched.

Catullus thinks so, too. He remembers Cynthia's words about Gorgo's 'protection'.

'Knock on the door, Antonius,' he says.

The house is as closed-up as the lid over a sleeping eye. Maybe Gorgo sleeps late. Ladies of her kind generally do.

'Knock again.'

The door opens suddenly, as if all its locks, bolts and hinges are oiled to soundlessness. A man stands there: a Numidian, tall, heavily muscled, feet planted apart. He wears a fine cream tunic with a border of gold thread. There's a chain of plaited gold around his neck. His earrings and nose stud are set with rubies.

And you can walk round here, dressed like that, thinks Antonius. That's worrying enough in itself. Antonius has met a few such men in his time. Not *met*, strictly speaking – you don't ever want to meet them, as such. But seen and known of. Such men can walk from one end of Rome to the other with a bag of gold in their hands, and no one will touch them. Their reputations are stronger than armour.

The Numidian folds his arms, regards them all, and laughs a deep, liquid laugh. 'You're early,' he says, as if he's been expecting them.

The man is a head taller than Catullus. What strength could he release, should he choose to stir himself. He's no stock bodyguard, all muscle and attitude. He is poised like a prince, and for some strange reason he reminds Catullus of Lucius. For a moment he's nine years old again, gazing up in trustful admiration at a Lucius whom he believes capable of separating a pair of fighting mountain lions with his bare hands.

'Greetings,' says Catullus, 'to you and all the household. We are here to see Gorgo.'

'You've an appointment?'

'No. Her name was given to me.'

'I see.' The man sucks his teeth reflectively, and then says, 'You'd better come in.'

He shows them into a dark downstairs room, and goes upstairs.

'It's the right house, anyway,' says Antonius. No one answers. Even Niko is twitchy, and the younger two slaves glance nervously around the room and at each other, before deciding that it's safest to stare at the floor.

Not that there's anything unusual in the room. There's no furniture apart from a shabby couch pushed back against the wall. The plaster is plain. It's a room where nothing happens except waiting.

But a lot has gone on here. You can sense it. The atmosphere is thick, enclosed. Antonius catches himself checking the door, to make sure no key has turned in it. They've got the trick of silent locks in this house. You wouldn't want to be trapped in here. There's a smell which is all right in itself, except that it reminds him of funerals. He wonders what it is. You wouldn't want to carry a cat in here either. It would bristle and spit in your arms, and claw at you to get away.

Antonius' hands are sweating. Maybe it's because it all feels so closed in. The window's too small and too high up, and it's barred. You'd need to be half the size Antonius is to have a hope in hell of squeezing through there. And now the master's found the house, he doesn't seem to know what he's doing here, any more than Antonius does. So who is this Gorgo?

A shiver passes over him. He'd thought the room was airless, but it's cold. Damp as well, he shouldn't wonder. And there's that smell again, spicy and strong, and somehow cold, too.

Now he's got it. It's like the whiff you get when the corpse of a high-up is carried past in a funeral procession. Must be something to do with the embalming. It's the kind of smell that goes straight to your stomach.

Sweat breaks out on Antonius' forehead. His chin has started to itch. Ever since he was a little kid, that's been a sure sign that he's about to throw up. Got to get out in the fresh air for a minute. But he daren't leave, not after what Lucius drummed into him about sticking to the master as tight as a leech, come what may.

Get a grip. The smell's nothing. It'll be coming from one of the workshops near by. They use all sorts in the tanning process.

The door opens. It's a woman this time, a big redhead who looks like a Gaul. You can smell her, too. That foxy Gaulishness.

'You come upstair,' she says to Catullus. 'No you,' she adds, nodding at the others, 'he only.'

That bit of air coming in with her makes Antonius feel better. It's only a room and she's only a Gaul bint. The room's got a door and they can be out of it, back in the street, free, any time they like. But the master's going off with the Gaul, on his own –

'We've to stay with you, master, Lucius told me we weren't to leave you –' begins Antonius, but the woman shakes her head contemptuously and makes a swatting gesture at him and the other three.

'Slave not go upstair,' she repeats.

Gaulish bitch – who does she think she is? She's a slave herself. Probably been living in Rome half her life and she still hasn't learned proper Latin. The master won't stand for her telling him what to do.

But he does. He says, 'Wait down here, all of you,' and looks so set and frowning that Antonius doesn't say another word. You never know when someone will turn on you, even a good master like his. It's like trying to make a pet out of a guard-dog, then one day there's a slash of teeth and the side of your face ripped half open. You've got to make sure they never have cause or chance to do it. However easy-tempered – or stupid – a master is, he'll catch on the instant you forget that you're a slave. It's not what you do, it's the way that you do it. 'Cheek' – 'getting above yourself' – 'insubordination' – he's seen lads with their backs in ribbons: not in this house, fair enough, but you have to believe it could happen anywhere.

Antonius hopes the lads are looking and learning as he bows his head obediently, and prepares to wait. At least it'll give him time to think what to say to Lucius if anything goes wrong.

Catullus turns to the woman. 'Can you bring them something to drink? They've had a long walk.'

Oh, very nice. Don't bother to remember that we'll be flogged near to death if anything happens to you. A master dies in a dirty hole like this and it's the slaves that get the blame every time. It'll be no use us legging it, cos we're dead meat anyway. Conspiracy, they'll call it, and have us tortured to find out who we've been plotting with, and then we'll be crucified, me and Niko as well as the lads. You ever seen a crucifixion? I have. Stop us doing our duty and looking after you, get that red-haired bitch to bring us a cup of poison instead, why don't you? Poor old Niko, just look at his face.

'I'm all right, me,' says Niko.

'We got no thirst on us,' chorus the lads.

'It's not worth troubling you, thank you all the same,' says Antonius hastily, 'given we won't be long here. So we'll listen out for you then, master, should you need anything,' he adds, loud and clear, for the sake of the Gaul and anyone else who might be out there, listening.

The upstairs room is so large that it must run across two houses. The shutters are closed, and the room lamplit.

He steps forward. The place appears to be empty, but the Gaul places her hands together, bows low and announces loudly, 'I bring him, mistress,' before she backs out, bowing once more in the doorway.

His eyes adjust. The room is sumptuous, decorated with a luxury that belongs to the East rather than to Greece or Rome. He has never been to Egypt, but this is the Egypt of his imagination, all silk and flowing colour. The room smells of roses, and a spice which he knows but can't immediately identify. And of lamp-oil, and jasmine.

He spots the clawed silver feet of a couch, almost hidden by curtains, which quiver in the draught from the door. That's where she must be.

'Come forward,' says a woman's voice, very calm and sure of itself. He walks across the floor. The embroidered carpet has a border of ibis, and inside that, a border of flamingos all facing the same way, against the background of a lapis lazuli lake – or perhaps sky. More silk hangings cover the walls. He would like to stop, and look at the detail in the carpet, but the voice says, 'Come here, to me.'

He steps around the screen of curtain. She's reclining on the couch, resting on one elbow. At her side there's a small table, with a silver pot and two chased silver beakers on it. There is a second couch, which he hadn't seen before because of the curtain.

'Forgive me for not rising to greet you,' she says, 'but I am tired. I received too many visitors yesterday.'

He would never have imagined that an abortionist and poisoner could look like this. If he'd imagined anything, it was a den full of sinister medical instruments. He'd expected the reek of herbs simmering with toadskin. If he'd imagined Gorgo, it was as a crone; cunning and plausible, keeper of a thousand dirty secrets.

Her eyes are light blue. Her gaze seems to float over his face, resting nowhere and missing nothing. Her skin is pale, her hair dark. She doesn't look like a Greek. She's dressed like a barbarian in a loose blue silk tunic over silk trousers. A long string of amber beads hangs between her breasts, as heavy as hailstones. Her hair is uncovered.

'And so here you are,' she observes. 'Please, make yourself comfortable.'

He settles himself on the second couch, facing her.

Sixteen

He has his story ready. He's a visitor to the city from Cisalpine Gaul. (He can easily bring back the accent that he has flattened from his speech since coming to Rome.) He's the adopted son of a wealthy knight who had no male heir. All seemed to be well. He loved his adoptive father, and cherished the good name of the family that had been entrusted to him and to his descendants.

(With a rush of creative satisfaction, he gets into character. Perhaps he really ought to write plays.)

But when his adoptive father was in his late fifties and already an old man, he married again. The woman was younger, twice widowed. She came of a good family in Ostia, and the omens were propitious. She was rich in her own right, having inherited from two estates.

At first things seemed to go well. But it happened, a few months after the wedding, that the son's duties took him to Ostia, and while he was there he heard disturbing rumours. The woman's reputation was bad. She was said to have been unfaithful to both her husbands, and it was even whispered that she'd had a hand in two very convenient deaths.

'So I went home to my father,' Catullus continues, looking straight into Gorgo's eyes, 'and my heart was torn in two, wondering if I should warn him. If it was just evil gossip, then I'd be ruining his happiness for nothing. My inclination was to wait until my stepmother gave me cause to act, but then I consulted a soothsayer. She listened to the whole story, divined in the blood of a fowl, and convinced me that I must open my heart to my father. If I did not, I risked blood guilt for whatever might happen to him. My stepmother had profited from death too much to be afraid of it any more.

'With a heavy heart, I sought a private talk with my father. Instead of listening as I had hoped, he was enraged at the first mention of my suspicions. He would not hear me out. He accused me of jealousy, and of unfilial behaviour. He said to me that his wife had already warned him that I had shown an improper interest in her. He had tried not to believe it, because he loved me. But now I had shown my true colours and my desire to destroy his happiness.

'I saw how clever my stepmother was. Nothing I said could convince my father that she had lied, or that he should trust me.'

He pauses, waiting for Gorgo's reaction. It's a good story. He can see the characters so clearly: the angry father with dangerous blood rising in his cheeks, the son outraged by the stepmother's lies, but still desperate to protect his beloved father –

Cynthia would love this. She'd be leaning forward in her seat, soaking up every word.

Not like Gorgo. She looks calm and cool. Perhaps his story is a little too well made. Truth has a more ragged edge.

Perhaps it's simply that nothing surprises her. Murder, death and desperation must be her daily bread. Perhaps she's become immune. People who swallow tiny quantities of poison each day can make themselves poison-proof. Parricide, matricide and fratricide all rolled into one might not make Gorgo sit up.

Gorgo stretches out her arm, and her silk sleeve falls back. The skin of her inner arm is as pale as a peeled mushroom. She lifts the silver pot, and pours a stream of transparent pale green liquid into the beakers.

'Jasmine tea,' she says. 'Will you have some?'

He takes the beaker. He doesn't like jasmine tea, but he's not going to refuse to eat or drink in her house, like the slaves. He takes a sip. Not pleasant. It reminds him of perfume on unwashed flesh. He takes another sip, forcing the liquid down his throat. Gorgo waits in silence. He hears himself swallow, and wonders if she hears it, too.

Her arms are at her sides again. Her fingers are elegantly

languid, but they are not white, like the skin of her inner arms. They are stained. Maybe the juices of the herbs she works with have also worked on her and made their way deep into her skin.

He sips again. Now that the actors have left the stage of his mind, the story sounds hollow. Why not just cut to the truth, and ask the questions that crowd out sleep, night after night –

Did Clodia come to you? Did she ask you to help her? What do you know about Metellus Celer's death?

He must get back behind the mask of the story. Make it hide those ugly, appalling questions. He steadies himself and takes a long slow breath, as a poet must do before a recitation.

'I could not stay in my father's house,' he continues. 'My stepmother set her own slaves to watch me, and carry tales to my father. I left on a voyage to Bithynia on family business; we are in the timber-export business there. I was away for almost a year, and when I returned I was greeted by two slaves of my father's household. They were dressed in mourning, and they wore caps. I knew them well: they loved my father. I guessed immediately that he was dead, and that their loyalty to him had been rewarded with freedom in his will.

'And so it was. My father had died suddenly, within two days of becoming ill. There was no time to send word to me. His funeral had already taken place.'

'No one sent word to you?' asks Gorgo.

'My father had been dead for a month, but my voyage had taken more than six weeks.'

'I see.'

'They also told me that my stepmother was pregnant. Fortunately these two slaves had been at my father's side throughout his brief illness, and they were able to give me a detailed account of his sufferings. They insisted that he had been perfectly well until after dinner on the day he was taken ill. In fact he had ridden out to our largest estate to discuss business with the steward that morning. He went to bed after dinner, they told me. At around midnight he tried to get up, feeling unwell, and collapsed. The slaves were roused with the rest of the household, and Mironus rode for the family doctor.

'Immediately I heard this, I suspected that some crime had taken place, and had been covered up. My stepmother has since given birth to a son, who bears the family name. And yet my father, in a long marriage, had only daughters. That was why he adopted me.'

'A strange story,' says Gorgo.

'Yes.'

'And you have come to me to tell it. Why?'

'I'm told that you have great skill in herbal medicine. I've come here in the hope that you can identify the cause of my father's death.'

'I see.' She drinks more tea. Her eyes are no longer fixed on him, but shrouded and inward. 'You've been told a lot about me.'

'Your skill and knowledge are well known.'

'In certain circles. Go on with your story. Tell me exactly what occurred when your father was taken ill.'

He reaches into a pouch at his belt, brings out a small roll of papyrus, and spreads it out. On it he's written down every detail of the symptoms he has gleaned from the Metelli slaves.

'I wrote down the symptoms in order, exactly as Sextus and Mironus gave them. I questioned them closely, and they were eager to help me. They'd been freed by my father's will, as I had guessed, and they had saved enough money in his service to go into a silphium-trading business. They loved my father, and were loyal to him. They had no motive for lying.'

They seem very real, his Mironus and Sextus, counting their gold and planning their future. He hopes that their silphium trading is a success. They'll have to be careful. The stepmother has power.

'They told me that my father was taken ill some hours after eating. First he suffered stomach and chest pains so severe that he fell to the floor when he tried to get out of bed. His breathing

178

became laboured. He swallowed as if there were an obstruction in his throat. The doctor arrived, and immediately applied leeches and gave him cinnamon tea. By this time he could barely swallow at all. They had to wipe away the excess of saliva that streamed from his mouth. Mironus said that my father also wept until tears ran down his face. Yet he was a man who never wept.'

'The pain must have been severe.'

'Sextus assured me that his tears flowed like rain, not like a man's tears. My father could barely speak, but he complained of numbness and tingling in his hands and feet. His breathing grew worse and he became very cold. He died just before dawn on the second day of his illness, after great suffering. On the first night, the doctor asked to see the dishes my father had eaten from. He must have been suspicious of poison from the outset. But all the dishes had been scrubbed, the copper cooking pots scoured with sand, and the kitchens swept clean. Not a particle of food remained from the dinner. Besides, all the slaves swore that my father, my stepmother and all the guests had eaten from the same dish.'

'What was that dish?'

'Roast partridge, stuffed with chestnut mushrooms, served with oyster sauce. My father loved oyster sauce.'

'And everybody ate from the same dish?'

'Everybody.'

'What about the sauce?'

'Of course I questioned them about the sauce, that was obvious. But it was poured from the same jug for everyone at the table.'

He has indeed checked all these facts. It wasn't difficult. Kitchen slaves will talk to kitchen slaves, and he paid well for the information about the last dinner eaten by Metellus Celer. Clodia's husband always took oyster sauce with roast meat. His tastes were simple, and he didn't like new dishes. Naturally he provided all the expected hors d'oeuvres, savouries and sweetmeats for his guests, but he could be relied on to eat only the one main course himself. He insisted on the very best meat and game. The partridges (perhaps his favourite bird) must be plump and perfectly cooked so that their succulence retained a gamey hint of blood.

Catullus knows exactly what was on Metellus Celer's plate at his last dinner. Two whole partridges, stuffed with mushrooms, coated with oyster sauce. The man's appetites were large, as well as simple. Did Clodia's glance stray to her husband's plate, checking that all was as it should be?

Suddenly he remembers the first time he was invited to dine at her house on the Palatine. It seems a hundred years ago. He can remember feeling a little bored at the prospect of an evening with Metellus Celer and all the other bigwigs who were bound to be there – and reminding himself that he could always slip away early and go to Ipsitilla's –

It wasn't the first time he'd seen Clodia, but that night she burned herself on to his mind like a vision sent by the gods. How gladly he'd surrendered. He was where he had always longed to be, inside the fire.

He'd borrowed Sappho's poem to describe it:

a subtle flame
burns beneath my skin,
my blood thunders
my ears ring
night covers my eyes

His heart clenches. That's how it was. If he could forget all that, he could survive anything. It's the way she keeps reminding him of her former self that tears him apart. She can be cold, calculating, treacherous, until he's almost free to hate her, and then suddenly she is his girl again, incomparable. She turns to him, as if for the very first time.

That first time. He made her laugh, she said. He laughed at everything and he was afraid of no one. He had come to Rome to make his name, and already his lines were caught up and repeated almost as soon as he'd finished writing them. His epigrams were famous. He exposed pretension, deceit, opportunism, folly. But he could be tender, too, with an intimacy that took your breath away and stripped words to the bone. She knew all these things about him before she knew him. They met once or twice, in crowded parties where there was no time to talk. Her attention was quickened, her pulses ready to beat faster. She would invite him to the next dinner at her house on the Palatine. She said to her husband:

– Rather a coup, we've got Catullus coming tonight.

– Really? Is the family visiting from Verona? Her husband spoke absently. He knew everyone's genealogy, and where they belonged.

– No, he's living in Rome now. His poetry is making a tremendous stir.

– Can't say I've heard of the poetry. But he comes of a good family.

She'd smiled at her husband. Of course he hadn't heard of Catullus' poetry. He relied on Clodia to keep him 'abreast of cultural trends' as he phrased it. She always knew what was what: she knew what would bring distinction to their house.

The dinner came. Dull at first, Catullus thought. A small, select gathering. Dutiful conversation about poetry, so crass that it made his eyes narrow like a cat's. Keen, knowledgeable talk about the relationship between Pompey and Caesar. Catullus could not concentrate. He watched the mouths, the lips moving, the slaves moving in their intricate dance of service. Suddenly he felt himself come to life. He told a story about a thief at the Baths, and now everyone was laughing. Clodia's mouth opened, showing her small white teeth.

He saw her; really saw her. The laughter died away. Clodia's pupils dilated as if someone had poured a drop of antimony into each of her eyes. They recognized each other. It was sharp as a stab but he still doesn't know whether what he recognized was her power to make him love her, or her power to make him suffer. But he wasn't alone; not then. Clodia was caught, too. They were both harnessed and they could do nothing but bend their heads to the yoke as it dropped over them.

His girl, his bright-shining goddess. If it's possible that she could watch her husband shake out his napkin, watch him try the flesh of the partridge with his knife and then nod with grave approval, watch him dip a chunk of meat into oyster sauce, and then turn to talk and laugh with another guest; if these things are possible then anything is possible.

Oyster sauce is strongly flavoured with garum. You would not be able to detect mushrooms in it if they were pounded to a paste. Sometimes he's amazed that all his tormented thoughts can be held inside one skull. He puts his hand to his forehead and expects to feel a vibration like the fury of trapped bees.

If she can do that, then nothing and no one can be trusted.

'But you still suspect that he was poisoned,' says Gorgo lightly, as if such a suspicion were the most natural thing in the world.

He can't answer. He doesn't trust himself. The death of a man by poison: you can't get away from that. He meant his story to shadow the truth, but it is becoming the truth.

No. It will happen only if you believe it. His girl, who broke her heart over a sparrow, she couldn't plan a death like that. She wasn't capable of watching calmly as her husband was dragged to the grave. And such a death. Such a degradation hour after hour until he must have longed to die, as a man broken by torturers doesn't even notice the reek of shit when he's thrown into the Cloaca Maxima. No woman could act her way through such horrors. She must be innocent.

But he can't leave it. Doubt is alive in him, clutching, killing him.

'Your father was previously strong and healthy?'

He nods. She turns on her couch and lamplight ripples over her clothes.

'Did the slaves mention the smell of your father's breath? The same smell would have been on his skin, and in his sweat and urine.'

He is back in the bedroom, with Metellus Celer. There is the smell of shit and vomit, so strong that it overwhelms every other smell at first. But as he comes closer to the bed, he smells something different. A familiar smell, but in the wrong place. The smell of brown, rotted apples lying in the long grass under the trees. Their skin is stippled with white spots of decay, and when you stamp on them they give off a sharp smell of fermentation.

'There was a smell of rotten fruit. Of apples.'

She swings her legs off the side of the couch and sits upright. 'Stomach pains, difficulty in breathing, sweats – did you mention sweats? Excessive salivation and uncontrolled weeping.' She ticks off the symptoms on her fingers. 'And, finally, the smell of rotting apples. Your father was unlucky. Either he suffered from a rare, sudden disease which mimicked exactly the effects of eating certain mushrooms, or he ate those mushrooms and died from their effect.'

'But that's not possible. The slaves swear that everyone was served from the same dish. Even the sauces were poured from a common jug.'

'Then there are only three possibilities,' says Gorgo. Her light, bewitching eyes shine like barbarian seas in the far north. Amusement plays on her face without settling into anything as definite as a smile. 'Either you're mistaken in your suspicions, and your father died a natural death; or the slaves are lying about the dish; or we must find a third explanation. Nothing is *impossible*. It only seems so because we haven't yet uncovered the explanation.'

She springs off the couch in a sudden, supple movement, and claps her hands above her head. Immediately, another slave enters. This time it's a boy, dark and slender. She speaks to him in a language Catullus doesn't know. It's not Greek.

'I have ordered him to fetch us some cakes, to sweeten our discussion,' she says. 'He will bring more tea, too. I hear that your slaves are refusing to eat or drink in my house. You should train them better.'

Almost instantly, it seems, the boy is back with another silver tray, this time one with a high border. The cakes are no bigger than his thumb, lying in a blue dish, glistening with sweetness. There are two little plates, and two embroidered linen napkins.

'The cakes are a speciality of the house, made from honey, almonds and cardamom,' says Gorgo. 'Serve yourself.'

He chooses three cakes, and puts them on his plate. They are still warm from the oven.

'There's a syrup of rose water and honey to go with them.' She indicates the jug that the boy is holding. It's the same blue as the plates, with an image of a leaping hare on its side. 'Some people like the flavour of rose water, others prefer the cakes as they are.'

'I'll try the syrup,' he says. The boy pours a thin stream over his cakes. The jug is so close to him that Catullus notices a tiny chip on the rim. The boy passes behind him, goes around to his mistress and pours out syrup for her before placing the jug on the tray. She lifts a little cake, dripping with syrup, and bites into it. Her teeth are small and white. She smiles.

'Delicious. Why don't you try one? They're not so good once you let them grow cold.'

He is no slave, but even so he's glad to see her taste the cake before he eats his own. He lifts the sticky, syrupy morsel. A golden drop falls on to the plate. His mouth waters. At that instant she leans forward and strikes like a snake. The cake flies from his hand and splatters on the tiles.

'I'm afraid they may have used the wrong kind of rose water in the syrup,' she says calmly. 'It may not be wise to eat your cakes.'

'But you've already eaten yours.'

She laughs softly, and says a few words in the foreign language to the boy. He smiles like a clever child, glances shyly at Catullus and then back to his mistress.

'He will show you,' says Gorgo. With a slight flourish, the boy brings out the jug from behind his back. But it can't be the same jug he used to pour the syrup. That jug is still on the tray.

Of course, there are two. They are identical, with the same distinctive blue glaze, the same leaping hare, even the same tiny chip on the rim.

'Yes, there are two,' says Gorgo. 'He has a pocket in his tunic. He holds one jug, like this, and serves you. There is just enough syrup in it for one person; a special syrup. He goes behind you, puts the used jug in his pocket, takes out the second jug and serves me. It takes some skill, of course, and a certain amount of practice. It is important not to spill any of the syrup. But it is not a difficult trick.'

She smiles at the boy, and says something to him. He opens his mouth. She pops a cake from her own plate into it, and dismisses him.

'You've proved your point,' says Catullus, 'but I'm still hungry. Is it safe to eat my cakes?'

'You may do as you wish.'

He watches her for a moment. Her fingers are relaxed. She's intent, but not afraid. Not expecting trouble, then, and with four of his slaves downstairs and his whole household told where he's going, there would certainly be trouble. Deliberately, he picks up a cake, puts it in his mouth, and bites.

'Delicious,' he says.

It is not a difficult trick. Metellus Celer always asked for oyster sauce with his roast meat.

He doesn't want to know any more. A healthy man can be struck down between one day and the next. A fever can seize him, or an inflammation of the brain. Philoctetes is a good doctor, but he can make a mistake. Rome is a stew of rumours, and there isn't a great man in the city who doesn't have enemies attached to his heels like shadows. So, if a man like Metellus Celer dies suddenly, everyone cries murder.

Clodia has no motive. She had nothing to gain by it. Freedom? She was free already. She did what she wanted. It's true that her brother and her husband are political enemies – but no one, not even Pretty Boy, would expect that of a sister –

The pale blue eyes are watching him.

'You are not in the timber business,' she says.

'No.'

'What are you?'

'I'm a poet.'

She nods. 'You wanted to know what had happened,' she says.

'Yes.'

'You want to know what will happen?'

He shrugs.

'I have some gift for it,' she says, 'or perhaps you don't believe?'

He's been to half the fortune-tellers in Rome in his time.

– Fortunes told with peacock feathers! Get your fortune told here, my handsome, with authentic, guaranteed feathers from the shrine of Holy Aphrodite at Kos!

– Over here, gorgeous! The amazing Rufa will trace your future on the one-and-only chart of divination, brought from the walls of a Pharaoh's tomb in Egyptland!

Ipsitilla says it's all vanity. *You just like the way they concentrate on you, darling, I don't think you care tuppence what they actually say.* But there's such a thing as second-sight. You shiver, and the hairs rise on the back of your neck. You mustn't cross a seer. She has the power to bring down light or darkness into your life.

He stretches out his hand. Gorgo puts one hand beneath his, lightly supporting it. Her other hand sweeps over his palm, barely touching it, as if wiping away everything that might hide what she wants to see.

'Now look at me,' she says.

His hand seems to tingle slightly as she passes hers over it again.

'I see a long journey,' she says. Her accent is more pronounced now. 'They have already seasoned the timber to build the ship in which you will sail. Keep still. I am feeling for the thread of your life.'

Her fingers flutter, then settle.

'You will live long,' she says, her voice thickening. There is a film of sweat on her forehead. 'No hand I have seen possesses a longer lifeline. But there's more –'

She pauses, sweeping his palm again and again. The veins in her forehead bulge. Lines deepen in her face, her nose grows sharp and her lips thin. She looks like a ravaged old woman as she draws in her breath harshly and says in a rapid monotone, 'You have two lives. You hate and you love. You see and you remain in darkness. You live and you die. You die without children but your offspring carry your name for ever. Take your hand away.'

He takes back his hand.

Seventeen

Gorgo leans against her cushions.

'Wait,' she mutters.

Sweat prickles the palms of his hands. Gorgo has crawled inside his life like a thief. But she can't really know his future, or his past. No one has the power to cancel the work of time. Without time, you have nothing. It's the one thing that's sure. A door opens and you come into the world; it closes and you go out of the world. Otherwise, life would be unbearable. He's always hated the thought of immortality. No wonder the gods have such cold, hard smiles.

He stares at Gorgo. She looks as if she'll live for ever, preparing poisons for Rome's convenient murders.

It's Clodia he needs. His girl, his Clodia. Every day another tiny smudge of a line around her wonderful eyes, a new softness to the skin inside her elbow. They're dying together, holding hands as they move through time. That poem he wrote about Clodia's sparrow, hopping into the blackness: it was about the two of them, him and Clodia, already on the dark path and always knowing where it ends for them. But not caring, because they've got what they wanted from time and death.

His girl.

'You don't look well,' says Gorgo. 'Does your chest always make that sound when you breathe?'

Gorgo is sapping his life. He can't breathe right. This room is stifling. Why doesn't she open the windows?

He breathes out slowly, and drops his shoulders to relax, as Dr Philoctetes has taught him.

'If you were my patient, I would be able to help you,' says Gorgo.

'I have a doctor already.'

She shrugs. 'Anyone can call himself a doctor. Most of them are quacks. Give me your hand again. Let me feel your skin. All I need is a hair from your head, a drop of your sweat; perhaps some urine. The rest is a matter of observation. I learned this art of diagnosis in Egypt, and I studied six years for it.'

'I don't think I want to be diagnosed.'

'You prefer to take your chance,' says Gorgo. She yawns, stretching her arms so the silk of her tunic moulds against her body. She looks tired now, and older. He's just the same when he's written for too long, written himself out. Empty, ready for any piece of folly his friends want to think up, wanting escape at all costs.

You prefer to take your chance.

I do. *You live and you die.* Who doesn't that apply to? *You hate and you love.* That one hit home. She might have read the words out of his mind. *Odi et amo.* He feels exposed, as if Gorgo has penetrated the part of him where his poems are made.

Hatred and love all tangled together, like Clodia's hair tangling across his mouth as she straddles him and leans forward with open lips.

There is something in Clodia that he has never found in any other woman, no matter how lovable or fuckable. Clodia is not as lovable as Cynthia. She's not as fuckable, strictly speaking, as Ipsitilla. She's like a taste that's never been known in the world before. It shocks your mouth and turns it into the blind mouth of a baby, rooting for the nipple that it's got to have no matter what, because the nipple is life.

He's tasted her and he can never give her up. It was folly to come here. He isn't looking for the truth about Clodia, because he doesn't want it. If she's done wrong, let her hide it. It's Clodia herself he wants: only her.

Her husband is dead, and the dead don't come back. Why torture himself over how Metellus Celer died, when all that's left of the man is a mask which hangs alongside the masks of his ancestors? His sufferings are over. No one can help him or hurt him. He'll never taste a fresh spring morning on the Palatine Hill again, or see that sharp blue edge of the distant hills. He walked about in solid splendour all his life, but death broke that like eggshell.

Catullus won't ever know if poison killed Clodia's husband. Gorgo might give him an answer if he asked her, but he won't ask.

No, Clodia, he thinks, no more pretending. I'm speaking to you now. Let's not hide from each other, playing at grief and conscience. Our time is short enough. Let's seize the golden ball that fate has thrown towards us, before it rolls away for ever.

He is free, and Clodia is free.

Funny to think he used to be in the habit of thinking himself sensitive. He would walk over corpses to get to Clodia.

But he doesn't need to, because Clodia is a widow now. It's all over, that part of the play where Clodia was a wife, Catullus her secret, desperate lover, and Metellus Celer either knew or didn't suspect, either cared or was indifferent. They'll never know now if he'd intended to put an end to the affair, punish Clodia, and make Catullus pay.

Those early meetings in Manlius' little villa look as innocent as the games of children when he stares back at them down the narrow passage of time. But they were never innocent. They carried seeds of knowledge and destruction in them from the first moment. He always wanted her husband out of the way.

Yes. Everything was leading to this moment. He can have what he wants. After a year of mourning, she'll be free to marry again. People are calling her a murderer as it is. Marriage may even protect her. At the very least it'll be something new to talk about.

– Have you heard? Our Lesbia's actually marrying her devoted poet.

– Let's hope he's got a strong stomach.

Catullus winces. There are thoughts so raw he doesn't want to touch on them. He's lost the right to the kind of marriage where everyone rejoices and the oldest, corniest, crudest jokes in the world are nothing more than water thrown against the fire. What if they really could both go back, he and Clodia, and be their untouched selves and then meet each other for the very first time . . .

It's self-indulgent fantasy. They are used, both of them. That's the whole point. That's why he can never have enough of her. She seems to gather up his whole life in her hands and make it mean everything he's ever longed for.

She's had men, and he's had women – and men, too: Cynthia, Ipsitilla, Ameana, his honey-sweet Juventius, Rufa, a dozen and then a dozen more with whom he's slept, teased, got drunk, gossiped and whiled away long stifling afternoons. All those afternoons seem to melt into one endless afternoon with the shutters keeping the sun at bay, a pitcher of wine, a plateful of cakes, the bed a mess of sweat-soaked linen. And a naked body sprawled beside him, or straddling him, as intent on its pleasure as he's intent on his own.

Clodia's afternoons have been just the same. It would take an abacus to reckon up her lovers. That's why he and she understand each other, because they're equally compromised by all the promises they haven't meant a word of. They've got so much in common. They share a stock of shifts and stratagems. They know about lies, their own and other people's. They know about scenes and storms of tears. They've both sworn by love on the understanding that love is whatever anyone chooses to believe in at the time. What's real is the hot body and the cold observing heart.

But then he saw her, his bright-shining goddess, with her thighs still wet from another man's semen.

They're both saturated with experience, like ground that can't take one more drop of rain without flooding. He wants to go straight to Clodia and swear to her that he's never for a second doubted her innocence. A rose grows in shit but it is still a rose. She'll believe in his belief in her. They'll create their own kind of innocence between them.

Why's he waiting?

He'll go to the Baths first, and steam the stink of Gorgo's house out of his skin. A masseur will pummel his body until all his thoughts are driven out of his head. He'll plunge into the cold pool and then start the cycle again and repeat it, hot, cold, hot, cold, until he's so clean and empty that one of the slaves will have to wrap him up in his towel like a baby.

It's going to be a new life. There will have to be a decent interval, but Clodia's a free woman. They'll be happy.

Gods! What if she says yes?

He rises.

'You must forgive me. I've stayed much longer than I intended.'

But Gorgo puts out her hand, arresting him. 'Wait. You wanted to know about poisons,' she says.

'I must go.'

Her eyelids droop, almost covering her eyes. 'Someone who poisons once will poison again,' she says. 'You told me you were a poet. Poets deserve protection. We don't cut out the throats of nightingales.'

'Even though their tongues make excellent pie.'

'Poisoners don't care if they repeat a line which has served them well.'

He laughs. 'That's not my kind of poetry.'

'Come with me. It will only take a few moments.'

She stands, and he stands too. He still hasn't made up his mind – he might leave at any moment. He tells himself it's pure curiosity that makes him follow Gorgo.

In the corridor outside, the Numidian is lounging against the wall. He smiles at Catullus, the kind of smile a man gives to a boy.

'You want anything?' he inquires of Gorgo.

'We're going to my workshop.'

The Numidian raises his brows. 'You want me to come?'

'No. Those slaves downstairs – are they happy?'

'They're very happy.'

'Eating and drinking?'

'Eating and drinking now.'

Her little pointed teeth show in a laugh, and he laughs, too, stretching his lips soundlessly, as he turns, and walks away. Gorgo lifts the latch on the door opposite.

One wall is lined with wooden drawers which stretch from floor to ceiling. On the long table are a pair of scales, several pestle-and-mortars, a set of knives, a rack of golden spoons and another of silver spoons, all precisely ranged. There are stacked bowls, rows of glass jars and sealed pots, papyrus holders and wax tablets. A small, sleepy fire lollops in the hearth. Copper pans stand close to it, their bellies full of reflections.

On the opposite wall, where there are no drawers, dried snakeskins hang from racks against the plaster. A python skin droops, so long that it has had to be doubled over on a padded hook. There are rows of teeth bored through and strung on gold wire.

'Tiger's teeth,' says Gorgo.

A high shelf holds jars of liquid, in which formless shapes float darkly. The room smells of resin, burning hair and incense.

Gorgo pulls a handle, and one of the drawers glides open. It's subdivided into dozens of compartments, each as wide as two thumbs. The compartments are protected with oiled papyrus. She lifts a corner of one, and he sees a pinch of fine, black, familiar seeds.

'Yes,' she says, 'poppy seeds.'

He's glad that the compartment should contain something so harmless.

'Poppy seeds can do nothing alone,' says Gorgo thoughtfully, stirring the seeds with her little finger. 'They must be combined with other ingredients.'

'I see.'

'I've spent my life here, and I see perhaps a little; not much. Do you recognize this?'

She uncovers a larger compartment at the right side of the drawer, revealing sections of dried, withered root.

'No.'

'If it were whole you'd know it. Mandrake. Tear it from the ground and it screams like a man. Swallow it and you'll be asleep and awake at the same moment, while your heart races and your mouth dries out until you can't even croak for help. But mandrake can be too slow. We combine it with these dried mushrooms here: muscaria.'

The drawer slides shut silently. She fingers another handle, hesitates and seems to change her mind. Suddenly she drops to her knees and pulls open the wide bottom drawer.

'This is thorn-apple. Its advantage is that your victim will remember nothing, if he survives. Thorn-apple swallows the memory. Its drawback is that he may survive. Here's hemlock. Everyone knows Socrates' fate. Well, my countryman was lucky that he could speak calmly to his friends after taking hemlock. It's rarely so gentle. You won't break your bones in convulsions, but you'll suffer. You may not be able to philosophize.

'Now here's the autumn crocus. See how well it dries, the flower as well as the corm. Look at the perfection of the stamens. Colchis is so much more beautiful than hemlock, but not as kind. Your mouth knows as soon as it's swallowed the crocus. It burns and freezes. That's the beginning. You'll choke for breath, you'll shit out your own guts in blood. You'll die within six hours.

'Come closer, you can't see from over there. Now the yew. When you see a flushed face and a pupil so huge that the iris vanishes, that's yew. You can't breathe deeply, you can only pant like a woman who's desperate to give birth.

'And here's white hellebore. She works even faster than the crocus. Your heart gives way and your lungs fill with water.

'Mushrooms you know. But there are a hundred varieties and

a thousand thousand combinations. With mushrooms, you can play on the body like a master musician sweeping the strings of his lyre.'

'But the results are not quite so beautiful,' he says, forcing the words past a tongue which feels thick in his mouth, as if one of her poisons is already working in him. His heart beats in slow, heavy strokes. Her words touch him where he doesn't want to be touched.

'Which would you choose?' he asks.

'What?'

'Which poison would *you* choose? For yourself?'

She frowns. Her fingers play with shavings of dried mushrooms as she ponders the question.

'I would not choose poison, if I had to die,' she says at last. 'I would jump from a high place. I have even chosen the place.'

'But suppose you had no choice?'

'Then it would be hemlock,' she says.

'But would it touch you? You might be immune by now.'

She laughs. Her quick fingers replace the cover over the mushrooms, without her needing to look. Her hands remind him of Dr Philoctetes' hands.

'The thing to remember with all poisons is that the results can be anything you want,' she says. 'If you have the skill.'

'I'm not interested in poisoning anyone.'

She straightens up slowly, surveys him. 'You Romans,' she says.

'I'm from Verona.'

She shrugs. 'Rome, Verona. What I mean is that this city lives by benefitting from the crimes of others. But you Romans are careful. You are never quite party to them. You remain pure.'

'I'm a poet, not a politician.'

'And you have never benefitted from a crime. So there we are: a Roman who is not a Roman.'

'I've taken up too much of your time. I must go.'

'You're a young man and a rich man and a Roman. Look at

me. I am neither very young nor very rich and I am Greek. Believe me, I know the ways of Rome better than you'll know them. When the grain ships come into Puteoli, and grain from Alexandria fills the warehouses of Rome, I know whose mouths are left empty, and I know who benefits. When a beautiful Greek boy stands on the auction block, being felt up by an old man who needs a new "secretary", I know whose home is empty. And I know who benefits. Now let's go downstairs and see what has become of your slaves.'

He follows her down the stairs in silence.

When he enters the waiting room, a smell of sour wine hits him. His slaves are reclining on the floor, surrounded by cups, dishes and leftover food. The two lads loll on their elbows, their faces glazed with drink. There are dice on the floor between them, but they're not playing: too drunk even for that. One of the cups has overturned and a dark stain of unmixed wine spreads over the tiles. No one has tried to wipe it. The boys stare up at their master with dumb surprise, as if they'd forgotten that there was any such person in the world.

Niko seems not to notice his master at all. He grasps half a roast chicken and he's tearing off chunks of breast and cramming them into his mouth. His lips shine with grease. A flap of chicken skin is caught, ridiculously, over his nose. The Gaul sits beside him, her thigh touching his. The front of her tunic is pulled down and her nipples are exposed. Niko must have broken off his work with her halfway through, to get busy with the chicken. Only Antonius stands rigid and apart, by the wall, looking at nothing.

'Antonius, what's all this?' asks Catullus.

Antonius clears his throat, looks down at his feet in their rough slave boots, then up again at his master, avoiding Catullus' eyes. He stands condemned, this efficient, easy-humoured man whose capacity for work has brought him steadily higher and higher in Lucius' regard. Antonius has been putting money aside for years, saving slowly to buy his freedom. And now he's lost. He sees his future vanish like coins poured into the sea.

'It's not the fault of the lads,' he says huskily. 'The way it was, they had no choice. *He* give them the wine. *He* tells them if they was real men and wanted to know what a man knows, they'd drink it. They're only country boys.'

'And Niko?'

Antonius gives Niko a quick, fearful glance. 'He's not himself,' he whispers. 'Anyone can see that. I tell you, master, he's bewitched, he's neither seeing us nor hearing us. There was something put in the drink, I swear on my life, master.'

'So you didn't eat or drink?'

'I never touched it.'

Gorgo stands by the door, her arms folded, watching the scene as if his men are animals in a field. Her face is cold. She's indifferent to them all, and if they'd been lying dead on the floor she'd have had them dragged away and cared nothing for it. And the same for him. All that attention she turned on him like a lamp meant nothing. What a fool he was to go so deep into her world. He was confused, like Niko. Bewitched, he could say. Gorgo's attention flattered him. He's used to women liking him.

Getting the slaves drunk is part of it. Maybe she fancies herself as the Circe of the Subura, turning them all into her swine. *You Romans*. How many Romans has she helped to their death, he wonders. How many Roman babies has she shucked from the womb before they can grow to men? And all so subtly done. What she does is measure the desire, and provide the means. It must be very satisfying, as she weighs and mixes, to know who is going to benefit.

'Your slaves are dead drunk in my house,' she says. 'You should have trained them better. Such behaviour is a punishable offence. If I were to call the authorities . . .' She's watching Antonius out of the corner of her eye. She knows that he's the only one left who's still capable of feeling fear.

You won't call anyone, thinks Catullus. Not to this house, with what it contains. For the first time he's aware of exactly how far he is from his own world, deep in a maze of streets where wealth and rank don't count except to make a man a target. People disappear every day. His protection has dissolved in alcohol and whatever else she had put into those cups. He must not let her sense it. He must appear not to be aware.

'You'll need to order litters,' he says. 'They're not fit to walk.'

'You think that litter-bearers will come to the Street of the Master Tanners, to take home a party of drunken slaves and their master?' asks Gorgo contemptuously.

But she's gone too far this time. Catullus smiles, suddenly liberated by her open hostility. If he's been enchanted, the spell's broken. There's no mystery, just a dirty trade.

He's had enough. Enough of walking away from his girl instead of towards her. If there's any poison in the case it's in his own mind, working against him and against Clodia. That's what Gorgo has done for him.

How Clodia would laugh if she were here in this room. She would never allow Gorgo the whip hand for a second.

'What? You let that second-rate Circe push you around?'

Clodia is equal to anything and anyone. A suspicious husband? A Forum humming with vicious rumours? Death? Face them down. She's Roman enough, his girl, born to breathe the high air of the Palatine and to look out over the clustered antheap of those who serve her. If she ever doubts herself, no one knows it.

It's all a game, an enormous throw of the dice. Rome faces down the world and demands grain to feed the plebs of Rome for nothing. Clodia faced down the hostile stares of the Metelli and the propped, embalmed corpse of her husband, and now she has her freedom. He has got to play too.

First, he's got to get himself home, drunken slaves or no drunken slaves. Tedious and inconvenient though it may be, it won't hurt him to make use of Gorgo's waiting room until Niko and 'the lads' have had time to sleep off their drunkenness. Gorgo will have to order those litters, or extend her hospitality. Her usual clientele of pregnant matrons and murderous spouses can wait on the stairs.

Lucius will be suffering already because they're not back. Well, there's nothing he can do now to ease Lucius' mind.

'You had better go,' says Gorgo suddenly. 'I will organize for you to go.' Her Latin suddenly sounds much more foreign. She reaches out her slippered foot and gives Niko's thigh a light, scornful kick. He doesn't even notice. 'Are they men, or beasts?' she wonders aloud.

The hours in Gorgo's house seemed endless, while they lasted. If anyone had said to him, 'How long have you been here?' he might have said, 'A hundred years,' and believed himself. But as soon as he was home, time slipped and those long hours collapsed into an incident, a visit. It was over now and had no further power, he thought. The visit had made its mark, of course, but he didn't have to consider how deep that mark might be, or where it touched him.

What stayed in his mind was the expression on Antonius' face. Shame, fear, an exhaustion of hope that went beyond anything Catullus knew about –

– He thought of all that feeling packed inside Antonius, and no way out. And then, because Catullus was Roman, his thoughts swerved.

Eighteen

The sun breaks through, becoming strong. The clouds fly away, leaving a stretch of freshly washed blue. Suddenly it's no longer late winter. Spring has come.

Birds sing in the olive thickets as Catullus climbs the slope of the Palatine Hill. A pure, warm breeze blows in his face, and carries a distant sound of hammering from the perpetual building site up above him. Men shout warnings, and then there's a squeal of metal against metal. Another dream villa being built for someone rich enough to afford the costliest land in Rome. This property boom has been going on for as long as he can remember. He listens, and it seems that the birds and the hammer are making music together. Perhaps the birds of the Palatine have learned to imitate the sounds that the workmen make.

(The thought stretches, and begins to fly. Nightingales might learn to bubble curses into summer nights. Poets could bring the noise of change into their poems: the groan and squeal of cranes unloading the grain ships, the rumble of wagon wheels when the city's streets open to them at dusk –)

He loves this high place, especially the steepest parts of the slopes where the rock crumbles and it's impossible to dig foundations. Here there's only the sharp green grass that will be lion-coloured by late May. Wild thyme and lavender cling to the rocks. A little further up a pair of olive trees rustle in the breeze, their leaves shivering with silver light. Viburnum is in flower by the path, its white clusters glowing against dark, leathery leaves. Its scent blows towards him, then vanishes as the breeze turns.

A sparrow flies across his path, settles briefly by a puddle to drink, and then flies off. More sparrows chitter in the bushes.

A butterfly clings to a stone ahead of him, its veined wings open and palpitating. He stops. It would be impossible for the butterfly to spread its wings more widely. It looks as if it's feeding on the small patch of sunlight where it has settled. Poets write that butterflies feast on nectar, like the gods. It's rubbish. He and Marcus once saw a dead dog on the rubbish tip at home, its belly split open by the pressure of the gases within. There were six or seven exquisite pale blue butterflies among the cloud of insects fastened to the seam where the dog's guts spilled out. He and Marcus stared and stared, with the buzz of the flies thick in their ears, then they backed away around the side of the outhouse.

Maybe the gods also feast on death and gloat over every shade of putrescence. Our sufferings are their nectar. They'll put up with incense and the smoke that rises from a sacrificed bull, but they prefer human pain.

(*Again he sees Metellus Celer's face. It keeps coming back, just as a debt-collector keeps coming back to the house of a man who owes him money.*)

It's not much of a climb, but he's already out of breath. He wipes sweat from his forehead, and looks back over the Forum, and beyond it to the ochres and terracottas of the seething city.

There's a cypress trunk growing out of the side of the hill, almost horizontal. Maybe it thinks the sky is in that direction. He smiles, thinking of horizontal skies, and skies underfoot. He feels better now. He'll sit here for a while.

This is good. Calm and quiet. Only the closest things seem real: the ants tussling with a crumb of soil, the sunlight that filters through the leaves and freckles his cloak. It's warm in the sun. He's glad he took this little hidden path, rather than the main road past the Temple. It's good to rest here, alone for once, without slaves or friends.

He's unfit; he should exercise more. In a minute he'll go on. Up above him are the villas in all their raw, pluming splendour. Imagine if you could look back seven centuries, when the Palatine was a wooded hill where the she-wolf suckled Romulus and Remus. And Rome was about to be born . . . How strange to think that this huge modern city of more than a million souls was once a circle of bare hills around a marsh. If he looks down, like this, through the flicker of leaves, he can almost imagine that Rome has vanished, leaving nothing but a heap of white and tawny stone.

How his chest aches: just there. He's got a stitch. He climbed that slope too fast. He'll rest for a bit; he doesn't want to come to Clodia sweating and out of breath.

How Marcus would laugh to see him puffing like this. When they were boys, he and Marcus would swim and row and run races all day long in summer. Up at dawn, padding barefoot through the silent house, hoping they were up early enough to get out without Lucius catching them. Once they were outside they'd buckle on their sandals, and Marcus would say, 'Idiot! You've gone and forgotten your cloak again. Here, have mine.' Catullus was ill every winter, feverish and coughing. In summer he was fine, but Marcus fussed just like Lucius.

That curve of shingle was their own beach. You ran down through the olive groves, slipping and sliding, taking care not to trip on their knotted roots. You plunged out into the dazzle of the sun rising over the lake. There was a chill in the air and mist over the water. Even the shingle was cold.

They stripped off their tunics, kicked off their sandals and ran straight into the water. That was the rule, to run without stopping until you were thigh-deep and couldn't run any more, and then you'd topple forward into the lake. You didn't feel the cold that way. Marcus would always dive straight down. The water would be bare and bald when he'd gone in, and Catullus would start to count. He'd count slowly at first, treading water, scanning the surface, but then he'd begin to panic and count more and more quickly, because the surface was still smooth and his brother had been gone too long, much too long, so long that in a few more seconds he'd have to call for help –

– And just at that moment, Marcus always surfaced. Never where he'd expected him; Marcus would be close to shore sometimes, coming up as subtly as a frog taking air, or at other times he'd burst out in a surge of water behind his brother, flicking his hair so that more drops spattered around him.

Marcus knew his little brother got scared.

'I always come up again. I'm not going to drown, idiot. Why don't you dive, too?' Marcus said it was better to be part of things than to watch them. A fight always looked much worse than it was when you were standing on the edge. If you were in the fight, Marcus said, you got so angry you didn't notice the blows. Not until afterwards, anyway.

He was sure Marcus would be a great general when he grew up. He was the leader of their gang, the Lakers, which was at war with the Hillers. The Lakers were him and Marcus and all the boys from the fishing hamlet just down from their villa. The Hillers were mostly shepherd boys, tough and wild with big dogs that they tried to set on you. Marcus knew about tactics and strategy. The Lakers used to hold secret meetings at the fort they'd made in the olives just above the shore. That was where they planned their raids on the Hillers.

The good thing was that the Hillers usually couldn't come off the hills, because of having to stay close to the sheep and goats. The bad thing was their dogs. Marcus learned the Hillers' dog calls, and secretly gave the fiercest dog, the leader, pieces of meat stolen from the kitchens.

But Marcus hadn't become a general. Someone had to learn to manage the family estates. Someone had to go out to Bithynia regularly, to oversee the management of the family's enormously profitable timber-export business there. Their father was getting past the age for long sea voyages.

Catullus' thoughts shift uneasily. Marcus seems happy enough. He's not much of a one for poetry, but he recognizes that poets have to live in Rome. Last time Catullus was back in Sirmio, he recited to his brother a piece in dactylic hexameters, a mock epic about those battles with the shepherd boys who lived out on the hills from early spring until the winter came, wrapped in their rough cloaks, sleeping against the flanks of their dogs for warmth. Marcus smiled when it was finished and said, 'It pretty much makes you see it.'

'I want to write more about Sirmio but I can't find the right approach.'

'Maybe you should come back here.' The pause lengthened, then Marcus said, 'I'm not serious. I know you're settled in Rome.'

Marcus knew about Clodia, too. Didn't want to talk about her, though: he wanted his little brother to marry, as he'd married. There were no children yet.

Marcus isn't stuck in Sirmio all the time. He travels to Bithynia regularly, and he's there at the moment; in fact he's been out there since the previous summer. He's established tax-collection rights alongside the timber business. He's visited the Troad, and the sanctuaries of Cybele, where he actually saw one of the goddess's devotees castrate himself at the height of a ritual dance. He observed the ceremonies minutely, he wrote. How Catullus wanted to read those 'minute observations' – but Marcus gave little further description, beyond saying that the man appeared to feel no pain. Marcus' letters can be frustrating.

He writes in his latest letter that he's in good health, although the winter seems long. Julia wasn't able to accompany him. After her third miscarriage she'd been advised to rest, make offerings to Bona Dea, and avoid pregnancy for a year.

'You must come out, my dear brother. It's a tedious journey, but once weather conditions improve, the voyage should take less than a month. I don't have to preach to you about the benefits of sea air. Come in May, and we shall be able to travel in the Troad together before the summer heat sets in. That should give you some material. I don't speak of the happiness which your visit will bring to me.

'There is heavy snow on the mountains as I write, and the sky is as dark as a cooking pot. It has been a long winter, my dear brother, and I am troubled with a cough. A family weakness, as you know . . . But I had a letter from Julia last week, and she is well.'

Marcus wrote rather formal, correct Latin which didn't reflect his speaking voice. *I don't speak of the happiness which your visit will bring to me.* But no, that wasn't entirely true. A sky *as dark as a cooking pot*; I'd have been pleased with that myself, thinks Catullus.

He has gone back to the past, because now that he is close to Clodia he is afraid of what he will see in her. He would rather stretch out the moment. How long has he been sitting here? He must go on.

He walks slowly up the last few yards of the path, and comes out on to the level. The marble facings of the Palatine villas glisten in sunlight. They are raised up, magnificent, seeming to float above the city. But the air is full of building dust. A gang of slaves, shackled together, are laying the foundations for a new piece of road.

Niko has been flogged: Lucius wasn't slow to smell the alcohol on his breath, or to get the story out of him. Or part of it, at least. The two boys were lucky to escape with a flogging. Lucius had been all for sending them back to Sirmio, to a lifetime of field work.

Catullus didn't intervene. A steward must be left to manage the household.

He turns, and looks down on the city. So many people wanting so many things. So many knots of connection down there below him. The Forum this morning full of people he knows, criss-crossing, greeting each other, in a rush, on their way to client visits, analysing cases in the law courts, pausing to congratulate an orator on his latest speech, discussing their investments with the hard discretion of the rich.

He'd seen Clodia's brother, as usual surrounded by a knot of admirers. Pretty Boy, a handsome parody of his sister. Everything that was enchanting in her became repulsive in him. His wide eyes that stared so arrogantly and unseeingly; his carefully curled fringe; his oiled, golden, pummelled flesh; his ruthlessness.

He greeted Catullus civilly, smiling. The smile seemed to say: Oh yes, my sister. We both know about her.

And there was Cicero. He'd stuck his neck out too far when he made that speech against Pretty Boy in his trial for profaning the rites of Bona Dea. Pretty Boy is watching him, biding his time. Old Chickpea seems surprisingly unconcerned. He makes cracks about Pretty Boy's thugs, as if their staves aren't capable of spilling his brains, or their knives of cutting out his tongue. A man can be so clever, thinks Catullus, that he stops being clever at all. He loses the ordinary alertness of the ordinary man.

Or maybe I'm the one who's too clever. I can roast and skewer the bastards with an epigram, recite it to Fabullus or Calvus, and then watch it do the rounds of Rome, from mouth to mouth until everyone who considers himself a wit has trotted it out. And nothing happens. I'm safe enough. Who breaks a butterfly on a wheel? Powerful men with gangs of armed, paid thugs aren't going to change their behaviour because I write a poem about them. They shrug their shoulders. Maybe they're even a little flattered.

He remembers how he used to stare around when he first came to Rome from Verona (trying not to, trying to look cool and unimpressed, but he could never keep it up). The Forum was a treasure-house then. All those great speeches, by men whose names rang round the world! All those swift, busy figures moving in an intricate choreography that he longed to learn. He loved Rome at first sight and his one aim was to belong. Not to be part of it, perhaps – he was a poet, and that came first – but to move as easily and surely within it as others did, to know the bookstalls, the bathhouses, and above all to know what lay behind the rattle of names, as Rome's gossip flew.

He belongs now. He's learned how to breathe in Rome's soup of hatred, mistrust, temporary allegiances and considered betrayals. He doesn't expect politicians to be anywhere else than halfway up each other's bums: literally so, in certain cases.

He used to think that satire was a weapon. He knows better now. They want to be noticed, these men. Even insults are taken as compliments.

– Better to be written about than not.

– All publicity is good publicity, as they say.

– Have you heard Catullus' latest?

– Who's he written about this time?

– Oh, I must say that's really awfully good.

And then sometimes, quite arbitrarily, they'll decide that a poem has 'gone too far' and demand apologies. He's had that, too. If the man who demands the apology has enough swords and staves at his disposal, of course you give it. It means nothing. Soup, all of it.

> *Nil nimium studeo, Caesar, tibi velle placere,*
> *nec scire utrum sis albus an ater homo.*

> *Not wishing to know what you are*
> *or how to please you, I blank you, Caesar.*

But it's not quite true. Caesar itches in his mind, forcing him to write. 'A great man,' his father says admiringly. How can his father be so naive? But perhaps in the end it's Caesar who is the most naive of all. These great orators and generals and politicians, even the most cynical of them, they have faith. They really believe that if they work, plot, bribe, conspire and manipulate enough then they will eventually get what they want. Throw in courage and vision (which he has to admit that Caesar possesses), and they'll be invincible. Why don't they realize that every other man of ambition in Rome thinks exactly the same? And, therefore, they are bound to end up cutting one another's throats.

There they all were in the Forum this morning, walking about in the sunshine, polishing a connection here, blackguarding a rival there. Each one, in his own eyes, the leading chariot with the crowd roaring him home. But one of the chariots is bound to clip the post, overturn and disappear in a thrash of metal, wood and flesh – it's inevitable –

– For heaven's sake, enough empathy! You don't want to end up feeling sorry for Caesar, or a viper like Pretty Boy. Besides, are *you* really so pure and uninvolved?

It's true. He's part of it all. The Forum's flow of people knew him, greeted him, gave way for him and took him in. Pretty Boy all but winked at him. Gorgo was right. He certainly was one of *you Romans*. The city's transactions were all for his benefit. Even the dirtiest tricks of politics had him in mind. For him the ships docked at Puteoli, for him the slave-markets opened long hours, for him the brokers discussed the speed of ships and the weight of their cargoes. Caesar dined at Catullus' father's house, and so he could write what he liked.

Fate had touched him lightly at birth. The world was his, and his language blossomed everywhere. He was so lucky, wasn't he, that he had to work hard to make himself unlucky . . .

When he walked through the Forum he was deep in its soup. He was a poet. He thought his head was free of Rome. He rubbed a line out in his mind, changed step, changed rhythm, but it was no good. He couldn't hear his lines through the roar of money-changers, shopkeepers and cheap-jack orators.

It was the noise of Rome working for him. The Catullan wealth had grown like its own small empire. It was already so far flung that it took weeks to sail to the end of it. His brother, in faraway Bithynia, hadn't come to the end of it. In remote valleys where even the gods had never heard of Rome, men were chopping down cedars for the sake of the Catulli.

He passed behind the Temple of the Vestal Virgins, tried a line-ending, dropped it. In there, too, they were doing the business on his behalf, keeping the flame, keeping Rome alive. Even old Chickpea, fresh from the rostrum, acknowledging his own success with such carefully calculated modesty that it made you want to laugh out loud – even old Chickpea had more guts than Catullus had. For Cicero, getting the Consulship had been like dying and going to Heaven. He never doubted the worth of his own contribution, or stopped reminding the world of it. Chickpea's probably worked on that air of exhausting himself in a higher cause just as hard as he works the honey-sweet plunges of his voice. He can whisper a thousand listeners into his confidence, make them feel part of the inner, brilliant mechanism of his mind.

It's a con, of course. That honey-sweet voice comes from hour after hour of voice exercises. Nothing's off the cuff. All his jokes are rehearsed, and he'll defend a liar and murderer in court as passionately as he'll defend an innocent man. But that's the job of a brief. At least Chickpea has the guts to define what he wants and try to get it. He's not been afraid to plunge his hands into the muck.

He must have been standing there for a long time, lost in his own head. One of the shackled slaves is eyeing him curiously, although he doesn't dare let up work for a second. The foreman has his whip out: perhaps they are behind schedule with this section of road.

'You there! Get on with it, you idle bastard, or you'll feel my whip across your back!' he yells, and then touches his forehead with his knuckle and calls across to Catullus, 'They're a useless idle lot, begging your pardon, sir, but we won't let up, we'll have this stretch laid by nightfall.'

He thinks I'm one of the villa owners who has paid for the new road and has strolled across to inspect its progress.

'Excellent,' Catullus calls back weakly, and the gang bends to its work again, shovelling gravel into the trench. The whip cracks down. It's a long time until nightfall, he thinks, and walks on across the hill.

He's almost there now, at her house on the Clivus Victoriae. Everything is ahead of him. Anything can happen. Clodia is all the perfection that he can imagine.

Fool, Catullus. You're such a fool that you're even a fool to yourself. Go in. Announce yourself.

I apologize, my dear Chickpea. You are no more a con than I am a man who can put together an argument, even with myself.

He goes to her doorway.

Nineteen

They sit side by side, on a marble bench overlooking the fish pond which was Metellus Celer's pet project, and which he saw completed a few months before his death.

Aemilia told him Clodia was out here in the new pool building. 'My lady spends half her life watching those fish these days.' Aemilia was tight-lipped. She looked older and angrier; there were brown stains under her eyes. 'Albus will show you the way,' she said, and called raucously for the slave, who came running. This wasn't one of the perfectly trained Metelli slaves who had made so many great parties appear as effortless as a dinner with a couple of friends. This boy with his shock of pale, matted hair looked as if he'd just finished digging a trench for beans. He stank of frightened sweat.

In fact there were signs of disintegration everywhere. Small lapses, but they'd never have been allowed six months ago. The girl who had washed his feet when he came in hadn't got the water at the right temperature, and it was plain water. The Metelli had always used lavender water. Someone had left a scrubbing-brush on the corridor floor. A reception-room door was wedged open with a block of wood. A great household like this couldn't run on Aemilia's bad temper. He wondered whether Clodia had just stopped noticing . . . or whether she didn't care any more.

'Come along with me, master,' said Albus, leading the way. Behind them, Aemilia began to bully a child who was cleaning the crevices of a stone faun.

'Dear gods, don't you ever listen, you imbecile. The *feather duster*, not that great clumsy brush. It's a valuable antique, one scratch and my lady'll have you sold into the salt-mines to pay off the damage.'

Albus winked as they turned the corner of the corridor. 'She's got a tongue on her, that one,' he remarked, as if to an equal. 'Where I come from they'd sew up her lips. No wonder missus keeps out at the pool.'

This was a new household, in which the slaves' attitude veered between a cringe and an overfamiliar grin. That 'missus' was a long way from the formal, mirror-smooth 'mistress' or 'my lady' of the Metelli house in the old days.

But Catullus was probably reading too much into it. This boy looked as if being indoors at all was a novelty to him.

'She's a lovely lady, though, my missus,' went on the boy, gormlessly.

'I can find my way from here. Get back to your work.'

He is with her at last. Aemilia's ranting and Albus' stupidity fade to nothing. The household is bound to be upside down after such a death. It's natural and there's nothing Clodia can do to prevent it. Everything will settle, he insists to himself, comforting himself with the repetition. Things will come back to how they were.

She's here, beside him. They're not quite touching, but she's there, next to him, breathing, being. He can rest his mind from its constant, painful search for her, from imagining what Clodia might be doing, how she might look, whom she might be with. But he doesn't try to touch her yet.

He was up in the hills with his brother once, early on a winter morning, and they found a little clump of wild hyacinths that had come out in a sheltered spot. But there had been a frost, and the flowers were sheathed in ice. Marcus said not to touch them, or they would bruise and blacken when the ice melted. *If you leave them alone, they'll be fine when the sun comes out.* He'd always remembered it: his brother, the leader, the fighter, caring that much for a flower.

'Clodia?'

'Yes?'

'What are you thinking about?'

'Oh, I don't know. The fish. They've been eating one another. We must have bought cannibals by mistake.'

'Surely not. They're carp, aren't they?'

'Yes. If we could have installed saline tanks, we'd have tried gilt-headed bream. They're terribly in demand. You can make a fortune farming them, apparently.'

'You don't need a fortune, Clodia, you have one already.'

She laughs half-heartedly. She's pale, dressed in a dark woollen tunic and a hooded cloak which shades her face so that he can't see it as well as he'd like. Such dull, plain clothes. Her face looks pinched, and she shivers as a breeze blows over the pond's surface.

'It's cold, isn't it?'

'How long have you been out here?'

'Oh, quite a while. I don't know.'

'You shouldn't be sitting on bare marble at this time of year.'

'Yes,' she says vaguely, 'I should have asked Aemilia to set cushions on the bench. There are dozens in the pool room. But I can't be bothered with having Aemilia out here. Everything's still so chaotic – we haven't begun to get the new slaves trained.'

'What's happened to the old ones?'

'Oh, well, you know, some of them were granted their freedom in my husband's will.'

But they would have stayed on. Freedmen stay on in the household. Why did they leave? Why did you want to get rid of them? No, don't think of that.

'Some of them went to my sister-in-law,' she goes on with the same uneasy vagueness, 'and I sent some to Formiae, and to the estates. We needed fresh staff here. They get into bad habits, you know how it is.'

'Not really. Most of our slaves have been with us for ever.'

'Well, that's nice for you, isn't it,' she says sharply, to close the subject. But he persists.

'You kept Aemilia, though.'

Something leaps in her eyes. 'Oh, yes,' she says quickly. 'Aemilia has to stay, of course.' She shivers again and huddles deeper into her cloak.

'Come here. Come here, Clodia. Let me hold you. I'll warm you up.'

She allows him to put his arm around her, and draw her close. But she doesn't soften against him, and after a minute or two she pulls away.

'Would you like me to turn on the jets? It's quite impressive. My husband helped design the whole thing.' She waves her hand at the big oval fish pond, the formal flower beds, the fountain. 'He always wanted a fish pond here,' she says reflectively, catching her underlip between her teeth.

'All right.'

He follows her to the pool room. There's an array of brass levers, and he wonders if she knows what she's doing. She pushes back her hood and stands there, frowning.

'You could send for someone.'

'No. I do know how to do it. He showed me. I think it's this handle, on the left, to turn on the jets.'

She fiddles for a while, but nothing happens. Suddenly she exclaims, 'Of course, how stupid, you have to open the sluices first. It's this big lever here you have to pull down. Don't watch me, you're making me nervous. Go outside and you'll see in a minute. The water will come through.'

He goes back to stand beside the pool. The oval is more than ten yards long, cupped in the hands of a high-walled rectangular building which is open to the sky. A big project, a magnificent addition to one of the most splendid villas on the Palatine. There are mosaics of Neptune set into the floor of the pond. The images waver as fish pass over them, stirring the water.

'It's coming!' calls Clodia.

Water pours from a dozen niches set into the walls of the

pond. The fish spurt across the mosaic and it disappears in clouds of bubbles. There are many more fish than he thought. Some are sheltered beneath tiled overhangs, others hide in plants. He kneels down and puts his hand under one of the spouts. The flow of water is cold and strong.

Clodia has come out to join him. 'Isn't it lovely?' she says, her face changed and glowing. 'No one else has a pond with jets like this, not in Rome anyway. My husband commissioned the design after I told him about a pond I'd seen in a villa down in Baiae. He visited it last summer. You should see the architect's drawings: they're a work of art. There are about four hundred yards of pipes in the pool complex alone, you know, and you can adjust the flow any way you want. We're lucky, of course, we've got a wonderful spring that never runs dry. He was planning to build a second pool, for bathing. Of course we'd have had to buy more land for the extension.'

He glances at her. 'You could continue the project in his memory,' he says. She gives him a sharp look, but he keeps his face impassive. Just for a moment, he neither hates her nor loves her. What he feels is something new: a cold, dry sorrow, as if something has died.

Pale green water bubbles thickly into the pond. He listens to the sound of it gurgling through hidden pipes, rushing as it comes to the lip of the pipes. It sounds like a waterfall in early spring, when heavy rains rush off the hills to fill the lake at Sirmio. He always loved to sleep in the sound of water.

There was always a part of Clodia that was like his child. No one else saw it.

No one can see them here. The pool complex stands apart from the villa, joined by a covered way. High walls hold both sun and shade. The flower beds are not yet planted, but vines and roses are beginning to climb the walls. You can still almost smell the fresh cement. There are no statues yet, but Metellus Celer would have planned them. Perhaps he had already commissioned a sculptor. It seems that there was some artistry in the man after all. Or more likely it was all money, and a tactful architect who let the client believe he was the designer.

The flow weakens. A few more gouts of water spill from the niches and fall slackly into the pond.

'It shouldn't stop like that,' says Clodia, drawing her brows together.

'You could send for one of the slaves,' he suggests again. 'Isn't there someone who understands the system?'

'Of course there is. But I want to do it myself. I do know how, I've just forgotten.'

She goes back into the pool room and he imagines her wrestling with the levers, pulling at one and then the next.

'Is that working?' she calls.

'No.'

'And this one?'

'No. Nothing's happening.'

A long pause, then she comes out, her eyes bright with temper.

'He should have left me some diagrams,' she says. 'That's the whole point of this complex, it's somewhere we can come to relax, on our own. The slaves do the gardening and pool-cleaning first thing in the morning and after that they leave us alone. Somewhere that's completely peaceful, where you're alone with your thoughts – can you imagine what a luxury that is, when you're in the thick of public life?'

He's never heard Clodia talk such rubbish. She seems to pity her husband, now that he's dead. Catullus hates it. It's the same old crap you hear everywhere, the whingeing of rich politicians who have their hands deep in Rome's purse. *The cares of a consulship – the sacrifice of private pleasure for the sake of the city – the unique pressures of responsibility.* Every jack-in-office, every on-the-make politician, every puffed-up toady prates about their 'sacrifices'. What has Clodia to do with all that? It nauseates him to hear her praise her dead husband now in this way.

'He chose all the fish himself,' says Clodia.

'Individually?' he gibes, and she doesn't answer.

Clodia and Metellus Celer's shared, married life seems to spread itself before Catullus' feet, like the mosaic that is slowly clearing as the water becomes still. But it's false. They had no shared life. Their marriage was an arrangement and their life together a formality. They did not love each other.

'He used to skim the leaves off the surface with a net,' continues Clodia, and laughs. 'The slaves used to complain that there was never anything left for them to do.'

'Really,' he says. *You liar. I know you. You let him do whatever he wanted, you took no part in it. You went on with your own life. You weren't watching him, you were in my bed. Don't try to sell me this story of a pious matron, humouring her husband, allowing him his hobby because it's such a good form of relaxation, isn't it, for men who work so hard.*

'I'm planning to build a little studio out here,' she continues. 'I've been looking around for an architect. I haven't told anyone yet, not even Aemilia. But it's a perfect place to write, don't you think?'

'A studio,' he says flatly. The conversation seems more and more bizarre. First a fish pond and then a studio and then what? What's it all for? Her poems aren't free of talent, but they don't merit a studio. It's Clodia herself who is the work of art. But only when she *is* herself, his Clodia, his Lesbia, who holds a rarer spice than anything that comes from the East in every grain of her body.

A fish-pond owner with artistic inclinations, who respects the memory of her unfortunately deceased husband – that's a stranger. And not a very likeable one either. He takes in a sharp breath. The solution is so simple, so close. All he has to do is to stop loving her.

'I'll write out here, with the sound of the water,' she goes on, 'and I'm going to get another sparrow, did I tell you that? A little one born this spring, I'll take it as soon as it's fledged and then I can tame it.'

'No, you didn't tell me,' he says.

'You're very quiet,' she says. 'Don't you like it here?'

'Who could not like it? It's so beautifully designed. Once the flowers are growing, and those little trees have gained some height, it'll be exquisite. Your husband must have thought a great deal about the future.'

'Yes,' she says, 'he did.' Her lovely eyes gaze into the distance. Only the gods know what she sees there, he thinks, and he feels cold.

'You could come and write here too,' she suggests. 'It's very peaceful.'

'No, I don't think I could write here.'

'You're shivering.'

'It's damp out here. Why don't we go back into the house?'

'No,' she says, 'I prefer it out here. Aemilia follows me around the house like an old nanny-goat. It's not very restful. She's getting above herself. Sometimes I almost think she's in the pay of the Metelli – but never mind that. Here, come under my cloak.'

She spreads her cloak around him like a bird's wing. The smell of her hair, her skin and her perfume fold around him. Her face is only a few inches from his. He can see the grains of powder on her cheeks. She isn't wearing rouge, and she hasn't reddened her lips. She's in mourning, after all. The darkness of her cloak makes her look even paler and more fragile, as if she's been ill or wounded, and has ventured into the first sunlight of the year to recuperate. Her eyes are huge and liquid. Wide open, they hide everything.

He puts his arms around her, and draws her to him. He must never set his thoughts against her. She is his girl.

'I thought you'd come before this,' she says. 'I was waiting for you.'

'I thought your house would be full of the Metelli.'

'Not any more. Even my daughter's gone back to the country. But they still keep calling on me, the Metelli, at all hours – almost as if they're expecting to discover something.' She laughs very softly, in her throat, and glances at him so that he can share the joke. His face feels stiff as he moves his lips in a smile. He looks beyond her, and sees a splash of dark purple at the corner of a stone flower bed. He folds back the cloak, gets up and goes to see what it is.

'What are you doing?'

'Nothing.'

It's only a wild hyacinth. It must have come up in one of the prepared flower beds, and a garden slave has pulled it out and tossed it on to the flagstones. He stoops. The plant is limp and the flower crushed, as if a boot has trodden on it.

'Come back to me,' says Clodia. 'Oh, heavens, look at those fish. It's revolting. That one is actually swimming about with a chunk out of its side – look. It doesn't even seem to notice. I don't know what I'm going to do about them. He got so many, and now they're eating each other. And I'm sure that's some kind of fungus – look at that one there, those white spots on its side.'

'It doesn't look very healthy.'

'No. Maybe we should get rid of them all and start again.'

'Put poison in the water,' he says, 'that'd be quick. They'd all rise to the surface and you could scoop them up.'

Her eyes widen. 'I couldn't do that. I'll give them to the slaves. They'll be thrilled. I shouldn't think they've ever tasted carp. Oh, darling, this is such a morbid conversation. Can't you think of anything more cheerful?'

'One or two things come to mind.'

'Only one or two?'

They go into the pool room together. There are box seats with embroidered, cushioned lids. Clodia lifts one, and rummages inside. She throws out silk cushions and covers, and thick woollen blankets.

'One could even spend the night here,' she murmurs.

'Yes.'

They are together again. She spreads blankets on the floor, covers them with silk and pulls him down to her.

'No one comes here. No one can see us,' she whispers as if it's a magic spell.

He is back with her, inside the climate of her skin, her hair, her eyes, her lips, her soft warm waist under the wool of the tunic and her silk underclothes, her eyes that seem to slant as she rolls on top of him and her sudden way of grasping his face between her hands, pulling him to her and softly biting his lips, all over, not hurting but tasting him as if he were a fruit she could never taste enough.

Afterwards he has it again, that feeling, that rare feeling that he doesn't know where he ends and she begins, barely even knows if they're male or female any more, she is so close. Perhaps he's given birth to her, or she has given birth to him. He's never felt so new. They lie together, wrapped in each other, just breathing. His lips touch the pale curve of her jaw. He opens his eyes and sees hers, half closed, shining. He reaches down and pulls a blanket up over her, to keep her warm.

Suddenly there's a sound of water.

'Oh!' she cries, springing up so that the blanket falls, 'The jets! They're working again!' and she runs to the window.

'Is anyone out there?'

'No. But look, the jets are working, all on their own.'

He can hear it. Water plashes solidly into water. He looks at the curve of her back, her buttocks, her legs. Her body is tense, stilled. Suddenly he realizes that she's afraid. She thinks the spirit of Metellus Celer has stopped the water and then made it flow.

'You must have found the right lever, after all,' he says quickly. She turns and comes back to him, picking up a blanket and holding it in front of her. Her face is even paler now. Her eyes look like holes in a mask.

'Come back here,' he urges. 'Come and lie down.'

But she won't.

'The water's too loud,' she says. 'It drowns out everything else. I don't think I know how to turn it off.'

He gets up, wrapping a blanket around himself too. She's right, it's cold in here. He puts his arms around her and she doesn't resist – indeed she seems to give way against him, as if she can hardly stand. He holds her, bracing himself, feet apart, to take her weight.

'It's all right, listen, you mustn't get so upset, it's over, we have to think about the future,' he murmurs. Even as the words come out of his mouth he feels how idiotic they are, and she seems to think so too, for she puts her hands on his shoulders and pushes him until their bodies separate. She scans his face. She doesn't look angry, in fact there's a slight smile on her lips. Her eyes are weary.

'The future?' she says. 'What's that?'

'Our life together.'

'Look at me. Look at you. You're forgetting that I'm ten years older than you.'

'That makes no difference.'

'At your age I'd already been married for ten years. Can you imagine that? My daughter will be ready for marriage soon. We'll have to bring her to Rome and find a suitable husband for her.'

'So you're saying you're going to become a virtuous widow, a credit to the Metelli? Is that it?'

'Perhaps not quite.' She smiles, flicking a glance at the ruck of cushions and blankets on the floor.

'I want to marry you, Clodia. I want you to marry me.'

'Marry?' She says the word delicately, as if it's a strange new taste. 'You really think that you and I should get married?'

'Of course.'

'I'm cold. Quick, pass me my clothes. You should get dressed too.'

They dress in silence. As she fastens her cloak she says abruptly, 'You know there's no one I'd rather marry than you. You're the only man –' she pauses, frowning as she fiddles with the clasp of her brooch – 'you're the only man who really knows me.' The brooch is fastened, and she adjusts the fall of her cloak's folds, then pushes back her hair, smoothing it. 'It's no use, I'll just have to pull up the hood. I can't do anything without a mirror. Come here. Let me tidy your hair, you look as if you've been out in a storm.'

Her quick, soft fingers move in his hair, and she wipes something from his cheek.

'You'll be spitting on your sleeve and washing my face with it next,' he protests.

'There, you look respectable now. My handsome poet.'

'Stop that, Clodia. Listen. I'm serious.'

'Please don't be serious, not now.'

'I asked you to be my wife.'

'There's no one I'd rather marry than you. I've already told you that.'

'But it's not what I asked. You say I'm the only one who really knows you. It's true. All those others, they don't even want to know you, Clodia, not really.'

' "All those others," ' she repeats, as if picking over his words with tongs. She's all wrapped up again, maddeningly separate and maddeningly herself.

'Don't pretend you don't know what I mean.'

'I'm afraid I *don't* know what you mean,' she says haughtily, as if he's some supplicant for her favours. And now she's gone too far.

'This time you're going to listen to me. All those others, the ones I'm not supposed to know about, the ones who say that anyone can have you for fourpence and the ones who say you're a cocktease who does everything except deliver. Did you think I had my eyes shut? Did you think I was too blind or stupid to notice what you were doing? No, Clodia. I didn't love you *because I didn't know*, I loved you in spite of everything I knew.'

'And what do you think I loved you in spite of?'

'What?'

'Or rather, *who*. All those lovely girls, that's who. Your Ipsitillas and Cynthias and Aufillenas and Rufas.'

'That's absolutely unfair. I've never gone near Rufa.'

'And let's not forget honey-sweet Juventius.'

'Juventius is history. I'm like an elder brother to him. Or an uncle.'

'It's true that there are some very surprising relationships between uncles and their nephews these days.'

She's back on form. His Clodia, snapping like bright fire in a grate.

'There's nothing you can tell me, Clodia my darling, about very unusual uncles and their very unusual nephews. Gellius, for one. Not to speak of aunts and mothers and bro – Broken hearts, Clodia, that's what it all leads to, and a lot of tension within the respectable Roman home too. But I'm hoping that it's also going to lead to some very good poems.'

She smiles. 'Now you're like you used to be. You were always making me laugh. That's why I wanted you to come to our house. You made me feel as if it wasn't just another boring old dinner party, but the most wonderful evening of your life.'

'It was the most wonderful evening of my life.'

'No, don't do that. Don't get serious again.'

'But you're right. It *was* wonderful. It frightened me. Why won't you let me say it? No one else is ever going to love you like that. You're free now. Why waste your time with people who don't even know you, let alone love you? You can come with me. You can be my wife.'

She stares at him as if from a distance. She doesn't seem hostile, but she doesn't yield either.

'I've been a wife,' she says. 'That's all over. Don't complain any more. I hate men who complain. They should be soldiers –'

'Soldiers on your battlefield?'

'Well, why not? It has its own honours. And you like it, you know you do.' She leans forward, and kisses him fleetingly, warmly, on the lips. 'I don't know what you're making such a fuss about. I've said, haven't I, that we're going to be together whenever we want. But listen, you'll have to go now. The sisters and the aunts will be making one of their mass Metelli visitations before long, and you know how tedious they are. I'm sure you've got things to do, people to see –'

'Poems to write,' he finishes bitterly.

'Perhaps a *nice* poem about me this time, darling? Or am I asking for the impossible?'

'It seems that I'm the one who is asking for the impossible.'

'Don't be like that.' She's warm, laughing, conspiratorial. She knows that he can't and won't resist, and of course he doesn't. He smiles back, reluctantly, holding her hand tight so that he can feel her bones inside his.

'I'd rather marry you than anyone,' she soothes him. 'Even if Jupiter himself asked me to marry him I'd just say no thank you, I'm going to marry my poet.'

Twenty

Whenever he has a hangover he gets this jumpy feeling, as if something bad is going to happen. Or perhaps he'll find that it's already happened, if he can remember everything from last night.

He's drinking too much. But wine's good, it heats the blood and drives away his cough. Lucius says he should mix the wine more. Lucius feels entitled to say such things; maybe he is. But there's been an underground, rumbling quarrel between him and Lucius for months, because his father is ill and he won't go back to Sirmio, even though Marcus is out in Bithynia again.

Julia still isn't pregnant. She refused to stay behind this time. Marcus had written: *'She thinks that perhaps if she looks after herself a bit less carefully, and tries to forget all about having a baby, then it will happen. Besides, there's a shrine she wants to visit.'*

'Your father is growing older, and he's alone. He needs you there with him,' Lucius said.

'If he needed me, he would send for me.'

Lucius was silent for a while. One of those critical, vigilant silences that Catullus has never been able to stop himself from breaking.

'He has no desire for my presence, Lucius, and you know it. It would only make him uneasy. When I'm there, all he sees is a walking reminder of everything that I haven't done and ought to have done. Or perhaps everything that I've done and ought not to have done. It's not going to improve his health. Or indeed his temper.'

'Your father is the same age as me, and we are both past fifty. At your father's age, your grandfather was already dead. People change as they grow older. You think your father still looks on

225

you as he did when you were fifteen, or twenty, and living in his house under his authority. But he chose to free you from his paternal power before you came to Rome, just as your grandfather chose to free me from slavery. Every stone is worn away by time.'

'Lucius, I swear you should have been the poet.'

Lucius smiled, and looks down. 'Your brother has no children,' he observes quietly.

'I know that.'

'I have prayed and made offerings many times for his wife to conceive, as I am sure you have.'

But Catullus had not even thought of doing so.

'I am still hopeful,' said Lucius. 'Your brother and his wife are young.'

'Or perhaps the gods are looking the other way.'

'You must never say such things.'

'When did anybody get what they wanted through prayer?'

'I did,' said Lucius. 'When I was a boy and a slave in your grandfather's house, I prayed that I would earn his favour. I swore that I would work for your family as if it were my own, until the day I died. As you know, my prayer was answered. Your grandfather sent me to school with your father. When your grandfather died, he gave me my freedom in his will, and I will never forget him. When I die, I have arranged to have my gratitude to him inscribed on my tombstone.'

'You're not going to die, Lucius. Look at you. Strong as an ox.'

'An old ox who kids himself he can still pull the plough.'

'But, Lucius, listen, you earned your freedom yourself. It was your work, your loyalty. You earned the trust my grandfather put in you. It had nothing to do with prayer.'

Lucius shook his head. 'Lucky it's only to me you talk like this. Prayers have a force that you don't understand until a long time after you've made them.'

'But all the same, I'm not going to Sirmio.'

Lucius was looking at him intently. It was a strange look, penetrating and almost pitying, as if there were things Lucius understood but knew he could never communicate.

If Catullus' mother were still alive, she would look at him just as Lucius had done. She would want him to understand his father too, and even love him.

His mother had loved his father, in her own way. It was something Catullus had fought against for years. She'd known something in his father that his sons never experienced. He remembered how their parents used to sit together, talking quietly about things that sounded dull when he managed to overhear them. His father didn't like to be interrupted. His mother used to work at her weaving, like a model wife, but her clear, intelligent upward glance was what her son remembered.

But he could not love his father. The thought of him brought on hot, furious, impotent anger. He felt as if his father had read him long ago, and then tossed the roll on the fire as if it were worthless.

'No, Lucius,' he said, 'he thinks he wants to see me, but the son he wants to see does not exist. When I was ten I used to try to be that boy. You know as well as I do that it never worked, but I took a long time to learn my lesson. Years and years and years. I look back and I squirm. What did I think I was doing? I never understood that nobody feels anything but contempt for a performing monkey.'

Lucius put out a hand, as if to stop him, but Catullus went on, 'I kept on thinking that if my father knew me a little better, if I wrote to him about everything here in Rome, if he read my poems, if he would visit me instead of always, eternally, wanting me back in Sirmio, where he thought I belonged, then he might at last lose interest in the son in his head and learn to love the son he had. Laughable, wasn't it? But those are the ideas a boy clings to, before he becomes a man.'

Lucius said nothing. He looked old and tired.

'I'll go back to Sirmio one day,' said Catullus more quietly. 'But not yet.'

His head is banging. It's not good to think about all that. He'll send for a cup of mint tea in a moment; that will clear his mind. He should have left the party earlier last night. It's not even as if he was having a good time. Caelius Rufus was there, and as engaging as ever. Funny how the charm worked even when you saw through it and had learned to hate it. At a distance, Rufus could still seem like the idea of a handsome and charming friend.

Rufus clearly thought he still had the right to talk to Catullus as a friend.

'I have your elegy by heart. A great poem.'

No, you don't, you bastard, Catullus thought. He'd talked poetry with Rufus long ago, when they were friends, real friends. That was before Rufus met Clodia.

A long time ago, before he'd really learned to be jealous, when suspicion was alien to him. Otherwise, he'd have seen the warning signs. It was one evening when they were talking about metre. He hadn't realized Rufus had such a feeling for language. He'd made an astonishingly sensitive and knowledgeable comparison between Calvus' use of choliambics and Catullus' own. And he even had the sensitivity and knowledge to prefer the latter . . .

What a fool you were, Catullus. He can't think of it, even now, without flinching from the memory of his own flattered self.

He'd been touched, moved almost, that evening as Rufus talked on, revealing a love of poetry that was more than educated – it was passionate. And what was even more surprising was that Rufus wasn't a closet poet himself, with a roll or two of poems tucked away discreetly under his cloak – 'It's just an old thing I wrote years ago but I'd love to hear the opinion of an expert.'

No, give Rufus credit. He was that rare animal: a disinterested lover of poetry.

Catullus had talked too much. He'd given himself away. He still can't forgive himself for that.

It must have been about then that Furius had started asking about Clodia.

'And how are things with our Clodia? Same old same old?' His eyes gleamed with curiosity. Furius was a friend in his way, but there was always a touch of malice and rivalry there. He had none of the almost feminine delicacy of a true friend like Calvus.

Catullus had shrugged, and said nothing.

'Clodia Metelli?' Rufus had asked. Only two words, but how they grated. How alert the man had been, all of a sudden. His handsome eyes were narrow suddenly, stilled into attention. Why the hell was he looking like that, at the mention of Clodia's name?

He'd seen what Rufus was up to but he'd pushed the knowledge away. He'd told himself that Rufus was a friend, and his interest in Clodia's name meant nothing.

He'd convinced himself that the light in Rufus' face was well-bred interest, and that was all. Something to do with him being such a friend and ally of Pretty Boy. They were in each other's pockets politically; at the time, their ambitions meshed.

– Clodia Metelli?

He should have listened. He should have picked up the signals. But what did it matter, anyway – whatever he'd seen, whatever he'd said or done, Rufus would have gone ahead.

And then last night at the party, the same cast of characters assembled. Or pretty much the same, though he can't remember everybody. Furius was there last night for sure. And then Rufus had come in, hesitated, looked as if he was going to come across and try to greet Catullus. But Catullus had turned away.

'You look as if you could do with another drink,' said Furius to Catullus, signalling to the slave. Furius sat down, obviously wanting to be tactful while longing to talk about the whole business. What a tasty dish of gossip they all made. Catullus drank and said nothing. He wasn't going to give Furius an opening. Without looking at Rufus, he could feel exactly where he was in the room. Why couldn't Furius stop looking at him like that?

You and Clodia – Why won't you listen to your friends? She's not worth it. The things I could tell you about her –

I know you could, Furius. Do you really think I'm that stupid? Let me tell you something. Keep on behaving as if something isn't real, even when it is, and after a while – quite a long while, I have to admit – very slowly, it becomes less dangerous. It won't work with a lion or an elephant, obviously, but for the more subtle terrors of life it is very effective.

Catullus drank down his wine, aware that Rufus' eyes were on him from across the room, sharp and measuring. He could hear Rufus' voice, but not what he was saying. People were talking to Rufus, laughing, treating him as a friend. Catullus felt as if his head was on fire. He had to get out of there.

That was when Rufus came across.

'I have your elegy by heart,' he said quietly. 'A great poem.'

'I'm leaving,' Catullus said, too loudly. He stumbled as he stood up. People were watching and he thought Rufus was looking at him with something close to pity. He shut his mind.

Why go over and over an evening that tastes of acid? It's not going to get him anywhere. He should be tough. He should make up his mind and stick to it. Months and months have gone by since Clodia said those golden words that so far have meant nothing:

'If I married anyone it would be you.'

And why shouldn't she marry? There's nothing to hold her back. It's more than a year since Metellus Celer's death.

Lesbia says she would rather marry me than anyone . . .

He's still going to believe in her. He's going to trust that she means what she says. *Or rather, you're going to take what you're given*, says a cold, unhappy voice in his head.

There's been plenty of evidence this past year, if he's needed it, of just how ruthless that family can be. Pretty Boy enjoyed his dish of revenge against Cicero at last, no matter that it was served cold. With a certain amount of bribery, corruption and general leaning on the body politic, he finally succeeded in getting old Chickpea banished on the grounds that Roman citizens had been put to death illegally under his consulship. As soon as Cicero was on his way, Pretty Boy's thugs had worked over his property with the expertise of a demolition gang. No one dared stop them. Even that big house on the Palatine, that piece of pretension that had been Chickpea's pride and joy, the symbol of his arrival at the very summit of Roman society – Pretty Boy had it knocked down. He went even further and started to build a temple on the site, so that once it was consecrated Chickpea would never be able to rebuild there. Pretty Boy's vengeance was as neat as it was ugly.

It doesn't make you feel so good about yourself, to know that a power-crazy psychopath like Pretty Boy has got a soft spot for you, not just on account of his sister but because, apparently, 'He really likes your style.' Pretty Boy intimidates the Senate, bribes juries, beats his enemies to death in the streets or sets fire to their houses, and Clodia just smiles and says, 'He won't bother *you*, darling, he's incredibly sweet and loyal to the people he likes.'

She's even let him know, to his horror and astonishment, that her brother was 'rather hoping you might write something about him, darling'. But she must have picked up his lack of enthusiasm, and so far no more has been said.

Clodia has settled down to being a widow. Perhaps 'settled down' is not quite the correct expression –

He gets up, and begins to pace across the courtyard and back, as if he's trying to get away from himself.

With a woman like Clodia, you have to accept certain things. She is never going to live according to the conventions –

– No, you stupid bastard, and you're never going to stop thinking in clichés and circumlocutions.

How his head hurts. Lucius is right, he ought to take more water with it. But it's around the fifth or sixth cup that everything seems to lighten, and he feels himself again. The trouble is that he doesn't stop, he goes on drinking past six cups, and then seven. Darkness settles around the corners of his mind, and creeps slowly inward.

He is never going to stop Clodia sleeping with other men. The best he can hope for is that she'll be discreet enough not to shove it in his face. And if he's lucky, she'll stop that trick of staring at him wide-eyed and saying: 'But, darling, why do you take it so seriously? It's got nothing to do with how I feel about you.'

The best he's got to look forward to is that she'll let him pretend. What you don't know doesn't hurt you; or, at least, there are subtle shades of knowing. You can put up defences. You can stop knowledge getting into the fibre of your being, where it hurts most. Rufus was never a real friend: dismiss him, cut him off, and then he'll have no further power. It is only through Clodia that Rufus has power, because she seems to delight in forcing 'her dear poet' to know everything.

He feels like a town with its walls battered by siege engines. He can hold out, though. He can continue to believe in her, because he's got no choice. Once his walls are down and the invaders have swarmed all through the streets, then he's dead anyway. He'll have nothing.

It's beautiful here in the courtyard, with the morning sun just strong enough to warm and not yet fierce enough to burn. Clusters of new leaves are spreading out on the vines that cover the pergola above his head. A pair of blackbirds nests there every year. Lucius has ordered the slaves not to disturb the nest, on pain of punishment. They'd have the eggs out in five minutes otherwise, and suck them dry.

Even the low box hedges are bright with new growth. His favourite tree is the mulberry, over there in the corner where its fruits won't drop on anyone's clothes. Mulberry stains don't come out. The planting is simple and traditional. Dark, slender cypress; broad mulberry; precise rows of box around ornamental beds. No ostentatious topiary, no specially commissioned statues. He likes everything to look as if it's been there for ever, and has just happened to grow this way.

The air smells of thyme, rosemary and marigolds. Once, back in Sirmio, Lucius discovered a rosemary bush with the darkest flowers they had ever seen. Their blue was so rich and deep that it was almost purple. Lucius took cuttings, and now they have bushes all around the courtyard, thick with bees all summer long.

There are four wall fountains, and a simple marble bowl in the centre of the courtyard, where water bubbles to the brim and spills over in skeins to the larger bowl below. A toad usually squats between the stone columns that support the bowl and the falling water. Lucius talks about replacing this fountain with a larger, more ambitious piece of engineering – he fancies a statue of Juturna – but the sound of water falling is all Catullus wants.

He closes his eyes. The air smells of bruised thyme, of stone, of water and of the rosemary he has just rubbed between his fingers. He should be happy. He will be happy, and plan his future as other men do, confident that what he wants will happen.

'*I would rather marry you than anyone.*'

(Night is sleep. *Nobis cum semel occidit brevis lux, / nox est perpetua una dormienda.* Our sole short day is set / into enduring night. A long, forever sleep, a night that never ends. Unless you're a fool, you must seize the day.)

He smells rosemary and the lost lines come back to him, a light touch on the mind at first and then suddenly they're sharp, insistent, already forming themselves into shape.

You mean, my life, that this love of ours
this bliss between us can live unchanging?
Great gods, let her mean what she says,
let this be the truth her soul speaks,
and let us go through our whole lives
never breaking the blessing.

Clodia is here with him now. She is the Clodia that only he knows. She carries the torch of herself as she brought it out of the darkness of non-being before her birth, and will carry it away into the blackness of her death. Lucius is wrong. The gods listen to us with indifference, because to feel like human beings is not what they were made for. The minds that made the world are not warm and soft and fertile, like a woman's body, but hard.

He must give that money to Cynthia. He had forgotten her. She will think it was just talk. He must get Lucius to arrange it –

And just at that moment, as if Lucius has heard his boy's thoughts, he comes into the courtyard. He stares round as if he doesn't recognize the place. His eyes light on Catullus. Lucius is pale, with staring eyes.

'Lucius!'

He comes closer. Catullus sees that his chin is trembling. In his left hand he holds out a scroll. A letter, still sealed. Catullus recoils.

My father is dead, he thinks. Nothing else would make Lucius look like that.

'From Sirmio? Something's happened to my father?' he asks, holding out his own hand and noticing that it's steady.

But Lucius shakes his head. 'The letter's from your father,' he says. 'Demetrius is in the house, he rode down from Sirmio by relay.'

'It's not my father.' The words take a moment to settle into his mind and begin to make meaning. Suddenly his heart thumps twice, heavily. His skin prickles as if fire were running over it.

'Who is it? What's happened, Lucius?'

Lucius knows already, that's why he's so pale and why his face is working like that. Demetrius has told him.

'Marcus?'

And Lucius nods.

Catullus takes the letter, and breaks the seal. The formal greeting is in his father's writing. '. . . *to his son Gaius Valerius Catullus, greetings*'. Words jump about in the text as he tries to read it. He smoothes the scroll carefully, but the words remain the same.

Marcus had been ill for several days with a cold and a chest cough, but it didn't appear serious. He seemed much better, and he was tired of being stuck in the house. The day was warm. He insisted on riding out with the surveyor to inspect a possible site for the new bridge. The weather changed suddenly, and they were caught in a violent storm. That night Marcus developed a high fever, and three days later, in spite of everything that could be done for him, he died. The doctor said that it was pneumonia.

Very faintly, Catullus hears Julia's living voice through his father's letter. '*He was tired of being stuck in the house . . . he insisted on riding out . . .*'

He can see them both. Julia, standing by the mounting block, wrapped in her cloak in spite of the sun. She's reaching up to make sure Marcus has fastened his shoulder brooch securely. '*You must keep warm.*' She pats his boot. '*Don't wear yourself out. Remember, you've been ill. Just take a quick look at this wonderful bridge site and then come straight home.*' He smiles down at her, at the untidy brown hair which is being blown out of its knot, and at her soft, round, upturned face. The horse shifts, and whickers impatiently. '*I'll be back long before nightfall,*' his brother says. Julia smiles. She's thinking of the hot spiced wine she'll order when Marcus returns.

Catullus smiles too, looking at them, and then a jolt tears through his chest. It's over. Marcus has gone.

He gropes forward, as if reaching for his brother, but it's Lucius who is there. Lucius doesn't open his arms to embrace his boy, to offer the comfort and support he's always given. He feels hard, like old, brittle wood. Catullus holds him tight.

'Lucius,' he says, 'Lucius.'

'He's gone,' says Lucius, his voice muffled. 'Our boy's gone from us. We'll never see him no more.'

Catullus has never heard Lucius speak in such a voice. It's as if the death has shocked him back into his child self, and he's the little slave boy who first came to Verona forty-five years ago. How old was Lucius then – six, seven? He would have talked like that. He would have wanted his mother. *I'll never see her no more.*

It happens again. Marcus dies, the shock hits him, then ebbs away, and leaves him trembling. He lets go of Lucius, and moves back.

'Marcus had pneumonia,' he says aloud. 'Julia's letter to my father came by sea. It took six weeks to get there.'

Lucius nods, collecting himself. 'The funeral's done, then,' he says.

'Yes.'

But when did it happen? When he was drinking, or when he was writing, when he was in the Forum, or when he was with Clodia –

When he was with Clodia, perhaps his brother's body was burning on the fire. I'll never see him again, he realizes. He won't see Marcus' body, he won't call his name for the last time, he won't open his brother's eyes for the last time, before his body is released to the fire. All that was over before they knew that Marcus was dead. He tries to imagine Julia negotiating with undertakers and hired mourners, while he and Lucius thought of Marcus as alive, and waited for his next letter.

'My father wants me to go out there.'

'To bring my lady Julia home?'

'No, she'll have taken ship already, with the Governor's wife. That's what my father writes. Here, Lucius, you must read it. And later, I'll go. There are things that have to be attended to.'

236

The words sound strange in his mouth. This isn't his language. He feels as if he has been catapulted into another world.

'He acted for your father in everything,' says Lucius quietly, as if to himself, as if beginning to measure what had been lost to the family.

'Lucius! If Marcus had had Dr Philoctetes, he might not have died.'

'My lady Julia would have made sure he had the best doctor.'

'I never went to see him. He kept asking me to go out there.'

Lucius says nothing. He's an old man, shoulders bowed, big hands hanging down. He holds the letter without looking at it. His eyes are red. 'No,' he says, 'I can't read it. Thank the gods your mother never lived to read it. Let me think of him as he was,' and he hands back the letter.

Suddenly he grasps Catullus by the shoulders, as if making sure that he's still there, solid, alive.

'Your father's alone. We'll go to Sirmio first, to let him know that he still has a son.'

'Yes, I'll go to Sirmio first.'

'When you go to Bithynia, I'll go with you.'

'No, Lucius. Come with me to Sirmio. I need you to stay there, and take care of my father. You know what you were saying about growing older? You were right. I can't risk losing you.'

Late in the day, he leaves Lucius packing his things, and goes to Clodia. He sends in his name, and a brief note he has written, telling her that Marcus has died, and that he is leaving at dawn, first for Sirmio and then, in time, for Bithynia. He will be gone for months, perhaps a year or more.

He knows exactly why he wrote that note. He wanted her alone, entirely his, thinking of no one and nothing else. He knows that she can do that for him, for a few hours at least. He looks at his note before he hands it to the slave doorman. Is it a betrayal of Marcus? he asks himself. Perhaps it is. Perhaps he is exploiting his own sorrow. He's made sure that she knows of his brother's death before she sees him, so that he will get his Clodia, alone, warm, tender. He has got to have her. He's got to touch her and taste her and then he can carry her away with him in his heart. His Clodia: that one.

They are in the pool room. It's growing dark and through the window he can see the stars coming out, one at a time at first and then so thickly that he can't count them. He turns back to Clodia. He can hear her breathing, but it's too dark to make out her face. She didn't want to light a lamp.

'Aemilia will pretend she thinks I need something if she knows I'm out here.'

'Where does she think you are?'

Clodia shrugs.

Quickly, he turns his mind aside.

'Lie down again,' says Clodia.

She wraps her warm, slender arms around him. He smells her body, feels her breath against his cheek. She rocks him gently.

'You're happy, aren't you?' she asks. She sounds uncertain. Not the sure, confident Clodia everyone else sees, but his Clodia.

'Yes.'

'You make me feel so different,' she says. She catches her breath in a laugh. 'If anyone who knew me came in, they wouldn't recognize me.'

He strokes her hair. He doesn't want her to think about other people.

'My Clodia,' he says, 'my life. My girl.'

'I shouldn't have asked if you were happy. Of course you can't be happy. You loved your brother. It's terrible, when you love someone and they die.'

'Who are you thinking of?'

'Livia. My friend. I told you about her.'

'Yes, I remember.'

He keeps on stroking her hair. As long as he does this, Marcus is not dead. He is somewhere in the darkness, warm and amused but saying nothing because there's no need to talk. Marcus would understand about the note. He would not be angry.

Twenty-one

His father had been so determined to send him out to Bithynia 'on a proper footing'. He'd pulled strings, and got Catullus a plum posting as aide to Governor Memmius.

'Extremely valuable experience for a young man.'

The prospect of sending another son out to Bithynia seemed to lift his father's spirits. His difficult second son would be transformed into a mature representative of the family, who would look after its interests, advance its cause, and incidentally enrich himself while forming a close relationship with a man in an influential and powerful position –

It was the story of the ideal son all over again, only perhaps this time there was a grain of reality in it. Catullus had even felt a certain pride as the responsibility was placed in his hands. Lucius was right: his father had become old. He had a perpetual tremor in his hands now. He rarely spoke of Marcus, but his bowed, shuffling silence was eloquent. Catullus had never imagined that the fearsome uprightness of his father could change so suddenly.

An old man, weak but still obstinate. They got on no better than they ever had in those long weeks in Sirmio before Catullus left for the East. He stayed out of the house as much as possible during the day, walking the hills, seeing nobody. If he found Marcus anywhere it would be there. He could almost imagine that he would come round a bend in the path and see the two boys squatting in the dust, heads together, watching a slow-worm make its way into the scrub. Or they might be hiding in an olive tree, concealed by the dapple of sun and shade. But he was tired of his own imagination. He wanted Marcus, not some shade in his mind.

He heard the shepherd boys calling each other from hill to hill. Sometimes he came on them, wild, dusty, ragged, their matted hair down to their shoulders. He would greet them respectfully, and they would stare. He wondered if they still fought the boys from the fishing village, and if the Lakers had a leader to plan raids on the shepherd boys' camps.

He would sit for hours in the shade of an olive tree, thinking of nothing, listening to the sheep in the distance, the cicadas and busy sparrows. Once or twice he heard a boy playing a pipe he'd whittled. It was a harsh sound, but it had its own sweetness as the wind carried the note away.

He never felt his brother's presence, although he longed for it. 'Marcus?' he asked once, but he heard his own voice fall away into the silence.

Julia had gone to her father's estate. He would visit her and ask her about Marcus' illness and death, but not now. Later, when he was back from Bithynia. First, he wanted to walk where Marcus had walked, and see the places he'd seen.

There was no baby. He realized how much his father had hoped that Julia might be pregnant, when he received the news that she was not. She put it delicately: '. . . *our sorrow that the gods never chose to give us a child*'. His father seemed to sag. Later he tried to be bluff, announcing: 'It's all on your shoulders now, my boy.'

It was becoming real to Catullus that soon Sirmio would be his. There was no one else to lead the family, or to ensure that the line continued. His father expected it.

Lucius was right. His father would not live more than a few years. They had never been a long-lived family. It was almost impossible to imagine Sirmio without his father there, directing the management of the estates, always vigilant, making greater what was already great. But Sirmio without his father would be a different place in another way. Slowly the pain and disappointment might leach out of it, leaving the linen clean. He might find himself eager to be there. He certainly wouldn't have to entertain his father's friends. No more lengthy visits from Caesar –

Impious, he was. Unfilial. Imagine having a son like him. Catullus smiled. The thought of a son was beginning to gain on him, just as Sirmio was changing in his mind from somewhere that had his father's identity branded on to it to somewhere that might become even more to Catullus than the lost and beautiful home of early childhood: his own place, here, now. He would like to show Lucius his son. And his father too, naturally, before he died. It would be like saying: *Don't be afraid. All this will go on.* He could see himself putting the child into Lucius' hands.

He would call his son Marcus.

Suddenly his mind stalled with grief. There was no Marcus. He could call his name for ever, and hear nothing but sheep and cicadas. His father was busy writing letters, making plans for the Bithynia trip, calling his son into the study every evening to go over contracts, contacts, figures and possibilities. They'd gone into everything, except the one thing that haunted both their minds: Marcus' grave. That is, until last night, when his father suddenly started rubbing his eyes as if the lamp smoke was irritating them, and said, 'Of course you will make the offerings.'

Catullus couldn't speak. He bowed his head, and his father snapped, 'You heard me? *The offerings.*'

'I heard you.'

His father stopped rubbing his eyes and almost glared at him, his eyes inflamed. 'You'll do everything that is proper?'

'You can trust me, Father.'

Catullus turned away as soon as he could do so without giving offence. He felt as if he'd been running a long race, until his heart was swollen in his chest and close to bursting. All he wanted was to fall to the ground that covered his brother's ashes. To kneel and cut a lock of his hair with a sharp knife, and place the offerings, and talk to his brother.

Through many lands and over many waters
I come, brother, for this sad leave-taking
to give you what the dead ask of us
and speak to your silent ashes.
Since fate has torn brother from brother
shamefully parting us for ever
here, now, I follow our ancestors' custom
and tender your grave-offerings –
take them, soaked with a brother's tears.
I greet you, dear brother,
I say farewell to you for ever.

'Ave atque vale ... ave atque vale ...' He said the words aloud, kneeling on the earth by his brother's grave. The words moved through the air, shadowing it. 'You understand, Marcus,' he said, 'that words are all I can give you.'

Twenty-two

Shafted, both of them. A right royal shafting they've had, his Fabullus and Veranius too. Now they're both back from Macedonia, where they thought they'd make their fortunes. They are poorer now than they were when they went out, utterly buggered by serving under that skinflint Piso.

Get a staff job and get rich. And so off they'd gone, full of high hopes, optimism and greed, dreaming of bribes, private arrangements with tax farmers and lucrative little levies on exports. What the hell else do you go out to the provinces for? as Fabullus had remarked. They'd wangled the posting, just as Catullus' father had wangled the posting for him in Bithynia, with good old Governor Memmius. And now they are all back with nothing to show for it. What a thorough buggering they've all had. Skinflint Piso has done the dirty on Catullus' friends out in Macedonia, while incompetent, corrupt, tight-fisted Memmius has done the same favour for Catullus in Bithynia.

Turned over and shafted to the hilt, it's the same story with all of them. And now Fabullus and Veranius have lugged home their sackloads of zero, poor bastards. How do men like Piso and Memmius get away with treating their staff so badly?

It's like the old times tonight, all of them back together in Rome. Catullus isn't here for long. A couple of weeks, and then he must get back to Sirmio. He'd been shocked, on his return from Bithynia, to see that the months had shrivelled his father as quickly as years might once have done. It was Lucius who ran everything now, deftly, with a tact that mastered his father's uncertain temper.

His father had welcomed Catullus. Not warmly, that would be too much to expect, but correctly.

'You'll find it good to sleep in your own bed,' his father had said.

The night before Catullus left again for Rome, his father had stayed up late, not really talking, because they never had anything much to talk about, but seeming to want to be with his son. Just before he went to bed he said something Catullus had never thought he would hear.

'Don't stay too long in Rome, my boy. We need you here.'

He'd expected that Lucius would stay at Sirmio. After all, he was needed there, and he knew Catullus was coming back soon. But Lucius wasn't having it.

'You don't look after yourself unless I'm keeping an eye on you,' he'd said. 'Look at you. You've lost weight out there. And how long have you had that cough?'

'I'm not staying in Rome, Lucius. It's only for a week or so.'

'All the same, this time I'm coming with you, to make sure I bring you home. I can't tell you how many times I've cursed myself for giving way over your going out to Bithynia alone. I couldn't help thinking, when there was a storm, of all the salt water that lay between us.'

Lucius' phrase jolted through him. *All the salt water.* The dark sea, its crests plunging like horses. He'd stood on deck and stared out over the wastes of water, as spray made a fur of bubbles over his cloak and blew salt into his face.

Marcus was in Bithynia and he would never see him again. Salt water would lie between them for ever.

'You're right,' he said. 'We separate from one another too easily, all of us. We don't believe that the storm will come, and then it does. It was good to get your letters, Lucius. We've hardly ever written to each other, have we? I suppose it's because we're not often parted.'

A faint smile crosses Lucius' face, ironic and questioning. 'In my view,' he said carefully, 'it's better to be near those you love than to write to them.'

'Maybe,' says Catullus, also smiling, thinking of Clodia and those dozens of poems written to her. 'You know, Lucius, when I read Sappho I think I'm uncovering the heart of the past, as if I could see through flesh and bone. But maybe it's not true. What about all the others who stayed so near to what they loved that they never wrote a word?'

'Yes,' says Lucius, 'write your thoughts down in words, and they're not safe any more. They don't belong to you.' His boy will never understand that. The habit of silence that you get, being born a slave, is one of those things that gets into the grain of you. You don't even want to let go of it. It's a kind of power, that no one can ever see into your heart. Not even his boy, whom he loves more than his life.

'I shan't stay long in Rome,' said Catullus. 'Look after my father.' *You are my father*, he didn't say. *My true father, who has given me everything that a father can give to his son.* Even to him, it sounded impious, dangerous, one of those truths that should never be put into words.

'No,' said Lucius, 'I'll come with you.'

'Gods, it's good to be back in Rome,' says Veranius, stretching luxuriously.

'I'm not back here for long.' Catullus doesn't look up as he says it. Fabullus already knows, but no doubt Veranius and Camerius will make a meal of it. Sure enough –

'Not back for long? What do you mean? Rome is home, have you forgotten? You can't leave. Besides, you won't want to miss the trial –'

'Which trial are you talking about?' he asks sharply.

'The trial of the noble Marcus Caelius Rufus, of course. You can't have not heard about it. Even *we* have, and we've only been back in Rome five minutes.'

'It's not even certain that there's going to be a trial, from what I heard,' says Catullus.

'Oh, yes, there will be,' says Camerius. 'And guess who's going to defend Rufus? Old Chickpea. I wonder how much that's costing.'

They are all looking at Catullus, waiting for his reaction.

'Mind you, even old Chickpea will have his work cut out on this one,' goes on Camerius ruminatively. 'Sedition, assault, theft, murder . . .'

'And conspiracy to murder,' adds Veranius, watching Catullus.

They think, of course, that he knows much more than he knows. But they are wrong, because he is not an insider in Clodia's life any more. Rufus is alleged to have plotted to poison Clodia. Clodia's position has shifted while he's been away in Bithynia. The talk about her has a jeering tone that sets his teeth on edge. She has gone far away from him, into a highly coloured world of plot and counter-plot, poison and antidote, threat and counter-threat. It is her brother's world, the element where Pretty Boy swims like a fish.

And now, it seems that Clodia swims there too. She claims that Rufus tried to have her poisoned after she refused his request for money to get hold of poison to kill someone else. A conspiracy with as many layers as Hell itself.

It would have sounded to Catullus like a melodrama written for the plebs, had he never met Gorgo. The scandal is swelling. Since he arrived in Rome two days ago, everyone's been fighting to be first to tell him all about it.

He refuses to react. The Clodia they talk about is not his Clodia. That is his only defence.

'The word on the street is that it's pretty definite there's a strong case against Rufus,' says Camerius. 'Witnesses, and circumstantial evidence, and all that kind of thing. Clodia has made a deposition about the plot to poison her.'

Poison. How has she allowed that word to rub against her name? Does she not realize how dangerous it is? Clodia seems to think that she's invulnerable. But then, he doesn't know what Clodia thinks any more.

'It's all politics, when it comes down to it,' says Fabullus quickly.

'Pretty Boy will be at the back of it somewhere, and half these allegations will collapse before they ever come to court.'

'Of course they will,' say the others, rather too quickly.

'But all the same, old Chickpea defending Rufus is going to be too good to miss,' adds Camerius. 'You've got to stay for that at least.'

'The estates need managing. I'm the only son now.'

They are silent. Perhaps they think that he's running away. Perhaps they are right.

'But you'll come back to Rome. Bugger it, you've got to come back. Your old man can run things, can't he?'

'He's not well; they need me there.'

He doesn't want to spoil the reunion by talking about how much things have changed for him. It feels like a betrayal of them and of himself. He has made a life here in Rome, and it's the life he dreamed of all the years of his adolescence. He's become Roman, and what his life will be back in Sirmio, he can't really imagine. Only his poems are left. Clodia has destroyed many things, but not his poems.

No. Be truthful. She's in them, part of them, indestructible. He won't get away from her, any more than he can escape from the self that is in love and in hate with her. But in Sirmio, maybe he'll find a little peace.

> *I don't ask for the stars*
> *for a return of her love*
> *for what cannot exist*
> *for truth or faithfulness –*
> *all I want is to be free from this sickness*
> *this soul-sucking corruption –*

He changes the subject away from his own future.

'We ought to have taken lessons from Caesar and Mamurra,'

he says. 'They could have taught us a thing or two about profiting from the provinces.'

'Those two know how to fill their boots with gold.'

'And we never even got any dinner invitations, while others –'

'*Others* – Always others, never us,' laments Veranius. 'We get fucked over when every other aide comes back loaded –'

'Maybe we made the wrong friends –'

'We were serving under the wrong man, that was our problem. The meanest bastard in the whole of Macedonia just happened to be our boss –'

'*We* were paying *him* for the privilege of licking his arse on a daily basis –'

'And that's certainly not why we chose to put up with the horrors – No, let's put it more strongly – the deadly, tedious, vile abomination of provincial life. The only variety you've got to look forward to is an uprising by some tribe which refuses to get the point that *it's been conquered*. All they want to do is stick a javelin up your arse –'

'He went down on his knees as soon as we were off the gangplank and kissed Italian soil, didn't you, Fabullus?'

'I'm never leaving Rome again, I swear it. They get you out there on false pretences, with all this crap about how you'll make your fortune from taxes and concessions –'

'And then you're forced to watch while all the gravy gets carried straight past your plate, hot and steaming.'

'Yes, I had your letters. Did you like the poem I sent you?' inquires Catullus.

'The poem! That fucking poem went the rounds. *We* were entirely discreet, as you can imagine,' says Fabullus, 'but somehow it got copied and then someone else made a copy of the copy, and so on. I'm amazed no one got court-martialled. In the end it was being scrawled on walls by the infantry.'

'Let's hear it!' shouts Camerius.

Catullus looks around. 'I'm not going to recite from a couch. It's unworthy of our noble calling.'

He stands, strikes a Ciceronian pose, and runs up and down a couple of octaves.

'I need to prepare – ahem! – my inestimably valuable vocal instrument –'

'Get on with it, you cocktease, before I start throwing these inestimably valuable quails' eggs at your head.'

> *O empty-handed aides-de-camp,*
> *Piso's idiots, ready for action*
> *with your keen little backpacks –*

– You remember how we loaded ourselves up with luggage?
– Because we thought we'd be bringing it home rammed with stuff.

> *Veranius, dearest of friends*
> *and Fabullus, my own,*
> *how are things going?*

– Absolutely fucking grim from start to finish.
– Fucked over to the highest degree of fuckdom.

> *Had enough of the dregs, the cold*
> *and the crappy food over there?*

– Goat casserole five nights running.
– Wine that makes your teeth hurt.
– Ice on the latrines.

> *Are you in negative equity, as I was*
> *in Bithynia with that bastard Memmius?*
> *O Memmius, how you turned me over*
> *and did me slowly, tho-rough-ly*
> *with that super-long member of thine!*

– 'Super-long' – you had it easy. I could feel Piso's prick coming out of my mouth –

> Now I see you two have met
> the same fate, you've been done by Piso
> with a tool of equal size
> while following our fathers' advice
> to 'make connections with the great'.
> Gods and goddesses, punish
> bastard Piso and bastard Memmius
> who dirty the faces of Romulus and Remus.

'Yes, "bastards" is the word for them,' says Veranius with deep feeling, while the others bang their cups on the table. 'I was terrified of dying out there. There's only one inscription that could have gone on my tombstone: *Here lies Veranius, fucked to death by Piso.*'

There's a sudden silence as each of them remembers the tomb in Bithynia. Fabullus clears his throat.

'He doesn't mean to be such a crass fucking fool as he is. Take him away, someone, and put his head in the fountain.'

Catullus puts his arm around Fabullus' shoulders. He feels raised up, glittering with wine and love for his friends. They are his. They have never betrayed him. They've come back older, harder, deeply tanned by wind and sun.

'Let's fill our cups,' he says. 'Let's drink to being fucked over.'

'You can't have done as badly as us,' says Veranius. 'I heard you had a boat built to bring you back from Bithynia. Very classy.'

'There's plenty of wood for boat-building out there.'

'I also heard she's a bit of a racer,' Veranius persists. 'Lucky devil.'

'Her racing days are over. She's in dry dock in Sirmio now. The most she'll ever do is take old ladies out for a turn on the lake.'

'*Old* ladies?'

'Yes, *old* ladies. Why does everything comes back to sex with you, Veranius?'

'Because I don't get enough. Even cross-eyed mountain girls wouldn't look at me –'

'We're forgetting our toast,' says Fabullus. 'Gentlemen, I give you: being fucked over!'

'And fucking,' says Camerius after the toast, draining his cup. Camerius has a new girl, who is – as usual – amazing-looking, incredibly witty, plays the lyre like a professional (which would be even more of an asset if Camerius weren't tone-deaf), and as for tits, you've never seen anything so perfect, round and rosy as pomegranates, just peeping through the sheer silk tops she wears – And crazy about Camerius –

– Her tits are crazy about you?

– I'd give a lot to find a girl with discriminating tits like that.

– Does she send them off questing on their own, Camerius, until they find someone to discriminate in favour of?

Camerius wasn't even going to listen. They weren't capable of appreciating a pure, refined, unworldly girl, the kind of girl you dream about –

– Before you ask her for a fuck.

– You bastards, you've got minds like the Cloaca Maxima. You think every girl's a clapped-out scrubber just because they're the only ones who'll take *you* on. A girl like Mucia's beyond your understanding –

– Mucia! Not *the* Mucia? Not All-comers Mucia?

– D'you reckon Camerius will be taking her home to his mother?

– Listen, Camerius, she plays the lyre like a professional because she *is* a professional.

Camerius protests, angry, but laughing too. He's always falling madly in love, spending everything he's got on the girl, and then when money and girl are both gone he writes up a storm of desperately ornate verse before recovering enough to start all over again. *'I've met the most incredible girl, wait until you see her . . .'*

Catullus loves them, loves them all. They're his. Fabullus, Veranius, Camerius. Beacons of friendship in a dirty world. He tries to tell them how much he loves them, but they're making bets on how long this new girl will last with Camerius.

The mood leaves him. All at once his friends' faces seem far away and inexplicably bright. How do they find so much to laugh about? His own mouth is stretched tight with trying to smile. Clodia once said he made her laugh, he made every evening wonderful. He can't do that any more.

'Are you all right?' It's Fabullus, leaning across the couch. 'Here, have another drink.'

He has another drink, and then another, and the evening goes on. At some point he recites a poem written to Clodia. When he's in the middle of it, new lines come to him. They are so good that he knows he'll remember them, and then Veranius says something about Cynthia and his attention snaps back to the table.

'How's Cynthia doing? I used to think about her a lot in Macedonia. I might go over there tomorrow – have you seen her?'

'You won't find her,' says Catullus, 'she's left Rome.'

'*Left Rome?* But she can't do that. What for?'

'Where has she gone?' asks Fabullus.

'She came into a small inheritance, and so she's gone down to the country, to be near where her boy is.'

'I shouldn't think she'll get much business in the country,' says Camerius.

'The inheritance gives her enough to live on.'

'Where the hell did an inheritance like that come from? A grateful client? I can't believe Cynthia still had any contact with her family,' says Veranius, clearly annoyed that Cynthia is not going to be there, the same as ever.

'I've no idea,' says Catullus, becoming aware that Fabullus is watching him.

'Cynthia gone . . . Why do things have to change? Why can't they stay the same?' demands Veranius.

'You're right,' says Fabullus. 'Only we should change while everything else stands firm around us. No doubt we'll find they've had the nerve to build a few new apartment blocks while we've been away, and change the Consuls. But let's not talk politics, it's too depressing. It seems as if we've come back to a madhouse. Well, if you ever hear from Cynthia, my brother, then greet her from me.'

He's forgotten that Fabullus sometimes used to call him that. *My brother.* No, not really forgotten. It comes as a shock, that's all, and then the words fall into place, hurting, but sounding sweet.

Twenty-three

He gives his name to the slave doorman. The man just stands there, doing nothing.

'Gaius Valerius Catullus, to see the mistress of the house,' he repeats sharply.

'I heard you the first time,' says the doorman.

Catullus' anger fights his disbelief that any slave should dare to speak like this. Since he came back from Bithynia he's heard nothing but rumours about what's going on in Clodia's house on the Palatine.

– A household turned arse over tip, where slave is master and mistress is slave.

– Or slave on top of mistress, even, you might say.

Lies, smears and slanders – but what do they add up to? Nothing, he tells himself on good days. Rufus' trial looks as if it will go ahead, because it's gone too far to stop. There are too many allegations and too many witnesses. He believes that Fabullus is right, and political machinations are at the back of the whole thing. Clodia has got dragged into it – probably because of her brother – but the essential Clodia, his girl: she remains apart.

On bad days, he believes the smears. She's a whore who is incapable of love or even the pretence of faithfulness. From birth she's been as hard as bronze: brazen. She couldn't keep away from Rufus. She had to have him, and then she hated him. The slaves know it, as they know everything. The mistress does what she wants. She doesn't care for the laws of the gods or of man, so why should they?

Don't think of all that now. Take one bastard at a time. He doesn't know this doorman. Rumour says that there are a lot of strange faces in Clodia's house these days, but this is the first time he's been here since his return from Bithynia. He wrote to her as soon as he arrived in Rome, and she wrote back to explain that it was difficult just now, her time wasn't her own. People were watching every move she made; she couldn't risk scandal.

Couldn't risk scandal! That's my girl, he thought. He wanted to write back and ask who her time belonged to if it wasn't her own. *Whose is it, then? Perhaps you'd like to tell me?* But he sent no more letters. Why ask questions, when you know you won't like the answers? Besides, even to think of what she might answer makes him feel exhausted, angry and ashamed. She has poisoned his mind. His suspicions are as detailed as those pornographic frescoes that old men keep curtained in their private rooms. Even though he hates himself for it, he can't resist looking at the pictures. He tosses himself off, thinking of Clodia splayed under another man.

'Running all the estates is a nightmare. It's like governing a province,' Clodia used to say after Metellus Celer's death. 'If it weren't for my brother's help, I'd never be able to manage.'

But Clodia has at least kept a façade of respect and order until now. This new cock-of-the-walk doorman is the symptom of a disease that's entering a more dangerous stage. Clodia isn't even bothering to keep up appearances any more.

'Who the hell do you think you are talking to?' demands Catullus, wishing for once that he'd brought his own retinue of slaves with him. No doubt this fellow is new, and thinks that because a visitor is unattended, he has no status and can be disrespected. He'll learn.

'Gaius Valerius Catullus,' singsongs the slave mockingly, 'but all the same my lady's not at home.'

The words 'to you' are so clearly intended to follow that they are almost audible.

A pure, hot flame of rage lights, deep in Catullus. 'You forget yourself,' he says, 'and Rome has her way of handling slaves who forget themselves. If you don't want to find yourself hanging from two pieces of wood on the Esquiline Hill, you'll speak to me with respect. Announce me to the mistress of the house immediately.'

Calculation moves in the man's eyes, and a shade of fear. 'She's not at home, she's at her brother's,' says the slave.

' "*She's* not at home, *she's* at her brother's"? Who do you think you are talking about?'

'The mistress,' says the slave, cowed and sullen.

'That's better.' Anger is catching his breath, making it hard to speak. That Clodia allows herself to be spoken of like this, by her own slaves, enrages him. And she's 'at her brother's'. Or perhaps somewhere else. They say she's got someone new. Catullus doesn't trust rumours about Clodia. He suspects that many of them start in her own house, and are intended to screen what she's really doing.

'She's always there in the afternoons,' goes on the doorman.

Catullus does not want to hear any more from this man. A slave doorman is like part of the door itself: he sees everything and knows everything. His fists clench, as he thinks of how much this man must know about Clodia. She doesn't even trouble to hide it. All the traffic of the house is exposed.

'I could find out more for you, about where she's gone,' says the doorman.

The slave wants a bribe. He could give him money, and he'd soon open his mouth. *If you want to know the worst of Clodia, this is your chance.*

'Fetch Aemilia here,' he says instead.

'Aemilia?' echoes the slave with an offensive show of astonishment. 'You're behind the times. There's no *Aemilia* here no more.'

'What do you mean?'

'If you mean the Aemilia that I know, she's gone. Left our service, so to speak.'

'You mean . . . she's been freed?'

It's not credible that Aemilia would ever leave Clodia's service willingly. She loves her too much.

'Freed? That's a good one. Sold is what she is. Sold in disgrace to whoever would take her, and lucky for her that she didn't get worse. She won't be giving orders where *she's* gone.'

'Where is she?'

A doorman slave knows everything. But this one shrugs. 'No idea. Your honour,' he adds with a barely discernible hint of mockery.

Catullus takes out his purse. 'Here's a sestertius that says you know.'

The doorman bends forward, peering at the coin. 'Sorry, sir, it's speaking a bit quiet, I can't make it out.'

'Here's another.'

The doorman glances around, slips the coins into his tunic and says quickly, 'Lollia's place.'

'Lollia's place?'

'You'll find it easy enough, it's a left turn off the Street of the Dye Makers, near the Twins' flower market.'

'You're sure? I'll have your hide in tatters if you're lying.'

'I heard them give the direction to the litter-bearers.'

'Litter-bearers for a sold-off slave! Now I know you're lying.'

'She wasn't looking too clever, if you get my meaning. The mistress wanted it that way, with the litter. Hidden, like.'

He doesn't want to know any more. It's like worms writhing when a stone is lifted. But the doorman is well into his tale now.

'She was lucky it wasn't worse that happened to her, stupid bitch. She ought to of kept her mouth shut. You don't talk about certain things that go on in this house, that's rule number one, not if you know what's good for your health.'

He'll go straight to this Lollia's house – it'll be a brothel, most likely – and get everything out of Aemilia. 'Sold in disgrace'. But Aemilia loved Clodia like a dog. She would never betray her.

(Didn't Clodia once say that she thought maybe Aemilia was spying for the Metelli?)

It's not possible. Clodia is her own woman, independent. The Metelli can do nothing to her. They can't even enter Clodia's house without her permission.

(But if some slave has opened his mouth about what happened before Metellus Celer died –)

Aemilia would keep Clodia's secrets, whatever they were. She would never betray her.

He walks back down the hill and across the Forum in a black dream. Fool, Catullus. Isn't it time you joined the real world? Anyone can betray anyone.

She couldn't keep away from Rufus, and Rufus, his own good friend Rufus, lover of poetry and listener to drunken late-night confidences – Rufus didn't make the slightest effort to keep away from Clodia, once he'd spotted she was interested in him. He wouldn't even admit that he was betraying his friendship with Catullus.

– All this business with Clodia has got nothing to do with our friendship, or the way I feel about you. Can't we be civilized about this? It's just a fling for both of us, not the end of the world.

Business with Clodia . . . Both of us . . . You bastard, you knew how those words would eat away at me. You want to make my love the same as yours – just a fling, although I found a lot of fancy words for it. As for friendship, you were never my friend, I know that now. You don't know what the word means. You stole my girl and then came to me and talked about poetry.

You knew my thoughts, Rufus. You chose to rip me apart, and then you pretended that it meant nothing. We were both men of the world, weren't we? – and 'our Clodia' – yes, *our* Clodia, Rufus! – we shared her, didn't we? – Our Clodia was a woman of the world and couldn't be expected to stick to the standards of the middle-class housewife.

You were always a liar, Rufus. You loved her because I loved her. You wanted her because I wanted her. It was my poetry that made you love her, if I can use the word 'love' for what you said you felt. She was precious to me, a jewel. Your eyes caught the gleam of it and you knew you had to have it. You were so greedy, weren't you? You saw something you'd never had, you envied a love which you'd never experienced. Maybe you thought you could have it too. Maybe you thought it would be fun to smash it.

And now your affair is over. You hate each other. It's degenerated into claim and counter-claim, and it's going to end up in the law courts. Every kind of vile accusation that you could throw at each other, you've thrown. That's all it added up to, and it didn't take long.

You haven't even got the wit to keep away from me. You smiled at me across the Forum this morning. You still think you can rummage in the shreds of my heart, and call it friendship.

Let me tell you what you know about friendship. You know about clambering over people, using them as stepping-stones to what you want. A friend like you is the worst sort of enemy. You crept close to me, you were so sympathetic, you wormed your way into my secrets. You learned all my weak points.

Did you love it, Rufus? Did you hug your intentions to yourself while I blurted out my soul in my poems? How you must have smiled to yourself. You were so handsome, so urbane, such a man of the world: but I know you. I know that really you're a greedy little boy cramming your mouth with cakes that you can't even swallow because your belly is already full. You wait until no one's looking and then you spit them out in the street.

And now you're tired of my girl. You've eaten her and you don't want her any more, is that it? Maybe all the accusations are true. You thought she'd treated you badly and you were entitled to revenge. That's the way a man of your kind always thinks. Perhaps you really did plan your revenge, so that you'd be back where you've always got to be: on top. You know as little about love as you know about friendship.

And don't come to me, Rufus, if golden-tongued Cicero can't get you off the charge. (Although I am sure that he will: what's a man like Cicero for, if not to turn black into white?) If you were starving in the street, I would take pleasure in seeing you die with a piece of bread held just out of your reach. I'd twitch it, to make you jump.

Lollia folds her arms, and looks him up and down.

'I think you've come to the wrong place,' she says.

He's not surprised. The frontage is narrow and dirty. Lollia's hair is brightly hennaed, but she's dirty too. It's a place for poor men who can scrape up a few coppers for their end-of-the-week fuck, and don't mind waiting while the girl wipes herself off from the man before them.

Catullus has picked up a trainee gladiator on the way, as bodyguard. He didn't want to bring any of his own slaves. The gladiator stands behind him, huge and impassive.

'I'm looking for someone,' says Catullus. 'A woman called Aemilia. I was told she's here.'

Lollia's face darkens. 'We've got no one of that name here.'

'I think you have. I think she's a former slave to the Metelli.'

'You'd better come in,' she says, glancing up and down the street. '*He* can wait here, just inside the door. That'll put the fear of the gods into the punters.' She laughs. 'Only joking. There's not much business this time of the day.'

Lollia takes him into a back room. The place is a warren and much bigger than it appears from the street. She shuts the door. There's a greasy-looking couch, but they both stay standing.

'She's not a working girl, you understand,' says Lollia.

He hadn't thought that she was, but when you came to think of it, why not? Aemilia was female. She was ugly, but not that ugly. And here in Lollia's house there didn't seem to be any other employment.

'She's going to do the heavy for me,' says Lollia.

'The heavy?'

'The cleaning,' explains Lollia, 'the scrubbing and washing and doing out the rooms and all that. I lost my house slave a couple of months ago, and it's all got away from me. Course, Aemilia's still recovering, but I've been told she's a good worker. She'd better be, the food she's eating and no return for it yet.'

'Still recovering?'

A flash of alarm crosses Lollia's face. 'I thought you'd come from the house?'

'I was there this morning.'

'Well, then, you know how she was.'

He nods. 'So she's here now?'

'Oh, yes. It's best she keeps indoors, that's what I was told. One good thing, the way she looks, none of the punters'll get any ideas about her. She'll keep at her work steady.'

'Can I see her?'

A familiar look of calculation and fear crosses Lollia's face. She glances quickly at the door. She wants him out of here. He digs out his purse, and gives her a denarius.

'It's worth that much to me, if we can have half an hour alone. No interruptions.'

She nods. The coin vanishes, a flash of silver into her dirty wrap. She goes out of the room leaving behind a smell of stale sweat and violet perfume.

Aemilia is unrecognizable. Her face is swollen, green and yellow with fading bruises. She has a bandage over one eye. Her hair has been shaved off at the front, where there's another bandage.

Her bandages are rags crusted with blood. She is wearing an assortment of clothes that don't fit properly and obviously don't belong to her.

'What happened to you?' he asks in horror, forgetting everything else.

Aemilia's one eye stares at him, hard and dark but somehow vacant too, as if she's given up registering things. She doesn't even seem surprised to see him here.

'Did my lady send you?' she asks. Her voice has changed too. It's hoarse. She wears a scarf wrapped around her throat. Perhaps she's got a cold, he thinks stupidly, then notices there are more bruises around the edge of the scarf.

'No, she didn't send me. The doorman told me you were here.'

'No one's supposed to know where I am,' says Aemilia, her voice quickening with panic. 'My lady swore it.'

'He heard the directions that were given to the litter-bearers.'

'Litter-bearers?' asks Aemilia vaguely.

'He said you were brought here in a litter.'

'I can't hardly remember it.'

This isn't Clodia's work. It couldn't have been Clodia who did this. She might slap Aemilia about, but she would never half kill her.

Aemilia moves her neck stiffly. 'I feel funny,' she says. 'I get dizzy when I stand up too long.'

'All right, sit down over there.'

He should help her but he can't bear to touch her as she lowers herself painfully on to the couch.

'Was it the mistress who did this to you?'

'She never would,' says Aemilia, and he hears a familiar possessive anger in her voice. 'She never would hurt me in her life. It was her who sent me here to keep safe.'

'Then who was it that hurt you?'

Aemilia hesitates. Slowly, her hands reach up and fumble at the bandage which holds in place the pad of rags over her left eye. There's a knot at the back of her head which she has to undo. It takes a little while, and neither of them speaks. The knot is undone. The bandage falls loose. Very cautiously, Aemilia eases away the pad of rags.

There is no eye. There is a raw, red, mashed swelling with a gap in the centre of it. Bitter liquid fills his mouth. He wants to turn away but Aemilia's remaining eye fixes him.

'My lady says that they make glass eyes in Egypt,' says Aemilia.

Her fingers are shaking. 'They paint them so you wouldn't know them from real. They cost a lot of money, but she's going to send away for one. They'll match the colour, she says.' There is a note of pride in her voice.

'Who did that to you? Who took out your eye?'

'My lady sent for a surgeon. He said the eye was past saving and had to be took out for fear that it would kill the sight in the other eye. He said that eyes have sympathies, one for the other. So he did that, he took it out. My lady held my hand. I squeezed so hard I was afraid I'd break her bones.'

'But the injury – who did it?'

'It was her brother,' says Aemilia. 'Him that they call Pretty Boy. You know him. Everyone knows him.'

Pretty Boy. *He likes your style. Don't worry, he'll never cause you any trouble. He's incredibly sweet and loyal.*

'And he tried to strangle you.'

'My lady stopped him. She come in and she stopped him. He didn't know she was in the house –'

'Never mind that. Tell me why he did this.'

Aemilia's one eye stares at him.

'That's why he went for my eyes, cos he thought I'd been spying on them. I would never have said a word. My lady knows that. She would of stopped him if she was there when he come back to find me.'

The room seems dark. Aemilia's eye socket gapes at him.

'You must cover your eye.'

'I can't tie the bandage myself, not at the back.'

He goes behind the couch. He has never touched her, and he doesn't want to touch her now. He waits while Aemilia settles the pad of rags back over her eye socket, and then takes the ends of the bandage, winds them to the back of her head, and ties the knot. Her hair smells.

'There,' he says, 'does that feel all right?'

She reaches behind her head, and tests the knot. 'It'll do,' she says.

'Listen, Aemilia, it isn't safe for you to stay here. That doorman knows where you are. He'll pass it on to the other slaves and Pretty Boy could come to hear of it. You don't want him sending someone down here after you.'

'I've been sold here. I can't run away, you know what'll happen to me. With this eye, I can't hide.'

He thinks quickly, and decides. 'I'll buy you. Lollia will agree if there's enough in it for her. I'll have you sent down to the country, where you'll be safe.'

She laughs, a hoarse disbelieving laugh. 'Why would you do that?'

'Because I don't like what Pretty Boy's done to you.'

She's silent for a bit, thinking it over, then she says, 'I would never see my lady, if I went away.'

'You won't see her anyway, Aemilia, if Pretty Boy sends one of his goons to finish the job.'

'It's only you who says he'll do that. My lady will have talked him down by now, made him see that I'm no danger to him. It was only in his anger he did this. It goes in the family. You know how she'll lash out and then she's so sorry after it.'

'She would never do such a thing,' he says quickly.

'No,' says Aemilia, 'she hasn't the strength. And not to me anyway, she wouldn't. I'm best staying here, where she's provided for me. I'll take my chance.'

He argues, but there's no moving her. He sees that she can't imagine a life without Clodia, any more than he can. Literally, she would rather die. He can't help but feel an unwilling respect for her, as if they were enemies who had slogged it out on the battlefield and ended up binding each other's wounds.

'She did do it, you know,' says Aemilia suddenly, as if she's paying him back for his offer of help.

'What?' His hair crisps with horror. He knows instantly, beyond intuition, what she means.

'You know. She did it. I was there. I didn't do anything to help, she didn't let me. It had to be done just right. I washed the crocks, that was all. But I didn't stop her. Why shouldn't she be free? She picks up whoever takes her fancy and then she puts him down. Maybe *he* didn't like it – maybe *you* don't like it – but that's the way she is. No one can hold her, it's not in her nature. She tells me everything.'

'You're lying, Aemilia –' But he knows she isn't. He feels it in the room now: her hatred. She's not grateful to him, she's not a defeated enemy, all that battlefield crap was in his head, not hers. She's powerless and a slave, half blinded but still stronger than him because she has the power to destroy him. She knows it. She's going to use it. Again, her lips part.

'I told her he never had that sparrow killed, but she wouldn't believe me.'

'Why are you telling me this?' he asks in a low voice, but she doesn't answer. She doesn't need to. Her work is done.

He should think of the man who died, but all he can think of is the sparrow. Clodia's husband didn't kill it. It died, that was all. Birds die. How long do sparrows live, anyway?

No. He sees it now: there's more. The mosaic is complete and he's standing above it, reading its images of frozen violence. It was Aemilia who killed the sparrow, because she was jealous. Clodia caressed it once too often. She must have turned her back on Aemilia to punish her, and given all her attention to the bird, murmuring to it in a voice so low that Aemilia couldn't hear the words, rubbing its soft body against her lips, her cheeks –

Aemilia killed it, and made Clodia believe her husband had done it.

He has moved away from her, to the other side of the room.

'You're taking a risk, Aemilia,' he says. 'Why are you so sure I won't go to the Metelli and tell them what you've said?'

'Not you,' she says. 'I know you. You won't do that.'

She is right. She knows him all too well. She looked ahead and maybe the eye which Pretty Boy had ruined saw more clearly than her good eye. Aemilia saw a future where she was separated from Clodia, and he was not. She saw a future where he would follow Clodia, no matter what darkness she led him into, as long as he could pretend not to know. She put a stop to it.

Twenty-four

Night-time on the Palatine. He's come here alone, but he wasn't afraid of being attacked as he threaded his way through Rome's simmering night streets. The gods are perverse. They destroy those who want to cling on to their lives, and save those who don't want to be saved.

All the same his blood quickens at a movement in the shadows. Pretty Boy's place is close by, and Rufus' rented house is more or less next door to it. And over there is the wall of Clodia's house. It's quiet tonight. No comings and goings. Her 'palace on the Palatine' that's no better than Lollia's tuppenny brothel. The same traffic, and the only difference is that it's less honest here. In they go and out they come. Pretty Boy, Rufus, even that bastard Egnatius who swills his teeth with urine and drawls, 'After all, our Lesbia's an experience everyone should have at least once in his life.'

Catullus' hand hurts. He has thudded his fist into the wall. He can do nothing. He's helpless. His body feels as if it's crawling with lice.

He must not think. He's got to find a way back to his own place, his lake, his Sirmio and the noise of lapping water that was there when he was a child and will be there when he is dead.

He will go back there, with Lucius. He thinks of Lucius at this moment, uneasily awake in the Roman night, watching out for his boy's return as he always does. Lucius will think Catullus is at some party, or with some woman.

'I never really drop off until you're home,' he said once. Catullus sees Lucius turn over in his bed, light his candle, and begin to read.

'I'm coming home,' Catullus promises in his head. 'We'll go back to Sirmio. I can't do this any more.'

Shadows flare along the house's façade from the lamps set burning at its entrance. It's late, but not too late. The entrance is not yet locked and barred. The doorman is still at his post. Catullus draws his cloak more closely around him, and hails the doorman, who stands up suddenly as if startled from the beginning of sleep.

'Falling asleep on duty,' remarks Catullus. 'I am here to see your mistress.'

The doorman fumbles for command of the situation. 'She's not at home.'

'Say, "My mistress is not at home."'

'Oh, it's you again.'

'Yes. Say it. You must have been deeply asleep, to forget how to address a visitor.'

'My mistress is not at home,' says the doorman.

'Good.'

No one's going to stand in his way tonight, because he's got nothing to lose. 'And now tell me the truth. Where is she?'

'She'll be back soon. I'm to keep the door until she comes home.'

'Back from where? The house of Publius Clodius Pulcher?'

'I don't know. Could be there, could be somewhere else,' says the doorman, with a touch of his former impudence.

'I advise you to think of a better answer.'

'All I know is, I'm to keep the door until she returns.'

Catullus moves back a few paces, thinking. He could get admission and wait in the house, but the doorman will give Clodia his name as she enters, and she'll be prepared for him. He wants to catch her off guard.

'I'll return later. Tell your mistress I called for her. You have the name.'

He turns the corner of the house and backs deep into its shadow. She will have to come this way. If she's in a litter, he can step out and stop the bearer slaves, but he doubts that she'll want to call attention to herself by using a litter for such a short distance. She'll walk, accompanied by a couple of slaves with torches.

His eyes are accustomed to the dark now. Of course it is never really dark or quiet here, among the great houses with their lamps and torches, their gangs of slaves on night duty, their rich owners coming and going at all hours. But it's dark enough. He feels as alone as if the Palatine were still a green hill, inhabited by a couple of shepherds living in rough stone huts. The wind would sigh just the same. The shepherds would turn over on their straw pallets, breaking a dream of happiness.

He is watching for the light of torches, and so he almost misses her as she flits past in a long cloak, her head covered by a hood. But it's her, he knows her from the way she moves.

'Clodia!' he says softly, and comes out of the shadow to stand in her path.

She gasps, but doesn't cry out.

'It's me,' he says. 'Quick, come into the shadow. No one can see us there.'

She does as he says. She's breathing hard and as he pulls her close he feels the bumping of her heart. She's been running.

'You came from your brother's?' he asks her.

'Yes.'

'You shouldn't walk alone at this time.'

'It's only a little way,' she says, her voice sounding surer now.

'There are some violent people around. Real thugs. You ought to be careful.'

'Darling, of course I'm careful.' She laughs. 'Why is it such ages since I've seen you? I heard you were back in Rome. Anyone would think you were avoiding me.'

'I'm serious, Clodia. Terrible things happen. I met a girl the other day who'd been attacked. She'd lost an eye.'

She freezes in his arms. 'What do you mean?' she raps out.

'And she'd been half strangled too. It's a miracle that she lived.'

270

'Why are you saying this to me?'

'Because it concerns you.'

'It's no concern of yours.'

'No, I see that. I begin to see that. I once thought otherwise, but that's what young men are like. They see only what they want to see. You must have laughed many times, you and Aemilia, after I'd left you.'

She pushes him away and stares at him. There's enough light for him to see the shining darkness of her eyes. Wide eyes, Hera eyes. The eyes of a goddess who loved her brother so much that she shared his bed.

'You are so beautiful,' he says.

She is silent, studying his face.

'We didn't laugh,' she said.

'It doesn't matter. I don't know why I said it.'

They are silent again. She is looking at him intently, and he allows her. He feels as if there's a mask over his face.

'I can't make you out,' she says at last.

'I know. It's too dark.'

'Not as dark as all that. The moon has risen,' she says, and she's right. A half-full moon is coming in the sky. He can see more and more of her.

'I came to say goodbye,' he says.

'Are you going away? I thought you were staying in Rome now.'

'My plans have changed. I'll come and go, I expect. Sirmio, Rome – and I might go back to the East. But I shan't live here permanently again.'

'You sound so strange, darling, not like yourself at all. So cold.'

'Aemilia sounded strange, after your brother's hands had dug into her windpipe.'

She takes a quick breath. 'Don't blame me for that. I didn't know –'

'You don't have to justify yourself to me, Clodia. I believe that you didn't know.'

She stretches up to him. Her lips touch his, quick and warm. They taste of wine.

'Who have you been drinking with?' he asks.

'Just with my brother.'

'You didn't pop in on Rufus?'

'That's over. More than over. I'm surprised you didn't know.' Her voice sharpens. 'We are enemies. He hates me, and I hate him. There's going to be a court case –'

'So I heard,' he says, stopping her. He does not want to hear it all again, from her lips.

She looks at him, trying to work out what he knows and what he doesn't know. But she can't read him. 'You've got nothing to be jealous about, my dear poet,' she says.

He is her dear poet again. She is turning the force of herself on to him, sensing somewhere deep in her instincts just how far he is from her – as she did with Aemilia, long ago on that day down at Baiae. Just as she does with everyone. *That's over.* It's Rufus' turn to suffer, if he's capable of suffering over her. No, he isn't the type. Vengeance is more his style.

Catullus cups her cheek with his hand, then traces the smooth warm line of her jaw. It is perfect, unbroken. He thinks of the swollen mess that Pretty Boy made of Aemilia's face. He thinks of Metellus Celer lying on his bed in a pool of his own liquid shit, while saliva bubbled from his mouth. What a long labour it must have been for him to reach his death. Clodia wasn't in the room. Surely if she'd been there, she'd have had to pity him.

'You remember your sparrow?'

'Of course – how can you imagine I'd ever forget him?'

'I was just wondering. Did you get another in the end?'

'No, not yet.'

my girl's sweet sparrow, her darling
for whom she'd have torn out her own eyes
and left herself blinded;

He quotes himself, still stroking her cheek. He feels her smile come under his fingers.

'I love that poem,' she says.

'I wrote it for you.'

'Much the nicest of the poems you've written about me, darling.'

She has recovered herself.

'I must go now,' he says, and his hand drops to his side.

'Let me know when you're back in Rome.' She can't quite hide her relief that he hasn't pursued the subject of Aemilia; or of her brother either –

– or of anything or anyone.

But suddenly she surprises him. She comes close, nestling into him, almost like a bird. He smells her warm hair, the perfume on it, and the sweetness of her body.

'If people ever said to you . . .' she mutters into the darkness of his body, '. . . if people ever said bad things to you about me – really bad things, I mean, not just same old same old – you wouldn't believe them, would you?'

He holds her. She is so warm, so soft. She seems to melt into him as if their lives are one life. *The last time*, his brain hammers at him, *the last time, the last time, the last time. Now you know what she is.* In a moment he will release her. He will never hold her again.

Or will he? Is there some present that doesn't end, where Clodia's sparrow always hops and cheeps, and where he kisses her, a thousand kisses and then a hundred more, and then another thousand –

Don't fool yourself. In a moment they will separate and become two people again. She will have to hurry, before the doorman gives up hope of her return and locks and bolts the main door.

He'll have to hurry too. He can feel time at his back, chasing him.

He'll let go of her. He'll see her flit away. He'll watch her out of sight, until he can no longer tell where the grey of her cloak ends and the black of night begins.

'No,' he says, still holding her, 'I wouldn't believe a word of it.'

Nulla potest mulier tantum se dicere amatam
vere, quantum a me Lesbia amata mea est.

My Lesbia, loved by me
beyond any woman
who calls herself beloved.

HELEN DUNMORE

HOUSE OF ORPHANS

Finland, 1902, and the Russian Empire enforces a brutal policy to destroy Finland's freedom and force its people into submission.

Eeva, orphaned daughter of a failed revolutionary, also battles to find her independence and identity. Destitute when her father dies, she is sent away to a country orphanage, and then as servant to a widowed doctor, Thomas Eklund. Slowly, Thomas falls in love with Eeva ... but she has committed herself long ago to a boy from her childhood, Lauri, who is now caught up in Helsinki's turmoil of resistance to Russian rule.

Set in dangerous, unfamiliar times which strangely echo our own, the story reveals how terrorism lies hidden within ordinary life, as rulers struggle to hold onto power. *House of Orphans* is a rich, brilliant story of love, history and change.

'Part love story, part tragedy ... Dunmore on dazzling form. Everyone should read her work' *Independent on Sunday*

'Outstanding, a sheer pleasure to read. Dunmore is a remarkable storyteller' *Daily Mail*

'Every character is richly drawn and makes for compelling reading ... top-quality fiction' *Daily Express*

'Richly ambitious ...there isn't a dull page. A remarkable achievement, firmly establishes Dunmore as among the best living novelists' *Scotsman*

HELEN DUNMORE

MOURNING RUBY

'Moments that bring the reader to tears … a fascinating – often brilliant – novel'
The Times

Rebecca was abandoned by her mother in a shoebox in the backyard of an Italian restaurant when she was two days old. Her life begins without history, in the dark outdoors. Who is she, where has she come from, and what can she become? Thirty years later, married to Adam, she gives birth to Ruby, and to a new life for herself. But when sudden tragedy changes the course of that life for ever, and all the lives that touch hers, Rebecca is out in the world again, searching …

'Bold and unusual … miraculously written, Dunmore's drama of loss and regeneration pieces together shattered lives' *Daily Mail*

'Emotionally restrained, beautifully observed' *Daily Telegraph*

'A tale of unbearable tragedy … prose and plot-lines as taut as hawsers. Dunmore is the most gifted novelist of her generation' *New Statesman*

'Beautifully told, intricate, powerful' *Independent on Sunday*

HELEN DUNMORE

THE SIEGE

'Remarkable, affecting ... There are few more interesting stories than this; and few writers who could have told it better' *Daily Telegraph*

Leningrad, September 1941. Hitler orders German forces to surround the city at the start of the most dangerous, desperate winter in its history. For two pairs of lovers – young Anna and Andrei, Anna's novelist father and actress Marina – the siege becomes a battle for survival. They will soon discover what it is like to be so hungry you boil shoe leather to make soup, so cold you burn furniture and books. But this is not just a struggle to exist, it is also a fight to keep the spark of hope alive ...

The Siege is a brilliantly imagined novel of war and the wounds it inflicts on ordinary people's lives and a profoundly moving celebration of love, life and survival.

'A Tolstoyan epic of love and war; life and death ... she writes beautifully' *Sunday Telegraph*

'Literary writing of the highest order set against a background of suffering so intimately reconstructed it is hard to believe that Dunmore was not there' *Sunday Telegraph*

'Utterly convincing. A deeply moving account of two love stories in terrible circumstances. The story of their struggle to survive appears simple, as all great literature should ... A world-class novel' *The Times*

'A remarkable parable of human survival against the odds' *Mail on Sunday*

He just wanted a decent book to read ...

Not too much to ask, is it? It was in 1935 when Allen Lane, Managing Director of Bodley Head Publishers, stood on a platform at Exeter railway station looking for something good to read on his journey back to London. His choice was limited to popular magazines and poor-quality paperbacks – the same choice faced every day by the vast majority of readers, few of whom could afford hardbacks. Lane's disappointment and subsequent anger at the range of books generally available led him to found a company – and change the world.

'We believed in the existence in this country of a vast reading public for intelligent books at a low price, and staked everything on it'
Sir Allen Lane, 1902–1970, founder of Penguin Books

The quality paperback had arrived – and not just in bookshops. Lane was adamant that his Penguins should appear in chain stores and tobacconists, and should cost no more than a packet of cigarettes.

Reading habits (and cigarette prices) have changed since 1935, but Penguin still believes in publishing the best books for everybody to enjoy. We still believe that good design costs no more than bad design, and we still believe that quality books published passionately and responsibly make the world a better place.

So wherever you see the little bird – whether it's on a piece of prize-winning literary fiction or a celebrity autobiography, political tour de force or historical masterpiece, a serial-killer thriller, reference book, world classic or a piece of pure escapism – you can bet that it represents the very best that the genre has to offer.

Whatever you like to read – trust Penguin.